"A masterful retelling of an Icelan[   ]e physical and intellectual landscap[   ].s excellent piece of historical fiction will find a wider audience than its esoteric subject matter might suggest. Highly recommended."
—*Library Journal*

"Janoda's book is a model of how to turn a saga into a novel."
—*Times Literary Supplement*

"If the mob bosses of the Sopranos spoke Old Norse and wore chain mail, they would feel right at home in this absorbing historical melodrama. Debut novelist Janoda paints a richly textured portrait of Icelandic culture, brimming with multigenerational cycles of bloodshed and violence. A gripping recreation of an ancient genre." —*Kirkus*

"*Saga* earns an honourable place among the many good novels developed from the Icelandic sagas." —*Globe and Mail*

"Readers will be mesmerized by the melding of myth with the everyday life. *Saga* resonates with the song of the sagas of old. For that alone, it is worth the read." —*Regina Leader-Post*

"Brilliant and unsparing in its depiction of a savage land. Janoda makes us smell the smoke, the peat, the half rotten beef, and feel the terrible cold." —*Historical Novels Review*

"A darkly grim narrative tapestry . . . compelling and ultimately rewarding." —*Paradox Historical Fiction Magazine*

"Janoda breathes a fiery and emotional life into this saga. He uses wisdom and craftiness to draw readers into the bloody feuds and intrigue of medieval Iceland." —*Logberg-Heimskringla*

Saga

Saga

A Novel of Medieval Iceland

JEFF JANODA

ACADEMY CHICAGO PUBLISHERS

Published in 2005 by
Academy Chicago Publishers
An imprint of Chicago Review Press Incorporated
814 North Franklin Street
Chicago, Illinois 60610

First paperback edition 2008
ISBN 978-0-89733-568-3
Copyright © 2005 by Jeff Janoda

Cover design: Sarah Olson
Cover photo: Courtesy of Heritage Image Partnership

Printed and bound in the United States of America

Library of Congress Cataloging-in-Publication Data

Janoda, Jeff, 1960–

  Saga : a novel of medieval Iceland / Jeff Janoda.
    p. cm.
  ISBN 978-0-89733-568-3 (alk. paper)
  1. Iceland--History—To 1262—Fiction. I. Title.

PS3610.A578S24 2005
813'.6—dc22

                                    2005003360

To my wife Jane, and my children, as well as my parents, Joseph and Gloria, and to the authors of the original sagas, who knew in their bones that it was just as important to tell a story as it was to tell the facts.

Author's Note

This book is not history. It is fiction, based on historical events. The goal was to show my understanding of the essential spirit of the Norse settlers of medieval Iceland, as I first appreciated it from the sagas, which I read long ago, and which began my life-long interest in all things Norse. That said, I have not significantly strayed from actual historical events described in the sagas, although there are minor changes to geography and timelines and events, to facilitate the storyline. All motivations and perceptions by the characters, both historical and fictional, are strictly my own invention.

The primary sources for the story were the Icelandic sagas, specifically *Eyrbyggja Saga*, of which the novel encompasses only a portion, the actual struggle between Snorri and Arnkel. The sagas were written down in the thirteenth century, but date from oral tradition that went back to the first settlement of Iceland in the tenth century. They are basically family histories, and contain much relevant information, but also much that is clearly not based on fact (ghosts and walking corpses abound). Despite the more fantastical elements, they remain one of the most complete, personal and detailed written descriptions of any medieval culture.

As to the elves . . . one has only to go to Iceland (even today, I am told) to sense them.

Jeff Janoda
Ontario, Canada

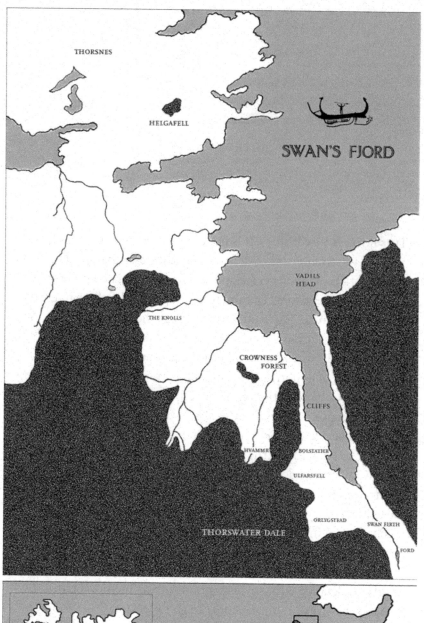

THORSNES

HELGAFELL

SWAN'S FJORD

VADILS
HEAD

THE KNOLLS

CROWNESS
FOREST

CLIFFS

HVAMMR

BOLSTADHR

ULFARSFELL

ORLYGSTAD

SWAN FIRTH

THORSWATER DALE

FORD

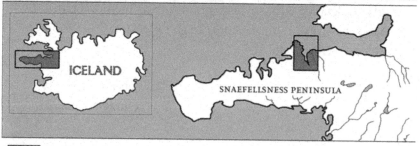

ICELAND

SNAEFELLSNESS PENINSULA

HIGHLANDS

GLOSSARY OF CHARACTERS

Arnkel gothi: the chieftain of Swan's fjord, the son of Thorolf Lamefoot, and a mighty warrior

Auln: the wife of Ulfar, occasionally host to visions, a fierce woman torn by her past.

Cunning-Gill: an war comrade and confidant of Thorolf Lamefoot

Dim: a slave of Arnkel's

Egil: a slave of Thorbrand, known to like a fight

Einar Gudson: the grandfather of Arnkel, slain by Thorolf Lamefoot in duel long ago

Freya or Freyja: there are two basic families of Germanic gods, who first warred against each other, and then reconciled and ruled together. Odin and Thor belong to the Aesir, while Freya belongs to the Vanir, a group of gods and goddesses concerned with fecundity and fertility, in contrast to the warrior nature of the Aesir. Freya was primarily concerned with love and endless childbirth. The great temple at Uppsala in Sweden was devoted to a cult centered on Odin, Thor and Freyr, the male counterpart of Freya. This is a very old theological construction, a triangle based on two parts strength and one part growth, found as far back as the ancient Vedic tradition, from where it probably rooted in the misty roots of time.

Freystein the Rascal: a large, powerful man, slave of Thorbrand, noted for his humor

Gizur: a Thingman of Arnkel the chieftain, a clever and happy man

Gudmund gothi: a wealthy and fierce chieftain, known to support any who could pay his high price

Gudrid: the resolute mother of Arnkel the chieftain, and once the wife of Lamefoot, but no longer

Hafildi: the second Thingman of Arnkel the chieftain, known for his temper

Halla: the eldest child and daughter of Arnkel, beautiful and strong of will

Hawk: the head Thingman of Snorri the chieftain, a tough, fearless and loyal man

Helga: the aging second wife of Thorolf Lamefoot

Hildi: the loyal wife of Arnkel the chieftain, and mother of four daughters

Hrafn of Trondheim: a merchant from Norway, and a friend of Snorri the chieftain and the sons of Thorbrand

Hromund gothi: an older gothi, given the task of keeping peace at the Thing

Illugi, son of Thorbrand: the youngest and most fierce of the sons of Thorbrand

Ketil, the fisherman: youngest of the so called "Fish Brothers," fierce sup-
 porters of Arnkel the chieftain
Kili: a Thingman of Arnkel the chieftain, cousin to Thrain, large of size but
 not of heart
Kjartan: a loyal friend of Oreakja, known for his good temper
Klaenger, the fisherman: a Thingman of Snorri the chieftain, known for his
 steadiness
Leif, the fisherman: the older of the two "Fish Brothers"
Njal: a Thingman of Arnkel the chieftain
Odin: He was the highest of the gods within the Germanic Pantheon, the
 god of war, of magic, of poetry. He is thought to come from Wode, the
 leader of the "Wild Hunt' which the Germanic people thought they
 saw and heard happen during storms, as long-dead warriors careered
 across the sky.
Olaf: a slave of Arnkel's, known for his laziness
Olaf Huskud gothi: allied with Snorri *gothi*, a chieftain and seal hunter
Onund: one of Hrafn's crew, a strong and violent man
Oreakja: the eldest son of Snorri the Chieftain, sixteen years old and fierce
Orlyg: the elder brother of Ulfar Freedman, dying slowly of a sickness
Rose: youngest daughter of Arnkel
Sam, the fisherman: a Thingman of Snorri the chieftain, a tough, angry man
 dedicated to his chieftain
The Slaves of Thorolf: Four kerns (men from Cornwall) brought to the free
 state by Thorolf Lamefoot. One of these men is called Baldy
Snorri, son of Thorbrand: third son of Thorbrand, namesake of their chief-
 tain, Snorri
Snorri gothi: a powerful and influential chieftain to the north of Swan's
 fjord, known for his wisdom and wealth, and chieftain to Thorbrand
 and his sons, among others
Styrmir: a Thingman of Snorri the chieftain
Svein Haraldson: A Thingman of Arnkel
Teitr: a Thingman of Gudmund *gothi*
Thor: often referred to as Odin's son, he was probably the favorite god of
 the Vikings, based on the number of place names and personal names
 incorporating his own. Less aloof and mighty than Odin, he was the
 true great warrior, carrying a mighty hammer, flinging lightning about
 the sky, and demolishing his enemies. Although Odin was the god of
 war, Thor was the god of the warrior.
Thorbrand: a wise old man, owner of Swan firth, and a follower of Snorri the
 chieftain
Thorfinn, son of Thorbrand: fifth son of Thorbrand, and called "the Holy"
 for his ability to see the elves

Thorgils: the head Thingman of Arnkel the chieftain, and his closest confidant

Thorleif, son of Thorbrand: eldest son and heir of Thorbrand, a good and brave man

Thormod, son of Thorbrand: fourth son of Thorbrand, aptly called "the Quiet"

Thorodd, son of Thorbrand: second son of Thorbrand, a powerful man trained as a smith

Thorolf Lamefoot: the father of Arnkel the chieftain, badly wounded in a duel years ago, a former viking still violent in his later life

Thrain: a clever Thingman of Arnkel the chieftain, though not from Swan's fjord

Ulfar Freedman: once the slave of Thorbrand, now a free man living on his own lands, married to Auln

Unn: third daughter of Arnkel

Vermund and Stir: two independent free men, acting as mediators at the Thing

Vigdis: second daughter of Arnkel

A glossary of places and terms can be found on page 359

ICELAND, THE FREE STATE

965 AD

I

SUMMER

THE TAKING OF THE HAY

THREE RIDERS PICKED their way in file up the narrow mountain trail. The pitch of the land would have killed them if they had slipped, but the horses were sure footed and canny, and each man knew the saddle. On their left, far below, was Swan's fjord, a deep rift driven straight into the mountain to let in the sea. Thousands of the white seabirds swam the ink blue water. Others flew about, a cloud of white specks circling like flakes of dust in sunlight.

The men came to Vadils Head, a small plateau dotted with the stone cairns of the dead, the highest point on the vast ridge of the mountain spur that fell steeply to form the eastern side of the fjord. Ragged, treacherous sheep paths scarred the slope, but no man could live there. The side facing north to the open ocean was sheer cliff. From it, the beaches on the narrow coastal plain below could be spied out for ten miles or more to the east and west. The men yearned for the good fat of whale, and it was in summer that the creatures most often stranded on the beaches of the Island, driven to madness by the Gods so that men could feast. But there was nothing except the Earth. The youngest of them bent down and idly rattled the iron ring bolt driven into the rock at the cliff's edge. The other two frowned darkly at him, shaking their heads. The shades of the men who had been hanged there would not like his mockery.

Two of the riders were brothers, called Thorleif and Illugi. The other was Ulfar, the Freedman. He would always carry that name, as a man who had been released from slavery by his master Thorbrand, the father of the two men with him. Ulfar's son would be a *bondi,* a free man, like the two brothers, but never Ulfar himself. He would always be the man who had once been a slave.

He could accept that. It was the Law.

If only he had sons.

He had not come to the high place to find whales.

Ulfar found a spot away from the other graves, back from the cliff. The sons of Thorbrand left him in peace, although they had come as witnesses to the burial. He tried to place the stones quickly, without thinking on what he did. The infant was wrapped many times in wool, but he had still sensed the round flesh of the malformed arms and legs through the folds as he cradled it on the long ride up the mountain. It had filled him with dread and despair. Auln, his wife, had begged him not to curse the elves when he buried their child and so he held his tongue and lay the offering of smoked fish near the cairn. He peered over his shoulder at the brothers to be sure they could not see him. They were strong men. Even in the idle moments of waiting for Ulfar, they stood testing their courage at the very edge of the cliff, Illugi the younger with his toes hanging in air. They would have thought him sentimental and weak to let tears fall onto the ground over a child too young to have been given a name. Ulfar covered his face with one hand as the pain wracked him for a time. Then he put it away forever, and went to join them at the cliff's edge.

He stayed one step back. The wind blew hard, and one blast could knock a man over.

There was nothing, nothing but black sand and pounding surf and wind.

The stark beauty of his land struck him then, there above the clouds, banishing for a moment all sadness. Towards the interior of the island were the white mountains, home of the God Under the Earth. Below was the sea, giver of life, laid out before his eyes as if he were Thor himself. Between them ran the thin line of green lands on which alone men could live. His soul struggled with it, forcing the wrenched agony of his despair into the rise of song.

A Face of the Sky God above
Face of the Sea God below
Stone and ice and water pressed between,
and man, the withered stem, springs from the crevice.

The others nodded, but said nothing.

They mounted, and rode for a while until they were out of sight and sound of the ghosts that haunted the cliff top.

On a vast slab of stone with a good view, they sat side by side to pass a bag of curd back and forth. Their eyes roamed the land, while the two brothers spoke idly of the weather.

Across the fjord was a gentler land, rolling green hills of rough pasture, and a solitary wonder standing out from the landscape; a forest of birch trees growing thickly near a shallow cliff, each trunk strong enough to cut for house frames, rare treasures in a land stripped to rock by men and sheep. The forest was called the Crowness. It belonged to the old viking, Thorolf Lamefoot.

Ulfar swallowed nervously at the thought of Thorolf. The man was his neighbor and the troll on his doorstep, the bane of his life. He winced at the memory of his booming voice, his vast angry face, and his drunken accusations. So he moved his eyes from the man's forest, to banish the beast's spirit from his heart.

Far to the northeast, on the flat coastal lands beyond the reach of the fjord, grew a solitary hill, surrounded by mist. That was Helgafell, the holy mountain, the farm of Snorri *gothi*, chieftain to the sons of Thorbrand, and many other men.

To the southeast, close by Ulfar's own farm within the deep body of the fjord, was a larger house, a true great Hall, the turf of its walls and roof thick and green with marsh grass. Bolstathr farm was the home of Arnkel *gothi*, chieftain of the fjord. He was the son of Thorolf Lamefoot the Viking, and also a man not to be trifled with lightly. Father and son had much in common. Arnkel's plot was smaller than Ulfar's, hardly more than a single home field and a garden, but a *gothi* could turn his hand to other ways of making a living. Men will always disagree and feud, and someone must be there to mediate. For a price. The *gothi* drew men to himself, and wealth, and respect.

To the south, at the very base of the fjord, lay Swan firth. It was the best farm in the region, split by a foaming, icy river running from the glaciers, full of sea salmon in the run, and other fish year round. Flat, fertile earth covered both banks of the river. The farm belonged to Thorbrand, and his six sons.

Thorleif and Illugi were the eldest and the youngest of the six, and far enough apart in age that the hatred of brothers had never risen for each other. Thorleif had almost thirty years to him, a respectable age, but his teeth and arms were still strong. Illugi was sixteen, full of young muscle and spit.

Illugi had the sharpest eyes. He raised a hand and pointed below.

"Ulfar, isn't that Lamefoot there, in your meadow?"

They peered down at the tiny figures moving on the ridge separating the old viking's half of the land from Ulfar's.

They were taking in the hay.

The brothers looked at Ulfar. It was far away, but the old man's lurch was unmistakable, as were the stacks of hay already piled high onto Lamefoot's oxen by his slaves.

"He's past the ridge line, into your land now," said Illugi. "Think he'll go farther?"

A spike of cold fear flared in Ulfar's gut.

"I don't know," he said. He shared the meadow with Lamefoot. Each of them was owner to the hay on their half of the meadow. He swore again. All his polite words to the beast had been wasted. "Auln said he was up to something."

Thorleif and Illugi looked up with wide eyes. "Did she *see* that?" Illugi asked nervously. Men and women sometimes came to Auln, even though she told them that her visions came at their own time, not at her call.

Ulfar did not answer. He chewed his lip worriedly.

"That old man would scare the piss out of a stone," Illugi said. "Why does he hate you so much, Ulfar?"

"Quiet, boy," said Thorleif, knowing Ulfar's fear. "We'd best get down to the ford and across the river."

They walked the horses until the trail became safer, and then rode as quickly as they dared along the hairpins to the valley bottom.

Ulfar and Thorolf had cut the hay together two days before, as their old agreement had said they should. It was a time Ulfar dreaded all year. The fallen stalks had been left to dry in the field. The old man had grumbled with disbelief at Ulfar's prediction that no rain would fall for several days. Ulfar peered up at the thin layer of cloud, knowing that the old man had panicked, and read the sky wrong, as always. It would not rain that day, or the next, and the hay would still not be dry.

Ulfar swore, his breath coming short. He did not want to fight. What did he know of fighting?

The ford was a quarter mile up the river, just behind the brothers' plot of land. The mountain trail wound down, down toward the valley, and led eventually to the ford. They waded across the river, the water soaking them to their thighs.

A boat floated in an eddy of river current, anchored fore and aft. Two men sat in it, fishing with lines. They looked up at the men crossing the ford, and one flashed a rude sign with his fingers.

"The Fish Brothers," Thorleif growled. He cupped his hand to his mouth. "One fish of every three is ours, you sheep lovers, that's the fee for putting your lines in our river. And not the smallest, either."

The men in the boat shouted insults back, standing.

"Damn their eyes," Thorleif said to Illugi. "If father allowed it, I'd cut them up into pieces and use them for bait. They rob us every time they drop a line here."

They rode wetly up the bank and cantered hard along the shore, throwing a final shout at the Fish Brothers. A short run along the fine gravel brought them to Swan firth. The other sons of Thorbrand came from their work at the sound of their horses, spilling out of the great turf house and the barn and the smithy. They shouted loudly when Thorleif and the other two did not stop.

"Lamefoot's stealing Ulfar's hay!" Illugi shouted back at them.

The brothers dropped their forks and buckets and ran after them, although Thorbrand shouted at them to stop from the door of the house, his grey beard wagging with the force of his calls. It was not far. A half dozen households lived less than two miles apart from each other, wedged together by the pitch of the land, the mountains and ice desert pressing them to the coast.

Ulfar reined in at the rock wall by the base of his side of the high meadow. Lamefoot had always gone a stroke or two past the ridge line, but now he was halfway down the slope, his four big slaves sweating and covered in hay slack, and grinning at him. They thought themselves as good as him, because he had once been a slave. There stood Lamefoot, pretending to look at the sky.

"Thorolf!" Ulfar said loudly. "Call your slaves off! I know you think it is time, but the hay is not ready yet. It will rot in the hay barn." He would pretend that Thorolf was not stealing his hay, that he was only doing Ulfar a service.

His horse shied from his loud words, and he should have dismounted, but he was afraid, and wanted the size of the animal under him.

Lamefoot picked his teeth and looked at Ulfar. He drank from the skin in his hand, and spat a mouthful out rudely. "Looks like rain."

The old beast was drunk again, thought Ulfar. Very drunk.
There would be no reason from him.

The other sons of Thorbrand began to arrive, running up
breathless to see the commotion. Thorleif's hand fell on Ulfar's
elbow.

"He's wearing his sword," Thorleif said quietly. "And look, his
slaves have their spears and shields. See them there, lying on the
ground?"

More hay was gathered.

"Lamefoot!" Ulfar shouted, his fear turning to helpless rage.

Thorolf reacted immediately. He marched down to the wall,
pitching away the skin, the sword scabbard banging his thigh.
Ulfar backed the pony away fearfully, and the slaves laughed at
his white face.

Lamefoot pointed a finger at him from behind the wall, eyes
red with anger and drink.

"Say that name again and I'll call you out and cut you down
like this hay," he said, his rough voice like stones rumbling down
a hillside. "I will take my fair share of this crop. Your side grows
thicker."

There was silence on the hill. Lamefoot was grey haired and
slow with age and his belly was a mound, but his shoulders were
as wide as two men, side to side and front to back. The finger he
pointed was a sausage, calloused and immense. He turned his eyes
to the sons of Thorbrand, who backed away nervously.

"He meant no insult, Thorolf, and if you take him to duel we
will witness that you do so with injustice." Thorleif said, his voice
hard. He made himself ride forward a pace or two. "You will lose
much, in land and property, paying for that killing."

Lamefoot's eyes were like embers on him, burning through
the vast whiskers.

"What do you know about duels, *bondi*?" he said, and spat on
the ground. "You have never fought one. I have."

"I know that, Thorolf," Thorleif said quietly.

"The Law says you cannot do this," Ulfar said, pleading now.

Lamefoot waved his hand toward the great turf Hall further down the fjord, where his son Arnkel *gothi* the chieftain lived. "There is the Law."

He turned away and spat to one side. Ulfar rode off with the sons of Thorbrand, the laughter of the slaves burning his back.

Thorgils came to Ulfarsfell the next day.

Auln watched him ride in to their farm, down the hill from Arnkel *gothi*'s great Hall of Bolstathr, pushing through Ulfar's roiling flock of fat and healthy sheep. She boiled clothes in a pot, driving out the lice and nits and fleas, stirring the sodden mass slowly with a pole. Outside the small barn, Ulfar stood braced before the fleshing log, cleaning the fat and meat from a ram hide. He looked up and smiled when he saw his friend.

Thorgils was a short man, but strong, with shoulders like rock from a life of work. He was the chief Thingman of Arnkel the chieftain.

He came often to Ulfarsfell, riding in when his duties at Bolstathr farm allowed, and always he brought a gift. Only once, a year past, had he mentioned Arnkel, and the idea that Ulfar should consider becoming a Thingman of the *gothi*, instead of keeping his attachment to Thorbrand. Ulfar's shocked face had been all the answer he needed.

Still Thorgils would come. Ever since Auln had arrived, he had come, and shared their fire and food.

She felt his eyes on her.

She did not know if it was her Sight that revealed his interest, or just ordinary intuition. It did not repel her. He was reasonably handsome, with a good beard and jaw, and clear green eyes under his reddish blonde hair. She had laughed at herself once, tying her hair up as he came down the hill. It meant nothing, she had told herself. It was simply good to know that she still could draw a man's eye.

Still, she knew the dark roads lust could take a man down along.

She put away the thought of her father and his haunted eyes and the smell of drink on his breath.

This was her new life. That was the old, and she had escaped it.

There was a shadow behind Thorgils. Some kind of falsehood or deception walked with him, although he himself seemed honest. The Sight moved behind her eyes, like some other person behind her shoulder, whispering into her ear.

He nodded to her as he dismounted.

"I'm sorry for your loss, Auln," he said, his voice gentle.

She nodded. "Thank you, Thorgils," she said, and began to stir the pot again. He handed her a small package, wrapped in leather. "Some herrings the Fish Brothers caught by net the other day. They will speed your healing."

She took them without a word, and laid them at her feet.

He squelched through the drying mud over to Ulfar. They talked for a while about the skin, and Thorgils felt the thick mat of fleece, whistling in appreciation.

"You have always raised the strongest, finest sheep, Ulfar," Thorgils said. The freedman ducked his head, pleased. Thorgils took a turn at the skin, scraping gently with the fleshing tool, a sharpened thigh bone, Ulfar guiding him with a few words. The two men spoke for a while of the flocks, and the weather. Auln brought out a pitcher of *skyr*, thick fermented cow's milk thinned to liquid with whey, and the three of them drank the refreshing sourness from wooden cups, sitting on the home field wall.

"I have heard of your trouble with Thorolf," Thorgils said carefully. "He has most of the hay from your meadow. What will you do?"

"I will go to Thorbrand and ask for his help," Ulfar said. "What else is there to do? All of his sons saw what happened. They must help me."

"Why?"

Ulfar looked at him. "He was my master until he freed me. He is bound to me."

Thorgils sipped from his cup. "He does not have to fight for you. I was at the Thorsnes Thing eight years ago when you were freed by Thorbrand, and I heard Arnkel *gothi*'s words on it, speaking the Law. A manumitted slave who falls into poverty must be supported by his former master. You are not in poverty, Ulfar, far from it. Look at this farm! You have done well for yourself, and now Thorolf Lamefoot is jealous of you. You bought his land and made it a source of wealth, and he hates you for it. You know how he is."

Ulfar nodded glumly.

"I also remember the words Snorri *gothi* spoke," Thorgils said, his voice full of reason. "That this land you bought with your own wealth would go to Thorbrand if you died without children." Thorgils eyes were hard as glass. "Do you remember that?"

Auln looked from one man to the other, appalled. "Is this true?"

Ulfar nodded. "It is the Law."

"So now that Lamefoot has robbed you, and threatened you, who would profit most if he were to slay you?" Thorgils spoke without passion, his voice full of persuasion.

Ulfar stood, his face rigid with disapproval. "My wife should not hear such things, Thorgils. Also, I do not like that you speak so badly of Thorbrand."

Auln looked at Thorgils. "You seem to know much about a freedman's rights," she said suspiciously.

"Thorgils' father was a freedman, Auln," Ulfar said absently, frowning with thought and worry. "Gunnar served Arnkel's grandfather."

"I see."

"You are stranger to these parts, Auln, and some things may be unknown to you," Thorgils said mildly. Auln stared at him angrily, thinking he spoke to her with condescension. Thorgils turned to Ulfar. "I speak only as a friend, so that you should see these things clearly. You must make a decision."

"Thorbrand is an honorable man," Ulfar said uncertainly, as if he did not believe his own words.

"This farm is a treasure, as is your meadow," Thorgils said. "You have made it so. Wealth will sometimes turn a man from honor. If you die without an heir, it is his. Think on it!"

Ulfar said nothing. The wind gusted along the ground, blowing up the dust of the yard into their faces. Clouds were coming in from the north, wet from the sea.

"I cannot believe that Thorleif would allow his father to let harm come to you," Auln said firmly. "He and his brothers are good men and I trust them."

"So do I." Ulfar turned to Auln. "I must speak a while with Thorgils, wife."

She stood from the wall, hands on hips.

"This concerns me as well!"

"I will speak to Thorgils alone," Ulfar repeated stubbornly. Auln glared at him and then stalked off to the house. In a few moments they heard the clatter of the loom, banging angrily.

Thorgils and Ulfar looked at each together. "I remember the storm when she came over that mountain pass three years ago, all alone," Thorgils said, smiling slightly. "No dowry, no family, and yet every man in the valley without a wife was hungry for her."

"Sometimes I wonder if I made the right choice giving her a ring," Ulfar said, looking at his feet. "She is so willful."

He glanced up at Thorgils, who stood quietly, listening.

"It is not Thorbrand I fear, my friend," Ulfar said finally.

"I understand." Thorgils took Ulfar's arm. "What man except Arnkel *gothi* has the strength of arm to match Thorolf? He has me, also, and the Fish Brothers, and Gizur and Hafildi, and many other Thingmen. Let him advocate for you in this. That is what chieftains do. There will be a price to pay, but that is only some wealth and then you will have peace."

"I must speak to Thorbrand first," Thorgils said hesitantly. "I owe him that much."

"Then do so. But remember my words." Thorgils turned and mounted his horse. He paused in the saddle and looked down at Ulfar with gentle eyes.

"There will be other sons, friend," he said. "But I know your pain."

Ulfar nodded quickly, face set.

Auln watched from the doorway, hidden by the shadow.

Thorgils rode off.

Ulfar went into the house, and squinted his eyes in the darkness. His wife worked in the corner at the loom, eyes locked on the warp and weft of the strands.

"What will you do?" Auln asked. Her anger had faded.

"I will ride to Thorbrand," Ulfar said. "Now."

"That is good. Ulfar, I do not trust Thorgils," she said. "Something surrounds him." She could not bring herself to mention his eyes on her. It would only hurt Ulfar to hear that.

"He is my friend, Auln," Ulfar said gently. "All his words were true, although I hated hearing them," Ulfar said. He peered at her, knowing she spoke of her vision. "And Thorbrand? What do you see in him? Will he help me?"

She shrugged. "My Sight is not like that. You know that." She knew it was not Thorgils himself that disturbed her. A menace followed him from Bolstathr like a trailing scent and she could hear the elves hidden under rock and sand chitter at it as he passed. They thrived on falsehood and evil and that was why they hovered about the dwellings of men.

"Then I will go," Ulfar said. "It would be best."

He saddled his horse and mounted. It was not a long ride to Swan firth, but he went slowly, so that he would have time to think of what he would say.

He rode along the shore, letting his mount nibble the grass where it grew thickly by the beach. The turf roofs of Swan firth came into sight. It was a large farm. The wide delta of fertile silt built up by the river supported many fields of crop and pasture. Ulfar had often worked there with the sons of Thorbrand. Every spring before he had purchased his freedom he had watched over the slaves and servants as they planted the seeds of cabbage and peas, making sure they gave each one the right depth, the correct covering of earth, the precise pressure of fingers into the ground. They were too precious to waste, and Thorbrand shook his finger at him for every one that did not sprout, walking along the furrows and pointing accusingly at every empty spot. If the hay in the fields was not thick as fur he complained and took money from Ulfar's meager wages.

He was a hard man, Thorbrand, grasping and ungenerous, thought Ulfar. What relief it had been when he had finally saved the wealth needed to buy his freedom.

Ulfar had told Thorgils that Thorbrand was honorable, but he was not, really. It was his oldest son that Ulfar respected, and it was for him that he now rode to Swan firth.

What a surprise it had been when Thorbrand had offered to loan money to him and to his brother Orlyg, to buy the farms and meadow from Thorolf the viking. Thorbrand had come himself, all smiles and nodding head, and they had discussed the terms.

Ulfar had asked why Thorbrand did not buy the land himself, suspicious of the old man's sudden generosity.

Thorbrand's face had turned hard as ice. "Thorolf Lamefoot will not sell to me. He claims that I will become too powerful if I own both Swan firth and his land, too. He announces to all the world that the lands he cannot care for himself are for sale, but from my money he turns away. It is that ambitious son of his, Arnkel. He is the one who guides his father."

Ulfar had thought long and hard about becoming a neighbor to the rough viking, but the offer was too good to deny. It was his chance to have a life for himself as a free man and not as someone's servant.

As he came closer to Swan firth, he heard the faint echo of shouting, words thrown across the water in anger.

A boat floated close to the shore. It was the Fish Brothers, followers of Arnkel *gothi*, fighting their daily battle with the sons of Thorbrand. They both stood in the boat, casting rude gestures at an enraged Illugi on the shore.

He knew the Fish Brothers, and tried to avoid them. They were fierce men, full of black mischief and cruelty. One of them stood with a fish held between his legs and pretended to mate with it, before he threw it roughly onto the mud bank to pay his dues for using the river.

They were as similar as twins, although a year stood between them, with long red hair and short beards. The oldest was called Leif, the other Ketil. Thorleif and Illugi had begged their father for permission to ambush and beat them for their insolence when Ulfar had been at Swan firth last.

Thorbrand had sneered at them.

"What will Snorri *gothi*, our chieftain, have to say about that?" the canny old man had told them. "Will he risk his reputation to support men in the Thing who assault other men who have paid their legal fee for the right to use my river? Your anger will mean nothing in a court of Law. What will you say? That you do not like the *style* in which the fee was paid? No, he would call you fools, and so Arnkel *gothi* would have no opposition. He could levy a fee from us for the dishonor and harm we caused his Thingmen. Would you want to pass over our best cows for the pleasure of knocking their heads together? Then your empty bellies could growl their contentment this winter."

Yes, fierce, Ulfar thought, to dare the sons of Thorbrand, although there were six of them.

Such men could stand up to Thorolf.

Thorleif and his brothers had watched meekly as Thorolf and his slaves had ridden off with his hay. How could they help him?

He reined in his horse.

All about he was hemmed in.

He turned the horse and headed back to his farm. There was only one thing he could do.

———————

"Are you mad?" Auln, said, later that evening when he told her his decision. "You go to Arnkel *gothi*? Did I not tell you my feelings on this?"

They sat on the wall benches within his house with Ulfar's brother, Orlyg, tending the smoky peat fire. His brother was sick, bent and toothless, and barely able to work the farm he held next to Ulfar's, but he had cared for Ulfar for many years as a child. So Ulfar did the heavy work on his plot, and made no complaint. He had finished gathering Orlyg's hay that afternoon, driving himself to take it all into the barn before Lamefoot went completely mad. Luckily it had been cut first and was dry. It filled Orlyg's barn to the rafters.

"What choice have I?" Ulfar said. "I cannot fight Lamefoot. He was a warrior and his slaves will fight for him. I have no one. What if they waylay me out of sight of witnesses, in the pastures? It is said that he served with the armies in England before coming home. Thorgils told me that he has *armor*. Little rings of metal all sewn together, and even a true war helmet. No, I must go to Arnkel *gothi*. He is the chieftain here and can intervene and his men are strong and many."

"He is Lamefoot's son, you fool!" Auln rapped the pot sharply with a wooden spoon, and drips of hot milk sprayed Orlyg, who protested with a grunt and wiped his face. The beef was still not fully warmed by the roiling curdled milk. Fillets of fish sat above the smoke, spread on wooden racks.

Ulfar shrugged. He had thought on it the whole day. "They do not get along well."

"Father like son," she said with a grimace. "So they do not visit each other. What of it? Blood will back blood."

Orlyg held out his cup. "Pour me some of that tea you made, Auln. It settles my stomach. What is in it?"

"Barley root and fennel," she snapped, knowing he only asked to divert her attention from Ulfar. But then she softened and tipped the little kettle up. She liked Orlyg even though he was a burden. "And juniper berries."

Ulfar took the slices of beef she handed him and chewed, trying to savor the sourness of it. But his worry made it taste like wood. He had slaughtered the oldest cow in the spring, when the last of the hay had run out, and butchered it into barrels of fermenting whey. This year there would be no hay at all, except Orlyg's, and his brother was greedy enough to ask him for payment. If he did not recover what Lamefoot had taken, most of his animals would have to be slaughtered.

It is hunger that must be kept away, he thought, that is what is important.

But in his heart he saw the faces of the sons of Thorbrand, watching as he was shamed by Lamefoot.

He could not abide that.

Nor could he stand the fear that filled him everyday, now.

"What of the old man, Thorbrand, and his whelps?" said Auln. She stood to fill the kettle from the pail in the corner, and winced from the pain in her abdomen, and the nausea. Her face was lined and dark with the peat smoke, but still she had beauty to her. The last pregnancy had been the hardest of all her failed ones. She had lost weight and there was pain the whole time. Food had been agony for her, except for sweet things without texture. Ulfar had spooned hot water and honey into her mouth every night. The child never woke to suckle after the early birth. The tiny limbs had been twisted, the spine warped. Ulfar had cradled the little body until its meager spark of life had burnt out because Auln had been too weak. They both knew he should have just left it out on the rocks to die from the first. But he could not.

It had been a son.

"They do not have the strength to fight Lamefoot!" he said, irritably. "Or the will."

She glared at him, and he instantly regretted his sharp words.

"But you said Thorbrand must help you," she said angrily. "He was your master!"

"Wife, I love you, but these are hard matters." Ulfar tried to touch her shoulder. She slapped his hand away.

"He must help you," she pressed.

Ulfar lowered his hand and nodded. "Yes. He must help me, in some things. But that keg of honey he sent this winter is all the help he will ever send, and I was surprised he sent even that. You do not know him as I do. He gives nothing without cost. It is his way."

He stood, to end the argument, and went to carry more bricks of peat to the side of the fire, feeling his way through the dark. Torches and lamps were for rich men. The pile of bricks in the side alcove was small under his hands, and he sighed. Another chore, a hike of a full day to the fens, a day of work, and another day returning with laden ponies. Three days, to make fire for a month.

He lay himself down on a bench and pulled the blanket to his chin. It was silent for a time, and he began to drift into sleep. Orlyg crawled up onto the guest bench, and soon his steady breathing whistled faintly as he slept.

A movement beside Ulfar's bench opened his eyes. Auln knelt near him, her blue eyes reflecting the dim light of the fire.

"It will not go well," she whispered, close to his ear. "I see it. Can we not stay alone, by ourselves, away from the world?" Her voice was so forlorn that Ulfar reached out to hold her hand.

"I would like that, Auln," he said softly. "You and I and our children together, only us."

She wept, the tears falling from her cheek to his hand as she held it close to her face.

"I am sorry, Ulfar," she whispered, her head bent. "My womb cannot make life, and you deserve so much. You gave me a home and a ring, and I have brought you nothing but pain. I am cursed."

"Do not say such things!" he said. "A child will come."

She wiped the tears away and forced a smile. "Yes. Yes it will." She frowned. "Do not go to Arnkel. Do not!"

Ulfar lay back, letting her hand drop. He looked at her with wide eyes.

"I cannot stand Thorolf's abuse any longer, wife. He means to kill me one day," he said. "I see it as clearly as one of your visions. Only one man can help me."

He closed his eyes to sleep.

She drank a cup of hot water mixed with Thorbrand's honey to settle herself before bed, and then crawled into the sheets next to him, arms wrapped warmly around his chest.

Ulfar lay on his side, watching the last dying embers of the peat fire burn out to darkness. He lay awake a long time.

———

The next day he walked up the hill to the great house at Bolstathr, a small box of carved driftwood under his arm. In it were gifts. There was a bundle of smoked salmon, wrapped in fragrant sea weed. Two cabbages lay on top of it, the green leaves hanging out to show how the box was overfull. A cheese went beside them, then several wild mushrooms, and the last of his rotted shark, reeking of the piss he had poured on it long ago. The best of the gifts was an infant sack of oiled seal skin, lined with fine wool. Auln had hated seeing it go, but Arnkel *gothi*'s wife was expecting. After several daughters, the first son was anticipated, and the *gothi* would treasure a gift that protected his first male heir.

Ulfar turned aside when he saw Arnkel *gothi* out in the home field with his men, checking the sheep for clemming.

The *gothi* turned when Ulfar walked in the gate, and stood with his hands on his hips watching Ulfar approach.

They were peas in a pod, he and Lamefoot, thought Ulfar as he stepped forward nervously. Arnkel was a younger version of the old man, the same thick neck, the same cold blue eyes, but the hair was blonde, not grey, and the bulk was muscle. It made him nervous to look up into the *gothi*'s face, towering above him. Arnkel had size, but there was a quickness to him, too, in speech and step, as if impatient with the pace of other men.

Then Arnkel *gothi* smiled, his teeth like huge white stones, and held out his arm, stepping forward. Ulfar took the arm. It was like holding the branch of a tree.

"Ulfar Freedman," the *gothi* said, as if announcing him to his men. "I have heard about the death of the infant in your home. Life can be hard, sometimes."

Ulfar blinked, confused, not expecting sympathy from a chieftain. He bowed, not sure if he should speak. So they stood for a while until Arnkel *gothi* turned to grin at one of his men and then waved a hand to the turf house.

"Come to my Hall, Ulfar. We will speak there. It seems you have business with me, although your tongue has left you."

They slipped through the mud of the paddock, and then scraped their feet for a few moments on the wall stones. Arnkel *gothi* walked ahead of him. The turf Hall was three times or more the size of Ulfar's home. Many flagstones surrounded the doors at the north end, and made a path down to the stables further on. They scraped their boots again and walked in, the stones continuing into the Hall. Through the door the gloom descended, but it was much less gloom than Ulfar's home. Two smoke holes pierced the long roof instead of one, and each of these let in a cone of pale sunlight through the arched loft above, the meats and herbs hanging from the rafters twisting slightly in the updraft from the long banked fire in the middle of the floor. An oil lamp of stone burned on the wall to their right, and Ulfar wondered at the wealth that let a man burn a lamp even when no one was using it.

"Have you ever been in my Hall, Ulfar?" Arnkel asked him. Ulfar shook his head, but then answered when he realized that he could not be seen well.

"No, *gothi*," he said.

"Not even at the Autumn feast?"

There was a breath of corruption in the air. In the dim light, Ulfar saw the wool curtain blocking off the alcove of the latrine. The jacks were directly attached to the Hall, and he gawked at the splendor of not having to bundle up in the cold winter to void oneself.

"No, *gothi*," he said, and then decided to be bold. "My former master Thorbrand is a Thingman of Snorri *gothi*. I have attended only his Autumn feast, at Helgafell."

Arnkel *gothi* turned, the lamplight steeping his face in deep shadow. "Of course. And yet you are here, and not at Helgafell." He walked into the Hall, and sat himself in the High Seat that stood along one long wall. It was raised onto a low dais of black basalt. From its height, a man could watch both doors. The upright beams of wood that formed the seat's back went up into the rafters that held the turf above them, each post carved with the curling, crossing lines and swirls of the Gripping Beast. Ulfar followed, and then stopped several steps away. Arnkel *gothi* lit another lamp, and the doubling of light showed many things. On the wall were weapons, hung openly; spears, and unstrung bows, a half dozen shields, and two swords, the blades gleaming with oil. The *gothi* saw his eyes on them.

"My father Thorolf brought those blades back from the wars in the south and taught me their use. They are Frankish. Do not ask to touch them or know their names."

Ulfar swallowed. He took the box from under his arm and thrust it forward, suddenly full of doubt and fear. He was dabbling in strange waters, with violent men, and felt his courage melting away. "I bring gifts to honor you, Arnkel *gothi*, and to ask a boon of you."

Arnkel leaned forward, his hands mounding the arms of his chair like vast spiders.

"I see. We'd best get witnesses in here then, if we are to strike some kind of agreement. Did you bring anyone?"

Ulfar shook his head uncertainly. Witnesses?

The *gothi* called out and three men came in from outside.

"Here are Thorgils and Hafildi, whom you know," the *gothi* said, waving a hand at the two of them. "Both are *bondi* in my service, and honorable men. They can act as witnesses, but it would be better if you had a man, too. Nine men is best, of course, but it would be difficult to gather them all quickly." Thorgils nodded civilly to Ulfar. Hafildi was a red faced man, with the defiant angry cheer of some large men. He looked at Ulfar with a cold curiosity. "This is Thrain," Arnkel said, raising his hand to the last man, a smallish fellow with bright eyes and a quickness to his movement, like a bird. "He is not from Swan fjord, but he is my Thingman."

"Witnesses for what, *gothi*?" Ulfar had found his voice somehow, but nearly lost his nerve again at the frown of irritation on the man's vast face.

"You ask for an intervention in some matter, correct?" said Arnkel *gothi*. "You seek to resolve an issue in your favor yet you need help with this, for one reason or another. We may help each other, then. But each of us must be protected."

"Can I not just tell you my trouble, *gothi*, and let you decide if you can do something about it?" Ulfar said nervously. Once more the frown, but it was followed immediately by a smile.

"Ulfar Freedman, I hear you, but a credible witness must know all of a bargain, not just the agreements at the end. Name a man or two and I will send for him, if it is not too far."

The three Thingmen men settled onto a bench with folded arms. From behind Ulfar came footsteps as man after man came into the Hall until there were six of them. They sat along the benches, one going into an alcove to fetch a skin of ale, which he carried between them, pouring it into their drinking horns. The men stared at Ulfar, whispering to each other. It was the first meal, after the morning work. Several women and a pair of slaves brought out small trays of cheese and meat and set them on trestles. A slave walked along scraping curds into each of the men's bowls from a large iron pot.

"My brother?" Ulfar suggested tentatively, but there were hoots at this from the eating men.

"Not close kin, Ulfar. His word would be suspect, should it come to court."

Court? Did the *gothi* think he would ever take him to court? The thought appalled him.

Ulfar thought quickly. He knew almost no one except the sons of Thorbrand, and so he said the names of Thorleif and Illugi, since they had first seen the wrong that Lamefoot had done to him. This seemed to please Arnkel *gothi*, to his relief. Ulfar simply wanted the matter over and done.

The *gothi* waved Ulfar to a bench to eat, and then nosed through the box Ulfar had brought while they waited for men to fetch the brothers. "I smell something worth having right now," he said, and fetched out the shark. He drew a knife from his belt and cut long slices of the gelatinous meat on a slab of wood and handed it around to the waiting men, spearing the biggest piece for himself with the tip of his knife, and popping it into his mouth. He whistled thoughtfully at the vegetables, and then held up the infant sack and nodded to Ulfar in thanks.

Ulfar picked at a bowl of curds without appetite.

A grey haired woman came out from the private living space, a curtained enclosure at one end of the long building. Arnkel *gothi* nodded to her, standing, and took her hand. She was dressed in good red cloth, and a fine robe of fur. Age had not stooped her at all, though she coughed forcefully into her hand at one point, her shoulders hunched with the force of it, and the pain in her face was clear. Her eyes were dark and proud and full of a direct confidence that made Ulfar flinch, as if she could see into the weakness of his heart.

"You know Gudrid, my mother, do you not? Mother, this is
Ulfar Freedman. He has a problem and desires my aid."

"He is not a Thingman of my son, the Chieftain, is he?" she
said haughtily. "Why should my son help him?"

Arnkel *gothi* raised his hand, as if to soften her words. "All
good men within my reach may have my aid, mother, if they are
to be true friends to me."

"You are too generous, Arnkel *gothi*," Gudrid said disapprov-
ingly. "Ulfar Freedman, do not take advantage of my son, who
only thinks of the best interests of his neighbors, and rarely his
own desires."

Ulfar's eyes had followed the words back and forth, and he
nodded, eyes wide at the oddness of the drama. He said nothing,
glancing at the other men for some clue. Thorgils looked at his
feet, while Hafildi sat with crossed arms, pursing his lips tightly,
as if fighting a smile.

Gudrid whispered a few words with the *gothi* before disappear-
ing behind the curtain of the sleeping area.

It was rumored savagely that Lamefoot had gone viking soon
after marrying the woman, because he could not tame her, though
to Ulfar's mind Thorolf Lamefoot needed no special reason to go
out to a life of fighting. It was in his soul.

Arnkel *gothi* waved over the rough-looking pair of men who
strutted into the Hall. It was the Fish Brothers, looking for breakfast. Ulfar glanced up nervously, and then put his eyes back on his
curds. Arnkel whispered a short command to them. They looked
at the *gothi*, frowning, shaking their heads, until he grew angry
with them, and pointed imperiously. They left grumbling. Ulfar
could make out nothing of what was said.

After a long while, with Ulfar sitting awkwardly listening to
the jokes and rough gossip of Arnkel's men, there was the sound
of horses outside. Thorleif and Illugi were ushered through the
door. Thorleif was cautious, looking around at the men, while
Illugi walked with a dark frown, daring the men to stare at him.

Ulfar felt envy then that such a young one should have the courage he lacked even if it was just foolishness.

"The sons of Thorbrand," Arnkel announced, seating himself again as if he were a king. "Ulfar the Freedman has asked that you be witnesses at our agreement, if there is to be one. Are you prepared to do so?"

"What agreement, Arnkel *gothi*?" Thorleif asked.

"I myself have yet to hear it, Thorleif. If you do not agree to it, you may withhold your witness."

Thorleif mulled it for a moment, and then nodded without enthusiasm. A place was made for them on the wall bench. But first Thorleif came forward and offered a large clay jug to Arnkel *gothi*, saying it was a gift from his father, Thorbrand.

The *gothi*'s eyes brightened. "Yes, we have heard of your father's honey, Thorleif. My wife would enjoy it very much."

"This is a slightly different kind, *gothi*. Darker, fuller of taste, so my father tells me. A woman with child craves the sweet." Thorleif's mouth was twisted. "It is his gift, not mine."

Arnkel *gothi* nodded, and called out to the living alcove. A girl came out, no more than fourteen years old. She walked forward, unafraid under the eyes of all the men. "Halla, take this to your mother," Arnkel said, and handed her the jar. She took it, knowing the men ogled her long blonde hair and her slender waist. Arnkel shook a finger at her for her immodesty, fighting a smile.

He turned back to Thorleif. "You and I played together as children, Thorleif, but I do not see much of you these days. Did I beat you too soundly when we wrestled?"

Thorleif said nothing. The *gothi*'s Thingmen laughed. Arnkel waved them to silence. "Come again to my Hall, and we will play a few games of board, and share a cup."

Thorleif nodded and sat down. He noticed Illugi staring at the girl as she vanished behind the curtain, and that she looked back at him. He smiled at Illugi's wide eyes, and how they followed the girl until she was gone.

"So now, Ulfar Freedman, all the witnesses are gathered. Tell me your need," Arnkel said, and leaned forward to listen.

So Ulfar told the story of the taking of the hay.

He faltered for a moment when it became clear that it was Thorolf, Arnkel *gothi*'s father, who was the cause of his complaint, and the black frown again descended onto the man's face. Ulfar's words came faster, thinking that rage would soon take the man, and he realized how foolish it had been to come the Bolstathr. But the *gothi* waved encouragingly to Ulfar when he hesitated.

"I do not seek revenge, *gothi*," he said hurriedly. "Nor any kind of satisfaction except the return of my share of the hay. I will even pay a fee to your father for the use of his slaves to reap it into cocks and gather it." Now that it was done, he wanted only that the *gothi* refuse, and send him away without harm for the insult of persecuting his own father.

There was shouting outside, as if cued to his final words.

It was Thorolf.

He stormed into the Hall, limping heavily, the two Fish Brothers nervously behind him. He saw Ulfar standing in front of his son. The old warrior's eyes went narrow and pig-like and he strode forward, fists like rocks.

"Hold, Thorolf!" Arnkel *gothi* shouted. He stood and reached to the wall behind him to take down a sword. Then he turned and held the sword high, the tip at eye level.

"There will be no man attacked in my Hall, Thorolf," Arnkel *gothi* called out, and his face and voice were both grim.

Ulfar had stumbled back, not quite hidden behind the High Seat. Lamefoot carried no weapons, but he would need none. Ulfar stared from the *gothi* to the old man, eyes wide.

Lamefoot stopped.

"You would draw steel on your own blood, for him?" Lamefoot said darkly, looking through his eyebrows. Ulfar trembled when those terrible eyes turned his way. "It is witchcraft he practices on you, swaying your mind. Did not one in every five sheep last summer have the clemming and die, all except his, although all our sheep mingled on the pasture? When the storms killed some of the sheep of every man, were his not spared? Magic!" Thorolf stopped, panting from his long words and glared at Arnkel. "What do you want of me, son?"

"He says you have taken his hay, and there are men here who also saw it."

"I have taken what is rightfully mine," Lamefoot growled. "The hay on his side yields three times that on mine. Another magic. I did him a service to take in the hay before the rain came, and he gave me only harsh words."

"We did not *handsal* sharing the hay after harvest," Ulfar interrupted, voice trembling. "We settled on that half of the meadow yours and the other half mine." Ulfar's skin crawled at the defiance in his tone, but he had to speak. "Whatever came off our own half was our property alone. And there has been no rain."

He saw Thorgils bob his head, urging him on.

He turned to face Arnkel, aghast at his own daring.

"*Gothi*, you witnessed this, the sale of the meadow, eight years ago at the Thing, when I first bought the land from your father. It was then you heard that we had split the meadow, along the ridge line."

The *gothi* would deny it, and then it would be over.

Arnkel nodded.

He pointed the sword at Thorolf's feet. "Ulfar speaks the truth, father. It seems you have taken all the hay from the field instead of just from the half you can claim."

Ulfar was stunned. The *bondi* around them watched open mouthed as the *gothi* turned on his father. Only Thorgils and Hafildi seemed unsurprised.

It was very quiet in the Hall.

"You will return three of four parts of the hay, Thorolf, without even payment for use of the slaves, to offset Ulfar's dishonor in having his property taken," Arnkel said. His tone was cold and final.

Lamefoot sputtered and stammered in protest. Then he spat on the ground, and shouted that Thor would grow rabbit's ears before he would give back the hay, and he would kill any of Arnkel *gothi*'s men who came to claim it, and Ulfar in the bargain. Ulfar had never seen the man say so much at once.

Thorolf stormed out when he was done speaking, splintering the door of the Hall with his foot before Hafildi could open it for him.

The hum of conversation began again.

Ulfar sat down, legs weak. It staggered him. He had won.

Arnkel *gothi* hung the sword up, whispered words to it, and then sat. He beckoned Ulfar closer, and bent his head to the Freedman.

One hand reached into a little leather pouch tied to his belt. There was a jingling of coins and metal.

He took hold of Ulfar's hand and dropped money into it, enough to pay for the hay, all of it real coin from Norway, with the head of the King on one side. Ulfar had only held money for a short time in his life, when he had sold all his stock to pay for his freedom. It made him nervous to have so much wealth, so small and easily taken, with all these eyes on it, and he said so to the *gothi*. Money was for warriors and chieftains, he said. But Arnkel only laughed, as if he meant it as a joke.

"I shall pay you for the hay as I think my father may harm you if you try to reclaim it yourself. This is my duty as chieftain of this fjord although you are not my Thingman. I do take on the dispute to myself and do so without fee. I hope that you and I may be friends."

Gratitude swelled in Ulfar's heart. The fear dropped from him. Arnkel *gothi* was a good man, a man of honor, who would face the monster for him. He dropped to one knee, and clasped the *gothi*'s hand, feeling light fall again on his head. Words had been forming in his mind, and now they poured out as a song. His voice was clear and strong, full of intricate harmony. In his song he compared Arnkel *gothi* to the sword hanging on the wall, telling how the two edges cut for the sake of others, one against enemy and the other for friend. At first the *gothi* frowned at the presumption and pulled away his hand, but then the magic of it took him and by its end he was smiling and nodding. The men rocked and clapped throughout the song, even the Fish Brothers, and they called out for another.

"Ulfar is well known as a *skald*," Thorgils said.

Arnkel waved them down, smiling.

"Yes, you have a way with verse, Ulfar Freedman," Arnkel *gothi* said. "It is said that Odin is the God of war, but that He is also the God of poets for he is clever and wise as any king must be, on earth or in the sky. If I had known of this talent before, I would have had you in my Hall sooner, to bless my home." Then he sent Ulfar away with a smile and hand on his shoulder.

In the gloom, Ulfar could not see the *gothi's* cold eyes follow him, or the hard face of Thorleif, who did not like at all that Ulfar had gone to a man not their chieftain.

Thorleif said nothing, except to agree to witness the agreement. The *gothi* had acted with immense honor and generosity. How could he argue it?

It was best to say nothing. They had no weapons with them.

———

A month passed.

Hard rain fell and so most of the men of the fjord stayed indoors, burning peat. Women worked the looms, the clacking of the wood a constant rhythm. The merchants from Norway could come any day in their ships, and they always gave more for whole cloth than for bulk wool or spun. *Vathmal* the cloth was called, and it was a woman's duty to make it as all the other women of the Free State did, so that there could be a standard. Ulfar had thirty bolts of it stacked under the sleeping benches, and the last of their sheep's wool would give them a few more. It was a good reserve. With it he could buy barley and hops to make ale. A bolt would buy more honey from Thorbrand to sweeten Auln's temper. She had rubbed the last of it out of Thorbrand's jar with her finger three weeks ago.

She was healthier, with color in her face and she worked longer. In time she would be ready for another child. Ulfar wanted the bedding very much. It had been a long time since he had touched his wife that way.

He busied himself within the house after the dawn feeding of the stock, oiling a blanket carefully for rain wear, sharpening his peat shovel, but taking care not to intrude on duties that belonged to Auln alone. He spent time in the hay barn stopping a leak in the roof. By afternoon though, it was hard to find tasks that would not undo good and Auln had begun to slap his hand back from things. She frowned at his idleness by the fire.

Ulfar sighed.

He threw on the newly oiled blanket to test it and walked out into the rain.

There was no point in soaking boots, so he went barefoot. It was not too cold. He loved the summer, especially when it hung on longer than usual as it did that year. Thor, the Sky God, smiled on them. If only the season lasted a month longer, the things he could grow! Even wheat could be teased from the ground. He walked over to the hay barn again and scraped the floor of all the loose hay he could find, before taking a bundle from the short pile in the corner.

Arnkel *gothi*'s money lay in Auln's locked chest, the key hanging from her apron. He would have to buy hay and that meant another trip. Some he could get from the sons of Thorbrand, who had large fertile meadows on both banks of the river that gave up much hay. If he was lucky he could have all of their surplus and probably pay a fair price, if they were not too angry with what he had done. Thorleif had seemed alright with what had happened, although Illugi had come to visit and told him that his father Thorbrand had been angry.

"Angry?" Ulfar had said. "Why?"

Illugi had shrugged. "He said we had been tricked, and that was all. I don't understand that old man. He spends his time hunting up roots and mushrooms in the hills with my brother Thorfinn and pretending he's bed-ridden when he's not."

"Mushrooms are good."

"Not these kind. They're all the poisonous ones, you know, the flatheads, and the spikes. He said the elves told him to do it." Illugi tapped his head knowingly, mouth quirked in contempt.

Then the boy had shown him the bow he had made from a yew branch bought from a farmer in the next valley, and the pine wood arrows, grinning evilly as he pulled them from their oiled sack.

"Can I store these here, Ulfar? Thorbrand forbids me from having them. He says I'm too hot headed and I'll shoot someone, and he'll have to pay blood money. I'll stop by to get them when I hunt." He winked. "Lamefoot might not be so brave with these in your hands."

Ulfar had been horrified. Loose arrows at Lamefoot? That was madness.

He showed the boy a place to hide his bow and shafts in the rafters of the barn, out of sight, so that Auln would not find them. He wanted no questions and Auln might get ideas if she knew he had such a fine weapon near, one that could take down even the mighty Thorolf. Illugi left, running inside to take a bite of cheese from under Auln's nose and to steal a kiss on her cheek. She slapped his arm, but let him have both the cheese and the kiss, laughing at the impish face he had made to her.

As he worked, Ulfar kept an eye on the meadow, near the ridge line. The rain was good and it was bad. It was miserable enough outside that Lamefoot would not feel like coming out to bother him yet it also meant he would spend the day drinking and who knew what could happen then? It was said that all of Lamefoot's money went to drink. He liked ale and wine, though never mead, which sickened him. Most of the plunder he had brought back from the southern wars had gone to pay for it. But the last two years, he had been paying in *vathmal*, and produce, what little he could grow, and trying to make his own drink. Thorolf was not a good farmer, nor were his slaves. They were Kerns, not noted for labor, only good in a scrap. So Thorolf had told him told him long ago, before he had started to hate Ulfar for being three times the farmer he was, just after he had sold the land to him. Ulfar's money had lain thick in his pocket then and the glow of his stature in the valley filled him.

Everyone had feared Lamefoot after his slaughter of Einar.

He stood and looked toward Bolstathr. A circle of stones lay hidden in the grass of the home field. It had happened there, fifteen years ago. The grass grew a little thicker around the stones, where the sheep could not get their teeth in.

His name had been Einar Gudson. He had owned all the land in Swan's fjord except Swan firth at the river mouth. Many men thought of him as wise, and his greed was hidden well since could strike a deal that left both sides content.

Einar had been no warrior, but he was a brave and strong man and even as he collapsed at Lamefoot's feet, bleeding from half a dozen stab and slash wounds, he put his blade into Lamefoot's leg, and given the old bastard his name forever, along with his lands.

That was the old way, and Ulfar was glad that he had not owned land back then, when a man could challenge in the *Holmganga*, the duel, and take all you had with a sword, if you had no sons.

Ulfar watched their ghosts fight within the circle, drawn by the horror of it, but knowing he should pay it no mind. It would give Lamefoot strength if he dwelled on it. His memory of the fight was not clear. He had been far off, still slave to Thorbrand and so Einar and the younger Lamefoot hopped about strangely, fighting only the bits Ulfar could remember. Einar fell to his knees.

His arm came up and plunged the sword into Lamefoot's calf. Thorolf's head went back in agony.

Behind the ghosts, men came out of Arnkel *gothi*'s Hall.

They carried spears and shields.

The spirits faded as Ulfar stared at the men, mouth open. There were a dozen of them. Some were farmers from the next valley, including Thrain. Thorgils led them, his face grim, and at his side was a tall, quick stepping man called Gizur who had grinned warmly at Ulfar after his song in Arnkel's Hall, and wiped the tears from his grey eyes. Last of all came the Fish Brothers.

Arnkel men turned right out of the pasture gate of Bolstathr and marched in single file along the rock path that led up into the meadow.

Hvammr, Lamefoot's farm, lay over there.

Ulfar dropped his shovel and hopped the stone fence of his home field. He ran after them, keeping low. It was grey and misty and none of them looked back. A man came out of the rocks to join them. He had a spear, too.

Had he been watching Lamefoot's farm?

The men rounded the ridge and went down into the valley along the trail that led to Hvammr. Ulfar followed. He crossed onto Lamefoot's land with a swallow of fear.

He hid behind a rock and looked down into the valley. Hvammr was an unkempt farmstead. Valuable patties of manure lay scattered where the sheep and cows had dropped them, simply because no one had scooped them up and put them into the pile. The rain would wash them into the mud in a short while and all would be lost. The walls of the Hall and barn were tattered. Four slaves, and the place looked abandoned. He shook his head.

The dozen men walked toward the farmstead. Their spears came down and they moved cautiously, fanning out into a line. Gizur called out and a man came out of the turf house, one of Lamefoot's slaves, called Baldy for his bare, gleaming scalp. His eyes went wide. The words were faint but Ulfar heard Thorgils ask if

Thorolf was home. The slave only shook his head, mute with caution. A woman came out of the door of the Hall, Lamefoot's second wife, Helga, stooped and grey haired. She pointed an angry finger up the long hill to Thorswater dale, a narrow cut in the foothills where the stream that ran through the farm began from a spring, far away and barely visible through the mist.

"He's gone to see his do-nothing friend, Cunning-Gill," she complained. "To drink and laugh and remember the English wars with that pauper, while his slaves loll about. He should be watching over their work! He cares more for his old comrades than for me!"

"He'll have less to laugh about after this day, woman," Gizur said.

Gizur pointed to the stock barn, and some of the men went in. They came out leading seven of the cows, ropes about their necks. The slave said nothing, although he stepped forward. Gizur pushed him back with his spear. Helga watched with wide eyes and then shrieked in horror when she saw the men begin to lead the cattle away, and hung pathetically from Thorgils' arm. He shook her off gently, and she fell into the mud and wept.

Ulfar ran back ahead of them as they began to climb back up the hill with the cows. He scrambled along the rock on his hands to keep from being seen. His heart pounded.

A part of him reveled at what had happened. Lamefoot had been hurt, and though it was Arnkel *gothi*'s men who had taken the cows, everyone would know it was because of Ulfar. It was revenge and he tried to savor it.

But his heart was filled with terror. Lamefoot would blame him, not Arnkel.

He was a dead man.

II
Winter

Of the Fire And the Hangings

Arnkel gothi sat dozing on his High Seat, chin on one hand. His stomach was full, but with meat and porridge only, because he did not like ale to cloud his mind, and there might be need to move quickly later. He drifted in the land of dreams, hearing sounds around him but seeing other things.

He fished by the water off a great rock jutting out into the fjord, and Einar was beside him, preparing his hook with bait. It was odd because Arnkel was a man in the dream, and yet still he looked up into the craggy face. The lines around the mouth and eyes bent into that crooked smile the old man had always worn whenever he saw his grandson. Einar nodded to him and winked, as if he knew everything in Arnkel's mind and approved.

He startled awake to a burst of laughter.

It was the Yule tide feast, and there was feasting in his Hall.

Many Thingmen had come, some from the other valley, and the Hall was full. Men sat tightly together on the benches, elbows on the trestles, drinking and eating. An entire side of beef hung from the spit over the great hearth fire, the yule log in the middle of it, burning down to coals. The smell of roasting fat filled the air like perfume. A dozen torches and lamps burned, and there were shadows in the deepest corners only. New straw had been laid down to keep their feet warm.

36

Ulfar Freedman sat at a bench near Arnkel's hand, a wary eye on the *gothi*'s roughest men. He kept his eyes down whenever Hafildi or one of the Fish Brothers looked his way.

One setting at the trestle table had been kept empty, by the *gothi*'s order. It was not at his right hand, the place of honor, because Ulfar sat there, but near the end. It was left for Lamefoot, who had not arrived.

That was expected, Arnkel thought. He was still pouting, although it had been four months since Arnkel had taken his cows.

The fat old man had stormed into his Hall a week after Thorgils and Gizur had claimed his fee. His bellowed threats and his sword had forced every man out of the Hall except the Fish Brothers, Thorgils and Hafildi who stood their ground and threatened him with lowered spears. By then Thorolf was out of breath and he left them alone to stand in front of Arnkel.

"The deal was one cow. One!" Lamefoot had snarled. "Give the other six back."

"They are slaughtered, old man," Arnkel said, the hidden laughter like a pain in his chest. "My meat stocks were low and I have many Thingmen to feast. They are in the barrels now, all but one." He had stood and picked up his own sword and then his shield and looked calmly at his father.

Lamefoot's eyes bulged.

He had pointed a trembling finger at his son, too angry to care if the other men heard. "You betrayed me. You said you would use your position to guard me when I took that bastard Ulfar's hay. For one cow. For one. But you meant only to cheat me."

"The hay was worth much more than one cow, old man," Arnkel said. Again Thorolf had reddened at the insulting name. "My men saw the stack of it in your barn. Ulfar has a way with the land as you do not, and I had to pay him the worth of it in money. That was my duty as *gothi*, and I needed to recoup what I had lost. How is this betrayal?"

Thorolf pointed his finger again. "All you have now is because of me, boy. You would not be chieftain if I had not put up the gold for it and bought Snorri *gothi*'s support eight years ago."

Arnkel had stood suddenly, teeth bared. The sudden transformation had startled the men, and even Thorolf stepped back. "Snorri tricked you, old man. He made you sell half my inheritance to the slaves of another man for that support. Ulfarsfell and Orlygstead are my land. My land!"

Lamefoot had stared at him. "It's that Ulfar. You've been seduced by him, by those damn songs of his. I've heard the others tell of it. You have him here each night, like some bird in a cage."

Arnkel *gothi* glared at him, despising the man for his stupidity, for his predictability.

"He's a better man than you, Thorolf Lamefoot," he said.

"I'll tell everyone," Lamefoot said, suddenly cold. "I'll tell them of our pact."

Arnkel spat out his answer. "Yes, make false accusations with no witness to what you say. Do that and I will persecute you in the Thing for your false words and take the rest of your chattel as fine. One lone *bondi*, without friends, persecuting his only son who is chieftain. You will be mocked. Old man."

The Fish Brothers' eyes had been going back and forth between the men behind their spear tips, and they braced, ready to go at Lamefoot if he charged.

Thorolf had said nothing more. He turned and left the Hall.

Arnkel *gothi* had followed after a few moments, to watch where his father went, beckoning the Fish Brothers, but Thorolf had turned toward his own farm.

That was good, Arnkel thought. It was too soon then for his father to play out his last use in life.

Everything in time.

His grandfather had said that to him many times, and finally, as a man, he had come to understand it.

Arnkel waited, while his men feasted on Thorolf's last cow.

He had sent the Fish Brothers and their sharp tongues to Hvammr a little while before. They had not liked leaving the warmth of the Hall and ale for the snow outside. They liked it even less when he told them that they were to go to Thorolf's Hall and invite the old man, and to speak of the great half of beef strung up for all to share, and the endless skins of ale that hung from pegs.

At the door of the Hall, far from the others, he added another thing.

"And tell also that Ulfar is here, singing songs, at my right hand. Be sure to say that."

They sobered quickly when they heard that and looked at each other. They took their spears and shields.

A while later there was a draft of cold wind from the main door and the stomping of snowy feet. Thorolf staggered in, draped in a lambskin and wool. He swayed drunkenly, stared for a moment at Arnkel and Ulfar, and then went to the fire pit. With his knife, he cut away a haunch of meat as large as his head and tucked it into a sack at his waist. He threw a brace of ale skins over his shoulder.

"Do you now leave, father? Is this how you repay my hospitality, to come in like some raider to pilfer my feast?" Arnkel's voice silenced the murmurs of outrage from the gathering of his Thingmen. "While I honor my good friend and Thingman, Ulfar?" Then, as if overcoming great anger and showing manly restraint, Arnkel stood and stepped down from his High Seat to put a hand on Ulfar's shoulder. "Come and listen to my good friend, for he is a singer of much talent. Let there not be anger between us, father."

He kept his face open and friendly, although his soul wanted to laugh madly at the rage that spun the eyes of Lamefoot like saucers. The old warrior stared at Ulfar's hanging head for a very long time.

Arnkel stepped forward. "Your scowl darkens my Hall, Thorolf Lamefoot. Do not think you can harm my good friend, Ulfar. It is beyond your strength."

Lamefoot backed away, his face taut with madness, and left.

He stopped once, to throw another skin over his shoulder, this one of mead, and smash away the Thingman who tried to fight him for it. Then he was gone. Hafildi held the jury-rigged door open for him, so that he could not kick it again. It was too cold for broken doors.

Thorgils met Ulfar's wide eyes. He turned away.

The bones of the cow were dragged outside when there was little left but dog pickings. Most of the visitors had found a place on the benches or the floor to sleep when Ulfar had sung his last song and gone home carrying gifts from the *gothi*.

"He'll be bolting his door tonight," Hafildi said loudly as Ulfar passed by them. Arnkel stood and led him out.

"Don't let it trouble you, Ulfar," the *gothi* said quietly. "Lamefoot is sleeping under two skins of ale now."

A few men stayed up.

The mass of embers from the cook fire would burn until dawn, and made the Hall too hot to bear with their coats and boots on. The *gothi* had insisted they stay dressed and ready. They sat in the entrance way to keep cool, but it was still too warm so they went outside to stand by the wall with Thorgils, who had the watch. The cold, clear air bit at their skin and revealed the stars fierce and sharp even through the moonlight.

Arnkel looked at his men approvingly. There were eight of them altogether, the best of his Thingmen in a fight. Gizur, the Fish Brothers, Thorgils and Hafildi he knew would not run. The other three were farmers, called to stay the night, and they knew nothing except what the others had told them, but they all seemed stout.

"How do you know he'll come tonight?" Thorgils asked Arnkel softly, so that none of the others could hear. "That was enough drink to put away even Lamefoot."

"He took mead." Arnkel *gothi* said shortly. "Thorolf hates mead. His wife drinks not at all. He wanted strong drink."

"So?"

Arnkel tapped his temple with one finger. "My father will not try to kill Ulfar himself. He knows that he would be outlawed, a year at least and probably three, and he is too old to wander anymore. So he will send his slaves." He shrugged. "Of course, anything is possible. If nothing happens within the hour, we will watch in shifts."

He looked down at Thorgils. "I need to know if you are behind me, old friend," he said, his voice low and private. "Things will happen soon."

Thorgils looked at him, and then away. He stared down the slope to Ulfar's farm, as if struggling with the thoughts in his mind. The dark of the night pressed in like a cold sheet on his heart.

In his mind he saw Auln, her hair moving in the breeze.

"I am with you," he said finally, his voice tense.

Arnkel frowned at him. "Are you sure?"

"Did I not say it?" Thorgils snapped, and the other men looked over, surprised to hear the sharp words toward the *gothi*.

Arnkel was calm, however. He nodded, satisfied.

Hafildi came up to them. "Do you think Lamefoot will offer them their freedom to do it?" he asked. His voice was loud, full of ale, and Arnkel put a finger to his lips, frowning.

"There," said Thorgils, pointing. A large black mass moved against the white of the snow at the bottom of the hill and they squinted to make it out. It moved toward Ulfar's farm.

Arnkel *gothi* picked up his shield and spear and leapt over the stone wall. His men followed. They ran quickly down the long slope to Ulfar's farm.

One of the farmers became fearful of ghosts or elves and made to stop, but was hissed forward by the others. They squatted behind Ulfar's home field wall and peered over it.

Three men dragged a tangled mass of branches and brush behind them down through the hay meadow. They came from the direction of Hvammr. It took some heaving to get it over the wall, but finally they tumbled it across with one great effort, grabbed the ropes holding it together and pulled toward Ulfar's house. They came to the little open space in front of the turf house, panting.

"Those are Lamefoot's slaves," Hafildi said quietly in Arnkel's ear, marveling at the wisdom of his chieftain. "Should we take them?"

"Wait."

The slaves huddled down, whispering. There was a rapid clicking of metal on flint, and a shower of sparks lit up the dark. A small flame grew larger until it began to consume the pile of brushwood. The slaves pushed it up against the house.

"Now?" Hafildi hissed, and the men looked at Arnkel anxiously. He shook his head. The dry grass of the turf wall and roof would catch any moment and the place would burn up in a heartbeat. The flames lit the slaves as they scrambled to either side of the door with spears in their hands, waiting.

There were voices from inside. Ulfar and his wife, confused and sleepy, and then crying out in alarm. The fire was as tall as a man now and its light could be seen through the doorway. Smoke clung thickly to the roof as it rose.

Arnkel *gothi* went to one knee, and hefted his shield. "Get ready," he said.

The door of the turf house was wrenched open. At that moment Arnkel leapt over the wall.

"Murderers!" he shouted. "Put down your spears!"

His men swarmed after him, yelling loudly. The terrified slaves threw down their weapons at the sight of the charging men and knelt in the snow, hands over their heads, their mead courage gone.

In the doorway stood Ulfar. He wore his nightclothes and was barefoot, eyes wide as he watched Arnkel knock the slaves flat to the ground with the haft of his spear and then lead his men in pulling the flaming brush away from the house. It continued to burn, lighting the open space.

Ulfar stumbled out into the snow, and fell onto his knees before Arnkel. Auln watched from the door, hands to her mouth.

"Thank you, *gothi*, thank you." Ulfar stammered the words, trying to speak.

Arnkel *gothi* held up his hand and helped Ulfar to his feet. He hated the touch of the craven man on him, thinking some of his coward's sweat would soak in to his own flesh. "You are safe for this night, Ulfar Freedman, but it was only by chance that I was smelling the night air with my men before bed or you and your wife would be dead now. Your life is in great danger here."

"What can I do?" Ulfar said, desperately.

———

Two days later, after a long snowstorm that had kept everyone penned indoors, the sons of Thorbrand were invited again as witnesses to an event at Arnkel *gothi*'s Hall. The messenger, Hafildi, was vague about the details and claimed to be in a hurry to invite others. He smiled from the saddle as he wheeled the horse away, and said to come with empty stomachs. The brothers thought there would be a feast and drink and that Arnkel's friendly words of before to Thorleif meant the first of many free meals and happy times. It was better to get along with neighbors than to argue, they said to each other, especially when the neighbor was a chieftain, and so they would put behind them their dissatisfaction with Ulfar going to Arnkel for help, instead of Snorri *gothi*, their own chieftain. Only Thorbrand, their father, seemed uncertain.

"Be careful," he warned, shaking his finger at them. They laughed at him.

Thorleif led them. Behind him rode Snorri, named for their foster brother Snorri *gothi* because he had the same white-blond hair. Then came Thorodd, the thick necked smith. Riding side by side came Thormod the Quiet, who never spoke more than one or two words at a time, and Thorfinn the Holy, who first saw ghosts and elves when they appeared and could tell the brothers where to leave their sacrifices to best effect. Last of all was Illugi, full of fire as always. He refused to stay at the rear of the line even when his brothers frowned and hissed at him. It was a formal occasion, after all. They came dressed in their colored shirts under lamb-skin coats and robes, wearing their best boots.

As they passed by Ulfar's farm, they saw a mass of burned wood partly hidden by new snow in the middle of the home field and the charred edge on the roof of the house. The animals were low-ing in hunger. They dismounted, calling for Ulfar, and then fed and watered the animals and cleaned the stalls of the worst of the manure, taking care to keep their clothes clean. Thorleif went to the house, thinking he might find the Freedman dead and lying in blood. There was no answer, but no body, and he sighed in relief. He rode over to see Orlyg but the old man was lying on his cot, more sick than usual, and he knew nothing. Thorleif helped him out to the jacks and then brought him cheese and water.

They came to Arnkel *gothi*'s Hall and tethered their horses out-side. Many spears and shields lay against the thick turf of the Hall and the brothers frowned. They had brought no weapons.

Inside the Hall it was noisy, warm and crowded, men laughing with cups and horns in their hands. The brothers smiled, their spirits rising as they were greeted in a friendly enough way by Thorgils and led to the drink and the food. Thorleif saw two of Snorri *gothi*'s Thingmen there, a pair of fishermen called Sam and Klaenger, and he waved to them across the press of bodies, glad to see friendly faces. He wondered why they would be at Bolstathr. Perhaps they were related to one of Arnkel's men, he thought. It was a common enough thing. Thorgils and Snorri *gothi*'s head-man, Hawk, were cousins.

Thorleif saw Ulfar through the crowd, seated by the *gothi*.

He called and raised his hand in greeting, but Ulfar would not meet his eye. Thorleif frowned, but was turned to the food in front of him by Hafildi's hand on his shoulder, and so he cut away some meat and then ate a small heel of sour bread, unable to resist the rare treat. Hafildi was there again as he moved through the press towards Ulfar, pressing a cup of mead into his hand. His brothers talked with other neighbors not seen in some weeks and all was friendly. Illugi had made his way to where the women sat and put himself in the sight of Halla, who smiled shyly when he waved at her. Ketil, the youngest Fish Brother, hovered near the girl and he frowned when Illugi drew her eye.

"Piss off, boy," Ketil said loudly and Illugi came at him at once, without thought. He was held back by the arms of men around him, who spoke well of his rage and tried to jolly him. Sam the fisherman was one of these. He put his lips to the boy's ear.

"Not the place for a scrap, Illugi," he whispered.

Arnkel *gothi*'s deep voice cut through the din of talk suddenly, calling them to quiet.

Thorleif turned like the others to listen and through the mead mist in his blood saw that somehow spears had come back into the Hall. Gizur stood near the *gothi*'s High Seat with Hafildi, Thorgils and Leif, their weapons butted and shields on their arms.

Illugi was at his elbow then, whispering through gritted teeth. Thorleif shushed him.

Arnkel *gothi* called Ulfar to stand before him.

Ulfar walked out in front of the High Seat. Men parted around him to make a space.

"A terrible crime has been prevented," Arnkel said loudly. "My friend and Thingman Ulfar Freedman fears for his very life and for the safety of his family."

Thorleif's blood turned cold.

Thingman?

"Thorleif!" Illugi hissed. "What is happening?"

Thorleif gripped the boy's arm. "We are betrayed."

So it was that in front of many witnesses Ulfar stood before Arnkel *gothi* and offered his hand, saying the ancient words that gave his land to another man. Arnkel slapped down on it, saying that Ulfar would forever be under his protection, and then Ulfar slapped Arnkel's palm, and the *handsal* was done. His land was given to Arnkel *gothi*. Ulfar would come to live with his wife at Bolstathr, as Arnkel *gothi*'s man, with all the rights and protection of a Thingman.

The Hall was silent. Many eyes turned to the sons of Thorbrand.

Thorodd stepped forward angrily. He shouted that Arnkel had robbed them. Then Thorleif and the others shook their fists and cried out against Arnkel so loudly that no clear words could be heard. The *gothi*'s men shoved them back and there were fists thrown by both sides. In moments the Hall was filled with cries of anger and pain. Illugi booted Ketil hard behind his shield and the man collapsed, hissing as he clutched his groin. Illugi was grabbed from behind and thrown down to the ground. Men kicked him many times. Halla screamed through her hands at the sight of Illugi writhing on the ground. He crawled away through their legs, bleeding from his face but others seized him. His brothers were tackled and brought down, and held by many hands.

The sons of Thorbrand were carried to the doors by Arnkel's men. They writhed and tried to break free.

Thorleif cried out clearly through the struggle.

"This is not Law, Arnkel! We have claim to Ulfar's land, not you! This is *arfskot*! You steal our inheritance!"

Outside, they were pitched into the drifts and spears pointed at them until they mounted their horses and left. Illugi, hunched painfully over his saddle, spat at them as he wheeled his horse away, a bloody wad that colored the snow.

Arnkel *gothi* had drink served to all of his men when the sons of Thorbrand were gone. Then he had the captured slaves brought out.

They were consumed by terror and begged for their lives on their knees, and even after the boots of the Fish Brothers laid them flat on the straw covered floor. They whispered pleas to Arnkel *gothi* in broken Norse—barely understandable through the Cornish accent and the terror—as he pronounced the sentence.

Quick fire, the burning of a man's home, was punishable by outlawing for free men, he said pitilessly. For slaves, it was death by hanging.

Three boats had been readied at the water's edge, called for especially on that day by Arnkel. One boat was the property of the Fish Brothers but the other two belonged to the fishermen, Sam and Klaenger. They had not been told in detail what their service would include, only that they would have feast and drink and two silver coins each for the day's work. Ferrying, Hafildi had hinted, and that seemed easy enough work. Boats were priceless and rare in the Free State. The large pieces of drift wood to make them were a chance find. Arnkel *gothi* had no other men with a vessel.

Sam and Klaenger had watched in horror as their fellow Thing-men had been abused and humiliated. They learned that they were to be used to take doomed men and their executioners across the water to the waste shore on the east side of the fjord where no man lived. The hard looks of the spear men kept them from complaining, but they were not happy to risk the haunting of their boats and the fishing luck that would suffer.

Arnkel, the Fish Brothers and the slaves rode in one boat. Thorgils, Hafildi, Gizur and eight spear men went in Sam and Klaenger's vessels, to act as guards and witnesses. Ulfar came also, face white and grim. He had said nothing to anyone since the ceremony.

There was only one easy place to land on the steep eastern shore, a tiny inlet directly below Vadils Head. They craned their necks back to look at the height above them when they landed. It would be a straight, hard climb to get behind the cliff and the men grumbled about the work involved until Arnkel asked them if they preferred to ride instead through the lands of the sons of Thorbrand to reach the mountain path now that those angry men had returned to their farmstead and found their spears and rallied their servants.

Sam refused to go any farther when they landed. He had worked up his nerve during the crossing and said that he wanted no man's

soul on him for money alone. He crossed his arms and said nothing even when Arnkel *gothi* told him that his fee would be forfeit,
and his face became stubborn when the *gothi* quietly growled that
if he left and abandoned them on the shore that there would be a
settlement. Klaenger was not so determined and was more afraid.
Arnkel told him he would have the full four coins. A spear man
was left behind to make sure that Sam did not leave.

The men prepared for the climb. Lengths of walrus hide rope
were strung over their shoulders.

It took more than an hour to reach the top and they sweated out
the drink from every pore. The bound hands of the slaves had to
be cut so they could climb but they still went slowly unless struck
from behind. One of them wept constantly.

It began to sleet when they reached the top, a cold downpour
that sapped the heat from them. All about were the cairns of stone
and the men became nervous being near the dead.

"*Gothi*," said Hafildi, and pointed below.

The little shape of Sam's boat pulled out from shore. It headed
north under one pair of oars, out to the coast. Arnkel said nothing to this, although his face became hard.

"Damn that Njal," said one of the spear men. "He let the boatman get the best of him."

Ketil laughed darkly. "Not as many going back, anyway," he
said to his brother and they laughed at the horror and despair on
the slave's faces.

Ulfar wandered off to the grave of his child and crouched by
it. He lay one hand on the wet stones.

The coils of hide rope were tied together to make three long
lengths, but it was found that they were too short to hang far
enough over the edge to give a long enough drop to kill a man
for sure. There was some argument over this. The Fish Brothers
said it did not matter if they had to drop the men two or three or
four times to kill them, that they would be dead in the end, anyway. Some of the farmers did not like this. They complained to

the *gothi* that the men's shades would be restless if they were so abused before death. If they hung them one at a time, the shades of the first killed would watch the deaths of the others and gain strength for the haunting. Arnkel *gothi* listened without speaking for a while. Then he called over Ulfar.

"Freedman, the crime was against your home and person. What do you say? How should we go about settling this debt?"

Ulfar looked into the wretched faces of the slaves.

"I would set them free if it is left to me, as long as they swore never to try and harm me or my family again." At this the slaves' faces shone with hope and they swore by Thor and by Odin and by the elves that they would never again go near Ulfar. One even promised to pay for his freedom from Lamefoot one day and become Ulfar's slave. Their hope was cut off by Arnkel's chopping hand.

"You have committed quick fire and this is a crime not against one man but against propriety and our people. Ulfar, I only asked how you would want the debt settled, not forgiven." Arnkel thought a while, and then had every man take off his belt, and unwound his own sash of *vathmal*. These he added to the end of each rope so that they dangled twice a man's height down the cliff side from the iron bolt. The nooses were tied around each slave's neck and their hands were bound again. The other ends were strung through the iron ring bolt in the rock. Arnkel picked up the loops of rope in one hand and a spear in the other and made each slave stand at the precipice.

He waved the other men back and spoke quietly to the slaves, alone.

"You have a way to survive this," he said to their faces, his voice hardly loud enough to ride the wind. "If Ulfar says to stay my hand, I will allow it. But from each of you I want a public admission that you did this crime of your own will, that my father Thorolf had no part in this. You will speak that now, to these witnesses."

They all agreed, shaking with fear and cold.

While Arnkel *gothi* stood next to them, one slave declared that he had always hated Ulfar and that he had decided without any other man's influence to kill the Freedman. The others agreed and swore this was true of all of them.

For one long moment they stood there, as the words drifted on the air.

Arnkel raised his spear level with both hands, and shoved it suddenly into the three bound men. They fell back off the cliff, screaming for an awful instant. The strands of rope hummed tautly across the rock edge as the bodies rocked from the fall, out of sight over the edge.

They waited a good time to make sure that the men were dead. The ropes continued to move, and some men thought the slaves were still alive. Hafildi crawled to the edge and peered over but then rose and said that the movement was only the wind. The slaves were dead.

They were hauled up and the ropes taken off their necks. Two had died instantly, their necks broken. One had obviously strangled and the men did not like this at all. They would have run back to the boats then but Arnkel had them carry the bodies to a bare patch back from the cliff and laid out beside each other. They carried rocks to cover them and chose especially heavy ones for the strangled man so that he could not rise to avenge his terrible death. The ropes and belts were buried with him as a gift to the dead. No man wanted them back. An angry wind howled as they worked and men began to hear voices in it calling their names and speaking other words. Even the Fish Brothers began to hear them and look about with narrowed eyes. Most of them covered their heads with hoods so they could not be recognized. They left the cliff and climbed down, feet wary on the ice covered rocks.

Njal was found lying on the ground, bleeding from his head. He awoke when they shook his shoulder and bolted up. His head bent shamefully under Arnkel's look of contempt.

No one spoke on the long row across the fjord back to Bolstathr. It was crowded without the extra boat, even with the slaves not with them.

On the other side, Arnkel held back two coins from the boatman.

Klaenger looked at the two coins in his hand, frowning. He was a placid, steady man, not easily roused, but the smirks of the Fish Brothers and the hard face of Arnkel *gothi* stirred his slow anger even though he was alone on the shore.

Ulfar turned and left, walking up the hill.

"Why do you cheat me, *gothi*?" Klaenger said, and the Thingmen stepped forward with their spears at these words.

"It is I who have been cheated, fisherman," Arnkel said grimly, and he had his hand on his sword hilt for Klaenger to see. "My Thingman was attacked, and *handselled* services were taken from me without my will."

"That was Sam who did that, not me. You said his coins were to be mine."

"Then it is Sam you dispute," said the *gothi*. He turned away. "Take your fee from him, since it is his actions which have harmed you."

Some of the faces around Klaenger were sympathetic. Njal would have spoken, but he already had the *gothi*'s displeasure on him. Klaenger saw the hard eyes and sneers of the Fish Brothers and Gizur and Hafildi, though, and knew he would get no satisfaction that day. He pushed his boat from shore and hopped in. Well out from the shallows, far enough that an arrow could not reach him, he stood and cupped his hands and called to the men as they climbed the hill to Bolstathr.

"Land stealer!" he shouted. "Thief!"

He was shouted down at once by the men on the shore, but said nothing more anyway. He sat and pulled the oars, pointing his bow at the mouth of the fjord.

Ulfar watched him go from the door of Bolstathr and then turned to go inside.

Thorgils watched him, shivering in the chill, exhausted from the long climb.

The cold wind had reminded him of a winter afternoon long ago, sitting around Ulfar's fire with Auln nearby at the loom. It had been the day after Thorgils' father had died and been buried. Ulfar had suddenly lifted his voice in song. It was a good harmony, filling the silence well. It had been a song for Gunnar the carpenter, the verses praising his strength and his skill with wood and the fine son he had made to carry on his family into the future. Thorgils had wept for his father, hearing it, and somehow it made the death easier to bear. Ulfar had smiled, glad to have been able to help his friend, and Thorgils hugged him hard in thanks.

Thorgils never told Arnkel about that.

"You made an enemy over two coins," he said as the *gothi* passed him.

Arnkel spat on the ground. "A fisherman. He means nothing to me."

Two months passed.

Ulfar woke late one morning. He threw off his blanket, put on his woolens and walked out into the great Hall of Bolstathr, scratching himself. He looked around for some kind of breakfast, glad that the Fish Brothers and Hafildi were gone to work.

A man waited there, seated nervously among the children who played at his feet. It was Cunning-Gill, a friend of Thorolf Lamefoot, his hat in his hand. Ulfar backed away slowly but Cunning-Gill waved in a friendly way to him and smiled with his broken teeth.

"Do not worry, Ulfar. I have no business with you and would not harm you in any case. I remember the onions and mutton you gave me two winters ago when there was nothing in my food box. Lamefoot can fight his own feuds."

Arnkel heard this as he came in the door with his daughter, Halla. He looked at his father's friend for a moment without expression and then shot his toothy grin at him. "Would you like a horn of mead, Cunning-Gill?" he said, and the man nodded with bright eyes.

He sat on a bench at the *gothi*'s waved invitation and shot down the drink Halla poured for him in a few swallows, then looked up expectantly. Halla filled his horn again, frowning at his greed.

"What is your business with me, Cunning-Gill?" Arnkel said. The Hall filled with men, entering noisily for the morning meal and the *gothi* frowned, trying to hear. Ulfar sat close by the *gothi*, almost at his feet.

"Your father is ill, *gothi*, and busy with other tasks. He sent me to say that if his slaves did not return from Vadils Head, I was to ask for their cost, twenty Law ounces apiece." He said this with his usual grin that stayed always, like a shield held up to the gloom of the world, but his eyes flicked back and forth and sweat beaded his forehead. He had believed Lamefoot's words that he was only a messenger but now he knew what it was the old man asked because suddenly there were angry men shouting at him and calling him a fool. He drank the mead quickly so that no one could spill it from his hand.

"Quiet in my Hall!" Arnkel shouted, louder than the rest. When the roar had settled, the *gothi* looked around him. "I have business here with my neighbor, Cunning-Gill, who has never done me harm. Now I see many men here sitting idly about during daylight when sheep must be tended, fish caught through the new ice and meat prepared for the tubs. I see my property not tended. Go now and do that. You will eat your food later." His eyes were hard as glass. There was a scramble of men rising and hurriedly dressing.

"Ulfar. It seems that my father is abed and can do you no harm. Go out to Ulfarsfell, and tend the land there for me. I have sent a man or two there whom I could spare since then but it needs your touch. The sons of Thorbrand sulk on their farmstead and you will not see them. Return here by nightfall."

Ulfar was happy to be given the chore. The pall on him lifted slightly at the thought of work and he threw the robe from around his shoulders. He ducked behind the curtained area to tell his wife, and then left.

Cunning-Gill looked up at Halla again, and held out his horn. She grudgingly poured him more mead while he grinned and watched the men go grumbling back to their tasks. He lifted the horn in mock toast to the men and they flicked earth at him with their toes.

Arnkel and he were alone, except for Thorgils, who stood with crossed arms, eyes like stones, as if he resented every drop going down Cunning-Gill's throat.

"Twenty ounces each," the *gothi* said. Cunning-Gill nodded.

"And he expects you to take this back to him? What if I paid in *vathmal*? How would you carry it all?"

The farmer shrugged. "He said nothing of that. I was just to deliver the message." He leaned forward conspiratorially, the mead glowing in his face. "To tell the truth, *gothi*, I think he expects nothing from you. Just hoping for the best he can get. He's got another way of getting back at you."

Arnkel *gothi* kept his face calm, staring down at the capricious fool who would so easily sell his only friend in the world for a moment's importance.

"What would that be?"

Cunning-Gill looked down at his empty horn, and Arnkel *gothi* waved Halla over. She poured, and he grinned with his broken teeth when she turned away from him haughtily.

"Well, he's sick alright, damned sick. His heart hurt him the night that Ulfar's house was burnt. Too much drink, he said, but I think it may be something more. But he is up out of his bed, moving around, saddling a horse, and waiting for me to return before he sets out. As to Ulfar, Thorolf talks about nothing else lately except sticking a blade in him. Heh."

Thorgils looked up at the *gothi*, expecting to be sent to Ulfar's farm.

"He's packed gifts, has he?"

Cunning-Gill laughed around a swallow of mead, spilling a mouthful down his shirt. "No fooling you!"

Arnkel and Thorgils saddled a horse each and set out to go to Hvammr. They brought spears and shields, and Arnkel put on his sword, first checking the edge lovingly with his finger and rubbing a little seal oil into the metal to keep the water off in the sheath. Cunning-Gill rode alongside for a while, grinning, until the cold wind sobered him and he realized that Lamefoot would know that it was his words that had brought the *gothi* to see him if he arrived with the two men.

He waved and began to angle off across the hill, back to Thorswater dale.

"Cunning-Gill, I thank you for your help," Arnkel said to the man before he left and handed him a small package of smoked salmon. "In the future, my Hall has a place for you. I would welcome any news of my father's well-being. You know that he and I do not bide well with each other and that pains me, but I care for my father as any man might. I wish to know how he fares and you are his friend. Come to my fire when it seems there is a matter I should know about and you will have good drink and food, and my friendship."

Cunning-Gills' eyes lit up at that, and he nodded and smiled.

They rode on.

"You might come to regret that offer," Thorgils said to Arnkel dryly. "He'll be showing up every time Lamefoot breaks wind, if he thinks there's ale in it for him."

"Don't like him, eh?"

Thorgils snorted. "He's lazy and he's a liar. A thief, too, although he hasn't been caught yet. Sheep vanish and suddenly his whey bins are full of meat."

Arnkel looked at him. "I want you to befriend him."

"What?"

"Gain his confidence. He will tell more of the truth to you than to me and he is an ear around Lamefoot's fire. Does he know you despise him?"

Thorgils shook his head reluctantly. "I don't think so." His face twisted as if he had tasted meat gone bad. The *gothi* laughed, and reached to slap the man's shoulder. "It's not forever. Besides, you have experience in this sort of thing."

Thorgils glared at him. "How long?"

Arnkel's face went hard. "Until Thorolf dies. Then I care not."

Thorgils nodded.

He had held the goat that Arnkel had sacrificed the day after Thorolf slaughtered Einar. They stood on Vadils Head. It was a sacrifice to Odin, the God of revenge. Thorgils' father had pinched the animal from the barn for them under Thorolf's nose, his eyes still red with weeping over Einar's death.

"Go, lads," Gunnar had said to his son and to Arnkel. "Do what is right."

They were ten years old.

Thorgils had dreamed of his father the night before. Gunnar stood in the home field of Bolstathr and looked down sadly at the body lying within the overgrown stone circle, as he had long ago.

It was Gunnar who had carried Einar's body away and wrapped it in *vathmal* for burial after the duel. Einar had freed Thorgils' father from slavery and Gunnar had served him loyally, even past death.

Thorgils had walked forward to the circle of stones, the odd logic of dreams taking him to Einar's body in a moment from the cold heights of Vadils Head.

But it had not been Einar he turned over with a shaking hand. It was Ulfar, staring up at him with rotted, accusing eyes, and when he turned in fear to his father he saw the same look, the same judgment.

He had woken covered in sweat.

The two men rode up to the ridge line, leaving the trail slightly to gain an extra few feet of height, and looked out over the land.

Arnkel breathed in the chill air as it washed over him.

Much of the narrow valley was clear from the ridge. Ulfar could be seen in his yard, feeding the cows, and further on south of that was the farm of Orlygstead, hard up against the land held by the sons of Thorbrand. To the north ran the ridge line, and at its end was the rich Crowness wood, just hidden by the rise. Below them, to the west was Hvammr, Lamefoot's home farm.

"One way or another, it will all come to me," Arnkel said grimly, looking out over the land. "Nothing must stop that."

Thorgils watched him silently.

"Odin, you have always given me strength and courage and I love you for it," Arnkel shouted to the sky. "Hear me!"

His words echoed along the valley, repeating again and again.

They rode down the other side, into the vale, and onto Hvammr farm.

A saddled horse waited in the cold by the turf house with another behind it, carrying furs. They dismounted and Arnkel called for Thorolf loudly.

Lamefoot came out, dressed in lambskin and armed with a spear. He looked once at his son but said nothing. With a grunt of effort, he stepped onto a stone and heaved his bulk onto the unfortunate horse and it huffed its breath out in a great white blast of protest.

He rode off, trailing the pack horse.

Arnkel fell in beside him, far enough away avoid a slash of the spear.

"Do you really think that Snorri *gothi* will have anything to do with you, Thorolf?" Arnkel said, mocking the man.

Lamefoot's face was set in rage through the white pallor of his sickness. He spat onto the ground and said nothing. It was admission enough for Arnkel. He saw the furs and knew they were gifts to gain another man's support.

"Then go, betray your kin. Abandon them," Arnkel said through his teeth. "That was always your way, Thorolf Lamefoot."

That drew a sharp glare from Thorolf, but already his son was riding away.

III

AULN'S DISCOVERY AND SNORRI GOTHI'S ANSWER
TO THE SONS OF THORBRAND, AND THOROLF

ULFAR WENT TO WORK at Ulfarsfell, and Auln was left in Bolstathr.

She begged to go with him, but he denied her that.

"Your loom has been brought here, Auln," Ulfar said, sadly. "I can do all the other chores. There is no food to make there, or clothing to wash. It is not our home anymore."

The gothi had been very clear on that. Ulfar was to return each night to share the last meal with the family in the Great Hall and to sleep with Auln in the private family section of the house. Arnkel wanted him very near. Ulfar thought that it was for their protection from the old viking, but Auln knew the reason. Arnkel still feared the Law and the claims of the sons of Thorbrand. If they lived like tenants of the gothi each day, then that was what they would become in the eyes of everyone and eventually even themselves. So the old woman Gudrid had whispered to her son on a chill night weeks before. Auln was near in the dark, eyes closed and pretending sleep but listening with wool blankets pulled up to her nose. One handsal could be forgotten or argued away, Gudrid had murmured, but a life in the gothi's household was evidence that could not be denied.

She still saw the awful light around Arnkel gothi in her heart, but it was in tatters. With it came a strange certainty that he worked against Thorolf, and how could he be a danger when he fought Ulfar's enemy? So she worked hard to quell her misgivings about the man, telling herself that it was his very strength that made him seem so dangerous. He had the look of a man who could kill easily. It was natural to fear him.

When Gudrid was in bed with her wet cough, life was not bad at Bolstathr. Auln would work at her loom along with the other women and listen to their gossip. It was actually pleasant to hear the voices when they were allowed to speak.

Usually, though, life was little better than slavery at Bolstathr.

Arnkel's wife, Hildi, was quiet, dominated by her mother-in-law. She was bullied, and forced to eat constantly by the old woman, although she was often not hungry, especially in the last few months as the winter began.

"Will my grandson be a weakling, of thin arms and narrow shoulders?" Gudrid would rail from her seat, an imitation of Arnkel gothi's from where she was tended like a queen by the servants and by the wives of Gizur and Hafildi. "How will he have greatness without strength? Eat, child! It is winter."

The old woman hovered over every part of the house when she could bring herself out of bed, checking each man who worked the food barrels, or the state of the cook pot or the taut weave of each loom, her frown like a thundercloud when she walked by.

She reminded Auln of her own father and the hard edge of his hand when anyone went against his wishes.

She had tried to savor the look in his eyes when she had told him that she would not return to the homeland with them.

"So, finally the witch betrays her own blood," her father had shrieked at her. "Did you always see that you would do this? Of course you did!"

People had turned to gawk at their hard words. Many families had covered the south shore of the harbor. Broken by the deep ash of the volcano that had destroyed all they had, they waited to take ship to a softer land, the beach crowded with the few animals they had left.

Delicious shame had shivered down her back as her father's eyes widened at the awareness that he would have no one but his old wife to torment and no strong back to bring food to his table when he sailed back to Norway. He tried to strike her, but she was not the helpless child she had been, and he had grown weak with age. She held his arms and threw him down to the ground.

It had been glorious.

"You will not touch me again," she ground out as he moaned in pain at her feet.

Auln took her few things and ran, feeling as if the layers of shame and horror and fear in her life peeled away in the wind blowing over her. She had looked back only once. Her mother stood on the beach near the ship, her arm outstretched, beckoning.

The helpless terror in her mother's eyes came back to haunt the early hours of every morning.

Arnkel had four daughters. The oldest was Halla, fourteen years of age, who constantly fought her grandmother's grip. Auln loved her for it. Their arguments were one of the chief entertainments of the men who ate each day at Arnkel's table. Eleven year old Vigdis had given up and walked about with head hanging low, unable to muster any words when the old woman spoke angrily to her. The two youngest were seven year old Unn and a five year old everyone called Rose, despite the long formal name Gudrid had given her, a child so beautiful that Auln's heart would break to see her little face go by. She had made a doll for her of rags and old wool and buttons of shell, just to see the glow of happiness in her eyes.

All girls. That was another reason for Hildi to suffer under Gudrid's tongue.

But for the baby in the womb there were only tender caresses, as if the woman growing the child did not exist. Hildi would sit back, eyes down, while Gudrid would sing to the child, sing to her swollen middle and call in Arnkel gothi to feel the weak kicking.

He would always come at her call. It was the old woman who had bribed the elves with a sacrificed goat to encourage a pregnancy when it was clear that Hildi was past her prime (so Gudrid said in front of all the others), and it was she who lay the gifts for the Otherworld creatures at the doors each night so that they would not come in and cause their devilry.

It did not help.

Hildi sickened. Slight at first, just a lack of appetite. Then came the fever and the chills, in turn, and a great thirst, always the thirst. Auln remembered the thirst, and how the hot honey water had soothed it, for a short time at least. Gudrid watched this happen for a month and then two, constantly nagging Hildi for her bad health until one day Auln could stand the old woman's voice no more and snapped at her.

"Gudrid! She cannot help that she is sick."

Those dark, awful eyes had turned to her and Auln had shuddered at the malice in them. In a rush of understanding she saw that the strength of will in Arnkel gothi came from her as much as from the raw violence of Thorolf Lamefoot.

Gudrid's voice had been quiet. She hardly ever raised her voice and yet all her words were always clear. "You live here by the generosity of my son even though your ill luck has caused this. Mind that you do not have to find a new home in the winter months."

Auln said nothing to that. She suspected Gudrid might be correct. Hildi's troubles had begun roughly at her arrival and it was so much like her own sickness.

She watched Hildi lose weight, as she had done. Then began the little blemishes of the skin on the back of the neck and the face. One day a little bloody fluid leaked from her womb, and Hildi had come to her in fear. It would stop soon, Auln told her, and made her a healing tea.

It did stop. Auln did not tell Hildi that it would come and go, sometimes with great pain, spasms of sickness in her womb.

One day, while working the loom, she saw Hildi take down a little jar from a shelf, and spoon a mouthful of the honey into her mouth.

Auln watched at first, licking her lips at the memory of the sweet. Yes, it was Thorbrand's. She recognized the glaze of the jar. Hildi savored the taste and then resealed the jar and lay down on a bench to rest, curled around her stomach and covered in blankets. Auln turned back to her work.

The clacking of the loom paced her thoughts, covering even Hildi's moans.

Her gaze went back to the jar on the shelf. A pair of raised beads in the glaze seemed to peer at her, at first without meaning, and then with a twisted maniacal cheer, as if to share with her their evil joke. She stared at the eyes in growing horror as they winked at her and gleamed in the shadow of the wooden shelf.

The same kind of jar that Thorbrand had given to her, once.

She looked to Hildi, seeing herself, the same worry of the winter before as she carried more than just a child to term. All the care of the future rode on her shoulders, to make an heir, a male heir, with men standing to one side who wished that it were not so.

Her hands did not falter over the wool. The loom needed the rhythm or the weave would suffer. Vigdis leaned around the hanging threads of her own loom and whispered, afraid that Gudrid would hear her away from her work.

"Auln, why are you weeping?"

She ran to Ulfarsfell, ignoring Gudrid's hard words as she tore away from her loom, and she wept as she trudged along. By the time she reached Ulfar, hard at work in the barn, she knew she could not tell him.

The tears dried finally, and in their wake came a growing heat inside her heart.

She knew who had given the honey, and why.

She knew.

She went beneath her sleeping bench, and searched among her private things. There she found the knife, a thin blade given to her by her mother. It was handled in walrus ivory and silver.

"A woman must guard her honor," her mother had said. But her hollow voice had had no truth in it.

It was the only protection her mother had ever given her.

The blade shone dully with oil as she twisted it in the light, the divots from the smith's hammer like coin sized, imperfect mirrors, and in one of these she saw her face, and the red eyes, full of rage.

The sons of Thorbrand came to Helgafell.

The openness of the ground always struck Thorleif. Cloistered in their river valley at Swan firth, he forgot how sheltered their farmstead was, with the high mountains like the turf walls of their Hall. The wind blew free over many pastures near the coast. The Holy Mountain was just a hill, not three hundred feet high but on the flat of the coast lands it dominated. On one side was Snorri gothi's farmstead, with many worn paths leading to it like the strands of a spider's web. At the summit was the altar where Snorri gothi would make the sacrifices to the Gods.

A ship lay off shore, anchored from both ends. A boat made its way back and forth to the beach laden with boxes and sacks, all carefully watched by the crew of three men. A merchant come in winter, the brothers said to one another in surprise, and to a place not usually visited. Swan's fjord was not a trade harbor. The captain was either a brave man or a fool to risk his ship but either way the brothers were glad to see the vessel, packed high with the things of life. Luck, they said to each other, that they had loaded their pack horses high with many ells of vathmal, bolts of the cloth intended to honor Snorri gothi. Thorodd and Thorfinn began to discuss how much of what they carried could be spared from the gift to the gothi and used to trade and although Thorleif listened, he said nothing.

The gothi was not a man to take less than his due.

It would be up to him to speak with their chieftain and present their case about Ulfar, and that was a harder thing to do in some ways than fighting. His father waited in his bed back at Swan firth and he would judge every word spoken and hold Thorleif to blame if the cost of the Snorri's help was too high. They were very much alike, Snorri gothi and Thorbrand, Thorleif thought, the same tangled cunning, the same weighing of balances. For many days Thorleif had considered his words to the gothi. He still felt unprepared.

There were many shouts from the farm as they arrived, and then waves as they were recognized. Men ran from their work to the great turf Hall of Snorri gothi, shouting news of their arrival. One man came to greet them, grinning. His name was Hawk, a large man in both shoulder and arm, sure of his step, deeply scarred along one cheek. He carried a shovel like a walking stick and planted it to talk to them.

"Hello, Thingmen," he said. "You would think it was Autumn instead of the leanest time of the year, with all the guests arriving to eat the food."

"I'm sure you have eaten the finest of everything before we arrived, Hawk," said Thorleif. He jumped down from the horse and held out his arm, and as usual it was a test of strength with Hawk who liked to unbalance other men for a lark. Thorleif held his ground while his brothers watched smiling, proud to see his strength.

"Come," said Hawk finally, clapping Thorleif on his shoulder. "You see the ship. It came just this morning. Hrafn of Trondheim brings a load of barley, hops and wheat for bread. And many other things. The man winked, but would say nothing more about the cargo. "Seems he was making for the Skardstron to the north, to take on seal oil from the hunters, but the pack ice stopped him.

Even Dogurtharnes has ice floating about and now the winds have
blown it to the west of us. He will not risk his whole wealth and
his life to make a run to the west and then south. So he came here,
knowing Snorri gothi's reputation even in Norway. He knew Snorri
would give him shelter for the winter, for both him and his goods.
There, that's the last of his cargo coming off now. We'll drag the
ship up on the shore for him." Hawk laughed and made the sign
of Thor's hammer on his chest, which meant luck. The merchant
had lost his advantage and would need to rely on his host's generosity. One of the barns was being emptied of animals and hay,
and it was here that the bent men carrying sacks from the beach
went, harried and pulled by a large man in leather and fur.

"Is that him?" Thorleif said. Hawk nodded.

They went over to peer into the barn, eyes wide at the riches. A
man walked by with a long load wrapped in skin on his shoulder,
and the jostling triggered the sound of metal scraping on metal.

"Weapons!" Illugi said, twirling to face them. The rest scoffed
and pushed him down with their hands.

"Stick with your meat knife, little man," said Thorodd the smith.
"You'd cut off your leg with a sword. Or my head." The others
laughed. The merchant had been eyeing them, even as he watched
his goods stored in the barn. He was big, taller than most men,
and broad in the shoulder. The grey in his long beard and braided
hair gave him a look of wisdom, but he also had eyes full of humor
and life. He greeted them like lords, bellowing with open arms,
and then unwrapped the bundle of skin with a flourish and took
out a sword. It was plain, as long as a man's arm, the hilt wrapped
in copper wire, the pommel a simple cube of iron, but the blade
had been polished to something beyond the usual black of iron.
He held it up for them to see, flashing it in the sunlight that fell
through the open door of the barn and then put it into Illugi's
hand. His brothers watched silently. Any one of them would have
bought the sword but the cost was too high. Such things were for
rich men and they would rather have full bellies than a bauble to

hang on the wall. Illugi saw their eyes. He slashed once with the blade, surprised at how balanced and right it felt in his hand for its weight, and then handed it back to the merchant.

"Not fine enough for me," he said. "I want a silver one."

The merchant laughed dutifully along with the brothers, and then they were ushered out of the barn by Hawk, who closed the barn doors behind the last of the merchant's crewmen.

Thorleif recognized one of them.

He was a restless young man with wild eyes and scarred chin. Onund, that was his name, he thought, an Islander from Straumfjord, who had caused his father much grief by sending back the wife his father had arranged for him. The return of the dowry had taken a whole afternoon of the Thorsnes Thing three spring seasons back, as Onund's father was not happy to return the wealth that had come with the bride, including fifty sheep that made him good money in wool. Onund looked happy enough with his roaming ways. Some men were just not meant to be farmers, it seemed. He had the look of liking a fight.

Hrafn frowned as Hawk bolted the doors of the barn.

"I had thought my goods would be kept within the gothi's own Hall, for protection," he said to Hawk. "How will my property be warded if it is here and you are all over there around a warm fire?"

"The dogs will tell us of any thieves, Hrafn, but all the men about this place are Snorri gothi's men, and they know that whatever is taken must be made up by him. They will not want to hurt their gothi that way."

The merchant said sourly that he trusted the dogs more than the men, and they laughed.

Hawk looked over the sons of Thorbrand. "I could use your muscle, lads. Only have a dozen men here right now and we have to haul that beast of a ship up on the shore."

Thorleif looked doubtfully at the ship floating in the bay. It was a knarr, forty paces long and a dozen wide, and even without cargo it would be heavy. But he nodded and they rode down to the shore along the path. Hawk had most of his men there already. Onund and the other two crewmen took a small boat out to the vessel and pulled up the anchors. Two long oars were put out, one per side, and the ship began to creep in closer to the shore. Onund stood at the stern, his hip into the tiller of the steer board, peering cautiously into the shoals over the side.

"Slower, you idiots," Hrafn called out through cupped hands. He turned to Hawk. "I should have gone with them, They'll rip out the bottom."

"It's mostly sand and shell, here. Don't worry, man. It's high tide. We'll get your darling safe and warm."

A ship's length out from the high water mark the bow touched bottom and nosed gently into a furrow of sand. Hrafn shouted orders to the men, and they dived below. From the storage below deck they hauled out a dozen short logs, each no longer than a man, but scraped perfectly clean and round. They muscled them down into the small boat and took them to the shore, three at a time, along with two massive coils of stout coir rope, thicker than a large man's thumb, each rope tied to a post on the bow beam of the ship, one to starboard and the other to port, paying out the rope as the boat rowed in and taking care to keep tension so the ropes would not dip into the water. The ship bobbed sluggishly in the slight surf. Hrafn pointed and told them to lay out the logs one after another, running up the beach, no more than two paces apart. The first two logs actually floated in the water, held in place in front of the bow by Hrafn's men, who had thrown off their boots and trousers and shirts and stood shaking with cold while the men laughed at them. Onund stayed on the shore. He handed one rope to Thorleif and the sons of Thorbrand manned it with a few of Snorri gothi's Thingmen, in a long line, while the rest took up the other. They spat on their cold hands and rubbed them together.

"Alright, men, on my call, start heaving," Hrafn called out. "Don't jerk on the lines, now. Nice and steady. She has to come straight up. Now . . . heave!"

The bow forced the first log under the water, and when it had been pushed down into the sand the sailor ran around to the port side of the ship, and leapt up to hang from the rail, lifting his frozen legs from the water. Then the second log went under and the other crewman ran to the same side as the first and he hung there, too. The weight of the ship began to grow as more of it was lifted out of the water onto the rolling logs and the ropes became as hard as rock.

"Get over here and help us," Thorleif shouted at the men hanging from the side of the ship, but Hrafn waved at him, shaking his head, and he soon saw that they were not just escaping the cold water. The keel of the ship protruded slightly from the center bottom of the hull. The slight load of the hanging men on one side caused the ship to tilt a hair, and it was the side strakes on that side that rode up onto the logs. When it was clear that the ship had gone over to one side, the men dropped off and splashed up to the shore, shivering and blue, and jumped madly about on the sand to get warm.

The water-soaked sand was firm and packed, but as they drew the ship up onto the logs further up the shore, the sand dried and loosened, and so the logs would not roll well. They mushed down and locked in place, so that the ship only slid on the slick green wood. The two naked crew men waited until the ship cleared the first two rollers, and then they went into the water one last time to fetch them out and lay them ahead of the ship. Their arms and legs shook so much by then that they could hardly put their clothes back on.

"So that is your life?" Thorleif wheezed to Onund who pulled just ahead of him. The man frowned blackly, thinking he was mocked, and Thorleif remembered that he had always been quick to anger.

Finally the stern rose out of the water. Hrafn chocked the rollers by the water and then shouted at them to stop heaving. He pushed against the slimy, barnacled side with both hands, testing for instability, but the ship rested cleanly.

"Not far enough to escape storm waves but it will do for now," Hawk said. "Until I get more men here. Then we'll pull it up another ship length, to the smooth rock over there, and put it up properly on the keel, and brace it."

Hrafn nodded, and turned to look at the sea. He saw only mist quickly melting away in the sunlight. The drift ice was thicker now, a dozen blue-white chunks floating within sight. He nodded, satisfied. The last task was to heave up the three free logs onto the men's shoulders and carry them back to Snorri gothi's farm. Wood was as precious as the other cargo. Hawk was an ambitious man with a good eye for profit and he discussed the purchase of the rollers in the spring, when Hrafn would leave. The merchant handselled them to him as they walked and took two coins as advance payment.

The Great Hall was full of orange light, many oil lamps hanging from the rafters alongside the herbs and salted sides of mutton and beef and the endless rows of smoked salmon and dried cod. Hawk led them through the door and there was much stomping of snow off their feet as they entered. Many pegs lined the wall of the entrance. Each of them found a place for their coat and hat. Thorfinn, Thorodd and Illugi carried in the load of vathmal from the horses and laid it down carefully to one side out of the wet slush, at the entrance to the alcove holding the whey bins. The alcove was a vast space compared to Swan firth's, larger even than Arnkel's storage place. Ten whey bins lay in two rows along the walls with a narrow path between them, each big enough to bathe a trio of men to the waist, filled with fermenting meat. Along every wall were shelves stacked full of cheeses and clay jars of curd, and many small sacks and containers of glass and metal. Snorri was a rich man, rich beyond words.

The gothi waited in his High Seat, fingers crossed, smiling at his guests. His hair was fine and white and hung straight down on both sides of his face and although he was only in his early thirties and had good strength in his shoulders, it gave him the look of old wisdom. Beside him sat his oldest son, Oreakja, sixteen years old but already as strong as most men. The gothi stepped down as they entered and came to them, taking each of their hands in turn. He said nothing of the cuts and bruises on Illugi's face. Then he waved them into the Hall and sat each man down on the benches. He offered the place of honor at his right side to Hrafn the merchant. To make up for that to his Thingmen he personally took a skin of ale from the wall and filled Thorleif's horn, and so all the guests were at ease and felt comfortable.

Hawk smiled, watching his chieftain's sure hand with many men, as steady and careful as it was with one. That was Snorri gothi's way, he thought. It was said he could mediate between the bear and the seal, with the gothi getting the seal's oil and the bear's fur in the end and both parties sure they had cheated the other.

Snorri begged pardon of the sons of Thorbrand and began to speak business with the merchant. First they settled on a price for all the goods that would be sold as bulk, the barley and hops, and the wheat, both in money and in vathmal. It needed to be high enough to satisfy the Norwegian, but low enough to prevent grumbling among the people of the area who would trade their goods. It was a fine balance. Hawk huddled with the sons of Thorbrand, explaining the discussion with much stress on the gothi's concern for his people, speaking quietly while the other brothers listened to the bargaining with great interest. They felt rather important to be present at such an event and the reason for their visit became less pressing. Hawk filled their horns without asking and so they enjoyed the warmth and the diversion. Thorleif kept quiet but he knew there were other sides to the problem. The higher the prices, the more trade tax made by the gothi, but then his support would suffer. He could only smile at Hawk's sweetened version.

Well, that was the task of a Thingman, to support his chieftain, he thought. But there were responsibilities both ways and that was what Thorleif counted on.

A few moments of tension darkened the mood when the Norwegian merchant and Snorri gothi found themselves disagreeing on the current value of vathmal cloth, Hrafn insisting heatedly that the low summer price he had heard farther down the coast was in effect all over the Island, and Snorri gothi gently reminding him that prices always increased as the cold weather went on.

Spots of red colored the merchant's cheek. At this first sign of anger Snorri waved for food to be brought, and said that such mundane things could wait until they had eaten.

The man bent to the platter of cheese and meat, distracted as he was intended to be and the gothi began to speak with the sons of Thorbrand.

"It is a long, cold ride from Swan firth, Thorleif. Although it is good to see you, I wonder why you would come so far in hard weather just to send greetings? Is there something I can do for you?"

"We need your counsel and your aid, foster brother," Thorleif said, and Snorri gothi's eyebrow twitched at the formal mention of their relationship. "First I offer a gift of harbor vathmal to you, six good bolts of cloth, the finest quality."

Oreakja's eyes became bright with humor. "Strange. Hawk must have imagined some of your horses. He said you had much more than that."

They laughed together and Snorri gothi rubbed his son's head affectionately. He bent to Thorleif and whispered. "Let me have a third share of that wool on the other horses, and I'll bargain a deal for the goods you want."

Thorleif nodded reluctantly. He wanted Snorri in a good mood. If a few bolts of cloth could do that, then he would pay the price.

The door swung open and more men came in with the hard bright light and the cold. Hrafn's ship had drawn many eyes and there were farmers and fishermen who had come to see the merchant. Among them were Sam and Klaenger. Thorleif waved to them. The sons of Thorbrand each rose to greet the men and talk about what had happened the other day, although they were cool with Klaenger for his help to Arnkel. Word had come to them from one of Arnkel's Thingmen, a man named Kili, who had married a niece of Thorbrand's years ago. At Swan firth he told Thorleif what Sam had done in defying Arnkel gothi, and how Arnkel had cheated Klaenger. Kili's disapproval was clear, but he was nervous as he spoke, and left their farm by the long path far around Arnkel's plot at Bolstathr.

So he knows, Thorleif thought, looking up at the white haired gothi. He must know what happened.

It was relief of sorts. Thorleif would not need to be eloquent when the story had been told by another already. The gothi would obviously be outraged by what had happened and would help them.

He let himself relax and had another horn of ale. He saw that the merchant was well into his cups now. The life of a trader. It seemed so grand, traveling the world, and dining with chieftains.

Hrafn drank to quell his nerves. At dawn that morning he had been lost in fog as the first thick flood of drift ice floated past the bow. His crew had been terrified. They knew that even grazing one of the jagged chunks could rip the hull apart. Strange noises could be heard in the fog, not whales. Some monster hunted out there. The other merchants had called him fool when he had left Trondheim, but the first man to bring back the seal oil would have the highest price and that could have meant another ship built, for his brother to command. They could have been a fleet. But there he sat trapped. Warm and alive, but trapped, in the Hall of the shrewdest chieftain in western Iceland. It would be a cargo of vathmal in the spring, instead of rich oil, one for which he would pay dearly. Then there would be the cost of lodgings for himself, his men and his cargo over the winter. He would be lucky to break even that year. It was only his second voyage in the Iceland trade and he already regretted it.

A dish was brought out and he held his breath, dreading it, though he smiled with the others as they clapped its arrival. The reek of it filled the Hall. A vast tureen of wood held the flesh of rotted whale, buried in sand and seaweed last year or the year before. They loved to parade it in front of strangers. The best defense was to start an eating challenge and praise the others, so that he would need to eat none of it. Snorri gothi pressed him, though, and he swallowed a mouthful knowing he would be in the jacks for hours the next day. He made sure to give them many faces and they roared laughter.

Damn them all.

He reached into the pack at his feet and pulled out the bulbs he had plucked from the strand on his ship. He peeled one with a knife, and saw Snorri's head go back at the smell as he cut it.

"This is garlic, gothi. It is said among the Franks that only the strongest men can eat it raw."

"Yes, I know it," Snorri said with a grimace, and reached out for it reluctantly.

Ah, sweet revenge, Hrafn thought.

The merchant drank horn after horn, enjoying the life that had nearly been lost to him and telling himself he would do no trading that day. His head was too far gone. The pretty woman who brought the ale smiled at him and seemed not to be the wife of any of these men, and so he talked with her until he noticed through the fog of drink in him that the laughter had dimmed and that the six brothers he had met in the barn were now standing in front of the gothi. They were back to it again, after the interruption.

These Islanders!

They were always negotiating, wheedling, gossiping, forever immersed in their neighbor's business, never happy until they had all your wealth in their pocket. This gothi would try to wear him down all winter to increase his tax on the trade.

He squinted, making himself listen to their words through the drink in him.

It seemed these tough looking brothers had a disagreement with a chieftain to the south from where they came, a man who had disputed their rights to a piece of land. He whispered to one of his men to go to the barn and fetch one of the weapons bundles. Here was a grand chance to make a sale, he thought.

But Snorri gothi was not as willing to help them as they had hoped. His calm voice drew frowns and mutters. Hrafn was very drunk, and he looked from one man to another, rallying his wits as best he could, trying to hear the meaning. It was almost as interesting as bedding the woman. He beckoned to Onund, and the man came over to squat beside him.

"There is little that I will do in this case," Snorri gothi said, spreading his hands.

"Gothi, we have had the rights to Ulfar's land taken from us," Thorleif said carefully, looking to Thorodd beside him for support. "It is a clear case of arfskot. Ulfar is childless, and his land should come to us on his death because my father owned him. The handsal between Ulfar and Arnkel gothi was not legal, but we need you to argue this for us in the Thorsnes Thing when winter ends. We are only bondi and you are known to be a clever advocate for men's rights. You are our chieftain."

Snorri listened carefully, nodding politely at the compliment, and there was no doubt he sympathized with Thorleif. He listened with wide, caring eyes.

"This Arnkel fellow is a powerful lord?" Hrafn whispered to Onund.

Onund shrugged. "Not so I've heard. Snorri gothi has more Thingmen. But times have changed since I was here last, maybe. He's a big bastard, though. I know that much."

"Why don't they just march? Take it all and split Arnkel's lands." Onund looked at him as if he were suggesting running across the fire pit. He was not one with words and could not explain why the thought was wrong. Hrafn's other man came back then and put the bundle at his feet. The eyes of the gathered bondar went to it, even in the middle of their argument.

"It seems to me that there is a simple answer to your problem, Thorleif, son of Thorbrand," Hrafn said grandly, and threw back the cloth from the collection of swords and axes, a half dozen of each.

But along with the greed and desire he expected, there was also contempt in the faces as they looked at him.

"It is . . . rather complicated, Hrafn," Snorri gothi said, smiling a little. "This is not Norway."

"A man has taken what is your own," Hrafn said to Thorleif and waved his hand to the weapons. "Here is the way to take it back. And only two Law ounces per sword, and a single ounce per axe."

Their laughter struck him then and he flushed deeply. But the old instincts took over and he made himself laugh louder than all of them. He would be a clown if it meant selling a few items.

Snorri gothi smiled again. "War is for kings, not simple men like us. See my headman Hawk, there? He is the strongest of my Thingmen, and could face any man." Hawk smiled, and nodded his head. "Yet how well will he fight knowing that two of Arnkel gothi's Thingmen are his wife's brothers and Arnkel's chief Thing-man is his own cousin? It is the same with all my men and with Arnkel's men as well. We are too tightly woven in the Free State to march off and slay each other in long lines, shield beside shield. Our enemy is often our best ally's cousin, or uncle. It is good and wise and altogether a manly thing to protect oneself within the Law, with others to argue for you, and seek an answer that gives everyone honor."

There were many nods to this, as each man heard what he could not himself put so well into words. A true man was moderate in all things, especially anger. "Hear that, you Norwegian fool?" Sam shouted. He was an angry looking man, thick browed and burnt dark from the wind. "That is wisdom you hear."

Hrafn raised his horn in mockery. "Hail to the land of women, where no man fights." There was almost instant quiet at the insult. "Yet, you all carry spears."

Snorri gothi patted his hands down to quell the angry mutters of the men. "Men are men, Hrafn, and you are wise to see this. Men will argue and come to blows because that is their nature. Blood spilled calls for blood. That is what honor demands and honor is a man's wealth to himself. But like vathmal to coin, one kind of wealth can become another and so all wealth brings honor. It is not only for those with strong arms and weapons. Blood can be wiped clean with wealth. Every man of restraint can see that. We have a saying here, that no man should murder more men than he can afford." He looked down at the pile of weapons, and pointed. "I will take that long handled axe, there, the two-sided one."

Through the dark laughter, Thorleif stepped forward. He had kept his peace during Hrafn's interruption but now was impatient. He spoke now only for Snorri gothi's ears, because the men had turned to each other to talk about the weapons and it became noisy again in the Hall.

"Will you not help us, gothi? Can you not make it clear at the Thing that we were robbed?"

Snorri leaned forward, frowning. "It is not clear. Both Sam and Klaenger have told me that you all came in formal clothing to witness the handsal of Ulfar's land."

Thorleif sputtered in outrage. "We did nothing like that! We were invited to feast and to a witnessing, but we were told nothing of what was to happen."

Snorri frowned, and made a steeple of his fingers. "And yet my own Thingmen, who were present at the handsal, told the story to me as I just related it to you. If they were so unclear after only days, what truth will you expect to find after a whole winter, in front of witnesses prepared by Arnkel? Will you not then be shown to be men who went back on your word and so were rightly beaten for it?" Thorleif blinked angrily, confused, unable to answer. "How will my reputation suffer to be associated with such men?" Snorri spoke slowly and calmly, but he had dropped his urbane tone and showed the hardness underneath so that Thorleif would keep respect through his anger.

Hawk moved closer, eyes narrowed, stepping around the great hearth fire and brushing the knees of those who sat side by side on the benches, talking and drinking.

"Ulfar's handsal and your rights will be seriously disputed. There is arfskot on one hand, but a legal transfer of land on the other. Arnkel has some room on this and he will argue it. It will be much easier for him when he can imply that you surrendered your rights by being present at the ceremony of your own free will."

The gothi's eyes were pitiless. It was clear to him that Thorleif was not the match of his father in guile. Thorbrand would never have allowed himself to be so deceived and Snorri said that, not out of malice, but to see what it might spur in Thorleif.

Yes, there it was, Snorri thought. Anger, but also worry and self doubt.

So, Thorbrand still had much influence among his sons, he thought. That was a thing to remember. Thorleif was a good man but he had been outwitted and likely would be again.

Arnkel gothi worried Snorri. That man complicated life, he thought.

There was madness in his soul which made him unpredictable.

It had been that way since Einar Gudurd fell to Lamefoot's blade, many years ago.

Einar had been one of the original leaders during the Land Taking, the Landnam of a generation ago, along with Snorri gothi's father and Thorbrand, when whole families came to the newly discovered island from Norway and spread across the fjords and shores of Iceland in one pulse of migration, like chaff floating down from the breeze. A wide open land free for the taking. No kings or lords were there to claim it as their own and make a man pay tax to live.

It was luck that made Einar rich. He was the first in Swan's fjord and took all the good land except the mouth of the river, thinking his family was alone, and that there would be time to build fences there and claim it also. One day Thorbrand and his family sailed in while Einar was in the hills, and took that land. So there was bad blood between the two families and Thorbrand naturally turned to Snorri's father for alliance, although he lived farther up the coast near the open sea, on the Holy Mountain. He had already become known as a chieftain. The new kind of chieftain, who neither commanded or ruled, nor led a host of men in war, but instead helped men to resolve disputes without blood and so gained reputation and honor.

One of Einar's men had been Thorolf, a young tough who missed the homeland's quarrels and did not like farming and spent his time hunting seal and birds and bullying the other men into handing over their share of the ale. He and his master argued constantly. To tame him and bring him closer, Einar married him to his fiery daughter Gudrid and gave him a small slice of land that had been named Bolstathr.

He was gone within the year, savagely beating Gudrid one day for her spirit and then running before Einar could have his vengeance for the abuse of his daughter, while she shrieked at him from the door through broken teeth that she divorced him and would see him dead, and threw her wedding ring at his back. He took a merchant's ship for England and was not seen for ten years.

He left behind an infant son.

Gudrid was proud, and stayed in her home alone to raise her son, whom she called Arnkel.

Einar held a feast for the boy's tenth birthday, and his own fiftieth. Snorri was there, too, with his father. Hawk was almost a man then, with a wisp of beard on his chin. He drank ale at the party and amused himself making terrible faces at the younger boys. Only Arnkel stayed at the table, staring at him without trembling. When Hawk put his face too close, Arnkel slashed open his cheek. There was much shouting and apologies, and a gift of a goat in compensation, though Einar was said to have proudly rubbed the boy's head later when the guests had left and given him a fine dagger, handled in walrus ivory.

Snorri gothi remembered his own terror of Hawk. He remembered the awe that had struck him to see a boy his own age with the courage to do that.

Thorolf came back a month later, covered in gold and scars and wearing armor, armed slaves in tow. Every man stood back from him. He soon began taunting Einar about the abuse of his daughter and lived openly at Bolstathr, expelling Gudrid back to Hvammr, where Einar lived. It was obvious he wanted her father to challenge him, and as the wronged party, Thorolf could claim what damages he liked after the duel, as Einar had no son. That was the Law then, as in the old country. Einar sent his three best men to kill Thorolf. Their heads were found on Einar's doorstep the next day. Nothing could be proved. Thorolf and two of his slaves had cuts and bruises along with their grins.

Einar's sheep were found dead in the high pasture, twenty or more at a time, the heads stuck on poles as if they had been raiders caught in the act of plunder. A barn at Hvammr burned one night.

Einar went to see him.

There was no argument, no loud words, no waving of the arms. Many people saw them speaking in the pasture like two farmers discussing the weather, but the next morning Thorolf's slaves laid out a circle of stones in the home field of Bolstathr and Einar came down with his sword and shield.

It was said that Einar had asked the warrior what he wanted, and that Thorolf had replied, "All your lands." In return he would allow Gudrid to keep Bolstathr and live there with Einar's grandson, and so the boy would have an inheritance. As Thorolf's eldest son, he would take all the lands on Thorolf's death anyway.

Einar would have an honorable death.

They fought a long time as such things go, and the old man made a good account of himself. He left his sword sticking in Thorolf's leg.

The wound mellowed Thorolf. He tried to be a father to Arnkel, in his own rough way, but the boy would only go with the man if the viking showed him weapons and how to use them. They spent many days together until even Lamefoot tired of the clanging of metal. His taste for drink never left him and he thought himself rich, with no need to work. His temper, always bad, became worse from the constant drunkenness and the pain in his leg.

His son was a different sort, quiet, grim, distant, though his huge fists were like rocks and every boy in the valley soon learned that hard fact.

Snorri came back to himself, to hear Thorleif once again try to press his case, but the gothi gripped his shirt with one hand.

Thorleif looked down in angry surprise at the clenched fist.

"The son is not like the father, Thingman," Snorri gothi said quietly, as if to himself. He released Thorleif and sat back. "I made a mistake once, eight years ago, letting that man become a chieftain. Now it seems that we both must pay for that mistake. What the price will be will depend on how clever we are . . . foster brother."

He smoothed Thorleif's shirt. "Eat now, and drink, and in the morning ride back to your farmstead. Keep a clear eye when you are there. Send word to me of anything that Arnkel gothi does."

So Thorleif sat back down with his brothers.

Toward sunset the gothi stood and stretched his arms. From a box at his feet he brought out a knife with hilt bound in gold wire, and he stuck this in his waistband. He led the way outside to where a goat was readied by one of the men. On the gothi's head was a wide brimmed hat of oiled seal skin, which he wore out of doors in summer and winter and it was by this that he was always recognized when he rode across the fields to the farms of his Thingmen. The brothers and Hrafn blinked at the bright red sun that hung close to the horizon and shook their heads to clear the ale mists that a long day of drinking had made. Sam and Klaenger had left earlier, using the calm weather to fish, since storm could come at any time and good weather was not to be wasted if you work on the sea.

"Hrafn, you do not know this place, because you are a stranger," said Snorri gothi. "This is Holy Mountain. At the top can be found Thor, if your heart is pure and clean and strong."

Hrafn looked at them with wide eyes and saw the somberness in them.

"It's only a hill, and low one at that," he said doubtfully, looking up to the top.

"Much of the land can be seen from there," Snorri gothi said. They walked up the mountain.

Hrafn stumbled near the base and the others looked at him with angry eyes. A wooden cross had fallen out of his shirt, hung from a leather braid around his neck.

"Christian!" Thorleif said, mouth open in surprise.

Hrafn shrugged nervously. "The lands I trade in are all of the White Christ. It is good business for me to be as well." He looked around at them. "In the land of Thor, I follow his guide."

He used his thumb and forefinger to hide the top portion of the crucifix, turning it the hammer of Thor and the men laughed quietly. Hrafn prayed under his breath, asking forgiveness. He swore to the Lord Jesus that he would donate a silver cup when next he was in Trondheim.

Many paths led to the stone altar at the top and they took the widest one. The gothi led. "Do not speak as you climb," he said to the merchant, "Or look back down the mountain. Keep your eyes on your feet, and your heart on the thing that you wish to happen."

It took only a short time to climb the hill, and by that time the sun had just touched its bottom edge to the Earth. The gothi had led the goat up himself, and carried it the last little bit when it smelled the frozen blood that coated the altar and balked, bleating in terror, as if somehow in the beast's narrow animal vision it knew its fate.

There was little ceremony. Snorri gothi put on the silver arm ring that lay on the cold stone. Thorleif and Thorfinn pressed the goat down on the altar and the gothi stood before it with the knife drawn. He called to Thor and held the knife high. He called to the elves around them, asking them to gather and see what had been brought for them. To them went the blood and a part of the flesh, for that was what they were, of the Earth and bound to it. To Thor went the spirit of the goat, and he would consume it within his Hall in the great sky above.

Thorfinn the Holy peered into the dark behind the hill, even as he held the wriggling goat onto the stone, and then hissed to Snorri gothi. He turned away from the glitter of unnatural eyes and movement in the shadows. He knew enough to pretend that he had not seen them hiding, emerging from the hard soil like worms. They would follow a man to his home if seen, and wreak revenge for the sin of entering a man's awareness, thieving, ruining food, and even taking the life of a child within the crib.

Thorleif squinted out of the corner of his eye, terrified and fascinated as always, but he did not have Thorfinn's vision and saw nothing. Then he froze. A flicker of movement chilled his heart, no more than a mote of dust in his own eye. He had kept his heart on his wish the whole of the climb, watching only the ground in front of him, desperately hoping that his will would hold him to it, and he damned the elves for taking his mind from it even for a moment.

His business was with Thor.

The gothi plunged the point of the knife into the goat's neck, and held the head still as it bled its life out into a large copper bowl held by Thorfinn. When the pulse of blood became weak, Snorri dipped in his hand and sprinkled the surrounding men with it,

turning in a slow circle, calling the attention of Thor to the sacrifice with loud shouts at each shake of his hand, while the God-
blessed grace in each drop soaked into the men.

A sigh of relief came from all of them. They could speak again
and let their minds wander and laugh with the unbinding of their
wills. They chatted about little things while the gothi stripped the
goat of its skin and cut off the rear haunches and the tenderloin.
The elves had no need for clothing, and the best of meat was wasted
on them. The head and entrails were left. The men turned to head
back down the hill as the last crescent of sun set.

A eerie glow lit the landscape in orange and black, the seen
and the unseen. Far to the south was a dark patch crowned with
white, the Crowness of Thorolf, birch trees swaying in the cold
wind, the richest land in the fjord.

There was a rider. Far to the south, but nearer than the trees, a
large man mounted and leading a white pack horse, heading for the
gothi's farmstead. He disappeared into the shadow of the hollows
and then reemerged into light again as the path wound its way.

"The only man I know who owns a white horse is Lamefoot," said
Illugi, peering at the tiny shape. "Why would he be out here?"

Snorri gothi put his hand on Thorleif's shoulder as they trudged
down the path. They nodded to each other, knowing each man
had held the same kind of wish in his heart, and here might be
the answer sent even before they left the mountain.

"Our faith was strong, foster brother," Snorri said.

He had prayed for an answer to Arnkel.

Thorleif had prayed for vengeance.

———

Lamefoot sat on the left hand side of Snorri gothi, stiff and
uncomfortable. He had lain a half dozen folded seal skins down
before the gothi without a word beyond, "For you," as if the gift
alone was good manners enough.

The sons of Thorbrand had left.

It was not all that far back to Swan firth, a two hour ride, and three at night. So they said loudly to Snorri gothi outside the Hall and thanked him for his hospitality, while Lamefoot looked on, surprised to see the sons of Thorbrand there. They greeted him in a friendly way, and he nodded to them. Hrafn took them into the barn then, and by torchlight they talked over a few purchases. They bought a great sack of grain and a smaller one of hops, both to make ale, and went home promising to return again when there was more light and time.

Oreakja saw them off. Hawk had gone into the Hall with the gothi and Lamefoot, and stood beside his chieftain, arms folded. He frowned at Thorolf.

Hawk remembered the monster of old.

"I want to speak with you privately, Snorri gothi," Lamefoot said. "Not with this oaf staring down at me and asking to get his ears boxed. I don't trust him. I've left my spear and sword by the door. What have you to fear from me? I come asking for your help."

"He will bring us food to share, Thoro . . . "

"I want none of your food. I want no favors from you, except one."

Snorri gothi leaned back in his High Seat.

What does this beast want from me? The question rang in his mind.

It is Ulfar, Snorri thought suddenly. It could only be that. Thorolf wanted his help against Ulfar Freedman, or because of him. Thor's Blood, had he killed the man? Did he need legal protection against Thorbrand?

His mind churned, trying to see the implications of it. Where had Thor placed the opportunity in this?

"A favor?"

"Yes. You are the chieftain of this countryside, more so than any other that claim to be so, and so it is your part to set right the wrongs done to men who live here. That is your duty."

Hawk snorted through his nose at Lamefoot's rose glass rhetoric, and the old man's eyes went to him like black daggers. But he said nothing. Snorri gothi only nodded at the compliment.

"What man has laid your rights low, Thorolf, and what has he done?"

"He is Arnkel, my son."

Hawk looked sharply at Snorri gothi, but his chieftain made no overt sign of shock. He leaned forward, scraping a thumb on his chin. He stared at the floor, in deep thought for some time, until Thorolf shuffled his feet impatiently.

"Ah. You wish to have settlement for the slaves he has killed, is that it?" Snorri said softly.

Lamefoot nodded sharply. "You see my mind, then."

For another long while Snorri gothi sat with his hands clasped, face down. In his heart he knew he did it to hide the gleam in his eye. Thor had answered his prayer. He turned his head and quietly asked Hawk to bring in the merchant Hrafn and several of the other men.

Hawk left and they were alone in the dim lamp light of the Hall. The gothi breathed in, knowing the gamble he made.

He turned to Lamefoot and his face and voice were hard as stone. "You speak of my duties as chieftain. But they are nothing compared to the duty of a father to his son. You held that more highly eight years ago, when you came to ask my support of Arnkel when he sought to become gothi."

"Which I paid for with great wealth, you," Lamefoot said. "I always did right by my son, and now he abuses me."

"Bah. You thought it cheap, then. A treasure given to you for your wasteland," he said, purposely flaying his voice against Lamefoot's temper. "I made you sell two farms you could not manage, to Ulfar and his brother, and you took good money for it from them. That was my price of your son's chieftainship, for putting my reputation at stake for you and him. I did it only for the sake of my Thingman Thorbrand's freed slaves, Ulfar and Orlyg, so that they could start a new life. I received nothing but honor." He pointed an accusing finger at Lamefoot. "You are not the man Einar was. He ran those farms well. Nor are you the match of your son, who is twice the man of you. Where is your shame in attacking him, when you should be one in all things?"

Thorolf's teeth bared in rage, but the gothi showed no fear. The farms had been weed ridden and poorly managed under Lamefoot and a relief to him to let go for hard coin. The real cost had been to Arnkel, who had been forced to give up right of heir to the land of Ulfar and Orlyg.

That had been his price to pay for the honor of being gothi.

Arnkel had hated it.

His rage had been clear to see, as clear as the light coming down from the sun.

He had hated his stupid father, who acted the great lord in his gold and silver, drunkenly giving away the future with a slap of the hand without any idea of what he did, the many eyes of the Thing on him under the bright sun of spring, and no way to take it back.

Snorri remembered his eyes, the barely masked madness in them as Thorolf handselled the agreement with Snorri gothi, knowing there was no other way for him to come to power. Murder floated behind those eyes as his father pushed him forward to swear before all that he gave up rights to Ulfar's land, and Orlyg's. Contempt filled the faces of each man who saw that, hidden behind smiles as they witnessed the triumph of Snorri gothi.

How much should I tell him, Snorri gothi wondered, looking down at Thorolf's swollen face.

Should I tell him that in one stroke I legally cut his son's inheritance of land by half, and so reduced a future enemy?

No.

His anger would come to me then, not Arnkel, he thought. Boasting had no place here. That was for fools like him.

He would tell him nothing at all. He would just use this gift from Thor, a father's hatred of his own son.

Arnkel was trapped on his tiny plot of Bolstathr until Lame-foot's death. It had been easy to predict that the proud and self-ish Lamefoot would never give up any of his lands to his son, and Arnkel gothi could not afford to buy them. He had little wealth and should have been no more than just another successful farmer, a bondi with pretensions. Yet, somehow, in eight years, he had drawn Thingmen to himself, and made himself a power in Swan's fjord and beyond, wielding his chieftainship and his personal strength like a sword.

His power was outside the Law.

I cannot fight Arnkel there, Snorri thought, in the wilds of violence and feud, where he is strongest. He must be beaten on my ground.

He smiled.

"I will not take up this matter, a dispute between father and son," he said slowly. "Especially when the son is so much more important and powerful than the father."

Lamefoot sputtered in outrage. "I own the greater part of land within the fjord, not that pup. And I took it by strength! What he has, came by my generosity!"

"Yet here you are now seeking my help. It is said that many years have passed since you tested your strength against each other in the weapons drill. He is a powerful man in his prime. It is under-standable that you fear him."

Lamefoot's face became beet red with rage. His jowls shook with it, and Snorri prayed that the bastard's heart would last long enough to carry through. He knew that Lamefoot's training of his son had stopped the day Arnkel had beat the sword from his father's hand and knocked him to the ground, a year after Arnkel had become gothi at Bolstathr.

There were many years of petulant pride to milk.

He waited, while Lamefoot stewed and paced about, mumbling. Then the old man stopped and turned, and spoke darkly.

"If you take up this case, I will give up right to all the blood-money for the slaves. That will be your fee." His greed had fought with his lust for revenge and had lost.

Snorri gothi shook his head. "No. What are a few pieces of silver to me, if I make an enemy of your dread son?"

Lamefoot's eyes bulged, and he savagely kicked one of the benches, shattering it. Hawk came in then, frowning, a long stave of wood in his hand and it was obvious that he had been listening from the darkness of the entrance way. Snorri held him back with a finger. Hrafn was ushered in by other men and he sat down quietly with his crew, nervously eyeing the old viking even as he took a horn of ale. Five of Snorri's Thingmen trooped in, curious, and Hawk pointed them to benches with a frown to silence them. But Lamefoot ignored them all. He stood, deep in thought, chin on his chest, talking to himself in eerie mutters.

The old man looked up, eyes alight with a sudden idea.

"Alright, then. . . . alright. What of this, eh?" He growled like an animal. "Crowness. The wood."

Snorri gothi clenched his fist to still the leap of glory in his guts. He forced calmness into his voice, and bored disinterest.

"What of it?"

"Take up this fight. Make Arnkel pay dearly for my slaves and the shame he has brought on me. Do that, and here and now I will give you that land." Lamefoot walked forward, hand high, as if daring him to hold out his for the slap that would make it legal. His eyes were dark and mad.

Snorri gothi looked around him to the half dozen of his men, and to Hrafn the merchant, and then stood from his seat.

"Will you be witness to this agreement, men? Hrafn of Trondheim?"

The men called their agreement, and Hrafn nodded doubtfully.

"This seems a fair price for the task set before me, to take up Thorolf's quarrel with Arnkel gothi, his son, for the price of his wrongly hanged slaves, at the Thorsnes Thing, when winter ends."

His voice had deepened, and he spoke loudly so that no man could miss his words. It was quiet as death in the Hall. Each man there knew what was happening, heard the ritual in the words. Hrafn watched with his mouth open. Snorri held his hand out for the handsal. "And for this duty, I shall take into my hands the land of Crowness, the wood, as it stands now in Thorolf's possession, in its entirety."

Lamefoot slapped the hand savagely, a blow meant to hurt, but Snorri gothi had no thought for the pain. He raised his hand high and slapped down on Lamefoot's palm, and it was done.

Lamefoot stood now like a man who had just done an awful crime and wondered how he had come to it. He stumbled away into the darkness of the entrance alcove. The door opened and cold blasted in.

Hawk went to close the door.

He returned to find the gothi looking at the axe he had bought from Hrafn, testing the edge with his thumb. It had rested against the side of his High Seat the whole time, hidden by shadow and close at hand.

"You do not own a sword, do you, Hawk?" the gothi said.

"No, gothi."

Snorri looked away from Hawk and smiled down at Hrafn the merchant, who looked up expectantly. "Well, it is time we bought you one."

IV

SPRING

OF THE THORSNES THING AND THE
PAYMENT OF SILVER FOR BLOOD

WINTER HAD FADED away. It was Spring, and the blood ran quickly in people's veins.

Mornings could be cold still, and nuggets of dirty ice still held in the deep hollows behind stones and cliffs where the sun shone only a short time each day. But the wind was kind most days. Men went about their work nearly naked, letting the heat of the sun drive the lice and fleas from their pegged clothes, although it was still just too cool to be comfortable. Longer days meant longer outside and so the tensions of inside life eased. It helped that most of the ale had been finished months back and it was only rich men who drank too much and quarreled. Now there was work to be done. The sheep needed to be taken into pasture after shearing, their wool carded, washed and spun. Looming into vathmal was the long work of the winter. Cows had begun to make milk again as grass made its way out of the ground, and that was much labor, both to collect the milk and then store it in the vast barrels of the upland pasture sheds, where it would slowly rot its way into delicious curd and cheese. The making of skyr began, the staple of life, thickened whey white as a virgin's skin and luscious off the spoon. Frozen peat had begun to thaw, and could be dug again.

Turf from the marsh had melted and greened, and soon collection could begin to repair the storm damaged houses and Halls.

It was an awkward time to have the Thing, pulling men from their work, but many grievances had built up since the last year and for so many to gather good weather was needed. No man's Hall could be big enough, and any true issue of Law needed the Gods above to witness it. As soon as the sun shone enough to warm the air, the men would meet. The women worked twice as hard while their husbands went off with their spears and their best clothes, and the men always promised to settle things quickly and return to their farms.

But, of course, the men said to each other with broad grins as they met on the paths to the Thing, not too quickly.

The site of the Thing was a truncated hill, topped by a cluster of rock outcrops, gathered about a central grassy flat a spear throw across. Men could sit easily on the flat rock, or stand to get height above men so their voices could carry. The best spots were kept for the wealthiest men and the most respected of the elders, and there would be grumbling when a man took a better spot than he was entitled to by his reputation. In later years, there had been so many people coming that many had brought benches, and these circled the grassy hilltop. Snorri gothi did this, hating the usual jockeying for one of the rocks, although he always got his way as one of the three chief gothi of the Thorsnes Thing. Quarreling wasted time and often led to new disputes and aggravated old ones.

Tents littered the field below. All eight gothar of the region had come, with their advisors and Thingmen, and those with grievances to argue on some man's behalf or their own had brought many Thingmen armed with spear and shield to support them.

A man needed strength to hold onto what the Law said was his.

A vast store of driftwood had been found on the rock beach below, and now fires burned everywhere below. As usual the Thing became more than just a grim settling of disputes. Kin met here and there was always laughter and singing in the nights around the fire, with wedding plans made and alliances nurtured and born. News and gossip spread like plague.

Already the story of Thorolf Lamefoot and the dispute with his son Arnkel gothi had gripped the attention of men. There would be many watching when that was settled. But for that first day there was only the choosing of jurors, twelve good bondar to discuss and rule on cases that would come. It was likely they would never be called upon, except when compromise proved impossible and no men of good will would step forward to mediate. Many men were suggested and witnesses were brought forward to hear testimony to each man's character. A candidate not selected needed to be thanked and praised for his offer of services and carefully assured of his quality before moving on to the next. Some men needed more stroking than others. Even with a short list prepared ahead of time, and much prior talk among the gothi, they had to move slowly through these ambitious men seeking to improve their reputation and their honor by the dangerous duty of judging their peers.

It took time.

Snorri watched the sun.

Arnkel and he had spoken not at all, although the hulking chieftain sat only three men away. Even their choices of jurors had been without dispute. Several of these men were Snorri gothi's followers. It was as if they had no quarrel, and that was as it should be in a land of Law and Thing. This was no place for violence, Snorri thought. The dispute would come in its own time, and be settled with restraint. There was even the illusion of friendship. Thorgils and Hawk spoke casually behind the row of gothar, since they were kin, and all knew that they were the first men of both chieftains. That was remarked on favorably by many men. It showed that compromise and restraint were in the air.

Snorri gothi knew better.

Oreakja sat beside him, listening to the testimonials. The boy tried hard not to show his boredom. As each man was selected, he would peer expectantly at Arnkel from the corner of his eye. He had been excited by the sharpening of weapons before they had left Helgafell and Hawk's dark predictions had made him believe that the Thing was a place where men lined up and threatened each other.

Snorri patted the boy's knee to calm him. He tried not to smile. Oreakja had grown up with Hawk as an uncle. The man's hardness was in the boy's spirit and that was good, but he would need more than bile to follow in his father's path.

"Patience, son," he said quietly.

"Why is he not arguing the jurors, father?" Oreakja whispered back. "We've picked four of your Thingmen already, and he just nods."

"That was to be expected," he mouthed against the boy's ear. "Arnkel is no fool. He won't waste the good humor of the men here by unnecessary delays. He knows that the other gothar will argue against me if I try to add any more of our men."

His son nodded, disappointed.

Arnkel's refusal to pay for Lamefoot's slaves had been like oil spilled into a fire at Helgafell. Men began to practice with axe and sword and spar with spears when the work did not occupy them. New shields were made from precious wood. The children ran about delirious with excitement and fought each other with sticks and snowballs in imitation of the men, certain that fighting was to come in spring and ghoulishly predicting who would be killed or maimed. Hawk would pretend he was Arnkel and chase them about with a great roar as they screamed and ran.

Hrafn the merchant had been asked to go to Bolstathr with some of his goods in February. He did much business and while there he had delivered Snorri gothi's demand for the twenty marks for each slave asked by Thorolf.

"Are you sure you wish to take on this task?" Snorri gothi had asked him. "I cannot be sure of what kind of answer you will get, and you must know the fate of many messengers. I can send another man."

But the Norwegian had insisted, eagerly loading a string of borrowed horses, and pointing his crew men here and there.

"If he acts the tyrant with me, at least it will be a welcome change from the unremitting excellence of your hospitality, Snorri gothi." He had grinned impishly at the gothi's laughter, even as he hurriedly tied knots. "I really must get out and wander. A whole winter spent in one place is slowly driving me mad."

The answer had been no.

Of course it had.

Snorri had hoped the merchant's rough foreign manners would stir trouble in Bolstathr, perhaps even enough to add to his case. But it seemed that Hrafn had a talent for escaping anger.

The merchant had been given a ring of silver by Arnkel to thank him and was urged to tour the countryside and to say only that he had been sent by Arnkel gothi.

Yes, he was clever.

I must be very careful tomorrow, Snorri thought. He pulled the brim of his hat low over his eyes and peered at the world from its deep shade.

The day ended well, with all twelve men selected and the order of the cases determined for tomorrow's Court of Prosecution.

The selection had moved quickly in its last stages, and the clear sky above boded well for the next day. Men had walked about the base of the hill as the work had gone on, laying out bits of food on the ground and charms of woven grass and horsehair, so that the elves would be distracted and not devil men with wrong thoughts. The gothar led the horde of men to the flat killing rock on the next hill, and there a bull was sacrificed and its spirit sent to the sky to thank the Gods for guiding them through the hard task of dealing with the honor of men with restraint. The bull died well, bellowing mightily so that Those above would know of its coming death. The men murmured happily to see that. There would be sound judgement the next day, it seemed. Too often a sick animal was substituted for the sacrifice and that served no one.

Snorri walked back to his tent with Hawk and two of his Thing-men. A quick meal of smoked fish and whey and then he was off, promising to be back by nightfall. He let the Norwegian protest for a bit at this. Hrafn claimed he was abandoned by his host. Snorri let him join their procession to the other gothar, as he had planned. It was always good to have men feel that you have done them a favor.

In the last months he had come to feel an affection for the merchant. He had a true wit to him and could tell many jokes well, and so had been good company. More importantly, he was a distraction and allowed Snorri gothi to talk business with greater subtlety while Hrafn amused the many ears that always listened in the close air of the Hall. Even at the Thing, under open sky, he would serve the same purpose. The only fly in the ointment was his man Onund, who seemed to have a talent for squabbling with everyone. He made the mistake of insulting Hawk and had his lip split open for that, although Hawk himself nursed a sore jaw. Hrafn had left him behind at Helgafell. He would only cause trouble at the Thing, especially if he ran into kin of his former wife, which was likely.

Another fly was the sight of the sons of Thorbrand, camped far away from any of Snorri's men. They had come to the Thing out of duty, but the news of Snorri gothi's case with Arnkel on Thorolf's behalf had come to them, and they pouted.

Thorleif had confronted him earlier, feet planted widely.

"You advocate for the father of our enemy, but not for us!"

"There are other concerns here, Thorleif," he had said mildly, but Thorleif had chopped his hand angrily.

"A chieftain has duties to his Thingmen!" Thorleif had snapped, and stormed off.

The man's naivete worried Snorri. But he could not dwell on that.

There was much to discuss with the other chieftains.

He spoke first to his friend Olaf Hoskud gothi, known as One Hand, a burly seal hunter from near the tip of the Snaefellsnes peninsula, and a man with whom he had stood before. He had many, many daughters, and wedding these to good men had been a yearly task for Snorri gothi. With barrels full of oil after a winter of hunting on the ice, he would thank Snorri for introducing him to a merchant so early in the season. Olaf's Thingmen tended to be fishermen and hunters, hardy men full of spit from their life on the sea. Glowering behind their gothi with spears in hand, they could convince many a juror of the need to vote a particular way. Olaf was his first stop because the man would have been insensible from drink if he had waited until later. The evenings were for drink. Olaf was known as One Hand because he always held a horn of ale in one huge fist and so had only the single hand free.

They spoke head to head for a time while Hrafn set the men to laughing and showed them some of his wares. Of great interest was his collection of combs, pins and brooches of ivory, and jewelry of good Arabic silver, some set with rare gems. They sold quickly. He lay them on a large piece of black felt, flashing a piece in the air now and then as he talked of its history. It was all fancy. All the gems were glass. The same stories, but they changed from piece to piece, as if Hrafn himself could not keep track of his own lies. Snorri gothi had heard the man's hawking many times over the winter. If all the stories were true, then each had the potent magic to create sons in the womb and make men as large and hard as beach stones if their women wore it. Yet men clutched the pieces they bought with gleaming eyes.

Men will believe what they want to believe, he thought. It was a weakness to be used like any other.

From Olaf gothi, he went to Gudmund gothi, a neighbor to the east, whose hunger for money was legendary. He had thought carefully about going to the man, knowing the risks. He had already sent gifts to the man in the winter, and cryptic messages of his need for support.

"Enough of your fine words, Snorri gothi," the man said, a gleam in his eye. "Tell me what you want, and I'll tell you the cost."

Friend or kin, whether blood or by marriage, Gudmund gothi would go against them all if the profit was there to justify it, and his many Thingmen backed him. It sometimes made for bad feeling from those he persecuted, and the gothi lived on the fine line between wealth and cold steel. All gothar did to some degree, taking on the quarrels of others but where Snorri worked toward compromise from the start, Gudmund had a way of keeping the dispute very much alive and full of the original hatred. The approach had its merits, widening the feud to other relations, and so increasing the reward of the gothi when it finally was resolved. With Gudmund's support, Arnkel would see that Snorri could rally the warlike as well as the sensible to his cause.

A boatload of smoked salmon, a small fortune in vathmal, and pasture rights for a hundred of Gudmund's sheep on Snorri's land was the cost, and they handselled under the last rays of the setting sun. It was too much for a few words of support but Snorri swore to himself that he would recoup the price at some other time. The Crowness was too great a treasure to risk on misplaced thrift.

He paid one last visit to a lone tent pitched far from the others. Thorolf was there, with his single remaining slave, drinking. They talked for a short while.

Men stayed awake as long as they could, enjoying the bright sky of evening. Some danced to the sound of drums and pipes, some sang, some only sat about and enjoyed the leisure of the Thing, away from the nagging of wives who thought daylight an evil time for idleness. Many of the men watched the wrestling. Challengers would call on any to take them down. One large fellow called Wulf had defeated four men with ease, using his bulk to fling them to the ground. He was shirtless, covered in a thick fur of red hair. A new challenger came up, throwing his shirt to the side.

It was Arnkel, grinning. His men hooted him on and made bets with other men in the crowd. "Haven't thrashed a gothi yet today," the red haired man called gamely, grinning also, but Arnkel said nothing. They spat on their hands and took the positions, one hand on the opponent's belt, the other his arm.

There was a count of three and it began. Each man heaved on the other's belt, trying to upend his opponent. Wulf tried to get his leg behind Arnkel's but the gothi pulled it back and threw it inside the Wulf's legs, but that too was avoided by a quick step back. The two were well matched in bulk, but Arnkel seemed quicker. The grin was gone and he grappled with a grim, deadly look in his eye.

He feinted with a pull to the left, and then quickly reversed. Wulf leaned to one side, slightly off balance, and the gothi pounced. He ripped the man's foot out from under him with a heel and threw him hard into the turf with one great heave of his arms. A roar went up from his men and from the other onlookers. They applauded and yelled congratulations to Arnkel and insults to Wulf. Arnkel offered his hand to help the man up. The red haired man was grumpy from his loss and threatened one of his tormenters with a fist but this was quickly smoothed over by other men and soon Wulf was laughing and swigging from a skin of ale. He slapped Arnkel gothi's shoulder affectionately. "You're a good fellow," he said.

The gothi wore a vast look of satisfaction.

His eye caught Snorri's across the turf. The men looked at each other for a moment. Then Arnkel turned and left.

All the chieftains had brought with them the last of the old stock of ale and mead and these they shared out among their men. When the sun finally dipped below the horizon for its short sleep, the songs to the few faint stars began. The host of men gathered, loosely bunched about the tents of their gothi and each following in turn sang a part of the chorus of the song while the others listened, one group taking up with the dying refrain of the last, so that it became all one song from a thousand throats that rang out over the plain. The Gods listened, pleased by the harmony.

Snorri gothi sang with his men, but his mind was on the next day.

The Court began an hour after dawn, when the sun had risen enough to give warmth. One juror had slept late and was hissed at by the others for the ale-darkened pits under eyes. It would be a long day of deep thought, and a bondi was expected to be somber and sober if he were to judge other men. More men began to come in from their tents. They chewed dried meat or fish and chatted and joked in low voices. The circle of chieftains surrounded the grassy space, each backed by a mass of their followers, while the jurors sat on benches in one tight group with many of their kin behind to prevent intimidation of their relations.

The first case was brought against a man called Rolf, who had agreed to prepare and weave the raw wool of a neighbor named Sigmund into vathmal for a fee, when Sigmund's wife and female servants and slaves had taken sick in one long spell of illness and could not do the work. The dispute was over the share of the wool he had kept as his fee. As the farm was large there was a good amount of wealth involved. Rolf saw quickly that his neighbor had prepared himself, especially when Snorri gothi stood to declare his support for Sigmund and advocate on his behalf. The agreement had been witnessed properly and these men were trotted out one after another by Snorri to tell what had been agreed to and how much wool had been processed. There was a cold exchange of coins, many coins, and the contractor left, angry and embarrassed at his swift defeat.

The next case was highly charged with hard feelings in two families, one of whom backed a husband still in grieving for his new wife who had died only a month after the marriage, of a strange fever. The dowry had been extravagant, seventy good milk cows, but the dead wife's family argued that the husband had somehow caused the death of an otherwise healthy woman and so the dowry was demanded returned. Payment for the wife's death was also demanded. Improper sacrifices were suggested, the wife's family strongly implying that the lack of piety on the husband's part had caused the death, but it was only a legalistic ploy to return the wealth to the family of the bride. The husband's lack of enthusiasm for the affair and devastated face made it clear that he was in pain. He would not speak, holding his head in his hands, and so it was his rapacious uncles and cousins who pressed the suit to keep the dowry. They argued that all their sacrifices had been done according to proper ritual. Snorri gothi spoke during this case, as the husband was a Thingman of Olaf gothi, and he stated that the payment of the dowry had been made and received in good faith and that the issue of the wife's death was not something that could be conclusively put at the husband's feet. He declared that the dowry should stay in the hands of the husband's family, but that a fee of ten law ounces should be paid by the husband's family for the loss of their relative, if the wife's family would give up the claim of wrongdoing.

This enraged one of the wife's family, a bulky red faced man who had been drinking since dawn. He leaped across the green space and slashed at the husband with his spear, cutting him badly across the shoulder and chest.

There was much shouting and pushing. Hawk pulled Snorri back behind him. He and several Thingmen formed a wall and waited while Hromund gothi's sons, who had the duty of peace in the Thing, came in with shields to separate the two groups.

In the end, several men of good faith went back and forth between the two glaring families and arranged a settlement of ten of the cows to be returned. The issue of the fee to be paid for the wife was paid for by the blood of the husband, Snorri gothi declared. The jurors mumbled among themselves, with an eye on the wife's family to check their mood, and then agreed. The husband was injured, but not badly, and would recover. The groups of angry men retreated, neither full satisfied, but neither as angry as they had been, and so it ended.

Snorri gothi's heart beat quickly. That crazy fool could just as easily have run at him instead of the husband, he thought.

Old Hromund gothi, given the task of keeping the order of the cases, waved a hand at him and at Arnkel.

It was time.

He stood. Hawk came up to stand alongside and Oreakja also. A murmur of surprise and interest grew behind him. From the crowd of men, Thorolf stepped forward, shouldering aside the others.

He had braided his beard and hair and greased it, and wore his armor of mail. He had strapped a sword at his side, although he had no shield or spear. His great belly stretched out the mail links to their limit, but it still looked impressive, cleaned, oiled and glistening. He glanced once at Snorri gothi and then took his place where Snorri had told him, at his left hand shoulder and two paces back. He was nervous and stiff with all the eyes on him. Whispers flew about in the crowd of the man who persecuted his own son.

Hromund gothi stood from his rock and cleared his throat with a rheumy bark.

"We stand here witness to a dispute set forth by Snorri of Helgafell, on behalf of Thorolf of Hvammr, against Arnkel of Bolstathr. Declare your grievance." He sat, waving another hand at Snorri to begin.

Arnkel had stepped forward at the call of his name, as if surprised and a little outraged to find himself there and in this he seemed to gather a little sympathetic buzz from the onlookers. "Why am I called?" he said loudly.

Snorri smiled grimly.

"Arnkel of Bolstathr, I bring against you the slaying of three men, thralls of your father, whom you did hang without his permission from Vadils Head. Do you deny this accusation, and shall we have to bring witnesses to it?"

As expected, Arnkel quickly admitted to the hangings. There was no profit in denying them and then having witnesses prove him a liar.

"Then there is justice in your father's claim for compensation for your crime. You hung these slaves out of Law and thus did commit manslaughter of his property. Why have you refused to pay for their lives, as the Law and decency require?"

Arnkel gestured behind him. Ulfar walked out from between the Fish Brothers. He was white-faced, but his chin was set and he stood squarely. Snorri had met him several times in past years and knew him to be a good man, known for his knowledge of sheep healing and the growing of things. He was small, barely to the shoulder of the darkly glowering Fish Brothers who flanked him, a dark haired man of mixed Norse and Celt blood. The brothers snarled back the crowd of watchers like angry dogs.

"This is Ulfar Freedman of Ulfarsfell," Arnkel called out. "It was his farm and person that was attacked by the slaves. The slaves brought wood to his home and set fire to it and waited by his door with spears, to slay Ulfar and his wife when they fled into the night. Only by the luck of Thor was I in my field with my men, taking the night air after feast, and saw the blaze. We came forward and took the slaves in the act of quickfire and bound them."

Ulfar spoke briefly, confirming Arnkel's words in a monotone.

Snorri held up his hand to interrupt. "Why did you not kill the slaves that night?"

Arnkel threw his hands into the air, as if exasperated. "Who am I to give justice on a whim, without thought? At the time I did not even know the names of these men. It was night, and dark. I thought it best to wait until day so that justice could be better done."

"You did not recognize your own father's slaves, although they kneeled at your feet, yet your eyes were sharp enough to see them creep up to Ulfar's house from Bolstathr? That is five hundred paces away, if it is one."

Whispers and mumbles followed this, and Arnkel's eyes narrowed. "Starlight on snow can reveal many things, and hide many things."

"Yet starlight could not hide their crime." This was Olaf gothi, who stood to speak, his seal hunters glowering behind him with

spears in hand. "Quickfire of a man's home in winter, with murder in their hearts. The punishment for that is plain and clear."
He pointed a finger accusingly. "They could be slain in the act
only. Not later."

Gudmund gothi stood then, and he pointed his finger also.
"The Law is clear on this, Arnkel of Bolstathr. Men may be killed
without consequence only in the very act of quickfire, not a day
later at your convenience."

Arnkel looked quickly between the two men, caught off
guard.

The jurors whispered among each other and with the closest of
the gothar to them, assuring themselves that this was in fact the
way of the Law. Both sides waited for them. For a long moment
Arnkel stared at Snorri with his bright blue, terrible eyes. He saw
his defeat coming like an approaching storm. Snorri met the glare
evenly, but he thought of the fine axe he had bought from Hrafn
and wished he had it tucked in his belt at that moment. The lead
juror, a heavy man called Gorm, finally turned to them and nodded. He called out that the Law could approve of execution without
trial only in the moment of discovery of the crime, as with murder
and rape, and the theft of cattle and horses and sheep. It was an
arcane ruling, but it was Snorri's only ploy with Arnkel. Arson
was greatly feared and there would be a popular desire to support
Arnkel who had in most ways seemed to act like a restrained and
sensible chieftain. Luckily, the influence of other chieftains and
their pressure on the court weighed as much or more than the
Law. Still, he had the future to think of as well. His reputation
was as a man of Law, who could argue cases cleverly within it, and
that needed to be protected. Leave the bullying tactics to men like
Gudmund gothi, who had a taste for them, Snorri thought.

Of trivial importance to this court was the true reason that
Arnkel had not slaughtered the slaves that night. But it mattered
very much. The slaves had still had a role to play. On Vadils Head,
Arnkel had somehow made them admit to trying to murder Ulfar

on their own and so cleared his father of all wrong. Klaenger had told him everything that had happened.

It might seem a strange thing to do, to help a man whom all knew had nothing but ill will toward his own kin. The noble son, forgiving all wrong of the father. Yet not so strange or noble if one were to look ahead to the years ahead, and see Thorbrand and his sons take Thorolf to task for the attempted murder of their freedman Ulfar, and so get payment. A very great payment. Even land, that would be lost to a son who would inherit one day.

Oh yes, he was clever.

But he sees how he has lost, Snorri thought. It is in his eyes.

The next time we meet at this place, Snorri thought, he will not be so easy to master. He knows what I have done, gathering other chieftains to me, and will learn from it. So now I must act the man of restraint, so that none will say that Arnkel deserves his revenge on me, and so that allies will be harder to come by.

He called to the crowd. "Are there men here would come forward to intervene and find a path that all of us can tread? Who will speak between us?"

There were many shouts of approval for Snorri gothi's words, at this moment when he could easily have imposed a harsh ruling on Arnkel, and also many surprised faces, especially among Arnkel's men.

Thorolf gripped his arm, his large hand squeezing tightly. "What are you doing? Press it! I've won."

Snorri turned to face him. "No, Thorolf. I have won, not you. I purchased this quarrel from you and so it is mine to settle as I will." He shook off the man's hand. Hawk pushed himself between them and faced Lamefoot chest to chest, whispering fiercely until the old man settled into a grumbling silence.

Two men came forward, named Vermund and Stir. They knew both chieftains and yet were not Thingmen of either, but only independent bondar hoping to make a name for themselves as mediators. They were known to have smooth tongues. Hromund

gothi held an arm up to both sides to see if the men were accept-
able. After the nods, they went back and forth speaking with first
Arnkel and then with Snorri, haggling over a fair price to set for
the slaves, while the men crowded around and passed the details
of each negotiation to those standing farther back. Snorri asked
for thirty ounces each. He knew it would never be accepted, but
it gave Arnkel room to bargain and thus save face.

Thorolf still fumed behind him, spitting and letting out exasperated blasts of air when ever Stir and Vermund returned with
an offer only a pittance above that offered before.

"Pay a fair price, damn you, for what you have done to me!"
he shouted once across the green space to Arnkel gothi, only to
have one of the Fish Brothers flash a finger at him rudely. Thorolf
was held back by Hawk and the other of Snorri's Thingmen until
he lost his wind. He would never be content with a money price.
His goal had been the humiliation of his son and that hope had
faded away.

Snorri gothi allowed the price to fall to twelve ounces per slave.
It would hardly replace three full grown men and the work they
could do, but it was still a large amount of money. He could go no
lower and have men begin to question his dedication to Thorolf's
case. It still seemed too much for Arnkel, who had naively come
to the Thing expecting an easy victory simply because of the enor-
mity of the crime he had punished by hanging the men. He was
tight lipped with rage and struck an onlooker down, a man who
had drunk too much ale and had too big a mouth. Thorgils and
Hafildi watched this break in their chieftain's control nervously
and Thorgils hissed a warning in Arnkel's ear. Arnkel shoved
him away. Thorgils glared at the gothi, eyes wide with anger and
then at Hafildi, who smirked at his embarrassment. Olaf gothi's
men had now gathered with Snorri's. They watched the bargaining intently as they leaned on their spears. There were two hundred men behind Snorri and they greatly outnumbered Arnkel's
Thingmen.

Arnkel seemed to calm instantly, as if ice had suddenly frozen from steam. He turned to Stir, who was nearby waiting for an answer. He nodded, speaking quietly. A bag of coin went into the man's hands and he carried it proudly across the grass space while the men quieted to listen as the haggling ended. Stir placed the bag in Snorri's hand.

The gothi turned and handed the bag to Thorolf.

"Here is the payment for your slaves, Thorolf of Hvammr. You have had justice done, and so my fee is earned. Go in peace."

Thorolf held out his hand slowly and took the bag of coin. Snorri laughed silently at the struggle in his face. His greed forced his fingers to the cord holding it shut. The old viking struggled with the last remnants of propriety in his soul that held him back from counting the coins like a whore, in the open. Thorolf looked at him, his eyes watery and mad with sullen rage.

"Twelve ounces each," he said bitterly, his voice loud in the stillness of the Thing. "Twelve ounces. In time I could have had that little out of Arnkel by myself. I had no idea that when I gave you my land you would fight this case for me with so little manhood, white-hair."

The insult floated on the spring air, and many men heard it. There was a hissing of discontent, and cries of "Shame!", but Lamefoot heard none of it. Hawk stepped forward but Snorri gothi pushed him aside gently and put himself very close to the old man.

He deepened his voice to carry it above the heads of the men, but not so much that they would think he spoke to any man but Lamefoot. "You are the one without manhood, Lamefoot, to complain of lack of trust. I bargained well for you and now you have good money in your hand paid by your own flesh and blood. I will not stake myself on your behalf ever again."

Arnkel gothi's voice cut across the open space, harsh and deadly. "What lands did you give, father? What lands, without my call to allow it as your heir?"

Lamefoot turned towards his son, seeing with his shallow fox cunning a final way to hurt Arnkel. "The Crowness," he said, triumphantly.

There were gasps all around and the word of what was said flashed down the hill. The wood was known as one of the richest lands in the region. Many men looked at Thorolf now with glares of disdain and scorn. They saw then the true nature of the case, the simple pigheaded pride of a stupid and willful man. Thorolf looked around at the faces and frowned uncertainly, and then turned to force his way through the crowd.

"I would not ask for your service anyway, white-hair, knowing what little my coin would buy," he said as a parting shot to Snorri gothi.

Then he was gone.

Hrafn had set himself on one of the higher rocks, back from the main court. His hearing was very good and he had listened to the cases of the Thing with great interest. His two crewmen stood near, weapons held nervously. He understood why. They were Danes, used to a different way of settling disputes and like him they had expected the hundreds of spear men to wade in among each other and begin the killing, especially in the case of the dowry. Only one injured man in the whole mess was miraculous.

Hrafn had spent his life trading in the south waters along the Channel, to the Saxon lands and northern Francia. The pirates teemed like lice on the water and they came from all sides. The Saxons had found their feet again and were taking back the lands they had lost from the Northmen. It was war, and war, and more war down there and that was a younger man's adventure. In ten years he would settle into a farm in Norway, buy the local lord's protection and live out his old age in peace.

But perhaps he would come here, to the Free State, he thought.

He had heard many stories in the long winter. The strangest ones to his mind were of the killings that went un-avenged. A slaying, then a settlement paid in livestock or cloth or coin, and all parties satisfied. Unbelievable, as if blood could be soaked up by silver. There was wergild, the paying of blood money, in Norway as well but it never wiped away the feud, only delayed it. Men needed to kill to avenge killing there, but in the Free State it seemed to end at the payment.

Some of the answer to this place could be seen in Onund. He had found the boy in London, trading his strength for food and living like a beast as he fought with fist and club for one of the port merchants to keep the rich man's dock clear of beggars and thieves. London was a charnel; he never stayed more than a night there if he could help it. He quickly sold his cargo to the first bidder usually, but even then still got more for it than in any other port in the south lands. On his last trip, a brawl had started over his cargo of amber and whale fat and the city soldiers had come to take what they could. Onund had broken his leg in the scrap and so Hrafn had taken him on, out of pity for a fellow Northman and because the Christ God had said that men must be kind to those in need. Hrafn was devout, though he prayed quietly here in pagan lands where the elves still walked the ground thickly, and he made cautious sacrifices to Thor whenever he was out of sight of land and the Christian God. He had discovered the boy was from the Island. Seal oil, walrus hide rope, and fine cloth to buy and a land desperate for little luxuries easily carried. Onund had told him all that as he recovered on the sea. It had seemed a good idea to change his trade route. The boy had been vicious and tough. He terrified the other crew men with his strength and rage when he recovered until they simply accepted him as second in command. During the winter at Helgafell, however, he had slowly returned to what was probably his true self, a man like the others here, short of speech, tight lipped and sensible, suspicious of others, and generous. No word was spoken hastily and he always looked to others before taking meat from the pot. It was as if a blanket had been wrapped tightly around him to hold in his darker side.

But even then his rage and anger would burst forth sometimes. The Island only tempered him.

Snorri gothi had laughed at this when he had shared his revelations one evening over many horns of ale.

"We are men like any other, Hrafn," he had said. "There is greed and lust and selfishness in all of us. But the edge of life and death is very close to us here, much closer than in the homeland. Nothing can be wasted, or hoarded beyond reason, or all will starve and die. Every man knows this. Children will grab all of the food from the bowl if they are not restrained, but a man restrains himself. So when a man acts like a child we frown at him as if he is a child, and speak of him as if he is a child." He had smiled and looked at Onund. "It is not a way of life that would survive in a land of plenty. And there are some men who are not suited to it."

Onund had flushed furiously at this and ducked his head. Hrafn had marveled at humility from such a wild character.

Lord Jesus Christ, he was sick of eating curdled milk every damned day, and rubbery meat that tasted of whey, with no bread, and hardly a green thing to cut the taste of it, except seaweed, with only some foul rotten mess to break the monotony now and then. He was tired of dark turf Halls, and the greasy closeness of winter living and the smell and taste of peat smoke in his eyes and mouth. Still, if it was only this sort of life that would breed men who would not kill each other for greed at the drop of a hat, then he would pay the price and make this Island his home.

The Thing lasted a week. As the last case was settled men began to drift back to their farms and to the grind of life. Snorri gothi had arranged a betrothal for his son and the boy was excited and very nervous. Hawk teased the boy relentlessly as they rode back to Helgafell, claiming that the size of the dowry was linked to the ugliness of the girl, and a very great dowry had been hand-selled. A hundred cows, so that Oreakja would begin married life as a wealthy farmer, even without the inheritance from his father one day.

"Put her in with the cows, lad, and then you can see your wealth as you take her from behind and it will stir you," Hawk said, and the men laughed. Snorri gothi said nothing and only smiled at the good spirits of the men, who knew their chieftain had come away with great stature and wealth from the Thing and so protected them as well.

"Oh, is that your style, Hawk?" said Oreakja gamely. "Now we know why so many of the calves this year had your look." The men slapped their thighs as they roared.

Hrafn rode beside Snorri. The party had been almost a hundred men leaving the Thing, but pairs and threes had split off as they passed their farms, waving goodbye and each formally promised to the gothi that they would be at the Autumn assembly at Helgafell. At each departure there was much grasping of forearms, the ponies weaving in and out as the men made their goodbyes. It was a fine spring afternoon with clear blue skies, warm and delightful. A stiff breeze stirred whitecaps out to sea and cracked the trailing edges of their clothing like banners.

Near the back of the group rode the six sons of Thorbrand. Hrafn had seen little of them. They had camped far from the other of Snorri's Thingmen during the Thorsnes Thing and they had not joined the fire songs of the gothi. They spoke very little to any other men as they rode, and kept to themselves. Although Snorri had spent time with all his Thingmen at some point in the ride, even if it were just casual words, he avoided the brothers. Hrafn asked about it. He liked the brothers, especially Thorleif, and had spent a month with the family at Swan firth when he had delivered Snorri's demand to Arnkel during the winter.

"They are angry with me for taking on Thorolf's claim against his father," the gothi said. He looked over his shoulder at the brothers. "You will remember that I would not back them against Arnkel about Ulfar's land." This was said casually, as if it mattered little, while the gothi waved to a departing man. He smiled as he spoke.

"They seem good and loyal men," Hrafn said cautiously. His voice must have carried a sliver of criticism in it because the gothi turned to him and frowned.

"That they are, Hrafn," he said darkly. "Come with me."

Snorri wheeled his mount around sharply and rode back to the brothers. Hrafn followed. He wondered what storm he had awoken. Snorri gothi seemed angry, and the merchant swore silently. His ship was ready to sail, but he needed the gothi's men to get it in the water and to load the remaining goods he had left after a good winter's trading. Olaf's seal oil waited for him and perhaps he had jeopardized that as well.

You damned fool, he thought. When will you learn to keep your mouth shut?

The brothers stared with surprise at the gothi as he charged up to them and reined in. Hrafn came up then and he shrugged at Thorleif's raised eyebrow.

"Our friend Hrafn feels that I have not treated you well," Snorri said, his voice hard.

"Gothi . . ." Hrafn said, but Snorri waved his words away.

"Is that what you believe, sons of Thorbrand?" Snorri gothi insisted. "Have I mistreated you?" His straightforward ire was so uncharacteristic that the brothers were taken back and did not know what to say. Hawk rode up then and settled in silently beside Snorri, frowning. The horses milled about under them, disturbed by the tension in the men's legs and the hands on the reins and they called to each other in warbling snorts and nickers.

The brothers' uncertainty confused Snorri. He knew of the friendship between Thorleif and Hrafn and had assumed that Thorleif had put the merchant up to speaking to him.

But now it seemed that he was mistaken and it had just been words from the merchant, nothing more.

The brothers did not inspire him. If only their father had thirty fewer years. A greater enemy to Arnkel's south would be a blessing, but he had only these men. Why did they not do what needed to be done? They kept coming to him for an answer to Arnkel and should look to their own arms. He might help them if only they took that final step.

Perhaps not even then, he thought with black humor. There was nothing to be gained by sentimental attachments. Hrafn was a fool to speak for these men and receive nothing for it. Snorri would fight when fighting became the only choice. There was too much uncertainty in it. The wisest man in the world could still fall from an axe in his head.

"How long would I keep the loyalty of other men if I were to pitch my influence and wealth behind a case that was not certain? You sons of Thorbrand need to be watchful, since you are closer to things down there in the fjord. Do not let Arnkel fool you again, and then I will help you!"

There was only silence for a time. Then Thorleif said quietly, "We will keep your words in our hearts, gothi." He beckoned with one hand to his brothers and led them off. The trail that led south to Swan firth did not break from this trail until farther on. They would pick their way along the pasture lands and marsh and then into the highlands. The mountains inland were sharp teeth, streaked with black and white.

Snorri gothi watched them go.

I will do nothing to antagonize or challenge Arnkel, he thought.

Although the forest of Crowness now legally belonged to him, he would send no one to take wood, not until he needed its riches. The wealth of it beckoned him. All that timber! Perhaps the matter would settle. The land was as close to his own farmstead as it was to Arnkel's and with Thorolf's surprising but welcome public admission of handselling the forest, Snorri could take possession of it at any time, without legal wrangling and witnesses testifying. There was the remote chance of Lamefoot dying to complicate matters and raise questions of inheritance but he still seemed hardy. He could live for ten years or more.

Until then the land was Lamefoot's and he had given it away to
Snorri gothi.

Yes, the slow game was always best.

He turned to Hrafn, and smiled, calm again. The merchant
was relieved to see him friendly once more and this made Snorri
grin broadly.

They came to Helgafell, and even from a distance he could see
there was trouble. One of the thralls came at a run and grasped
Snorri's boot with both hands. His eyes were wide and he looked
back over his shoulder as he hung there.

Thor's Blood, it's started already, Snorri thought. Had Arnkel
raided the place?

The slave found his breath and blurted out the news. A man
was dead, one of the other slaves, a bad tempered Irish named
Rag. His skull had been caved in with an axe handle.

"Who struck him?" Snorri asked.

The slave looked up fearfully to Hrafn. "It was Onund the sailor,
gothi. He was drunk, and Rag spat near him without seeing him
in the hay. They fought and Onund knocked him down and then
beat out his brains. It was awful, blood everywhere." The slave
began to warm to the story, seeing he had an audience, but Snorri
cut off his words with a wave of his hand.

"Where is Onund now?"

"In the barn, gothi, I think."

He called in a half dozen of his men and Hawk to lead them.
They took up shields and spears. Outside the barn, he set them
into a line and then they went in, two at a time. Rag's body still lay
there stiffly. Flies buzzed around the blood. The men swore under
their breath at the sight of the gore that covered everything around
the body and had sprayed up onto the wall and a rafter.

"He must have gone mad," Hawk said, eyes wide.

Snorri stared at the blood a while and then turned to the others. "Find him."

Onund was asleep, sodden and snoring in one of the stalls, covered in dried blood, the axe handle still in his hand. There could be no doubt of his guilt. A bucket of water woke him.

"Damn you, man," hissed Hrafn, and kicked Onund as he scrambled backwards on his elbows. "Do you know what this will cost me?"

Snorri gothi smiled.

———

Late that night, when all the other men had curled up on the benches to sleep and the last of the children had finished their wailing and dropped off, Snorri and Hrafn sat at the foot of the High Seat, very drunk, leaning into each other's shoulders. It was not often that the gothi let his senses be taken fully by the drink but he had felt a need for it that night, and the next day Hrafn would set sail for Olaf's farm to get seal oil before he headed home to Norway.

The skin passed back and forth between them. They spilled as much from their horns as they drank. For some time they had said nothing and Hrafn's eyes had begun to close. Business had been ended earlier. Onund would stay at Helgafell to work off his debt to Snorri gothi for the death of his slave. Hrafn had been hard put to hide his joy at the small cost of his man's crime. Onund had blinked in surprise and relief, expecting some awful reprisal.

Snorri gothi had clapped a hand on his shoulder, although his frown was dark, and said in Onund's ear that there were many services a man might provide to wipe away the stain of blood.

"Hrafn," he whispered. The snores of men filled the Hall.

"Hmm?"

"Have you ever fought a man with blade or axe?"

Hrafn's eyes opened, and he looked at the gothi. He drank a swallow from his horn. "I served under Erik Blood Axe in Yorkshire when I was young and foolish and thought myself a mighty creature under the sun." He puffed a little breath through his nose. "When he fell, I had to fight my way to the coast with a band of his men. There were many Northumbrians to kill along the way, but they killed many of us, too. Three of us survived, running on stolen horses. We took a fishing boat and spent a week at sea with no water except rain.

"After that, I thought there must be better ways to spend life."

They drank for a time, and Hrafn's eyes began to close again.

"Hrafn," Snorri whispered. "My father told me once that a man was more than the strength in his arm. This I believe with my whole heart. Is not Odin the God of wisdom as well as strength? Do they not go together, as one thing?"

As answer, Hrafn pulled his crucifix from his shirt and dangled it.

The gothi snorted at the evasion and drank from his horn. "You do not see my meaning, Hrafn. You have gained wisdom, because you have come to know the difference between your desires and your needs. You have strength, too. What is strength? It is the ability in a man to act on what wisdom has shown him, no matter how unpleasant the task. They cannot be separated, and that is why Odin is God of both of these things in the hearts of men. Each is the scabbard for the other's sword, each useless or dangerous without the other."

Through the veil of drink, or perhaps because of its liquid intuition, Hrafn could sense the need for confession in the gothi's voice, and knew that the man spoke because of the mead and because Hrafn would leave the next day. He was a safe haven for words that might be regretted later. But there was trust in that, and he was touched by it.

"It is true that strength is more than just the flesh." He mumbled slowly, trying for eloquence through the scattered haze of his thoughts.

The gothi leaned into him. "Go to sleep, Hrafn."

The merchant stumbled off to his bed with mumbled apologies and was soon snoring.

The gothi stayed a long time in the company of a lone lamp. The orange light flickered across his face. He drank no more and nodded off several times but always awoke to sit up again. When he thought it was dawn he put on his hat and cloak and went out to the barn under the first glow of the sun as it watered the dark sky to the east. He found the best of the goats and tethered it.

He stood by the gate a long time and then pulled his seal skin hat from his head, dropping it on a fence post and leaving his head bare to the sky. He peered upward. The wind ran nakedly across his scalp.

The path was a smooth white line of packed snow amid the blackness of the rocks, seen better with the corner of his eye than the middle. He never looked down the mountain as he climbed. All about was the rustle of the elves. They whispered at the fatness of the goat and the reek of the mead off him. Only the summit was clear of them, where the Gods lived. The dark things lived in terror of the noble beings of the sky. He kept his mind away from their mundane lusts and looked to the altar at the top of the mountain and said the prayer again and again as he gathered his soul for the sacrifice.

The top was windswept and cold. The world below was covered in long shadows.

He waited for the sun.

The dawn was the time of Odin.

He begin to chant the prayer louder and louder as the glow became brighter to the east, and drew the knife from his belt.

Odin's name came clear from his lips now, and it seemed the elves about him hissed in surprise and dismay. Odin wanted the whole beast to himself, the body and the soul, and they had grown accustomed to their share of the sacrifice.

Snorri gothi always sacrificed alone at dawn.

"I come to you now, Odin!" he shouted to the sky. "My head bare so that you can see my face and know it is me!"

Brighter. Brighter.

He doused the goat in seal oil, spilling the precious stuff about as if it were water.

An arc of intense light leapt over the horizon, the first life of the sun. In the corner of his eye he saw the elves leap about in mad excitement, flickers of light and shadow.

He cut the goat's neck in one slash, and held it down till it died, draining the blood into the bowl. There was a handful of dried moss and birch bark in his pocket and he drew this out and put the flint and steel to it. The goat erupted into flame and greasy black smoke. Snorri stumbled back from the flames and held the bloody knife up to the sky. He scooped handfuls of the blood onto the burning goat.

"Odin!" He screamed the name, calling forth the spirit of the God of Cunning and Guile.

The great blue eye of the sky fell on him and he met the gaze. He let the God look into his heart.

V

OF THE DEATH OF ORLYG, BROTHER OF ULFAR

THE MEN CAME HOME.

Hafildi waved and hallooed as he rode up to Bolstathr. He was grim when he dismounted, though, and said to Arnkel's mother that it had not gone well at the Thing.

This set the servants and slaves frantically to work so that the Hall and everything in it would be put to order. No one wanted the angry eyes of Arnkel on them for some trivial matter of neglected housekeeping. Gudrid walked about like a hawk above a field, whipping men and women to their work with her tongue. Her hacking cough warned them of her approach and they bent over to double their efforts. It was said that Thorolf's beating long ago had damaged her ribs and lungs. Sleep within Bolstathr was something done to the tune of Gudrid's sickness. One either got used to it or left, and it steadily grew worse as the years advanced.

Auln packed her little basket with a few bites of meat and a little curd. She set out for Ulfar's farm, desperate for escape from Gudrid's bile and the panic of the gothi's homecoming.

She said goodbye to Hildi and the woman nodded tiredly. Dark circles colored the skin under her eyes. She still mourned her baby, born that winter and now dead.

Arnkel gothi had hidden his disappointment well. He held the little boy tenderly as it breathed its last and then kissed Hildi's forehead as she wept. Then he had gone off to brood. Auln had felt pity for him. It was hard not to like the man when he acted so nobly. Other men would not have been so generous to have their dreams shattered. The little thing had been like Auln's child, spine twisted and head deformed.

Hildi had wept the whole night after, a muted echo to Gudrid's cough.

Gudrid became a witch after the baby's death, cursing Hildi constantly, and so Auln had begun inviting Arnkel's wife along to Ulfar's farm, simply to escape the old hag's bitterness. She never accepted. Auln had finally realized, in a sudden moment of almost jealous insight, that the quiet woman had immense pride in her role as Arnkel gothi's wife. If that meant putting up with a hellish mother-in-law, then she would pay the price. Sometimes Auln took Halla in her place, because the girl would never surrender to her grandmother's dominance, and there was always argument. That day she was alone. Sometimes there was a man or two to spare and Arnkel gothi would send them along with her but they would do the work poorly, and she would need to check. It was better in the end to do the work by herself. Ulfar would come sometimes, although if there was rumor of Lamefoot being about, he would stay in Arnkel gothi's Hall. Another task was to care for Ulfar's brother, Orlyg. The man refused to come to Bolstathr. He spat through his few teeth that he would never betray his master Thorbrand and his anger would always lead to the wet cough that would convulse him. Auln knew he was near death, but Ulfar refused to see it. Orlyg even declined to stay in their house, insisting on lying on his own cot, in his own tiny Hall, even if it meant being in filth. He was too weak to do work.

The milking of the cows and goats came first. They lowed their pain at her as she entered the barn. Then came the feeding. Much hay was now piled high in the barn, bought from Thorbrand, and she pulled it down with the fork, using as little as she could. The animals would get most of their feed from grazing. The pastures were green again, thank Freya, and Auln whispered a little prayer of thanks to the Goddess as she worked. The newness of the Earth came from her loins each spring.

Ulfar had spent most of his money to fill the racks, going cap in hand to Thorbrand, and Auln had railed at him for that.

"If this is Arnkel gothi's land now, let him pay for the hay," she had said, but he would not listen.

It was not the thought of paying that bothered her as much as knowing the money went to Thorbrand. Her hands twisted on the hay fork. She imagined that it was a spear shaft and that she was a man in the prime of his strength.

Oh Gods, to be a man! Then she could take her own vengeance. She plunged the fork into the hay as if it were a living body. Her passion startled the cattle.

After the feeding she rested a little, sweating from the work. Piles of wool lay waiting to be spun on distaffs inside the house, but the thought of sitting alone for hours on end in the dark of the Hall seemed a dreary thing to bear. She had grown a taste for company in Arnkel gothi's house and Hildi had become a true friend.

Auln had waited until the others slept one cold night. She had forced her eyes not to shut, and when the snores and wheezes had sounded in the Hall she had crept up to the shelf above Hildi's sleeping bench and taken the jar of honey. She went to the jacks. In the private embrace of stinking darkness she gently pried open the jar. Her nose twitched at the bitter after-odor. Why had she never noticed it before? She knew herbs, even the poisons.

She pitched it into the hole where it belonged, among the shit of life. It whispered to her from the reeking dark, laughing at her misery. She wiped her hands against her apron again and again to rid them of the smell of sweet death.

Her hate she would keep to herself, and she would wait for a chance to have vengeance on Thorbrand. One day she would find a reason to go to the man's farm and when old Thorbrand turned his back, she would put her knife into it. That could never happen if she revealed what she knew. She would never be allowed within reach of the old man if she told Arnkel gothi of the poison in the honey. Arnkel would never slay Thorbrand on her word alone but then the story would spread, as gossip always did, and eventually it would make its way back to Swan firth. The old man would be warned.

She turned her back on the dark house and trudged off across the pasture to Orlyg's farm.

The two properties lay side by side, separated by a small creek and low esker of black gravel that guided the flow of the water, rising from one end where grass grew and passage was easy across, to twice the height of a man at its other, bare of growth and covered in wads of sheep dung. It was there that the big ram that ruled both of the flocks of Orlyg and Ulfar liked to perch. The shortest route to Orlyg's house lay across the highest mound, and Auln ran up this, still full of the juice of her anger and needing to breath hard. She came to the ram perch, and turned herself around looking in all directions as the big male would when he was searching for challengers.

It was good view. No wonder the brute liked it.

The rounded peaks of the turf roofs of Swan firth could just be seen to the south-east, a half mile away across green pasture. It was an easy walk and she imagined herself setting out there, knife under her cloth belt, basket over one arm, the mask of a smile on her face.

One day.

To the north she could make out her own farm, and also the long hill where Bolstathr lay, although Arnkel farmstead at the hill's base was partly hidden by the slow roll of the land. On the other side of that hill was Lamefoot's farm, and she cursed the man then, under blue sky, cursed his name to Freya, for how he had shamed her man.

She narrowed her eyes and peered at the top of the hill.

Riders, two dozen or more, little more than black dots from the ram perch as they rounded the top of the rise. So, they returned from the Thing at last. The party headed down from the path toward Bolstathr.

She thought then of heading back to welcome Ulfar, but she was already most of the way to Orlyg's farm and so decided to make a quick visit and bring the news to the old man. He would need hot food also, and she could cook a quick meal for him.

She turned to walk there and stopped.

The house was as it always was, a low mound of green turf merging into the deeper emerald of the pasture around it. Dead grass lay around the edge of the roof. The blades of it hung forlornly, dried and withered, as if they were the bodies of slain men draped over a wall. The wind moaned over her. It tossed her hair into her face, and the whisking tendrils of it caressed the house in her eyes, like the arms of women binding the dead.

She made her feet move. Every step plunged her more deeply into her dread.

The smell stopped her at the door.

It had been three days since she had come last.

She called for him into the dark of the entrance way. Her heart raced. She stayed in the bright daylight outside.

"Orlyg, can you hear me?"

But there was only the smell, of rot, of death.

She did not want to be the first to go in. His spirit might still be in there and that terrified her. But then, he might not be dead. He had soiled himself before, in the pain that kept him mostly bed ridden and perhaps he only slept.

"Orlyg!" she said desperately, into the dark. "I don't want to go in the house. Answer me!"

There was flint, steel and char cloth in a little tin in her apron pocket. A lamp of soapstone hung in the barn, and she took it down carefully without spilling the oil. She knelt outside the door and started a tiny fire of hay and dried grass and put the wick of the lamp into it. She blew on the twist of grass carefully, and stopped once to call Orlyg's name again. When the lamp was lit, she went in.

He was dead.

One arm fell from the wool blankets to dangle onto the dark earth floor. The mouth and eyes were open to the turf roof above.

Auln backed away. She prayed the lamp would not go out. Near the door she bolted and ran out into sunlight, throwing away the lamp, and kept running until she was past the paddock and into the pasture again.

Ulfar found her there, kneeling, weeping. He reined in the horse, jumped down from the saddle and ran to her.

"Auln! Auln! Are you alright? What is the matter?" He knelt beside her, facing her, holding her shoulders with both hands.

She pointed to the house behind her and then put her arms around his neck, glad to see him alive and well. He held her for a few moments. His eyes went to the house.

"He is dead?"

"Yes."

He pushed her back gently and they knelt facing each other, legs touching, looking into the grass, as if praying together for the soul of his brother.

Auln touched his hand softly, and in a moment was kissing his mouth. Ulfar returned it with wide eyes. Their passion became intense. His hands ran over her and he pulled away her dress and entered her as she lay with her back to the grass. It was over quickly. They lay quiet, breath heaving as they stared at the clouds and laughed a little when they looked at each other.

"I hope that we have made a child," she said somberly.

He nodded.

"I must go and tell Thorbrand about Orlyg," Ulfar said finally. He stood and cinched his belt.

Auln looked up at him. She grasped his hand tightly, still kneeling.

"Tell him what?"

"That Orlyg is dead. He has no children, and now the land becomes Thorbrand's. It is the Law." He looked at the house grimly. "First I must ready my brother for the grave. Then I will go."

Auln pushed herself to her feet. She still held tightly to her husband's hand. "What of you? Do you not have rights here, Ulfar?" She took his face in her hands, and spoke desperately. "You are Orlyg's kin! His only kin. The land must be your own and it will be your child's. Your brother's farm will become our home. Arnkel gothi has no rights to it, nor does Thorbrand."

Ulfar shook his head, frowning, confused. "No, I don't . . . I have heard of nothing in Law about this. Yes, kin do inherit, I know, but . . . "

Auln gripped his shoulders tightly, and shook them. "Arnkel gothi would know. He would tell you. Do not go to Thorbrand!"

Ulfar stared at her oddly, as if she had spoken a blasphemy to his face. He pushed her away gently and led his horse to the house, while Auln watched him.

A sudden rage took her. She dressed frantically and turned to run.

Back to Bolstathr. Back to Arnkel gothi.

It was a long run for her, a mile or more, and she was breathless and gasping when she climbed the rise toward Arnkel gothi's Hall and went through the gate. Two of the slaves placed stones on a section of the wall that the winter's chill had forced out and they stared at her as she ran by them. The broken door was chocked open to let in air and light. She ran through without stopping. The turf of the roof was being replaced section by section and men had opened a large part of the roof over Arnkel gothi's High Seat, so that sunlight poured down on him as he sat there, illuminating him like a king from some ancient legend, dry flakes of dirt floating down on him unnoticed and lit by the rays into fragments of white light. He held a horn of mead in one hand, but had no enjoyment of it, and saw only the dark thoughts in his own heart. The

sight of his immense, frowning face unnerved her for a moment
but then she stepped forward and called his name loudly.

"Arnkel gothi!" The women and men turned to look at her in
surprise, and even the workers above peered down to see who was
so loud when the gothi had so much weight on him.

The gothi blinked in surprise. "What is it, Auln Ulfar-wife?"

"Orlyg has died."

She said the words simply, without explanation, and he stared at
her for a long moment. She stepped forward and pointed through
the turf wall toward Orlyg's farm.

"My husband has gone to open the wall of the house and carry
his brother's body to burial, and then he will go to Swan firth to tell
Thorbrand that the land awaits him. My husband Ulfar has right
to the land of his brother Orlyg and I call on you as his chieftain
to guard his rights."

The formality of the words came easily to her. She had
rehearsed them on the long run with only her heaving breath
for company. Now all depended on the gothi. She did not know
Law, but he did.

His eyes were hidden in shadow cast by the sunlight above and
she could not read them. He turned to the wall behind him suddenly and took down the sword that hung there, and the shield.
He lifted the spear from its holder at the side of the High Seat.

"Hafildi!" he shouted loudly, and stepped down from the dais
of the seat toward Auln. Hafildi appeared in the doorway. Arnkel
gothi turned to him. "Get every man who is here now to arm and
come out to the paddock. Send a slave with a horse to the pasture
to fetch the men who are herding and turfing. Have them come
with weapons. Find Thorgils and Gizur!"

Hafildi ran off, eyes wide. He shouted out orders and his voice
passed to the outside, ringing dimly through the thick walls. Arnkel
followed him, sword in hand and the shield on his arm. As he passed
Auln, he stopped and looked down at her. He was like a mountain
beside her and reeked of the steel and wood he carried.

Thorgils came in behind her. He stopped, breathing hard.

The gothi's eyes searched her face, as if he looked for the reason she had come to him. He nodded and said, "I thank you, Auln, for Ulfar's sake. I am in your debt. I will not forget it."

"I will not let you forget it," she said, looking up at him, her jaw set. He smiled grimly and passed by her into the yard. Thorgils followed him. He looked at Auln as he went out, but she said nothing to him.

There were a dozen men at the farmstead, rallied by the calls of Hafildi. Another man ran down to the water and began blowing a horn. The Fish Brothers stood in the boat far across the fjord and looked back. The net was pulled in hurriedly and then the boat was wheeled about. A rider went out to the meadows surrounding the farm, into the common lands where all the farms grazed their sheep and there he pulled in another half dozen men with his shouts.

Arnkel gothi nodded when they had all gathered, satisfied. Almost twenty men. He sent one slave on a circuit of the farms of his outlying Thingmen, riding the best of the horses, for speed. What a surprise it would be for them, just come home from the Thing and called out almost instantly. Wives and children would cry their frustration at that, and he smiled a little at the thought of the domestic trouble he brewed for his men.

Ah well, that was life, he thought, rarely convenient. But on some days it was very good.

He smiled, the humiliation of his loss at the Thing already a faded echo in his heart. Snorri gothi was very far away. The sons of Thorbrand would need to fight for Orlyg's land or lose it, and he knew they would not fight. He toyed with the thought of bringing only enough men to equal the brothers, to shame them into a fight there on the spot, perhaps to kill a few to cow them forever.

No, it was not time for that throw yet, he thought. He could get what he wanted and still argue he had the Law with him. He remembered the hundreds of men gathered behind Snorri gothi at the Thing. It was a power he had underestimated, Snorri's ability to manipulate behind the scenes. It had kept that white haired freak alive all these years, and given him the win that day. Arnkel's rage had almost taken him when his bastard father had admitted to selling away the Crowness, coming on top of his defeat. Without the host behind Snorri gothi, he would have run across the grass and killed them both. Even with it there it had been a struggle for control and the thought of how he had almost destroyed himself brought cold sweat to his face.

Einar, his grandfather, had played nefatl with him every night. He would smile patiently at Arnkel's rage when he lost and laugh when Arnkel swept the game pieces from the board with a roar of petulance. The old man would rub his head when he had cooled down. "Use that anger, lad," he would say each time. "Don't let it use you."

Then he would let Arnkel win the next game.

By the Gods, he had loved that old man, he thought.

One day, grandfather, he thought. One day the vengeance will come.

Arnkel stood in the pasture, waiting for the rest of his Thing-men to gather, staring at the circle of stones where his father had killed Einar.

Lamefoot had toyed with his grandfather, using his skill with the sword to cut him and cut him again, trying to maim him, to make him suffer, to shame him. Arnkel had watched from the house with his mother's arms tight around him as she prayed to Odin to give her father strength. But Odin cared little for love, and less for justice. He loved strength and it belonged to Thorolf that day. The balance and grace of the cutting blade had mesmerized Arnkel, even as he stared in horror at his grandfather's blood, and he swore that he would learn to use the weapon that way.

Thorgils brought him his bay, saddled and ready. They mounted and he swept his hand forward.

A great joy filled him as he rode at the head of his men, their spears upright, and shields tight to their bodies. This was clear and simple, he thought. The strongest would win, and he knew Odin hung above him, his great blue eye watching with approval. He stared upward at it, meeting the gaze.

Not in defiance.

In brotherhood.

No one was at the farm. Cut clearly into the turf were the drag marks of a horse-drawn sling, two poles fastened to a collar and dragged behind. Ulfar had hauled away his brother's body toward Swan firth. Arnkel gothi sent men to the paddock and the hay barn to see what wealth might be found and had the house searched.

"Barn is full of hay, gothi," Thorgils said, coming back to speak to him. "Enough to feed many animals this winter. Thor knows why he had so much. A barrel of barley, mostly good. The house has three vats, one full of meat, the other half full, and one empty except for the whey. The full one smelt old, but I think it's good. No loom, of course. He had no wife. There are a dozen bags of wool. Not much peat. Almost no cheese. The garden looks well tended, and that's probably Ulfar's doing. He'll be pleased to hear what riches he inherits."

"Take the wool back to Bolstathr," Arnkel gothi said, looking at Thorgils oddly. "Hildi and the girls can card and roll it. We'll leave the hay here. What about stock?"

"Four cows, one ox. The sheep are in the high pasture, but Orlyg was known to have about fifty. Thorgils paused. "Gothi . . ."

"Send a man up to the pasture to find them and mark them for us," Arnkel interrupted, pointing to the hills. "Take the cows and ox back to Bolstathr." Arnkel's barn was nearly empty after the previous year's slaughter and the winter feasting. He looked over Orlyg's ox and saw that it was old and a little lame but still with fat. He ordered it slaughtered and packed in the whey vats. "Tell Hildi to boil out the leg bones tonight. I feel like having marrow."

Thorgils stood unmoving.

"What are you waiting for?" Arnkel barked.

"The stock is not yours, gothi. It belongs to Ulfar," Thorgils said quietly. "Does it not?"

Arnkel glared down at him. The nearby Thingmen stared open mouthed at Thorgils.

There was a shout from the lookout sent toward Swan firth and the men looked toward Arnkel.

"Pick up your spears," he said, with a final deadly glance at Thorgils.

A dozen men came out from Thorbrand's land. They rode without haste, in twos, as if in procession, and it seemed the men talked with each other, although the figures were small with distance. Another dozen pack ponies trudged in string behind them, led by a slave.

"Come to empty the place, but they don't know we're here," said one of the Fish Brothers gleefully, twisting the shaft of his spear in his hands.

"Yes," said Arnkel. "All of you, up on the stone wall. Make yourselves seen. Don't act like fools, just stand there." The men scrambled up on the wide stone wall that surrounded the home field of the farm, a long line of them, armed with shield and spear. Two men had bows and they strung arrows after a nod from Arnkel. The gothi rode through the vegetable garden and out the gate. He paced his horse back and forth in front of the wall.

They were seen almost immediately.

The horses left their long line and bunched together, milling in confusion as the men brought them together. One man waved to the slave leading the pack ponies and he rounded about and started back to Swan firth.

"Are they not even going to come?" Hafildi said, frowning. He carried an axe in one hand. The men on the wall began to hoot wildly, banging their spears on their shields, and shaking them in the air.

The milling about continued for a few moments, and then the horses spread out into a long line, and began to ride toward Orlyg's farm. The men quieted at this, and looked at Arnkel gothi, who said nothing. He sat his horse with spear butted on his foot, shield arm holding the reins.

"What do we do, gothi?" Thorgils said, not wanting to have to kill neighbors. He had known Thorleif and his brothers all his life.

"Stand," was the answer. "If they attack, fight. We have eight more men and it will go our way." He looked back at Thorgils. "Come to the front, man."

Thorgils flushed angrily at the words, because Hafildi and others laughed into their shoulders. He was only a step farther away from the sons of Thorbrand than the other men. Thrain began to run forward, thrusting his spear defiantly in the air. The others shouted at him, ridiculing his size, knowing the bravado was all for the gothi's eyes. He did not like that and spat back at them, calling them cowards.

One rider held back a little from the line. It was Ulfar. The line came closer until even the faces were clear. Arnkel's men became quiet, although it was obvious now that most of Thorbrand's men had not brought weapons, expect for Illugi who carried his spear with a bent, tense arm as if he meant to skewer the first man he came near. Ulfar's face was contorted with anxiety, mouth open, confused and anxious. The shouts of the sons of Thorbrand and their slaves filled the air, and Thorodd and Illugi shook their fists in anger again and again.

Ulfar rode toward Arnkel, his eyes wide with anxiety.

He reined in near Arnkel, who did not even look at him as he approached. The gothi's eyes were for Thorleif only, knowing he led, knowing that to cow him would be the quickest victory here.

"Gothi! Gothi, why are you here, with your men?" Ulfar said breathlessly. "This is not good. This is not good at all. You must leave!"

Ulfar spoke with desperation, unthinking, wanting only that the terrible situation would end. Arnkel's sudden glare silenced him instantly.

"It is not your place to tell me what I should do, Thingman," he said harshly. But then, seeing Ulfar's terror, he pulled back his rage. A chirrup or two brought his mount nose to tail with Ulfar's pony, so that the men's legs touched.

"Have I not protected you and your family, and stood for your rights? Taken you into my household, sat you at my side and given you honor?" He leaned toward Ulfar, his mouth hard with anger. "Well?"

Ulfar nodded, swallowing.

"Now you rail at me when I guard your rights again and try to hold your brother's land for you. That is my thanks. I expected more loyalty from you, Ulfar Freedman. I expected that you would turn away from this family that gave you no protection, but instead you stand with them, as they take away the only inheritance you have in life, as they take away the future of your family!"

Ulfar's chin sank lower and lower with every word.

Enough, thought Arnkel. Now for honey.

"This land is for you, Ulfar. I can think of no better man to work it. Let us fight together for what is your own."

The freedman looked at the gothi, blinking in confused despair, trying to understand.

"Take your place with my men," Arnkel said.

Ulfar rode slowly through the gate, the gothi's men watching him. The Fish Brothers elbowed each other gleefully, rolling their eyes and laughing. Thorgils hissed at them to shut their mouths.

There was an explosion of yelling from the sons of Thorbrand as Ulfar joined Arnkel. Illugi rode forward in rage, hefting his spear, but Thorleif shouted his name and the boy retreated sullenly.

"What have you to say about this, Arnkel gothi?" Thorleif called out grimly. "How do you stand?"

"I stand beside my Thingman, to guard his rights in this matter," Arnkel called back. "This is his land, through his brother Orlyg. We have accounted for everything on the property. If any goes missing, we will know where to find it."

There was another explosion of curses from Illugi and Thorodd and the other brothers, but Thorleif was silent. He turned his horse away. He did not go back to Swan firth. He led them up into the high hills and scree, along the outer paths, to the west, to the paths that then turned north to the coast.

"Running off to Snorri gothi," Hafildi said, eyeing them. He jumped down from the wall and butted his spear on the stone with a sigh of relief through puffed cheeks. Arnkel gothi looked down at him with a grin, and wheeled his horse around in a joyful circle.

"That will bring them no aid," he said. "Snorri is a coward, who only has power because of his tongue, and he will not stand against me. He didn't as a boy, and he won't as a man."

Arnkel followed the sons of Thorbrand with his eyes until they disappeared over the rise. He was satisfied. The fight he wanted would come, he thought. Not now, but it would come. It must come!

He had not spoken idly about Snorri. His words would find their way back to the gothi eventually. Maybe it would be enough to pull him from his hole in Helgafell, put a sword in his hand, and make him forget about Law for a little while.

Then there would be blood.

He turned to Thorgils.

"Go and visit your cousin Hawk, at Helgafell," he said. "Give him my greetings. Tell him what happened here today."

Thorgils looked up at him. "He won't turn. He is Snorri gothi's man to the grave."

"I don't expect him to turn. But he will tell you what Snorri says to the sons of Thorbrand. Take that big salmon the Fish Brothers caught yesterday for the gothi. He will not be able to say that

I have no manners." Thorgils mounted his horse and cantered back to Bolstathr.

Arnkel watched the man's receding back for a little while, frowning. Then he jumped down from the saddle with a spring, and landed lightly.

"All you men," he called to the others, who had begun to sit on the wall and talk. "Back to your work. There will be no fight here this day, and food will not leap onto the table by itself. Thrain, take your fierce soul up to the pasture and find Orlyg's sheep. Put my mark on them."

Then he pointed at two of the men, both slaves, one a Dane aptly called Dim whom Arnkel had taken as payment for his influence in a dispute a year back, and the other an Irish named Olaf, grandly named after a king, even though he was the son of a slave and therefore a slave himself. Neither worked well except under someone's eye. "You two will stay here with me. Get to work on those cow stalls and muck them out. The shit is knee deep. Mind you, keep that manure pile neat, and piled high. Then feed and water the stock."

They trudged sullenly to the barn while the rest of the men dragged themselves up and onto their horses. The gothi jerked his chin at Hafildi, who began to bellow with his great voice, and soon the farm was cleared. Arnkel shook his head, hating their laziness but not knowing how to make them better workers, beyond scaring the wits out of them. He enjoyed work himself, and always looked for another task to do, so it seemed natural that other men should be the same. Did they not see that the wealthier their gothi was, the easier their life would be?

Bah, he thought. There were better things to think about.

First he would explore Orlyg's farm and check in detail what wealth was there. Then he would have to get back to Bolstathr for the slaughter of the oxen. If he was not there, the cuts would be rough, and full of skin and hair when they went into the vats of whey, and that would make for bad meat later. The many little tasks filled his mind. The main door of Bolstathr needed to be reset on hinges, and that was a something he would do himself. His mother hated drafts, even in warm weather.

He was glad now of having the extra property to care for. Bolstathr was too small to keep him occupied. He spun around, hands on hips, to look at his new possession, smiling at the thought.

Ulfar watched him, slumped in the saddle of his mount, his eyes dark and unreadable.

Arnkel gothi felt a flash of irritation.

Oh, yes, he thought sourly. Ulfar.

He could not forget about Ulfar.

"Go to your own farm and work there, Thingman." he said, forcing respect and mildness into his tone and turned away, wanting that gloomy face gone.

The man left without a word. Arnkel glanced over his shoulder at him as he walked to the barn to check on the slaves. Yes, he would have to deal with Ulfar. Like any broken tool past its usefulness, if left under foot it would only trip and cause trouble.

———

Thorgils came to Bolstathr and cinched his horse outside the Hall. He went in and found the ladder and set it up to climb to the rafters where the great fish hung by a piece of twine, slowly twisting in the fire smoke. One slash of his knife and it came away. It was as long as his arm and heavy, even gilled and gutted, the twine he held it by digging into the flesh of his hand.

Auln waited for him at the bottom of the ladder.

"It's too early to cook that for the supper meal," she said.

"I am taking it to Helgafell," he said, and gave it to her to hold while he put away the ladder under the benches. He stood and faced her again. Her hair was long, and fine, and her lips soft. His eyes lingered there, entranced by their movement as the words came from her mouth.

"All went well?" she asked, handing him the fish.

He nodded. "Everyone is alive still," he said. "Thorbrand's sons ride to Snorri gothi. So I go, too."

Auln smiled, a terrible thing that reminded him of a wolf.

He turned to leave, but then peered at her over his shoulder.

"This is just beginning, Auln. There will be reckonings for what has happened today, and other days."

Still the awful smile held. "Yes, I hope so," she said.

VI

Autumn

Of the Slayings

The first chill winds had begun from the north. Summer was dying, and it felt the coming of winter like pain in its bones.

Arnkel gothi worked in front of his Hall, planing the rough logs that Thorgils had bought from his cousin Hawk. Wood was like gold, and he cursed every fragment he had to cut away as a waste, but the door of his Hall must be presentable as well as strong. His mother would insist on it. Still, he would make it stout, thick enough to keep axes at work at it a long time if it came to that, thick enough to bolt on a great bar along the back. It would be easier for an enemy to chop through the roof than come through the door.

The adze felt good in his hands, and he reveled in the heat coming off his body. He had thrown off his shirt so that the sweat would not ruin it. Nearby lay the great hinges the smith had made for him, and a bucket of long nails, and the spoon auger to drill holes in the ledge of the door before he hung it. Bjorn, the smith, had let him take over his hammer for the nails, as it was a simple task, and he was happy to humor the gothi. Arnkel's men had gathered around to see him sweating in the heat of the fire, until he threatened them with a glowing piece of nail wire, the grin huge on his face.

His mother heard of it later that evening.

"It is good that you have industry, son," Gudrid said severely. "But do not lower yourself like that. Your men will lose respect for you."

"This is not Norway, mother," he had said, patting her face gently. "All men must work here."

She had always been that way, he thought idly, locked in the ways of the old country, of jarls and lords, never realizing that her own father had left Norway to escape men like the ones she wanted her son to be.

The truth was that he would trust none other but himself to do some things, like the butchering, or the door. He trusted his own hand more than anyone's.

It was hard to find work for all his men. He knew that he would have to sell his slaves in a winter or two. They did not produce enough to justify the food they ate and he kept them only because of their use in a fight, if it were to come. Better to have Thingmen, each on his own farmstead. His mind plotted the future, seeing Gizur at Hvammr, and Hafildi at Orlyg's farm. Thorgils was too much use close at hand.

He smiled.

Thorgils thought himself hard to read, but he was like water.

He wanted Ulfarsfell. And he wanted Auln.

He could have neither.

Swan firth he would sell to the Fish Brothers, when finally he drove off the sons of Thorbrand. They loved the sea and the freedom of working when they wanted, but seeing Thorbrand and his sons dead and gone might tame them. Or maybe he would put the two slaves there and see if having their own land to run would spark some life in them, he thought. He would even free them.

But he would never let them marry.

Auln had ruined Thorbrand's plans, he knew. The woman had arrived in Swan's fjord like an answer to Arnkel's prayers.

Thorgils had wanted her from the first time she had walked into his Hall, her traveling pack on her back. It was clear in his eyes. Arnkel had made sure that she went to Ulfar. Auln at Bolstathr would have caused only havoc. His mother would have tried to cow Auln as she did Hildi and there would have been much unhappiness in his house. Arnkel would have taken her himself as a second wife but Hildi would have hated that, and he loved her too much to allow that kind of strife over lust.

The thoughts followed the rhythm of his strokes, and so deep did he go into them that he did not notice the strange man until he walked through the gate.

Arnkel straightened, the adze hanging from his hand.

He was a big fellow, with a scarred chin, limping slightly. A bag was thrown over one shoulder.

There was no one else about except the women in the house working the looms. He had sent men off to their tasks that morning.

Arnkel nodded politely as the man approached and the other man returned it.

"You are Arnkel gothi?"

"Yes. Will you take some meat and drink?" The habits of hospitality covered his suspicions. The man nodded again. Instead of bringing the stranger inside the Hall, Arnkel called to his wife, and after a few moments she brought out a platter of cheese and meat and a pot of ale. She startled at the sight of the stranger and looked nervously to Arnkel. Her belly was mounding again with child.

"Put it on the wall there, Hildi, and go back inside." She looked over her shoulder fearfully as she left.

The man dropped his sack and sat down on the stone beside the food. He began to eat, slurping loudly from the pot with a full mouth and making it unfit to share.

Arnkel watched him sourly, still standing. "I have not heard your name yet."

The man spoke around a mouthful of cheese. "Onund." His eyes went to the adze in Arnkel's hand and then back to the food.

"Onund," Arnkel repeated. The man only looked to the food, so Arnkel bent back down to work on the door. He jostled it to one side so that he could face the man as he stood chopping on the door but the man did not seem to notice. He belched loudly and kept eating.

The name bothered Arnkel. It seemed familiar.

When the food was gone, Onund stood.

"I'm looking for a place to live and work," the man said, but his tone was almost defiant, as if he dared Arnkel to accept.

What is this devil up to, the gothi thought. He finished the last smoothing slices with the adze and lay it against the wall of the house. He stood and faced the man, fist on his hip.

He pointed to the north. "Try Helgafell. Snorri gothi has a big farmstead. I hear he lost a slave a while back. He might need a pair of hands."

"Snorri sent me off. I don't want to work for that bastard anyway."

Arnkel shrugged. "No place for you here. I don't need any more help, and I don't hire landless out-country men in any case. Try Swan firth, down there." He pointed to the south end of the fjord. "You've eaten, so I'll say good bye to you now." He turned back to pick up his spoon auger from the ground, and heard the quick scramble of feet. He wheeled about and saw the man leap for the adze against the wall.

Sudden rage and fear took him. He jumped after Onund, yelling out loudly. The stranger grabbed the adze and lifted it high above his head in one great arc, but Arnkel was there under the swing and took him down with his arms around his chest. They crashed to the ground. Onund's elbow caught one of the walkway stones and he hissed with the pain, the adze dropping from his numbed hand. Arnkel scrambled up on him like a pouncing spider, pinning the other arm with his hands, and then his knee. His right hand came free, and he smashed the fist into Onund's mouth. The man was tough. Blood erupted from his torn lip, but he fought back, wrenching his arm out from under Arnkel's knee and twice throwing the fist into the gothi's ribs, short powerful punches that forced the spit out of Arnkel's mouth in a great spray of pain.

Arnkel reeled back, still perched on top of the man, and his hand fell on the adze. He gripped it, raised it high and brought it down through Onund's outstretched, desperate arms. The man screamed wetly as it crunched into his face. Arnkel wrenched it free and chopped down again. Onund's body shuddered and twitched from the trauma, but he was dead, his skull split open.

The yelling had brought the women. Hildi rushed out and stopped just outside the doorway, Auln behind her, gripping her shoulders. They stared down at the blood and brains, and Hildi put her hands to her mouth. Arnkel's youngest daughter raced outside, past the grasping arms of the women and stopped. Her mouth hung open.

"Are you wrestling, Da?" she said. Her eyes were wide, staring at the blood splashed across her father's face, and pooling around Onund's head.

He stood and picked her up to turn her eyes away. Gudrid came through the door, and glanced over at the body. Auln was nearest to the gothi and she held out her arms. "You're covered in it, gothi," she said brusquely. "Give her to me."

"Yes, just wrestling, little one," he said to his daughter, handing her over. "Go to the well and draw a bucket for Da, would you? Auln will help you."

Auln took her, using her shoulder to hide the slaughter.

Gudrid came near and put a hand on her son's shoulder.

Thorgils came back from Orlyg's farm an hour later with the two slaves in tow, ponies loaded with bundles of meadow hay from Orlyg's barn. He crouched down by the dead man and used a finger to tilt the hacked face. The two thralls gawked at the gore. Arnkel gothi sat on a rock while his mother re-braided his washed hair.

"Hard to recognize through all that mess, but that's him alright," Thorgils said.

"You know him?"

"In a way. He was at Helgafell when I went there in the summer. Tied to a post when he wasn't mucking out stalls. Onund, I think was his name."

Arnkel nodded. "That's right. So he was the one that killed Snorri's thrall?"

"Yes. I had a talk with him, while I waited for the sons of Thorbrand to finish shouting at Snorri."

Arnkel grinned. Thorgils had arrived at the right moment, after the brothers had gone into the Hall to plead their case but before they knew he had arrived, so he had heard everything through the turf walls. They came out angry, confused, and surprised to see the headman of their enemy standing waiting for them, and for a few moments Thorgils had feared for his life, seeing the murder in Illugi's eyes, and the massive clenched fists of Thorodd. Hawk had come then, and whatever might have happened ended in angry mumbles. Thorgils gave Hawk the salmon, gossiped a while and left, satisfied, and told the story around Arnkel's fire that night.

Once again Snorri gothi had refused to back his Thingmen.

They stood silent for a while.

"Snorri will claim he escaped, or that he forgave him and let him go," Thorgils said finally.

"Of course he will." Gudrid snapped, and she wrenched on Arnkel's hair hard enough to make him wince.

"Gah, woman. . . ."

"There must be an end to this," she hissed loudly into his ear. "Snorri gothi did not come to his authority without reason, and you underestimate him, as you did at the Thorsnes Thing, when you lost your woods."

Arnkel frowned darkly. "They are not lost, mother."

"You are the stronger," she said, ignoring his words. "Use that strength, before you are murdered in the night, or lose more land to those who know the Law better than you."

The gothi looked up at his mother. "The time is coming, but I will decide when."

He stood, snapping his fingers at the thralls, and ordered them to take the body up to Vadils Head and bury it, with the criminals and infants. The Fish Brothers would boat the body across.

"Better finish your door," Thorgils said as the thralls dragged the body away. Arnkel laughed darkly. He picked up the auger, reveling in the smell of the air and the feel of the wind on him. He felt calm and at peace, soothed by the killing, and he knew it was sign from Odin that his way was right. Strength of arm and wits would carry him to the end.

"I see you," he said to the great blue eye, and felt its love for him.

———————

It was the Autumn feast, and the household of Arnkel prepared to host all of the Thingmen and guests of the gothi. There was much work to do.

The summer had fattened the cows and sheep and the goats. One of the milk cows had become old and four of the sheep also, and there was little chance of them living the winter, so feed would be wasted on them. They were slaughtered. One sheep was given to Odin, on the great stone altar behind Bolstathr that Einar had built many years before. The animal was burned to ashes, every bit of it. The other three were skinned, and then mounted on spits, as was the cow. There was a great need for fuel, and Arnkel set the Fish Brothers to gathering drift wood from the beaches out beyond the narrow waters of the fjord. The open sea was hard on their little boat and pitched them enough to cause them fear, but they held to it and eventually dragged back a great mass of floating wood, bound together by coir rope. Along one desolate stretch of shingle they had found a small minke whale beached and still a little bit alive. It was another man's land, but they came ashore

and flensed great cubes of fat from it, thick as a sod of turf, enough
to fill the bottom of their boat, even while the creature flailed
weakly under them. They came back bloody and greasy and very
proud of themselves as they hauled the pieces of it up to the Hall.
It was enough blubber to feed the household for the winter. Dried
and salted, a few mouthfuls filled the belly. Some of it was eaten
quickly, but most was hung from the rafters of the Hall and left to
rot until it became black and full of smoke and flavor.

Hildi and Auln cleaned a dozen swans and stuffed them with
onion and sage. These were wrapped in seaweed and baked in pits
of glowing embers. Gudrid supervised the making of the ale, hov-
ering over the slaves as they milled the precious barley to a fine
dust with stones and minced the hops. She stood over the slowly
boiling pots, stirring the mash herself with a great iron spoon-
sieve, as long as a sword, beating back with it the men who tried
to steal hornfuls of the mash before it was ready. After a week in
the barrels it was done, thick and foamy, and strong enough to
turn a man's head if he drank too much of it.

The Thingmen arrived in twos and threes over the course of
the first day of the feast. Arnkel gothi dressed in his finest woolen
cloak, and red shirt and leggings. He would preside over the feast
from his High Seat later, but for that first day he sat on a rock outside his door and welcomed each man with thanks for his loyalty.
He poured ale into their horns, and sent them inside to the food
and fire, all the while counting who arrived. It was the gathering
of Autumn, held by each gothi in the same week, when a leader
could see who was with him and who was not. A man could not
be in two places at once and so it was impossible for him to split
his loyalties. Only a fool would miss the opportunity to gorge
himself to bursting, and drink till he could not stand. It was the
time of plenty. The hard time of winter would soon be on them,
when every man would keep a close eye on the food in the bins
and whey barrels, and would watch every mouthful of cheese and
meat that went down his family's throats.

Ulfar's vegetables filled a table and were eaten quickly while he looked on, swallowing his dismay at the sight of his summer's work vanishing in a few short hours. The men ate like wolves, fighting over the last small onions in a basket that passed around, wrenching joints of meat from other's hands. Somehow knives stayed on the tables, instead of sticking in men. Bones flew like missiles through the air, and roars of laughter would erupt when a man was struck unawares. Flurries of the things sailed across the Hall and the children shrieked with delight to see the men acting like fools.

The first day was a frenzy of hilarity and games, as if the cares of the world needed to be dispelled without delay. During the morning, wrestlers filled the yard, each cheered on by a circle of men. After the noon meal the men divided into two large masses and a red rag was tied to a spade handle. One group tried to carry the banner through the others, a wedge of driving shoulders and exploded breath and grunts of effort and pain. Arnkel nearly made the opposite wall on one attempt but was brought down by four men hanging on to him like burrs and he fell laughing. He wiped the blood from his mouth and handed the banner over and it began again. At the end, they sat on the wall and on the ground, covered in sweat and dirt, showing off their bruises and cuts and blood. The children stood on the wall, egging them on, but Arnkel sent them off with a roar. The women were ushered inside the Hall, where Hildi and Gudrid gave them mead, a special treat for a special time, and there were soon shrieks of laughter coming out the open door.

"Be a brave man to go in there, now," said Gizur, grinning through a swollen eye. Thorgils sat near Cunning-Gill on the wall, speaking quietly to him. Arnkel's mouth twitched at that, but he approved. Cunning-Gill was not his Thingman and the others had looked narrowly at him when he arrived, but the gothi's loud greeting and Thorgils' friendly words to him had silenced them all. He had played well, and shown that he was not afraid of tangling with other men, although he was nearly as old as Thorolf. That was not surprising, thought Arnkel. He had killed Saxons alongside Thorolf, long ago. One cheek was red and puffed from an elbow.

Ulfar sat near them. He had hovered around the pack of men, never really diving into the fray. The men rarely spoke to him, and then only in harsh words.

Ketil pitched small stones at his head, and he did nothing except raise an arm to ward them off.

"Stop that, you," Thorgils barked. The man spat sullenly and glared at Ulfar and at Thorgils.

Ulfar stood and walked back to the Hall.

"Yes, go and sit with the other women," Leif taunted.

"Bring me back a skin and serve me, wife," the other Fish Brother called, and in an instant the rest of the men were hooting and cat calling at Ulfar's back, until he disappeared through the door.

Arnkel gothi looked on.

Even the Thingmen who had shown disapproval of Ulfar's handsal to him over the rights of the sons of Thorbrand last year had joined in the baiting. Not a single man held back from the joy of expelling another from their company.

He nodded, satisfied.

It was a sign.

Later, when the men and women gathered in the Hall about the trestles for another meal, Arnkel waved Cunning-Gill over. The man came with a great leg of swan in his fist, mouth full, a horn of ale in the other hand.

"Yes, gothi?"

"When you have eaten your fill, I would ask that you take your horse and ride to Hvammr to ask my father, Thorolf, to join us here for meat. It is proper that my own kin attend the Autumn feast. Tell him that my good friend Ulfar the Skald shall sing tonight, of my victory over the man called Onund, and I would like him to be here for that and to see me honor my good friend with gifts."

He had spoken in a low voice, leaning forward, so that only those close to him in the long narrow Hall could make out the words over the loud conversation. Ulfar and Auln sat nearest. They looked at each other in alarm, remembering the last time Lamefoot had been summoned with a similar message. Thorgils heard it, and Hafildi, who thumped Ulfar's arm lustily, grinning at the freedman's flinch of pain.

"I will do it for you, gothi," Cunning-Gill said through a mouthful of meat. "I doubt he will come, though. His heart has been troubling him again. And his temper has been worse lately. Much worse. Like a dragon, he is. I hardly go to Hvammr anymore. He called me a leech the other day and took out his knife. Told me to never come back."

Hafildi spat out his meat, choking laughter, and made a great act of drawing his knife on the man. Cunning-Gill ignored him.

Arnkel shrugged. "What my father decides is his own concern. My duty is to make him welcome."

Cunning-Gill left a little while later, holding his bulging stomach. Arnkel jerked his chin a fraction at Thorgils, who wiped his mouth and followed the man outside.

He helped Cunning-Gill saddle his horse, speaking idly about the games that day, and held the reins as the man mounted.

"Gill," Thorgils said. "The gothi was impressed by your strength today, and your past friendship to him. I will tell you in confidence now, that he spoke to me about you and said that he would like you as his Thingman, if you were willing."

"Did he?" Cunning-Gill's eyes narrowed.

"Yes, he did." Thorgils said. "He needs only some sign of your loyalty, for him to make this a true friendship." His voice was flat and unconvincing.

Cunning-Gill leaned forward slowly in his saddle, as if to speak, but instead let loose from his lips a long line of spit that fell to the ground near Thorgils' foot.

"Get your hand off my reins," he said coldly. "You think I do not see through your falseness, Thorgils? You have always spoken badly of me, and suddenly you seek my company. Your father was a slave and you are hardly better than one. I am bondi, through my father! Ah, and now I am to be the gothi's Thingman. What honor!"

Thorgils let drop the leather, his anger sparked like a sudden fire.

"My father was a freedman, damn your eyes!"

"A slave, like you," Cunning-Gill repeated stubbornly.

Thorgils stepped forward, murder in his eyes.

Arnkel was there suddenly, holding him back with his arm. He had been standing out of sight around the corner listening, and he twisted Thorgils roughly and frowned into his face.

"Are you mad?" he hissed. "Stand down!"

Thorgils backed away without a word. The gothi turned to face Cunning-Gill, his eyes still on Thorgils.

"I wish to speak with you, friend," the gothi said.

"Enough of this bullshit about friends, gothi. You need something of me and I have no need of your warm words and company. There is no one here but the three of us. Speak plainly."

"Cunning-Gill, you earn your name." The gothi smiled, and did not seem insulted by the rough words.

"So, here is what I need of you. I wish to give Ulfar gifts, a shield and sword, once given to me by my father Thorolf. They are for Ulfar's protection and to honor his gift of song and sheep care to my house. They are fine work, of great value. The sword alone is worth at least twenty law ounces, but I own a sword, and several shields, and have no need of others."

Cunning-Gill said nothing. He spread his hands as if to say, what is that to me?

"Thorolf will be most angry when Ulfar receives these things. I have no doubt he will try to kill Ulfar when he hears of it."

"So you invite Lamefoot to your Hall to witness this gift giving," Cunning-Gill said, snorting in contempt. "I can think of no quicker way to see Ulfar dead."

Then his eyes widened.

He looked down at Arnkel with an open mouth.

"How can you say such a thing, Cunning-Gill, when I have treated my man Ulfar with such honor and largesse? I seek only to protect him from Thorolf's anger, and to warn my father of ill-considered actions." Arnkel gothi said this mildly, but his eyes were open, unblinking, and hard as ice. The wind rustled through the long grass of the turf roof behind him, a sibilant whisper of elves' voices.

Cunning-Gill looked up the hill that led to Hvammr, and then down the gentle slope to Ulfarsfell. His eyes came back to the Arnkel.

"I have no desire to see my father burdened by the murder of a man," the gothi continued. "The guilt of it, and the complications of Law and inheritance would be too much for his weak heart." Arnkel stepped forward and grasped Cunning-Gill's knee with his large hand. "It would be fortunate for Thorolf to have a friend who could take this load from his shoulders. Such a man would have my favor, and my friendship. And my protection. Such a man would be worthy to care for the farm of Hvammr when Thorolf finally passed from the world, and would prove a better owner for the sword and shield that Ulfar would carry."

They were silent a long time. The wind gusted louder, tossing their braided hair. The smell of storm was on the air, roiling clouds coming in from the sea.

Cunning-Gill nodded.

"Alright," he said.

"Come to me when it is done," Arnkel said.

Cunning-Gill rode up the slope towards Hvammr and disappeared over the rise.

The two men stood silently outside the Hall, watching the weather come in from the sea.

Thorgils looked at Arnkel. "Is there no other way?"

The chieftain turned to Thorgils. "I know I can trust you, friend Thorgils, to do what must be done."

Thorgils followed Arnkel back into the Hall without a word. He could not bring himself to speak to Ulfar.

———

Lamefoot was not at Hvammr.

His wife said he was away, her eyes downcast, thinking that she would have to make Cunning-Gill welcome.

"Where is he, Helga?" he said shortly.

"He said he went to his wood," she answered, pointing to the north. "To the Crowness. Men have been cutting wood there, Snorri gothi's men, and he went to see them."

Cunning-Gill sighed. A long ride and another back before he could return to meat and drink at Bolstathr. He thanked the woman, and turned his horse about.

The path from Hvammr to the Crowness lay along the west side of the ridge that separated Lamefoot's farm from Bolstathr. The wood had once covered the whole ridge, and there were still rotted cadavers of stumps sticking from the ground here and there on the slopes, but now there was only grass. Sheep dotted the slopes here and there in yellowish clumps.

He stopped when the trees came in sight over a slight rise in the land.

He had no wish to enter there. The elves lay thick on the ground inside the forest, everyone knew that, and there was no telling the power they might have. Sometimes they brought luck, sometimes misfortune, and he had nothing with him to offer as a sacrifice before entering, although he searched through his saddle bags to find a morsel of meat or cheese.

Nothing but dust.

He picked the horse's flanks a little with his heels and it walked ahead.

"Easy, girl," he whispered to the mare, and stroked the ragged mane. The horse eyed the wood nervously.

A man rode over the next rise. His long red hair blew back from the speed of his ride, but he reined in when he saw Cunning-Gill, and rode close.

"I know you," the man said. "You're a friend of the gothi's father. Gill, isn't it? Do you remember me? I'm Svein Haraldson."

"Yes, I do. Come to the feast?"

The man nodded eagerly. "Damn right. One of my cows went sick last night, so I was delayed. Any food left?"

"Piles," said Cunning-Gill.

The man went to ride on, and then turned. "Speaking of the gothi's father, he's just up the trail. Didn't say a word to me. Hear the wood being cut?" Svein Haraldson grinned widely. There was not a man in all of Snaefellsnes who had not heard of Snorri's price to Thorolf. He waved and vanished down the trail.

Axes worked on the other side of the wood, their percussion clear, a rhythmic beat. Cunning-Gill turned to circle the wood, taking the long way around. The Crowness covered a large patch of the fjord's flat land, ranging along both banks of a small river, with spurs running out here and there on rises of land. It was an hour to ride through at a walk, thousands of trees, and the thought of those riches staggered him.

What a fool Thorolf had been to give this away for the pleasure of sticking one to his son, he thought.

He found Lamefoot around one of the spurs.

The old man sat on his horse. He watched a half dozen men cut down the largest trees in a grove, no more than an arrow's flight away. They were hacking the fallen trunks up into long sections, trimming branches, and stacking them with spacers to season. Twenty trees or more had been felled. A dozen horses stood in picket nearby, some saddled and ready for instant use, and the others already loaded with trimmed lengths of birch trunk.

Cunning-Gill rode up to Lamefoot. The men with axes stopped working and peered at him, and then behind to the path, as if expecting more men. But it was soon obvious that he was alone and they bent back to their work.

Thorolf looked at him.

His face was grey with sickness, bags under his red eyes, and he slumped on his saddle. A thick robe of seal fur covered his back, even in the mild air.

"They ruin my wood, Gill," Lamefoot moaned. "They ruin it."

Cunning-Gill settled his horse beside Thorolf's and watched the wood cutters. Two men stood guard, doing no work, men in leather armor, holding spears and shields. They faced Thorolf. Another man stood nearby. He held an axe, a two-sided one, with a long shaft. It was a fighting axe and not made for wood. He wore a helmet.

"That's Snorri gothi, there. Axe and the steel on his head, when he should be feasting his Thingmen," Cunning-Gill, said, surprised. "Everyone said he didn't have the balls to take the wood from this place."

"And that is the bastard, Hawk, there, ready to skewer me if I come near," Lamefoot added. "Beside him is the gothi's son, and there are the two fishermen he keeps. Even if I had my armor and my weapons ready at hand . . . damn them. Damn them."

They watched for a while, saying nothing, but it was plain that the men were nearly finished. The last tree was sectioned and trimmed and heaved onto a pile, left there until the next year when it would be dry enough to work. Hawk waved amiably to Lamefoot as they hefted their weapons onto their shoulders and mounted their horses.

"Bastards," Lamefoot moaned again.

Cunning-Gill tugged at Thorolf's arm and finally convinced the man to turn about and ride away.

They traveled back along the path to Hvammr.

"I tried, Gill. I tried to stop them. Snorri laughed at me when I said that I had only loaned the wood, and that damned Hawk stuck his spear in my face." Thorolf pounded his saddle with a weak fist, startling his horse, "I never gave it up. I never did. That damn thief." His lips trembled. Gill stared at him, amazed at the lessening of the man.

Is this what sickness does to a man in the end, he wondered. He had no wish for that fate.

"I have more bad news for you, Thorolf," he said cautiously, and edged his horse away a little. The old Lamefoot might still lurk inside this shell of weakness. Thunder boomed faintly from the sea, where the sky darkened to grey.

He told Thorolf about the gifts to Ulfar, and Arnkel gothi's invitation to the feast.

For a long moment he thought Thorolf might have missed his words, so lost was he in his misery for the Crowness. Then he saw the man's eyes and knew that it was rage that blocked the man's speech.

They came to Hvammr. Lamefoot roared for his wife and Baldy, his single remaining slave. They came running, dragging a large wooden tub, and up-ended it beside the man's horse. He threw a vast leg over the saddle and slid down onto the tub like a walrus sliding down a wet rock into the sea. Cunning-Gill bent his head with silent laughter at the sight. Thorolf was helped down from the tub by the two of them, but shook off their arms the moment he was on the ground. He waddled into the Hall. Clanging and smashing echoed through the door.

He came out, dragging his mail shirt, and also a spear and a sword. Over his shoulder was a shield.

"Help me get this on, you idiot," he wheezed to the slave. "Quickly. Did you lose your brains when you lost your hair?"

After a long struggle they forced the bernie over his head and shoulders. It rested in a mound of links on the top of his belly, like a hiked-up dress. There was no stretch to the thing, and he could not force it down to his thighs. Lamefoot roared in frustration, his face red as blood.

"Get this damned thing off!"

The slave and wife desperately pulled on it, as Thorolf knelt in the dirt, head down, arms stretched forward. Cunning-Gill came to help, almost ill with the struggle of keeping in his laughter. Finally they peeled it over his head and off his arms, as if skinning an immense metal rabbit.

Lamefoot stood laboriously, puffing, and then his eyes clouded, and the blood rushed from his face. He clutched his left arm, and staggered, and then sat heavily on the still upturned tub.

His wife screamed into her hands, and rushed to him.

"Alright. . . . I'm alright," he mumbled.

Cunning-Gill crouched beside Thorolf. "Easy, man. My father had a bad heart, too. You must rest easy or you'll kill yourself with strain."

"Yes . . . yes . . . I'll rest. Gill, help me get to my bed."

He and the slave each put one of Lamefoot's arms around their shoulders, and half dragged Thorolf into the Hall. His weight almost broke them, even though the old man carried most of it on his shaking legs. Lamefoot lay down on the bench furs while Helga put more wood on the fire. Cunning-Gill sent her off to get water, and then pulled the slave over and told him to deal with Thorolf's horse, to curry it down in the barn.

When he was alone with the old man, he crouched near.

"Thorolf, what can I do for you?" he whispered in the old man's ear. "What can I do for you that you cannot do for yourself?"

Lamefoot's eyes opened in the gloom. He turned his head to look at Cunning Gill.

"I'm weak, Gill. I've never been weak, and I hate it." His eyes went through his friend, as if he were not there. "I should have died long ago. Maybe Einar's blade should have gone through my heart and not my leg. That would have been better than this."

"What can I do for you, my friend?" Cunning-Gill hissed again.

The eyes came back to him.

Thorolf's hand twitched. He pulled back the furs under him to show the wood beneath. "Under this bench, where I lie, is the silver Snorri squeezed from my damned son for my hanged slaves. Twenty ounces left, all in coin. Far more than enough to pay what wergild you will need for the killing. Keep the rest." He gripped Cunning-Gill's arm. "Kill Ulfar. Slay him. Cut off his head." He turned his face to the roof. "I will use all my influence to protect you, if I live. Do it today. Today! I want to hear of it happening before I pass."

His eyes closed and the hand dropped away.

Cunning-Gill went out into the yard and mounted his horse. It was short ride over the hill back to Bolstathr. He went in, took meat from a spit with his knife and found a horn and filled it. For a few moments he whispered to the gothi, telling him what had happened. Arnkel made no sign, and only waved his hand languidly to the feast, inviting Cunning-Gill to eat. He sat near Ulfar and Auln, and smiled and laughed. He cut meat for Ulfar who was grateful that at least one man in the place would speak to him civilly. Auln stared suspiciously at him until the gothi sent her off to help with the serving of the meat. The ale took Ulfar and he began to sing the verses he had made. The men listened at first because the gothi made them quiet, but the song was a good one, and they soon listened because of that alone. The lyric rang out, telling of the door that was unmade, and of the tool that made the door to the house being the tool to make a door to the Otherworld for Onund, the assassin. It was a clever rhyme and after the song was over men repeated it, singing the verses over and over.

The drinking went on as the storm rolled overhead, booming the rafters. Hours went by, the storm lessening and then waxing again with new strength. Rain poured down, pounding the turf roof. Cunning-Gill and Ulfar sat head to head talking. Ulfar heard with joyful relief that Thorolf was bedridden and even near death. He grasped Cunning-Gill's arms like a brother and asked if it were really true.

"Of course it's true, friend," Cunning-Gill said, and put his arm around Ulfar's shoulder. "You can sleep safe in your house tonight if you want, and soon any night at all."

Ulfar's eyes brightened. They sang together a while, and drank another horn of ale. Auln came to say that she was tired and going to bed, and Ulfar heaved her about and kissed her, giddy with elation. She smiled happily at the news he spoke in her ear, and she nodded to Cunning-Gill, as if it were he who had put Thorolf on his back.

Finally, the storm began to fade to remote rumbling, and the dark grey of the sky began to roil as the clouds thinned. The rain lightened, then trickled to a stop. It was late. The setting sun broke out from under the passing storm, near the horizon, and the sudden light brightened the Hall through the smoke holes.

Cunning-Gill whispered in Ulfar's ear, encouraging him, and finally the freedman stood and approached the High Seat. The ale gave him the courage to ask Arnkel gothi if he could go to his own farm, Orlygstead, to spend the night, explaining that it was very crowded with Thingmen at Bolstathr and the benches and floor would be full of men, many restless with piss from too much ale, and some ill with it. Auln was asleep in the family chamber already, so he did not wake her.

Arnkel gothi put his hand to his chin, as if pondering a move of pieces in a game, frowning thoughtfully.

"Normally, I would not allow this, Ulfar," he said loudly, so that many could hear. "Your protection is a responsibility I take seriously. But with Thorolf near death's door, I will allow it this night." He picked up the shield and sword that he had given to Ulfar earlier. "Wear this at your side then and put this shield on your arm." He tied the sword belt around Ulfar's waist himself and showed Ulfar the proper grip on the center bar of the shield. Ulfar's face glowed with the attention from the gothi, and with pride at his warlike appearance. He did not notice the hard looks of envy from many of the drunken men.

The gothi gave him a last affectionate slap on the shoulder and bade him good night.

Ulfar walked outside, weaving a little with the drink in him. The shield was heavy on his arm, but the weight was reassuring. Just out of sight of Bolstathr and near the end of the wall that separated his land from the hay meadow he shared with Lamefoot, he stumbled to a stop and let the shield slip to the ground to ease his arm. He sighed as the piss poured out of him onto the wet grass.

He looked up at the meadow, the place where his troubles had begun. What if he had worn this sword then? Would things have turned differently?

The spirit of the ale still drove him. He drew the sword, and held it tip up at the level of his eye as he had seen the gothi do in his Hall. Thorolf stood in his mind's eye, his slaves smirking behind him, the beasts loaded high with his hay. His hay!

A final crescendo of the dying storm thundered, the deep sound rippling across the sky. Sheet lightning fought with the light of the sun.

Ulfar leapt up to the wall, and cut the air with the sword, daring the spirit of Thorolf to challenge him.

"That's a fine blade," he heard, and turned quickly, mortified to be caught in his pretending. It was only Cunning-Gill, holding up another skin of ale and laughing.

Ulfar smiled with relief.

"Yes," he said, hefting the weapon. "It is that."

Cunning-Gill took a long pull on the skin, and wiped his mouth. He handed the skin to Ulfar, and pointed at the sword. "Mind if I give it a lift? Haven't held a sword since I came back home. I sold it to buy an ox."

Ulfar laughed, and handed over the blade.

Cunning-Gill took it in his hand. He cut in the two diagonals, and the two levels, his arm remembering the drill and Ulfar watched, eyes wide at his dexterity.

"I didn't know you had sword skill, friend Gill," Ulfar said, and leaned against the rock wall, arms crossed. "I am impressed."

Another cut, and another. Yes, his arm warmed to it well. He lusted for it, this blade, and that fine shield lying in the grass, trimmed in good bronze and not just black iron.

He stopped and looked at Ulfar, stepping close to him. A flicker of movement caught his eye, near the top of the ridge line.

It was a rider on a horse. He recognized the gleaming scalp of Thorolf's slave even from that distance. Ulfar saw his eyes go up and he spun.

"By the Gods," he burst out in fear. "I have to get back to Bolstathr. He's come to get me."

Cunning-Gill faced him.

Thunder shook the horizon again, and the sound came to them as a low deep voice speaking far way.

"It will come eventually, Ulfar, no matter how much you run," Cunning-Gill said, and his voice was almost sad. "Thorbrand and his sons want your land back, and so you must die. Arnkel gothi wants your land, and so you must die. Your ghost cannot haunt me for this." Ulfar's face drained of all color and he backed away slowly, seeing the tip of the sword come up. His legs struck the wall.

"You cannot blame me, Ulfar."

He drove the sword through Ulfar's chest.

It went in easily, missing ribs. Cunning-Gill twisted the blade and pulled it out with a wrench, pushing on the man's falling shoulder. The blood poured out, covering his hand and the blade.

Ulfar's eyes were open as he lay on the ground, the feet twitching, and then very still.

The slave watched it to the end, and then set his horse in motion. He rode down the path to Swan firth, to the sons of Thorbrand.

Cunning-Gill watched him, trying to order his thoughts after the passion of the murder. Why did he go there? Why not back to Lamefoot?

What do I do now? The killing had dulled his senses, as if it were a whole skin of wine. He felt heavy and inert.

A strange unease filled him, a sense of being watched. He spun around, but saw nothing, although the light was good. The clouds raced away with the dying thunder and the great blue of the sky filled the world above. It was a sheltered spot, seen only from the top of the hill, and the slave would have spotted anyone there.

No, somewhere else.

He peered up into the sky, bright blue, and rimmed with angry red along the horizon as the sun made its way down to its sleep. The sky watched him, the vast eye filled with rage.

He cowered down.

Who is angry? What have I done?

That great eye above.

It came to him, then, the memory of stories around the fire. Odin, the God of War and battle, was the God of poets.

Thor's Blood, had he offended the strongest of the Gods?

He whimpered in his throat. Not my fault, he thought. Not my fault. He backed away from Ulfar's cooling body, and then turned and stumbled off. Where could he go?

Arnkel gothi, he thought in sudden, desperate panic. He would go to Arnkel gothi, as had been arranged. If ever there was a man favored by Odin, it was he. He would advocate for him with the God. Yes, that was it. Just as if Odin were another man. A sacrifice. Perhaps a goat . . . no, two goats.

He ran, the sword clutched in his hand, and the shield on his arm. Yes, the gothi would want the prizes back. He would pay for his protection with them.

Arnkel stood and stretched after Cunning-Gill left his Hall. He
put his hands on his hips.

"I have been too long indoors and on my ass," he declared.
"Come on, men, let us go outside and use the last light to wrestle
by. I put a bolt of vathmal on Hafildi against any man here."

There was a cheer at this. The men stood up from the benches
and the floor, dragging those that were mostly asleep up to their
feet. There were forty or more men, and they flooded out onto the
home field of thick grass in front of the Hall like a herd of mad
sheep. Hafildi had already stripped his shirt, and a large canvas
was spread as the fighting ring. A large-stomached farmer from
the next valley named Kili challenged Hafildi, and they went at
it like bears for a good time before the farmer was thrown to the
ground. There was a roar of approval when the gothi waved aside
the need to pay the debt, and said that the fight itself had been
payment enough. The farmer was very relieved, knowing what
his wife would have said about losing such an amount of wealth
on a trivial wager.

The women had come to watch the men wrestle. Halla stood
by her father, who could not help but notice how the younger Fish
Brother looked at his daughter.

"Ketil is a fine looking man," he said, and she sighed.

"He has the smell of a pure red head on him, that copper taste
in the mouth," she said, cruelly, so that Ketil could hear. "And the
smell of fish."

Ketil's face crumpled, and he looked away angrily.

"Halla," Arnkel rumbled.

"You may arrange my marriage if you like, father, but I will
decide in the end if I will marry the man, not you."

Gudrid, standing near, heard this. The old woman and the girl
began to argue, and they stormed off, shrieking at each other as
they went into the house.

Gizur had been standing on the wall, watching the gentle slope
that led to Ulfar's farm. It was before dusk, in that strange light

before darkness begins its rule, but when light has not given up
its hold and the eye can still see clearly.

"Gothi, Thingmen, look!" he shouted loudly, pointing.

Arnkel and the men came to the wall to look.

"What is it you see?" Arnkel gothi said, speaking his lines
loudly. Gizur was known to have better eyes than any man in fifty
miles. It had been Arnkel's decision to play the game this way. Men
would believe Gizur's vision, and it was best that Arnkel gothi be
seen to be just another man out of doors.

"It is a man running with the sword and the shield that you
gave Ulfar. But it is not Ulfar. And there is a gleam to the sword,
a dark gleam. There is blood on it!"

"Yes, there he is!" another man shouted, and then they all saw the
man, sprinting madly along the trail that led to Bolstathr. They clam-
ored out, pointing at the small figure dashing along the cow path.

"Who is it?"

"Looks like he's coming here!"

The running man stopped suddenly, peering up at the row of
men standing at the wall, pointing at him. He heard their shouts
and spun suddenly, racing away.

"Murderer!" Gizur shouted. "After him!"

The spears and shields had been left against the turf wall, and
the men ran for them.

Arnkel gothi shouted loudly. "Wait! Hold!"

They stopped, staring at him, and glanced back anxiously at
the running man like dogs held at bay.

"Thorgils! Take these men from the next valley only. You eight
men, there. Chase down that man and find out what he has done.
The rest of you . . . we must go to see if Ulfar has come to harm
and to see if there are other raiders hanging about. Arm yourselves properly and saddle your horses. Gizur, bring my sword
and shield from inside."

Arnkel gothi caught Thorgils' arm, and put his lips to his ear.
"Make sure he does not speak," he hissed. "Understand?"

Thorgils nodded, grimly.

His heart ached.

You could not have lived, Ulfar, he whispered to the night wind, not knowing that he thought the same words Cunning-Gill had spoken. The prayer did nothing to ease his shame.

He leapt over the wall with the eight out-valley men. None of them except Thorgils knew Cunning-Gill well, and may not even have recognized him in the dark, and that was just as well.

Arnkel's men were soon ready. The horses high stepped about in the dusk, excited and nervous. The gothi put on his leather and a cap of wool and then strapped on the sword belt Gizur handed him. He led them down the slope to Ulfarsfell, the others fanning out behind him into a wedge of riders, the hooves soft on the turf.

"They will come again," Arnkel said quietly to Hafildi. "Thorleif and his brothers will come, and they will bring their weapons, and perhaps their courage."

Hafildi looked at the gothi, and saw his blood lust. Arnkel gothi ordered the men to be on a sharp watch for marauders and they peered this way and that, behind rocks and into hollows.

By the meadow they found Ulfar's body.

Arnkel ordered the bloody corpse taken back to Bolstathr. He sent two men who seemed very nervous to be running about in the dark with weapons, and told them to build a litter for the body.

"What do we do now?" Hafildi asked him.

"We ride to Ulfar's farm."

———

Cunning-Gill ran down by the cliffs that went north along the west side of the fjord, half way between Bolstathr and the Crowness woods. He gave them a good chase, but there was no easy way to cut from the pursuit along the rocky shore without losing time and being spotted. As the cliffs rose, the path went farther and farther down toward the water, until the ground was only a narrow band at the foot of the sea cliff. High tide had forced the water close, and Cunning-Gill's wind was gone. It would be a straight run of a half mile before the path widened and that meant speed. But he was blown already, and knew there was no hope. There was not even darkness to hide him. Night in early autumn was still full of light, a long dusk with a short spell of darkness.

On one glance back he saw Thorgils at the head of the pack.

He tried to find anger in his heart for the gothi's betrayal, to give him strength, but it was only himself he cursed, for his stupidity. He should have stayed in his poor home in the hills and never come down.

His heart went out of him a few steps later and he wheeled with his back to the cliff, bent over, gasping.

They surrounded him, a half circle of spear points and heaving chests. He tried to speak.

"The gothi . . . he sent me . . . " His words were choked, broken through a dry mouth and aching lungs. Thorgils pitched his spear at him, but he staggered aside and blocked it with the edge of the shield. They were on him before he lowered it and tackled him to the ground.

"Stop . . . please . . . the gothi," he gasped, but Thorgils was astride his chest then, and his knife was in his mouth, on his tongue, cutting it. Two men held his legs and the others his arms.

"What's that he's trying to say?" said one of the Thingmen. "Something about the gothi."

"Shut up, murderer!" Thorgils hissed into Cunning-Gill's face, his knife still pinning the tongue. "Now, you will only nod, or shake your head. Understand?"

Cunning-Gill nodded, terrified, choking, the blood pouring into the back of his mouth from the gash.

"Did you slay Ulfar?"

Thor, help me, he prayed, looking for shreds of mercy in Thorgils' eyes.

He nodded, and all the men saw it.

Thorgils pulled the knife out of his mouth and stabbed Cunning-Gill's throat. He stabbed again and held the metal in the wound.

When the man was dead, he pulled out the blade and stood.

"Take this piece of shit and throw it into the sea," he said, cleaning the knife in a puddle of tide water.

The Thingmen looked at each other.

"Do it! There will be no spirit to haunt you from this wretch. He was a mouse in life, and he will grow no greater in death."

The water was very deep close to shore, and the body sank without a trace. One man had put stones in the pockets, and in the boots. Thorgils picked up the sword and the shield and led the men back to Bolstathr along the wet, narrow path.

He had done his duty to his chieftain.

Ulfar's voice floated through his head, a sad song that would not leave no matter how much he shook his head, riding the wind.

VII

The Vengeance of the Sons of Thorbrand

Auln waited with the other women by the gate, the smallest children thankfully asleep inside the Hall. They stood by the home wall, watching toward Ulfarsfell. Hildi held onto Auln's arm.

"It will be alright, Auln, I know it will," Hildi whispered in her ear. "Arnkel will set it right." It was quiet, the stillness that follows storm, and sound traveled far. They could hear the shouts from far up the shore as the men chased a man, calling to each other like hunting wolves, faint brays and whoops. The stars had begun to come out to the east through the fading blue, but the sky would not really darken fully.

She had caught one glimpse of the fleeing man before Thorgils and the others had jumped after him. Cunning-Gill, his red shirt unmistakable. She had never trusted him, and he was a friend of Lamefoot's. It was all a fit. Her husband lay dead in the dark, that was almost certain, despite Hildi's words. Waiting for some word was like a burning pain. It was an awful kind of relief when the two Thingmen returned. They appeared out of the dusk at the bottom of the slope leading the horse that carried Ulfar's body behind it.

He lay peacefully on the poles, on his back with arms straight, head to one side, as if he slept. Auln rushed forward and knelt beside him, sudden hope welling up. Was he only wounded?

The eyes were open. She knew from the moment she touched his cold hand that there was no life. Then she saw the vast wound in his chest, and felt the blood, black in the gloom, the cool tackiness reminding her of Thorbrand's honey. The women were silent behind her. Then Hildi spoke quietly to Halla and Vigdis, sending them for water and rags and a bolt of vathmal, silencing Halla's complaint with a dark frown. She lay a hand on Auln's shoulder.

"Come, Auln. We will wash him and prepare his body."

Hildi had the two men unhitch the sling from the horse and drag it into the home field, well away from the house. She called for lamps, and by that dim light they swabbed the drying blood from Ulfar, and put a fresh shirt of wool on him. Auln combed his hair, carefully parting it in the middle, and bound it with a strips of leather behind into two thick braids. Gudrid came out to help, silent and grim. Hildi had her take the other side of a long strip of vathmal, and they wrapped the body in a winding coil, again and again, until the bolt was gone, and every part of Ulfar was hidden. She had the men cut long strips of leather from the great ox hide that hung curing in the barn, and with this they tied the cloth tightly to Ulfar's body.

Gudrid set the two spear men to guard the body. They glanced nervously at each other, hating the thought of spending the night near a dead man, and one of them tried to argue his way out of the duty. Gudrid chopped her hand down imperiously. "You will stay. I do not want the elves coming to do mischief before we cover him with stone tomorrow. I will have my son send others to relieve you, when he returns."

Auln stayed near the body, kneeling, her hand resting on the wool. She wanted to weep, but the tears would not come.

A short while later there were voices from down the slope towards the water.

A shape darkened out of the gloom, and Auln froze in terror and despair. It hulked forward, spear in hand, walking toward her. Her heart broke with grief and shame. It was her father, coming to avenge her betrayal. He was covered in dripping blood, his face hidden by the purple dusk, but his eyes glittered with greed and lust, pinning her to the ground beside Ulfar's body.

She sobbed, hands to her mouth, tears blurring her vision, distorting the figure until it stepped forward into the light of the lamps near her and became Thorgils, his face twisted and bitter. He stopped, seeing her for the first time in the poor light, and the shrouded body beside her.

Blood covered his hands and legs, and the other men kept their distance from him. They looked at each other for a long moment, as the fear left her, and the shape of her face came through his inward vision. He walked over to her and stood awkwardly, holding his spear in one hand. The two guards stepped away to the wall, and they were alone. Gudrid and the others had already gone inside to give her peace with her husband.

"I am sorry for your loss, Auln," he said. She was silent for a long while and he turned to leave.

"You have said that to me before," she whispered. He turned and looked at her, and then nodded.

"It was Cunning-Gill?" she asked.

"Yes. The greedy fool wanted the shield and sword."

"Is he dead?"

"Yes."

Her mouth trembled then, although her eyes were dry.

"I am with child, Thorgils," she said, hopelessly. "What will I do?"

Thorgils stood there tautly, staring down at Ulfar's wrapped body. He looked over his shoulder at the two men standing by the wall, but they spoke with each other in low voices and had not heard.

He stepped forward and touched her face with a finger. "Say nothing of it. To anyone."

She blinked, confused, first by his soft touch, and then by his words.

"Do you understand?"

She shook her head and looked up at him. "I see kindness in your heart, Thorgils. I know that you regret Ulfar's death." Her voice rang with a strange timbre, and his eyes widened, seeing the oracle in her looking out.

"He was a good man, and my friend." His voice shook slightly, and the rugged face whitened as if in sudden pain.

He glanced again at the two guards, and then knelt down on one knee so that his eyes were at her level.

"Do you have kin on the Island, Auln?" he said softly. "Someone you can go to now?"

She shook her head. "They went back to the old country. The ash from the fire mountain destroyed everything they had here. I am alone."

He used his spear to push himself up. "Say nothing of the child," he repeated.

She nodded.

At dawn, Arnkel led the men back to Bolstathr. He left a few behind at Ulfarsfell to guard the land. All the livestock came with them, driven ahead of the riders. The sons of Thorbrand had come again, Gizur said to Thorgils. "But they ran, like last time. I put an arrow into Thorleif's saddle bag, and off they went." The men were giddy with fatigue, and the strain of the night's tension. Sleep seemed far off, and with the growing light they began to drink again and eat the cold meat off the spits. Ulfar's body lay forgotten now, unguarded in day. The men avoided it. Gizur was the hero of the moment, and he recounted again and again how he had run forward roaring, and loosed the arrow at Thorleif. The gothi grinned, and filled his horn himself.

Arnkel was satisfied.

The night had moved from the hunt for a murderer to a fight for land without a single comment from his Thingmen, and now he had laid claim to all of Ulfar's land and Orlyg's. All the chattel had been taken here to Bolstathr. Only the land and building remained, and they could not be stolen.

He had taken back the riches his fool father had given away eight years ago.

It was victory and he savored it.

Even while he played the host, and roared and grinned with his men, his mind went to the next move.

The Crowness forest waited.

He could do nothing until Thorolf died. That was close, but not close enough.

He gestured Thorgils over from a bench near the door. Hafildi saw the gesture and came, too, thinking he was also called. Thorgils had sat glumly apart, brooding, and needed something to do. "Why the long face, man? I've done it. I've won, for now."

"Yes, you have, gothi."

"You did well with the chase," Arnkel said generously. Hafildi snorted.

"Didn't think you had it in you, Thorgils," he said.

"Shut your mouth, you," Thorgils raged, and stepped forward.

Arnkel looked at him, pursing his lips thoughtfully, and held up a hand to stop their argument. They still glared at each other. He pointed to a man with long red hair who sat at a trestle trying to eat as much cheese as he could.

"It seems that Snorri was stealing from my land yesterday," he said. "Svein Haraldson came through the Crowness and said he saw them cutting fresh wood. That white haired coward waited until he knew where I would be for certain."

Thorgils nodded and drank a swallow from his horn.

"He also said Thorolf was there, crying about it."

Thorgils sighed, knowing that some extra task lay ahead for him.

"Lamefoot gave up the land fairly, by handsal," he said harshly. "We all heard that from his own mouth at the Thing. Snorri gothi can do what he wants with it now." In his heart, he remembered Arnkel's hand on his chest at the Thing, shoving him aside like a child. He spat out the words scathingly.

Arnkel's hand slammed down on the broad arm of his High Seat and he stood abruptly, glaring down at Thorgils. "Snorri can do what he wants with the land? Is that what you said?" His voice rang out through the Hall, and the babble of conversation stopped cold. Every face turned to them. "Thorolf my father has given it up, and has no say in how the land is used?"

"Is that what you said?" Arnkel roared again and Thorgils saw for a moment the awful rage that filled the man. He looked the gothi in the eye, facing him squarely.

"We all heard it," he said.

"Fish Brothers! Ketil! Leif!" Arnkel shouted, and the two men leapt up from their trestle, mouths full, spilling meat and cheese on the dirt floor. "Take yourselves to Hvammr and tell my father the truth that Thorgils has said here tonight. Tell him that he has lost all rights to the wood of Crowness, and that Snorri gothi may use it as he wills."

He bent down to the side of the High Seat and picked up the shield that had been given to Ulfar. He stepped closer to Thorgils, until their faces were close, and shoved the shield roughly into his chest. "You, Thorgils," he said, roughly. "You take yourself again to Helgafell, and see your cousin Hawk, and when you are there, see what Snorri's answer to the sons of Thorbrand is to be. But first, give Snorri this shield." Arnkel's face was savage, the teeth bared. "Tell him to bring it when next he goes to take wood from my land, the Crowness."

His head twisted to see the Fish Brothers still untangling themselves from the food. "Go!" he shouted again, and they ran like goats, spilling the table. "My father will need to hear this news!"

"The gothi's gone mad," one of the Thingmen whispered as Thorgils passed him on the way to the door.

He went outside, saddled a horse, and left. The shield was slung from his saddle, knocking against his leg as he rode. He crossed over the ridge and turned up into the hills, following the paths high above the fjord. It was the long way, but he wanted to be above the problems below. Just going upland and into the sky cleared his head. To the east, across the water, rose the greater height of Vadils Head. The valley was spread out below him like a map drawn on skin. He could look right down into the Crowness, and see the new clearing made by Snorri. Sheep covered the green, all about, slowly growing back the wool that had been sheared in the spring.

An hour's ride later, he came to a pair of rounded hills, the Knolls, the last high land before the ground began to dip toward the coast. Sheep paths wound up to the top of each, and on the highest one he saw horses, four of them, saddled and readied, but tethered. They nibbled at the scant tufts of grass, and raised their heads to watch him when he came in sight.

He reined in, looking at them.

A thin column of smoke drifted up in the air from a pocket at the summit of the Knoll. He knew the spot, a good camp, out of the wind when it blew. If he were riding to Helgafell to see Snorri gothi, and wanted a moment to stop and think, that would be the place.

He rode up the path.

Four men came out of the bowl at the top, drawn by the sound of his horse's hooves, and stood there, looking down at him; Thorleif, Thorodd, Illugi and the largest of their slaves, a man called Freystein the Rascal, a man nearly as big as Arnkel, with braided brown hair and a vast beard pierced by an endless grin. Thorgils swallowed the cold spit that rushed his throat. No one would know that he was here. But he would not skulk by, and then appear at Snorri gothi's farm to pretend he had not seen them.

He jumped to the ground when he reached their horses, tethered his own, and then turned to peer upward at them. The last climb was a hard, steep scramble, not made for a horse. He lifted his hand and waved.

They looked down at him for a long moment, and then Thorleif beckoned carelessly with one hand, and they disappeared behind the rock. After a long moment of thought, Thorgils left his spear leaning against a stone and began to climb, using his hands at one point when the climb became almost vertical.

They squatted around a small wood fire, eating smoked fish, passing the fillet around and breaking chunks from it. Thorgils stepped down into the bowl of rock and walked forward slowly. Thorleif held out the fish to him when he came near, and nodded to a spot by the fire.

"That's a fancy looking shield hanging from your saddle," Freystein the Rascal said cheerfully. He was a favorite of Thorbrand's, and a close friend of all the brothers, especially Thorleif, who was his own age.

"It's a gift for Snorri gothi, from Arnkel gothi," Thorgils said simply, and ate a small bite of the fish. He passed it on to Illugi, who snatched it back angrily, glaring at Thorgils.

"A gift!" Thorodd snapped. "So Arnkel buggers us again, and gives gifts to Snorri. Why? So he will do nothing for us? He could have saved his gift. We all know what Snorri gothi will have to say, as he has always said." He looked over at his older brother. "This journey has no purpose."

Thorleif was silent, grim, staring into the flames.

Illugi still stared at Thorgils, and now he stood. Only then did Thorleif look up. He shook his head at his younger brother.

"He comes to taunt us," Illugi said, spitting at Thorgils' feet and stepping forward with his hand on his knife. "Stand up, and I'll show you what that will get you."

"Get your hand off your knife, boy," Thorleif said.

"One less of them."

"Auln is with child," Thorgils said quietly. "Ulfar's child."

The words stopped them cold.

"Truth?" asked Thorodd.

Thorgils nodded. "She told me today." He looked knowingly at Thorleif and the others. "Only I know this."

Illugi backed away, frowning in confusion, and glanced at his brothers. "What does it mean?" he demanded.

Thorleif ignored him. He looked at Thorgils. "Ulfar is truly dead? This is not some game of Arnkel's? Thorolf's slave came to tell us, but I did not trust him. Still, I gathered everyone and I went to his farm to claim it, only to find you-know-who."

"He is dead."

Thorgils told them all of the last night and of his chase through the dark.

"Cunning-Gill," said Freystein wonderingly. "Never made him for a murderer. Thief, yes, but not that."

Thorodd stared suspiciously at Thorgils. "Or it could all be a tall tale, and Ulfar's blood dries on Arnkel's blade . . . or his." He pointed a thick finger at Thorgils.

"It is truth," Thorgils said simply. "Although I will say that Arnkel is not without some guilt in Ulfar's death."

The brothers looked at each other.

"What is your meaning, Thorgils?" Thorodd asked cautiously. Thorgils did not answer. Instead he turned away, staring into the fire. After many long moments, he looked up.

"Thorleif, could you find a place for Auln at Swan firth?" he said awkwardly. "I would consider this a favor. A great favor."

The brothers looked at him, and then again at each other. Illugi frowned, peering from one man to another, trying to make the scattered pieces fit in his head. Thorleif laughed darkly at him, and rubbed his hair. "I will speak to my father about it," he said, finally. "Auln is a good weaver, and would earn her keep."

He looked significantly at Thorgils.

"It must be soon. Before she begins to show." Thorgils nodded.

Illugi blinked, suddenly understanding. "You think that Arnkel gothi will slay Auln, because she carries an heir of Ulfar's?" His voice was full of outrage. "He's a bastard, but he wouldn't do that." He looked at Thorodd. "Would he?"

The blacksmith shrugged. "That strength you admire so much in Arnkel, little brother, the strength our own gentle gothi seems to lack, allows many possibilities. A child of Ulfar's could have claim on the father's land, one day."

"Kill a woman!"

Thorodd shrugged coldly.

Thorleif stood and stamped out the guttering fire. "There is more to Snorri gothi than you give him, brother."

The last embers of the fire went out.

"Let us go now to Helgafell."

They rode down the Knoll and onto the plain and finally came to Snorri gothi's farmstead. A gentle rain had begun to fall, bringing up mist from the sea, and they saw nothing except the path ahead of them until they arrived.

There was a ship offshore.

Hrafn of Trondheim had returned.

The merchant was waiting with the gothi as they rode into the home fields, bellowing welcome. He hugged each of the brothers in turn, and Freystein, and they slapped his back and laughed at his bearskin cape, a massive thing that hung to his feet. Snorri gothi watched with a smile, Hawk beside him.

Thorgils stood apart, waiting quietly. The brothers then greeted Snorri. There was no humor then, just respectful nods and the grasping of forearms. Hawk came forward to greet Thorgils, but it was a cooler welcome than last time.

"Do you come yourself, or are you sent, cousin?" Hawk said quietly.

"Something of both," Thorgils replied.

The rain began to fall harder, and the gothi ushered them into the Hall. Hawk stacked their weapons against the wall for them, and frowned when Thorgils kept hold of the shield. But it was not like a sword or spear, so he allowed it. They steamed in the warmth, their wool soaked through. For a long while they stood around the fire that burned in the pit, drying their feet and legs, with children playing tag around them, while Hrafn sat by the gothi and raised his voice over their shrieking to tell them of his past year. They laughed at his stories, eager to hear any news of the greater world.

"I am a month early this year. No drift ice to trap me before I can leave, with Thor's aid." He grinned and raised a horn to the God, and they joined him, and spilt a little of the ale from their horns into the fire as a sacrifice.

Snorri gothi had sat quietly, listening. His eyes roamed over the brothers and across to Thorgils who sat apart and silent in a corner. Finally Hrafn yielded to the growing tension that even his exuberance could not cover. He bowed to Snorri, and begged pardon for speaking so long.

"May we speak much more before you have need to leave, friend Hrafn," Snorri said. "Now, if you would be patient, I must speak to my Thingmen and my other guest."

Hrafn bowed again, and sat, his horn filled by Hawk.

"Thorgils of Bolstathr, I will speak to you first, and then send you on your way, since it seems that my loyal Thingmen require my exclusive attention," Snorri gothi said, a trace of edge in his voice. He leaned forward in his seat.

Thorgils brought forward the dark blue shield, and lay it down gently at Snorri's feet. He said the words that Arnkel had told him to say, without emotion, hands at his side.

It was very quiet in the Hall.

Hawk stared at his cousin angrily, but Thorgils said nothing more, and would not look at him.

The gothi's face did not change. It was hard to read his mood by the weak flickering light of the fire and the few oil lamps.

Thorleif looked at his brothers, eyes wide with surprise and hope. It was a direct challenge. Snorri could not ignore it, at the risk of his reputation and his honor. Thorleif stepped forward then, eagerly.

"Gothi, we come to you about Ulfar's land, and Arnkel taking of it from us, as he did before with Orlyg's land." Thorleif's voice was full of triumph, strident with assumption. His head went back in shock when Snorri chopped his hand down and stood.

"Be silent!"

They stared at him. He stood with clenched fists and then lifted his hand and pointed it at Thorgils. "You will go now. Do not come to this place again, with your threats. He jerked a thumb at Hawk. "You and your kin here may arrange your gathering of the blood away from my sight and off my land."

Thorgils nodded. He turned and left without a word.

Hawk shut the door firmly behind him.

Snorri pointed his finger at Thorleif, his head down, the hair falling across his face. "So, you seek to shame me into action, by calling for me to come to your aid in front of Arnkel's head man?"

"No, gothi."

"Is this the loyalty I can expect from the sons of Thorbrand?"

Thorleif became angry, a sudden flame of resentment.

"Loyalty must be earned!" he said through his teeth, stepping forward. "We ask for our chieftain's aid against another who harms us, and always he refuses us. Always. Why does he not fight for us?"

"Why does he not fight?"

He stepped closer again, frowning deeply, peering into the gothi's face.

Snorri dropped his eyes from Thorleif's.

By the blood of Odin, Thorleif thought, stunned.

He is afraid.

Always he had thought that it was cunning that held back the gothi, the angling for position, guile, all the things his father urged on him. Although it was Thorleif and his brothers who suffered for the waiting, he had always trusted that Snorri only waited like a hawk above the hidden dove, waiting for his prey to break cover.

There is no subtle wisdom here, waiting for opportunity, he thought.

Snorri was hiding.

"Thorolf Lamefoot is with us in this," he said softly, as encouragement, trying to stifle his own gloom at the thought that the man he most depended upon was a frail reed. "It was his slave who came to tell us of Ulfar's death. And there are some, like Thorgils, who are not wholly with Arnkel."

Snorri raised his hand and stepped backward. He fell heavily into his seat. "I cannot help you, because you have not helped yourself, just as the last time you came here asking for my aid." His head hung down. "Arnkel has taken all the livestock and most of the portables, save the hay, and these cannot be brought out from him, since no one would know what is his, and what was Ulfar's. What could be argued in court?"

"Damn the court!" Thorleif hissed. "There is another way."

"There is only the land left," Snorri continued, as if he had not heard. "It lies between you, and the strongest only will take it. You must endure this, for Arnkel rules over every man's fortune in Swan's fjord, and will do so as long as he lives."

Thorleif stepped forward. "Gothi, we have our arms, and our weapons. Together, we have as many men as Arnkel, and more. Let us fight! If you are with us, we are not just brigands, but men with just cause. We cannot fight alone! We will lose everything! You must join with us."

Snorri shook his head, holding up a hand as if Thorleif's very words hurt him.

"Gothi . . ."

"Leave me!" Snorri shouted, and covered his face with his hands.

The brothers stood, appalled, silent, as did Hrafn, stunned by what they had seen. Hawk jerked his head to the door, his face set in stone, and so they left.

When they were gone, Hawk closed the door and came to the High Seat. He stood by Snorri, watching him, his tough face quiet, arms crossed.

He lifted an eyebrow.

Snorri smiled.

———

Outside, Hrafn put his hand on Thorleif's shoulder.

"Come down with me to the shore," he said quietly. "I have a gift for you."

"Thor's Blood, what will we do?" Thorodd moaned as they trudged through the rain to the shoreline. The brothers walked in silent dismay, shocked at their chieftain's despair.

"I don't know." Thorleif looked at his brothers, and at Freystein, and made himself grin.

"No matter. It will be our backs we must rely on, then. Let us go and see what Hrafn has brought us."

It was a boat.

"Oak planking, pine thwarts. Built two years ago and tight as a virgin." Hrafn held the steer board proudly while the brothers went around it with open mouths. It was ten paces long, with four oars, and a mast that could be put up, and a spar for it tightly wrapped in a sail. The boat rested heavily on the sand of the beach. "I got it for a song from the widow of a dying fisherman, in Trondheim. She hadn't a clue of the value. I was first there, and she needed quick money." They laughed. "Towed it from the mainland. Steady as a rock, but of course the weather was good. It's yours."

Thorleif stood with open mouth. It was a valuable boat in Norway, but in Iceland, with decent building wood rare as gold, it was priceless.

"I cannot repay you. This is beyond my means."

"As I said, it is a gift," Hrafn said, and put his hand on Thorleif's shoulder again. "I value our friendship greatly. But let me tell you something I discovered last spring when I went to see Olaf gothi to buy his seal oil." He rubbed his beard thoughtfully. "They had fish hanging from the rigging of their boats, drying in the air."

Thorleif nodded. "Cod. They dry well in the wind."

"Yes, and will not spoil for months when dry, I am told." The merchant smiled. "Thorleif, I am Christian, as are most of the people of Norway, except for the few who live in the high mountains. I eat fish because I like it, but also because my faith prohibits meat at certain times." He smiled, extending his arms like a man preaching. "There is great profit to be made here. Fish caught in these waters, and dried so as not to spoil, and sold to people who cannot get fish easily, yet require it for over a hundred days a year." He laughed then, and rubbed his fingers together. "Perhaps you can turn your hand to other tasks than sheep and hay."

The brothers talked with Hrafn excitedly about his idea for a while. "I suppose we would sell our fish to you exclusively, Hrafn," said Thorodd, grinning.

"Of course!" the merchant boomed. "For a very fair price."

Thorleif touched the firm strakes of the boat, loving its solid beauty. "Why not give this to Snorri gothi, if you wish to plan for a future here on the Island?" His brothers hissed at him. He ignored them. "A chieftain carries much more weight in these parts than simple farmers such as us. A noble gift like this may buy his friendship and influence."

Hrafn winked. "I have other gifts for the gothi, and other deals to strike." He pursed his lips thoughtfully. "You are a loyal man, Thorleif, as are your brothers. I knew this from our first meeting. That is why I trust you with this boat, and with the future."

He leaned forward. "And I shall work as best as I can here for your interests. I have met Arnkel gothi, and I know him to the soul. He would be better suited to Norway than here, and I think any business I make with him would suffer to my own loss. I will place my interests with Snorri gothi, and his good men." He winked. "But, of course, there is no need for Snorri gothi to know that. Not yet, at least."

They laughed.

After going around the boat and testing it in the water of the little bay, they decided to row the ship back to Swan firth, sending their horses back with Hawk, who offered to ride them in string when they walked back up the hill to Helgafell.

"I'll meet you in your Hall," he said. "It has been a long time since I have spoken with your father, and I want to pay my respects. Don't worry, I'll go high up in the hills, well away from Bolstathr."

Thorleif nodded, satisfied. It was good to see that Snorri gothi's strongest man recognized the danger of their chieftain's lack of action. A war council was needed.

They were not used to boats, and their rowing was inept, out of time, each man digging too deep or too shallow on the oars, and the boat zigged and zagged down the fjord. Hrafn and his men laughed at them until they were out of sight.

"That is a good friend for us," Thorodd said to Thorleif as they pulled the oars.

"Yes."

They clowned in the boat like children with a new toy, happy to be distracted for a little while from their troubles. They let Illugi take command at the steer board. He barked orders at them, and Thorodd and Freystein acted like fools, pretending to misunderstand, while the boat wheeled around in all directions. They leaned into each other's shoulders with laughter when his face became red, while Thorleif grinned from the bow.

A lone rider shadowed them for a while, heading south. It was Thorgils, riding hard, trying to keep pace, but then the rock and height of the land slowed him, and he fell behind.

Two hours hard rowing brought them past Bolstathr, and they held past the farmstead, looking in, just out of arrow range. By that time they had the rhythm of it and they had all learned to keep a straight course with the steer board. There was no one in the fields except children, playing in the puddles. A white horse stood tied to the post by the door. Illugi pointed to it, throwing off his stroke, and Thorleif nodded.

Lamefoot had gone to see his son.

"Maybe they're patching things up between them," Freystein said.

Thorleif shrugged.

They kept on down the fjord as it narrowed, and the mouth of the river that flowed through their lands became clear far ahead.

"There's a boat just down from the ford, in the river," Illugi said, peering over their shoulders at a cloud of seagulls circling hungrily over the rapids. "Must be fishing." He had taken a turn at the steer board again, and he stood with a hand over his eyes. "Yes, they have lines out."

"Who is it?" Thorleif asked, and for a few moments Illugi stared ahead, frowning. Snorri gothi's men sometimes came down to the fjord to get river-run trout. Then the boy spat over the side. He looked at Thorleif, his eyes hard and angry.

"The Fish Brothers?" Thorleif said. A sudden certainty gripped him.

Illugi nodded blackly.

Thorleif called to the others to stop rowing. He turned and peered ahead and then looked at the shore. The boat slid slowly past Ulfar's farm. It was deserted, a few sheep roaming about in the pasture.

"Is your bow still in Ulfar's barn, lad?" Thorleif said. Illugi's eyes brightened like lamps, and he grinned.

They landed him on the shore, at the base of a spit of land that jutted out into the water, fifty paces across and three times that long. He jumped past them to the grass. "If anyone is there, come straight back. We'll wait on the other side of this spit," Thorleif said.

Illugi ran hard. It was not far, but Bolstathr lay easily seen to his right, just up the slope, the turf roof clear in the light. He kept his eyes there as much as he could, but there were only the children and they did not see him, lost in the fun of splashing mud and chasing goats.

He hopped over the home field wall, and ran for the barn. It was dark inside, but he threw the doors wide, scrambled up to the rafters and pulled the bow case from where it was jammed between rafter and turf. It was a long jump down. He rolled, tossing the case ahead, then picked it up and ran out of the barn.

Auln stood in the door of the house, a bucket in her hand. Halla stood beside her.

Auln stared at Illugi, eyes wide.

He stopped, breath coming hard, and looked over his shoulder at Bolstathr, but still there was no man to be seen.

"Auln." His eyes went between the two women.

"You must leave here, Illugi. They would kill you if they found you here."

He ran up to her, the bow case in his hand. "This is mine," he reassured her. "Ulfar hid it for me."

Auln nodded.

"I'm sorry that Ulfar died, Auln," His own words brought water to his eyes. "He was a good friend."

One hand covered her mouth. "Go, Illugi, go," she said.

He swallowed, stepping forward. "Come live with us, Auln, at Swan firth, not with those bastards up there," he said impulsively. "They care nothing for you. There is a place for you with us—and for your child."

She stepped back from him, through the door, openly weeping. "Go!" she cried, and closed the door.

Halla stood there when Auln was gone. They looked at each other silently for a moment. "I will not say that you were here," she promised boldly. "Aren't you afraid of my father? Every other man is, you know. He'll kill you."

He stepped forward and kissed her on the mouth, and put his arm around her waist. She pushed him away, and slapped his face, but not hard. She grinned at his hurt look, and so he grinned back.

"He has to catch me first," he said. Slow steps backed him away from the door, still grinning, and then he ran, the mud of the paddock slowing his steps until he came to firm pasture.

There was a shout from the top of the hill, and he saw men standing at the wall, pointing down at him. Lamefoot rode off on his white horse towards Hvammr, his head hung low, slumped in the saddle.

They were no more than a bowshot away by the time he reached the boat, gasping. He hurled himself over the gunnels. His brothers had beckoned him forward frantically as he ran, seeing the half dozen spear men behind him. Freystein stood in the water to his knees, and he shoved the boat out into water, but waited too long and lost the bottom and could not get easily over the side when the boat went deep. He hung from the side, while they pulled at his shirt and pants and finally rolled his bulk into the boat, cursing his size, half laughing.

"Thor's Blood, row!" Thorleif shouted at them, and took the steer board. They had drifted away from the shore, but a thrown spear could hit them and he hoped none of Arnkel's men had bows.

He looked over at the boy. "Why are you so damned happy?" he snapped, but Illugi only grinned like an imp. He began to bend his bow and string it, bracing the tip against the thwarts and pushing down, but Thorleif shook his head at him.

"Save your arrows for a bit," he said.

They were clear now, the spear men running out on the headland, shouting insults, taunting them, shoving their spears into the air, and Thorodd and Freystein shouted back, rudely pointing their fingers although it threw off the stroke.

"Row," Thorleif growled.

They came to Swan firth, inside the mouth of the river. The Fish Brothers saw them now and stood in their boat, staring, a quarter mile upstream. They did not recognize the boat. Thorleif pointed the bow to shore and sent in the men to fetch the spears and shields when they grounded on the narrow gravel beach. While he waited for them, he walked along the shore, picking up good sized stones, each as big as a fist, and tossed them into the boat one by one.

Thorbrand followed the brothers from the house, lurching along with a staff in his hand.

Thorleif groaned inwardly at the sight of his father.

Thorodd, Freystein and Illugi piled into the boat, and laid their weapons and shields down along the seats and the hull, then turned to take their place on an oar. Thorfinn, Snorri and Thormod came running out with weapons, along with two slaves who ran with fear in their eyes, and one slave called Egil, who was known for liking a fight. A word from Thorbrand stopped them short, and they all fell in step with him, heads hanging more and more as he spoke to them in his soft, irresistible voice.

Thorbrand came to the shore. He looked at Thorleif scathingly.

"What nonsense is this?" the old man said. "To whom does this boat belong? And why do you march out?"

Thorleif set his jaw stubbornly. "It is our boat, now. We go to show our enemies that we cannot be abused any longer." He pointed down the shore to the Fish Brothers, frantically pulling in their lines. They had seen the brothers running out with weapons.

Thorbrand looked down into the river a long time, but he said nothing.

"Snorri gothi will not help us, father," Thorleif said. "That is clear now.

"He is a coward!" Illugi burst out. "A damned coward!"

Thorbrand looked hard at the boy, but Illugi kept his eyes up defiantly. Snorri, Thormod and Thorfinn shuffled their feet behind their father, unwilling to draw his wrath.

Thorbrand looked at Thorodd, the blacksmith, twisting the oar in his great hands. "What do you say, Thorodd? After Thorleif, you are the oldest, and I trust your sense more than his, though that is no great thing to say." The man grimaced. He did not want to go against his father, but he was tired of the shame his family had endured, and he said this.

The three brothers behind Thorbrand nodded silently, agreeing. Thorbrand looked at them all one more time, turning to stare into all their faces.

"I see. So you are determined to do this. You are men now, I suppose, and can take the consequences of your own stupidity," he said blackly. He faced Thorleif, and pointed upstream. "Bury them back there, past the ford, in the pasture where the brown earth goes down far. You know the spot. Bury them deep and leave no marks."

Thorleif nodded, eyes wide with wonder. He looked at Illugi, grinning, and the boy thumped his back.

"Listen to me, you fools," Thorbrand snapped. "Hide their boat until tonight. Then take it out full of rocks, and put holes in it. Right out there, where the water becomes deep."

"Why not sink them with the boat?"

"A man's body will rot under the water, sometimes," Thorbrand said. "Then it floats.

"If you could drown them it would be good. It would look like drowning. But those men will not surrender to you. You will need to put holes in them."

Thorleif nodded, seeing the wisdom in the words, wondering where his father had learned about floating bodies.

Thorbrand shook his fingers at them. "No bragging, no taunting. This is murder. We kill secretly, because we cannot afford to pay for these deaths. Understand that. You may put a grand name on it, call it battle among yourselves if you like, but Arnkel will take all you have at the Thing if it is ever found out that you took and slew his men. He is a chieftain and you are just men, and you will lose at Law." His eyes were like watery ice. "Only we know of it, do you understand?"

He made them swear an oath, there and then, never to speak of it with any but each other, and then he turned and limped slowly back to the house.

Thorleif pointed to Snorri, Thormod and Thorfinn, and one of the slaves. "Get mounted. They may put to shore to escape us, and we will need to ride them down quickly." They nodded and ran to the barn.

Freystein pushed them out again and they began to row up the river. The other slaves came in the boat with them. Thorleif put one of them on the fourth oar. To Egil he handed a spear and told him to be ready, and the slave grinned evilly, happy to be diverted from work by the fun.

"We'll take them deep in the river. Row, damn you. Row!"

They moved quickly. The slave on the oar was named Ragnall. He had sailed in boats all his early life, and so turned out to be the best rower of all of them. Thorleif praised him for it, but his face was white with fear. He knew the reputation of the Fish Brothers.

The boat cut through the water quickly, and Thorleif steered small, keeping the steer board tiller balanced against his side, under his arm. The Fish Brothers had just hauled up their anchor and were settling in at their oars, wheeling about their smaller boat.

"We'll get them at the ford, looks like," Thorleif said grimly. "Illugi, make your bow ready. We'll try to come up beside them, but if they get around us, I want you to loose at them."

"Aye, brother," Illugi shouted, full of feral joy.

Thorleif steered straight for the other boat, but the Fish Brothers were quick on the oars, and experienced. They dodged to the east bank, where the water of the river flooded fastest and deepest, and Thorleif saw he would miss them. He hauled desperately on the steer board, but could not turn the boat fast enough. They would pass a boat length apart, and the Fish Brothers would be past them, with headway, while the sons of Thorbrand would need to turn and gouge at the water to gain speed again.

"Illugi!" he shouted, and with one hand bent to pick up a stone from his feet. Illugi shipped his oar with one toss, and notched an arrow, while Thorleif stood, trying to keep the steer board against his leg. He threw the stone very hard, and then Illugi drew back the bowstring to his ear and launched the arrow.

The rock smashed Leif in the shoulder and he shouted in pain and lurched to one side, bumping his brother Ketil beside him. Illugi's arrow would have missed to the right, but the lurch put Ketil into the path. The arrow pierced his shoulder, just under the collarbone, and the man pitched forward, howling. Their boat spun now, pushed only by the river current, oars trailing loosely. Thorleif sat again, and steered to them.

Illugi stood with another arrow ready as they came close.

Thorodd and Freystein picked up their spears and came to their feet, balancing carefully, their oars loose in the water. Egil knelt beside them, spear point up.

The boats came together. Ragnall grabbed hold of the other boat's gunnel, peering up fearfully at the Leif, who stood with the spare oar held like a pike, hair wild across his face, teeth gritted in fear and rage, and pain. His brother lay in the bottom of the boat, moaning, clutching at the arrow, tangled in the fishing lines amid the dozen large trout that slimed the planks.

"Take the fish," Leif growled desperately.

"We will," said Thorleif. He stood with his spear.

"Arnkel gothi will kill you for this," the man said, seeing no pity in them.

Illugi put an arrow through his chest, and then the other men stabbed him with their spears, again and again, and also his wounded brother. The blood filled the bottom of the boat, and still their rage made them savage the bodies. Finally Freystein's spear broke at the head, and as he stopped, so did the others.

They stood panting with exertion while the river pushed them farther out into the water. Thorleif threw a rope over the bow post of Fish Brother's boat and they began to row for shore.

Later, they did as Thorbrand had said, and planted the men deep, carefully placing the pieces of cut sod back over the dirt to melt together at the first rain. Thorleif and Illugi knelt as they fitted the last slice of turf in, and then looked at each other.

"Is it good, brother?" Thorleif said, grinning, and the boy smiled widely.

"It is good, brother!" They hugged each other hard, thumping the other's back, and then stood, still with one arm around the other's shoulder, stamping their feet fearlessly at the elves who swarmed the grave from surrounding bushes, just at the limit of sight. Thorleif threw a small piece of iron onto the grave and pressed it out of sight with his foot, knowing the smell of the metal would keep them from tampering with the bodies deep below.

They rode back to Swan firth.

Hawk was there, with the horses.

He stood in the barn, staring at the boat he had found the brothers hauling up from the shore. Even buckets of sea water had not washed the smell of blood from it. He turned when Thorleif and Illugi came in, and they looked at each other.

"Thorbrand was not very happy to see me," Hawk said, grinning slightly. "It seems I have stumbled on secrets."

Thorleif led them into the Hall, and sat Illugi with Hawk and a skin to share by the hearth, and had his mother bring out food to them. Her name was Thurid. She was much younger than her husband, purchased by Thorbrand as a slave many years ago. She was welsc, from the wild lands in the east of Britain, her hair still black and mostly without grey, the same hair she had passed to Thorleif and Illugi. Thorleif passed her on his way to his father's alcove of the house as she prepared the food, and she took his arm.

She stood on her toes and pulled his head toward her lips and kissed him. "Your father and you have different ways," she said quietly. "But both of you are fine, strong men." She smiled. "You did well today, son. Your family is safer because of it."

Thorbrand's cough sounded from behind the curtain near them. "Do not encourage him, woman," the old man said in his scratched, rheumy voice. "His foolishness may mean the end of us."

Thurid stuck out her tongue at the curtain, and Thorleif smiled, loving her.

He pulled the curtain aside and walked in.

It was a small place, bulging out from the main house, barely wider than two men's outstretched arms. Shelves of wood lined every wall, except for the back where a large flat stone stood waist high perched on four rotting stumps of wood. Each stump bristled with bracket fungi of different sizes and kinds, and mushrooms and molds grew within the cracks. The shelves were crowded with clay jars and bottles of rare Roman glass, blue and green, and small sacs, tied with leather thongs. The smell struck him, as always, pungent, almost sweet, like the reek of death.

Thorbrand stood at the table, carefully grating a long, dried root onto a plate.

"What's that?" Thorleif asked, without interest, but only to divert the man's usual bitterness.

"Dwarf root," Thorbrand said. He peered over his shoulder at Thorleif. "It heightens a man's common sense."

Thorleif rolled his eyes at the roof.

"It's done, father," he said shortly. "I need your help, now, not cold words."

Thorbrand laid the root and grater down carefully, and sat on the stool nearby, moving with the slow frailty of age. He faced Thorleif and planted his stick on the ground, hands on the knob.

"It is not even a day, and our dark secret is out," Thorbrand said, nodding towards where Hawk sat laughing and joking with Illugi, around the corner.

"Hawk is with us," Thorleif said.

"Hawk is with Snorri gothi," Thorbrand said sharply.

Thorleif spread his hands as if to ask what difference that meant. "Perhaps now Snorri gothi will see that we are worthy enough to back. He will lose some of his fear of Arnkel, knowing that he is not unbeatable."

Thorbrand pursed his lips sourly. He leaned toward Thorleif. "Son, there is some good that will come from what you and your brothers have done this day. Arnkel's men will not be so free on Ulfar's and Orlyg's land as they were before, nor will they come near Swan firth lightly, out of fear of you." Thorleif nodded slightly, surprised by the encouraging words from his father, but knowing more was still to come.

"However, although there is no proof, Arnkel will know who killed the Fish Brothers. It is likely they told someone they came to fish in the river. He knows we have a boat by now." Thorbrand looked at him narrowly. "Now it is feud. Do you know what that means for us?"

Thorleif said nothing. Thorbrand turned to the shelf beside him as he spoke and took down a large urn of honey, the wax seal tight around the top. He broke the seal, took out the wooden plug and reached for a small sac high above him. He poured a brown dust from the sac into the honey, and then began to stir it with a long stick.

"None of you may be alone, anywhere. Even in the jacks outside. You must shit together, or not at all. They will lie in wait along path and trail. While you work, you must always look over your shoulder."

"It was like that already."

"No, son, it was not. Not really. Also, our sheep are scattered about the high pasture. They will be fair game. We cannot send a slave or two to tend them, not even Freystein. A man alone is as good as dead out there, now. You must all go. When you are there, who will be here, to watch our property? And the safety of your brother's children and wives?

"That is feud, son. That is what life is in the feud. That is why wise men such as Snorri gothi wish to avoid it to the last breath, if they can."

Thorbrand put his hand on Thorleif's shoulder. "Snorri gothi will never back you, until he sees no other way to defeat Arnkel, except the sword. It isn't cowardice, son. It's cunning, and guile and wisdom." He looked at Thorleif. "Now, you will have to make peace with Arnkel, and give him gifts to buy that peace."

He put the wooden plug back into the urn of honey, and handed it to Thorleif. "I hear that Arnkel gothi's wife is with child again."

Thorleif grabbed the urn and threw it away in sudden anger. It smashed against the shelf behind the stone table.

Thorbrand glared at him.

"I'm sick of your scheming, old man, and your poisons, and your fears," he said through his teeth. "I wish you had never told me about your elvish secrets, and I want no more to do with them." He gripped Thorbrand's shirt tightly and shook the old man. "Do you know what we did to Auln? To Ulfar? To Hildi Arnkel-wife?

"I will kill no more children."

"It must be, son," Thorbrand said calmly, even though his chest hurt under Thorleif's fists. His eyes were close to Thorleif's, his breath smelling of damp rot. "I tried to save Ulfar's lands for our family. I kept our greatest enemy from having an heir. One day, Arnkel will pass away, and his line will be no more."

Thorleif stared at him. "Do my brothers know? Have you told any of them?" He shook Thorbrand. "Thorfinn? Have you told him?"

Thorbrand shook his head. "Only you. My eldest son. My heir."

Thorleif dropped his hands. "You will tell no one. Or I'll kill you myself."

He tore aside the curtain and left, his heart full of sick rage. He brushed past his mother, who watched him with an anxious frown.

Out in the main Hall, he begged pardon of Hawk with gritted teeth and took Illugi by the arm. Outside, he found Freystein, and Thorodd, and he said to them all, "No one is to speak of Auln and her child to our father. Ever."

He made them swear it to Thor.

VIII

OF THE DEATH AND HAUNTING OF THOROLF LAMEFOOT

ARNKEL GOTHI WORKED his field.

Frost forced up boulders from the ground each winter, the crop of the Underworld. They needed to be pried out and put into the home field fence.

He set the two slaves to digging around the base of the largest boulder, a huge thing too large to put arms around. It had been rising steadily from the ground for years. When they were knee deep into the dirt around it and the under curve of the rock became exposed, he used the iron pry bar and a great timber of oak, wedging them under, with another rock as the fulcrum. Then he heaved, to wrench it from the earth, straining every muscle. It was work to keep a man strong, and he loved that.

He kept his eyes to the top of the ridge that led to Hvammr.

The messenger would come. He knew he would.

Lamefoot could not have lived the night.

He felt it in his soul.

The old bastard had come to him the day before, at nearly the same hour that the children told him of the strange boat that had floated by, the same hour that his men chased one of the sons of Thorbrand from Ulfarsfell.

Lamefoot's face had drooped along the left side, eyelid partly closed, the corner of his mouth and lips moving numbly, the left arm hanging limply, as if half his soul had gone already, and left that part of his body to rot.

He had stood before Arnkel in his High Seat, leaning on the shoulder of his slave. Thorgils, Hafildi and Gizur had lined the step to the seat, spears up, but it had soon been clear that Lamefoot's strength was gone and they butted the weapons and leaned on them. Gudrid stood beside her son, her hand resting gently on Arnkel's forearm, back straight and proud as she looked down her nose at her former husband, hating him, reveling in his weakness.

"I come to you, my son, so that the ill-liking between us should end," Lamefoot had said haltingly, the spittle oozing from the dead corner of his mouth as he slurred the words. "Your hardiness, and my good counsel together would make us great men in this place."

Arnkel had said nothing. He stared at his father, hands grasping the great arms of his seat. Lamefoot had peered up at him, bent over with the strain of standing.

"As a beginning to our new friendship," Lamefoot had continued desperately, "I say that we, the two of us, father and son, should claim back the Crowness wood from Snorri gothi, who ruins it each day. He claims I gave it to him, and in this he lies!"

Arnkel had leaned forward, looking through his eyebrows. "You gave that wood to Snorri to hurt me, Thorolf." His words had come through gritted teeth. "I will not help you slander him, or gladden you with strife between two men of influence, even though I know he has no title to the wood."

It was silent.

Thorolf panted with exertion. "It is your poor heart that makes you say this, and not even call me 'father,' as you cast me to the dogs."

Gudrid spoke then, glaring at him. "You are the dog, as you always were, Thorolf."

The old rage sparked in Lamefoot's good eye. "Still your teeth, old hag, or I will break them as I did before."

Thorgils, Gizur and Hafildi had looked at each other, seeing the coldness come over the gothi. He had lifted a hand to them, and sent them away, out of the Hall, and Thorolf's slave as well, leaving the old man standing painfully alone.

The door closed behind them. Only the gothi, Thorolf and Gudrid remained.

Arnkel sat for a moment, still as rock. Then he leapt from the seat and threw himself at Thorolf like a lion onto prey. His bulk smashed the surprised old man back off his feet and onto his back. Arnkel drove a knee into the man's guts as he landed, then reared back and smashed Thorolf's face with his fist, once, twice.

There was a flash of steel, and Arnkel's knife was at Thorolf's throat, pressing down, drawing a bead of blood as the tip entered the flesh.

Thorolf stared up, helpless, the wind gone from him. His mouth and nose bled freely from the blows and both his arms were pinned by the gothi's knees. He had frozen when the sharp metal touched his neck, and he moaned at the agony in his crushed arms.

"You would slay your own father," he mumbled through the blood in his mouth.

Arnkel had put his eyes close to Thorolf's, his breath hot in the man's face, two hands gripped tightly around the haft of the knife. "This blade has been at your throat before, Lamefoot, while you snored drunk in my mother's bed, and my true father lay waiting to be buried in the ground," he said in a harsh whisper, his face a mask of blinding rage. Thorolf stared up the walrus ivory handle of the knife in Arnkel's hand, the knife given him by Einar. "Not by my hand. By my mother's. I kept you alive and held back her hand on the knife because I needed you. But I need you no longer."

"You are nothing to me."

He had taken the tip of the blade from Thorolf's throat, and slashed upward through his cheek, and across the pulp of the eye into his brow. Thorolf hissed with agony.

"Die, old man. Go home and die. That is the only thing you could do for me, as my father."

The gothi stood. He sheathed the knife, and watched Lamefoot slowly roll onto his side and then onto all fours. Somehow he brought himself to his feet. He staggered out. Blood ran from his face, the one good hand clutched to the hideous wound.

He had not looked back.

The gothi had turned and found his mother beside him. They embraced, and she put her face into his shoulder.

"Is he at peace, now, do you think?" he had asked her, his voice shaking. "Is my grandfather at peace?"

Then he turned from her and retched onto the ground, holding one of the timbers for support. Gudrid watched, knowing it was not weakness, but only the strain of forcing himself not to slaughter Lamefoot when he was under his knife. That would have been madness, a self indulgence he would regret forever. A man who killed his own father would be pariah, and no man would follow him. Inheritance would become a legal matter, a complication that could last for generations.

One last heave loosened the boulder from the ground. Arnkel felt it move free of the ground's suction, his legs and arms and back straining. A shout came from the house, and there was Hafildi pointing to the top of the ridge.

A man rode down on a horse. It was Baldy, Thorolf's slave.

The thrall reined the horse in as he came to Bolstathr, scattering a flock of sheep in his way. Hafildi pointed to Arnkel out in the field and the slave picked his way across the rocky ground.

"Thorolf has died," the man said quickly.

Arnkel nodded. He saw the slave's terror.

"What is it?"

"Gothi. Your father. You must see him. His face . . . " The slave could say no more.

Arnkel called for water, and washed himself on the paving stones outside the door. Hildi came and braided his hair tightly, and his beard, and Gudrid brought out his fine wool shirt, the one dyed green, and his new leather pants. While he prepared, he sent Thorgils with the two slaves to prepare a team of two oxen, with a sledge. The men loaded a pallet of fresh cut sod onto it, at his order.

He drove the team himself, the others following. He rode the sledge as it slowly gouged a trail through the pasture, leaving bare earth and torn sod behind, the reins taut in his hands. The downward slope on the other side was steeper, and he nearly lost the team as the loaded sledge slid forward on the slick grass. Only a rough patch of jagged basalt slowed the mass of it before it rammed into the rear of the oxen. He had Thorgils and Hafildi tie off their horses with rope to the rear of the sledge, ready to take tension if it slid again, and so, with some trouble, they came to Hvammr.

Helga sat outside. She was drunk, as drunk as any woman they had ever seen. She stared at them dully as they came closer, and pushed unsteadily to her feet, the skin of mead hanging from one hand.

"I cannot live here anymore," she said, coming up to clutch at Arnkel's sleeve. "There is evil afoot, and it will take me here."

Arnkel said nothing. He stared at the Hall.

Thorgils gently pulled her back and sent her back with one of the slaves, telling her he would gather her things and send them to Bolstathr later. The woman hardly heard him.

"Burn this place, gothi," the woman shouted over her shoulder. "Burn it. He will come back. The elves will follow his lead, as they do all the angry dead, and things will happen."

When she was gone up the hill, half hanging off the arm of the slave, Hafildi looked at Arnkel. "Maybe she sees something."

"I will not burn my property because of the ranting of a drunk old woman," Arnkel said coldly. But the men around them looked at each other nervously and clutched their spears in fear. Three of them were farmers, come to see Arnkel about a dispute and pressed into this unwelcome duty, not suspecting that they would be handling the dead.

The gothi hobbled the oxen with twists of cord and went to the door of the Hall. There was no smoke from the hole. The fire had gone out.

"He came back last night and sat in his High Seat, gothi," the slave Baldy said in his ear. "He never left it, not once all night. I knew he still lived near the dawn, because I heard him muttering to himself, but with the light, well, I heard no more. I found him." He ducked his head nervously. "Don't let him look at you, gothi. His eyes are open. And they are mad."

Arnkel took a step into the Hall.

A single widening pillar of light from the smoke hole illuminated the fire pit brightly and cast weak silver morning light on the rest of the Hall.

Thorolf sat in his seat. He slumped over a little, head against the post, eyes and mouth open. A thin trail of blood ran from his mouth and nose into his beard, dried to crust. His eyes looked across at the opposite wall, not the doors, and Arnkel breathed a little with relief. "Stay out here until I call you," he said to the others. They agreed, happily, wincing their noses at the smell of shit and death coming through the door.

Inside, Arnkel slid with his back to the turf wall, away from the body's stare, going along the one wall, then the other, and finally sidling up to the High Seat from the extreme left. He kept very quiet, moving his feet slowly, breathing shallowly as he moved into the miasma of Lamefoot's stink. He came to the dais of black rock, and gently stepped up. Finally he was behind Thorolf. For a moment he paused and bent his head to peer at the old man's face, fighting the dread that shivered his skin. Lamefoot's face was twisted in agony. The awful cut shone redly wet, even in death, untreated, unsewn. He had let no one near him, Baldy had told him. Anger still lay frozen there, as if the man had raged at the cloud of death that rose up to take him.

Arnkel's heart betrayed him then, showing him the memory of one of Lamefoot's few warm moments with him, in this very Hall, many years ago. He had rubbed Arnkel's head with rough affection the first time his son had parried a sword stroke with skill.

"Get out of my mind, bastard," Arnkel snarled under his breath, wiping his hand across his eyes. "You will not mar my vengeance."

He took the vast shoulders, and pulled Lamefoot's body forward onto the ground, and with great effort, turned it on its back. From his belt he pulled a small sack of wool, and this he pulled over the body's head, and tied it in place with a length of twine around the neck.

He stood.

"Thorgils, Hafildi," he shouted. The anger was still on him. He shook his head, fighting Thorolf's image in his heart, laughing, sharing ale with him from a skin.

The two men looked in fearfully, heads to the ground.

"His face is covered, you fools," Arnkel said, irritably. "Set the Thingmen and Baldy to break the wall behind the High Seat. They brought axes? Shovels?"

Thorgils nodded.

Arnkel stepped behind the High Seat and picked up Thorolf's axe from the ground. He began to hack at the thick turf wall, ripping out chunks of the dirt and marsh grass. The wall was solid, compacted by the mass above. In a little while, he heard the dull sounds of axes sinking into the turf on the outside. The walls were as thick as a man's leg was long, and he burrowed in like a rabbit.

One last hack of the blade at knee height sunk his blade through and into space beyond. Sunlight shone through a hole, and there was a startled yelp from one of the men outside. Arnkel grinned without humor. The men widened the hole, chopping at the edges.

They had avoided the wooden supports, and pierced through a tunnel no higher than Arnkel's waist, and twice as wide as his shoulders. No need for waste. Any hole they made would need to be repaired, and quickly, if Lamefoot were to be prevented from

returning. The dead did not think. They always returned the way
they left and so it was easy to fool them. The men swept away the
clods from the ground, and Arnkel ducked through the hole to
the other side.

"Bring the team around. Put the sledge here."

Thorgils drove the team, the beasts lowing and complaining at
the sharp turn he forced on them around the corner of the house.
They pulled the sod from the sledge piece by piece and stacked it
neatly to one side. It was good marsh turf, the roots well matted
and still moist. When it was clear, Thorgils took a broom from
the wall and jumped up on the sledge to sweep the wood clean.
After a few swipes, Arnkel jerked his head.

"Never mind that. You and Hafildi, and Kili," he said, pointing at the largest of the Thingmen. "Come in here with me. We
will take him out."

"The sledge is covered in dirt, gothi," Thorgils said frowning,
still holding the broom.

"I said never mind." The gothi ducked into the hole. Kili would
not go in the house and only shook his head in terror, his extra
chin wobbling with the movement. Thorgils ordered Baldy in, but
had to drag the moaning slave by the arm to get him moving.

Light poured through the dust of the hacked opening, but it
was still gloomy inside. A putrid stench filled the air. The gothi
stood by the mass of Lamefoot's corpse. He pointed Baldy to an
arm, and Hafildi to another, and had Thorgils take the legs. Then
he himself gripped the collar of Lamefoot's leather jerkin, and
they dragged him off the dais, Arnkel, Baldy and Hafildi shuffling
backwards in small, awkward steps behind the High Seat to the
hole, pressing closely against each other as they went through the
tunnel, their shoulders rubbing great drifts of dirt onto the body,
and into their hair. The man's weight was immense and sodden,
hard to grip, and they clutched the clothing more than the limbs.
Finally they emerged into daylight. The Thingmen waiting outside backed away.

"Keep moving," Arnkel grunted. "Up. Up onto the sledge." The gothi looked scathingly at Kili through his eyebrows as he hauled, but said nothing.

It took all of them to lift the body the knee height onto the flat wood. Thorolf's leather coat sleeve tore open at the shoulder where Baldy held it, showing the red shirt underneath, and the slave moaned again, imagining his master's anger.

Once the corpse lay on his back, the three men lowered the arms and legs slowly, as if the man were still alive. Arnkel gripped the top of the sack covering the face and let the collar drop without care. Lamefoot's head thumped dully against the wood. The sack came off and his single terrible eye leered at them.

The Thingmen backed away, terrified, eyes wide at the sight of Thorolf's ravaged face.

Kili moaned. "Odin's Blood, he looked at me!"

"Gothi," Thorgils hissed, as the Thingmen looked on in terror. "This is unseemly."

Thorolf would surely rise and seek vengeance on them for his dishonor at the contempt Arnkel showed.

"Shut your mouth."

The men looked at Thorgils, eyes wide. He flushed deeply and felt sick with rage, his passion struggling with his inherent loyalty and he could say nothing, do nothing, except stand there while the men saw his shame.

Even Hafildi's caustic sarcasm seemed dulled by what had happened. He only looked away from Thorgils' eyes, perhaps seeing his own fate one day in a moment of prescience.

The gothi glared at the outraged faces around him, seeing their fear of him, despising it, but knowing instantly that he had misstepped.

"I beg pardon for those words, Thorgils," he said finally, the words awkward and false, still angry. "My father's death has unnerved me." He pointed into the Hall. "Would you do me the service of finding a bolt of vathmal to bind the body for burial?"

Thorgils ducked through the hole without a word. Before he went in, though, he bent down to Thorolf and gave the lyke-help, the closing of the mouth and the one good eye. Arnkel should have done that himself, and the other men looked at the gothi nervously, thinking that he would be angry at Thorgils' presumption. But he did nothing except tie the sack on the head again.

Arnkel set the men to repairing the tunnel, laying the sod in layers, grass down, until it was solid again. While they worked, Thorgils, Hafildi and Baldy wound the body in the cloth. The torso was almost impossible to lift, and the winding became uneven and loose, but the gothi waved that aside impatiently. When the head was covered, he cut the remaining cloth away with his knife.

"Hafildi, stay here with Baldy. Go through the barn, and the out buildings, and see what stock is here, and what feed. Drive the cattle to Bolstathr later. Never mind the Hall. I'll go through that myself."

"What are you going to do about Thorolf?" Hafildi asked. The gothi turned and pointed up into the hills. The Thingmen said nothing, relieved to hear that Arnkel would bury his father and his angry spirit away from their farms, but also thinking that a little effort could take him even farther away, perhaps towards the glacier. None of them would say a word. Arnkel was grim and dangerous, and no one wanted his wrath on them.

Arnkel gothi drove the team up toward Thorswater dale. He took only Thorgils with him, and two horses to back the sledge. It was a long, slow pull. The gothi drove the team, Thorgils riding behind him, dour and quiet. They said nothing to each other. The trail narrowed as it followed the stream, and the slope became more pitched and covered with split boulders, and razor edges of black rock, spaced here and there with clumps of grass and a scattering of gravel and sand. It was hard ground that only the toughest sheep would live on. They were close to Cunning-Gills' little house when Arnkel turned the team away from the stream bed of the dale, and drove it higher up the slope, into a cleft of rocks where natural caves formed dark pockets in the hillside along the wall of the cleft. Most were no more than indentations, hardly shelter from rain. The sheep liked them. One was longer and deeper than the rest, just higher than a man in height, and wide enough that three men could walk abreast, dog-legging thirty paces into the broken rock. It was said that Irish hermits had fled there at the beginning, during the Landnam, and their bones were scattered on the hillside somewhere, their ghosts long ago dispersed into the wind.

"This will be Thorolf's Howe," Arnkel said over his shoulder, pointing at the large cave deep within the crevice. He halted the gasping oxen. "We will block it with stone, and he will bother no one."

They tried to move Thorolf. His body had lost the stiffness of recent death, and he hung limply, almost impossible to grip. Arnkel put his hands under the torso finally, kneeling, and gave a vast heave, rolling the body off the sledge and onto the ground. For a moment, Thorgils thought the corpse's obscene paunch would rupture from the fall. They each took an end, but on the rough ground and with the body wrapped it was a hard pull, and they needed to go fifty paces or more. After less than a body length of struggle, they stopped.

"Bring a horse," Arnkel said, breathing hard. His words echoed off the rock walls around them. "And rope." A light rain began to fall on them from the narrow crack of grey sky above.

The horse was leery in the tight space, and smelled the body, fighting the lead, but Thorgils got it around somehow and into position facing into the draw. Arnkel lashed the rope around the widest part of the body.

The ground was a rasp of knifelike stones and gravel, and the shroud of vathmal quickly abraded away under the wear as they pulled the body along. By the time they reached the cave, only shreds of it held along the bottom of the body. Thorolf's jerkin was tough, and kept the rocks away from the flesh. Thorgils led the horse into the cave until the footing became too treacherous for the animal and it stopped, whinnying at the feel of the ground under its hooves.

They found a shelf in the cave, long and wide enough for a body. There were marks on it, as if it had been carved out by metal tools, long ago. They heaved under the body and somehow pushed it onto the shelf with one tremendous strain of their arms and legs, and then stood over it together, looking down, catching their breath. Arnkel tore away the remains of the cloth, now no more than a tattered shroud. Lamefoot lay with the mute indignity of death, face still hooded, his hands splayed slightly at his sides as if to ask why such a fate should be his.

"It's cold in here," Thorgils said.

"Always is," the gothi said. "Even in summer." He pointed at the mouth of the cave. "We'll put a wall of stones across the opening," the gothi said. "That'll stop his wandering."

So they did, heaving the great things from up and down the draw until they had built a wall waist high. They used the sledge for the largest stones, but it was still hours before they were finished blocking even the short span of the cave mouth. They found a patch of alders, and cut down many of them. These they planted in the top of the wall, braced with stones, so that even the open space was blocked by dense branches.

The gothi said no words when they were done. He turned the sledge, and began to drive it down the slope, Thorgils following again.

Cunning-Gill's wife watched them pass. She stood in the door of her house, three thin children about her knees, watching them with hopeless eyes. Arnkel's cold eyes turned to her, and then away.

"It will be hard for her, up here alone with young ones," Thorgils said.

The gothi looked contemptuously at him, but said nothing.

He sent Thorgils back to Bolstathr with the oxen and sledge, Hafildi riding behind.

"You're staying here alone?" Hafildi said doubtfully. "Swan firth is just a little way over there, you know."

The gothi slapped his sword and grinned. "I have Baldy with me. He will have to come to know his new master."

The slave swallowed nervously. He remembered the old days, when he and the now dead slaves had killed Einar's men at Thorolf's side. The young boy he had terrorized was in his prime and owned him like sheep.

When the others had left, Arnkel looked at Baldy, his hand on his sword.

Baldy fell to his knees.

"Please, gothi, please."

"Show me where my father kept his things," Arnkel said, his voice pitiless. "All his things, even the secret ones. If I find you have kept something from me, you will swing from that ring bolt on the cliff, just like the others."

Baldy took him from one end of the house to the other, desperately showing him the storage tanks, and the chests of cloth and clothing and gear. There were piles of iron tools, still oiled and ready, hoe and shovel blades, all valuable. There was even charcoal. Baldy showed him the sack of money in the sleeping bench and Arnkel took it, and nodded in satisfaction when the slave told him it was the last of the money Arnkel himself had paid. Then the slave took an axe and began to break into the turf wall over one of the sleeping benches.

"What are you doing?" Arnkel said, frowning.

Baldy pointed. "Treasure in the walls, gothi."

He pulled out a chest from the dirt spacer between the outside and inside layer of turf. It was a large chest, an arm's length long and half as wide, heavily banded in iron. Arnkel knocked the lid back with his foot.

There was some treasure. A battered chalice of silver rolled about, from a Christian church, the gems dug out with a knife long ago. A thin crucifix of gold lay inside it, as long as his finger.

"He was going to melt those down, gothi."

Arnkel nodded, but his eyes were on the bulky packages of oiled canvas below the trinkets. Two of them filled the bulk of the chest. He pulled them out and tore away the canvas.

In one fold of rough cloth was a mail bernie, made from tiny rings of riveted wire all connected. The other package was a helm of iron, with a long, broad nasal, and a sculpted bronze covering for the upper face, like a mask, pierced for the eyes to look out and shaped to fit the nose and cheeks. Arnkel lifted the mail, held it by the shoulders, and then bent and put it over his head and arms, letting the weight of it drop down on him.

It fit perfectly, draping down nearly to his knees. He took the helmet and lowered it on to his head.

Baldy backed away in terror. The gothi's face could not be seen, except the growth of beard that protruded, and some of the mouth.

"You have the look of your father, gothi," Baldy whispered.

"Is this everything?" Arnkel said, and the slave shivered at the sound of it. From inside the helmet, his voice was the youthful echo of Thorolf.

Baldy trembled and nodded.

Arnkel turned toward him. "You are the last of my grandfather's enemies," he said.

Baldy did not run. He knew he was dead, knew that running would only make the suffering last longer.

Arnkel killed him.

He cleaned the sword with the hem of Baldy's shirt and then took off the armor and helmet and put it back into the chest, carefully wrapped. Then he dragged the body outside by a foot, and left it in the dirt.

The chest rode awkwardly on the back of his horse, but he balanced it with a hand as he rode back to Bolstathr. Thorgils waited for him.

Arnkel ordered him back to bury the man.

The men working in the paddock overheard and looked at each other, and one man whispered a prayer to Thor. Thorgils only nodded, knowing that Baldy could not have lived the day. He had kept his horse saddled.

The sun emerged from under the blanket of grey above, far to the north west, and shone redly under the cloud, even while a light rain fell. The drops lit up like fire in the eerie light, and it caught all of them, a moment of intense beauty as the Sky God shone down his pleasure.

"You see," Arnkel called to the man who had prayed. "Great Thor tells us that he approves." The other men nodded and discussed it as they worked the last shovelfuls of the day. Soon it would be meat, and ale, and they could debate the sign from the Gods at leisure.

"No one will want to live there," Thorgils said, as Arnkel dismounted. "You should hear the talk. Baldy told everyone and they all saw Thorolf's face."

"It will be my seat," Arnkel said loudly, and this the other men heard, too. He pulled the chest down and put it under his arm. "Where I go, my family and my household go."

Thorgils mounted, and tucked the spade behind him under a strap. "Best talk to your mother about that, gothi."

Arnkel ignored the words. He pointed a finger at Thorgils. "When you get back, I want you to send a man up to the hill over the Crowness. Set up watches. I want to know the moment Snorri goes to the wood."

A month passed.

Summer began to fade, and each evening the chill became deeper.

Auln had begun to show, but she hid herself inside clothing, and bloused out her apron, and so it was not obvious. Gudrid was her usual nasty self, and constantly remarked on how much food she ate, the attacks relieved only by her tirades against Hildi and Halla.

Thorgils sat beside her at table when it was meat at Bolstathr. He would say nothing, only roll his eyes when the old woman raged, and it would make Auln laugh, and this would ignite a new attack. But neither cared about that. Their eyes met as they passed, and Auln began to touch his arm as he passed her in the barn, or out in the field, and both were happy.

Arnkel gothi never censured his mother, but his impatience with the constant bickering wore on him, and he grew abrupt and irritable. He ordered Hafildi to stand watch the whole night once when the man became drunk in the morning and fell asleep in the barn.

It was not a happy household.

Thorgils' interest in Auln was obvious to all, now. Hafildi and even Gizur taunted him relentlessly, but he said nothing, knowing that they lusted for her, too, but were watched by their wives, two plain sisters with red calloused hands and hard voices, acolytes of Gudrid, echoing her words in every matter to gain her favor. Everyone was together all the time now, out of fear of the sons of Thorbrand, and the close living wore on everyone. Thingmen would arrive to seek out the gothi and find reasons to leave early, dismayed by the poisoned air and the bickering. Hafildi beat any slave that looked at him crossly, and once swung at Thorgils, who stepped away from the drunken attack and drew his knife. Hafildi's whole side went by him unprotected, and Hafildi knew that he had only been spared by Thorgils' mercy.

The Fish Brothers had vanished.

The gothi sent riders up and down the shores of the fjord, looking for the boat or its wreckage, or bodies, but there was nothing.

"We should kill one of them," Hafildi said one night, as they sat around the hearth. Arnkel sat slumped in his High Seat, hand on his chin, and the others gathered around him. Gizur agreed nervously, and glanced at Arnkel for some sign of his thoughts. But the man was unreadable, as always.

"We'd have to trap one or two of them alone, without witnesses. Any more and there is a chance one could escape to tell," Thorgils said, reasonably. "That means setting out scouts, and we already have a man set out over Crowness. If we killed one of them openly, they could have the gothi's balls at the Thing, since there is no proof they killed the Fish Brothers."

"We know they did it!" Hafildi exploded.

"No, we do not. Maybe they tipped and the currents took the boat out to sea. Who knows?"

"I do," Hafildi said stubbornly.

"That's not enough for the judges, man, and you can be damned sure Snorri gothi would be there scheming."

They sat despondently for a while, drinking slowly. Gizur idly poked the fire. The wind howled outside, a lashing storm of rain and hail, and the sound of it shivered them.

"Kili says he saw Thorolf again, walking over the pasture the other day," Hafildi said. He had drunk a whole skin and spoke carelessly. Gizur again glanced nervously at Arnkel, but the man did not move. "Helmet and armor on, and that red shirt poking out at the collar. You know, the one he wore the day he died."

"Shut up, bondi," Gizur said anxiously. "I don't want to hear such things. It's tales. Just tales."

"Didn't all the oxen that carried him up to Thorswater dale die? Eh? Just fell over dead one night, both of them, in the barn."

"I said shut up."

Later that night, there were screams outside the Hall, and the men leapt up, grabbing dully for their weapons. They rushed out to find the gothi already there, sword in hand, holding Helga by one arm as she sobbed and writhed in his grip.

"I saw him!" she shrieked. "I saw him. Just standing there, plain as day."

Her feet were bare, torn and bleeding from her long run through the dark on the stones, her hair disheveled. She begged on her knees not to be sent back to Hvammr, and the gothi let her stay the night. Gudrid came out and sourly led her inside to a pallet in the family alcove, and gave her a horn of mead, although she smelt as if she had drunk much already. Arnkel had refused to give her a place at Bolstathr, claiming rightly that his Hall was crowded already and had sent her back after Thorolf's burial.

The men stood in the moonlight uncertainly, shivering with dread, looking about them, but none of them wanted to be the first to go inside and show his fear.

"Thorolf must be mighty angry, to walk the Earth so much," Hafildi said. The gothi turned his head quickly, and glared at him.

"Why would my father be angered, Hafildi?" he raged, but Hafildi wisely would not answer. Arnkel snorted in disgust and sheathed his sword. "I will go myself to see. There will be nothing but shadows, and an old woman's mead-addled dreams."

The gothi saddled a horse and rode off. The men went back into the Hall, and, because it seemed close to dawn, decided to stay awake. Gizur told the slave to light the fire and put peat on the flame, and so they sat glumly around the smoky heat, saying nothing. Luckily, the noise had not woken the children, and so they were undisturbed.

Arnkel returned a long while later. They heard the jingle of the harness and went out to meet him. Dawn paled the sky, and made the terror of the night vanish like smoke. The sun would not rise over the high eastern mountain for some time, but it was day and that was the time of men.

They looked at him, and he shrugged. "I saw nothing."

The work went on that day as if nothing had happened, but every man and woman looked over a shoulder as they bent to the work, especially when outside. No one wanted to be alone.

Little was said at the morning meal, and Arnkel only gave brief instructions for the afternoon's tasks, and they worked until the sun began to set again.

Helga refused to return to Hvammr, clamping her toothless mouth stubbornly shut at Arnkel's reassuring and then commanding words. They sat eating the last meal, curds and pickled goat, and rabbit.

Auln, watching, saw the irritation in the gothi's face, and stepped forward.

"Gothi, let Helga go to live at Ulfarsfell. I will go with her. The welcome of your Hall has been generous, but your land there needs tending, and the time I walk to and fro each day is wasted. Helga has the reputation of being a fine weaver, and my spare loom there stands ready."

She looked expectantly at the gothi, who said nothing. She glanced at Thorgils significantly, while Helga looked back and forth between them, her eyes full of hope.

"That seems a wise thing, gothi," Thorgils said hesitantly. "Ulfarsfell has begun to look ratty since Ulfar died."

Auln spoke again, as if the thought had just occurred to her. "Halla could join us there, at least for a while. It is feud between you and the sons of Thorbrand, but she would be more than safe there, as a woman, and Ulfarsfell is not all that far off. It strikes me that she would enjoy the change."

Arnkel frowned, shaking his head. "First it is too far to walk, then it is near and safe. Which is it? Also, I do not trust Thorbrand or his sons to stay away from Ulfarsfell. One of them was there not so long ago."

"Only to pay his respects to me about my husband's death, gothi."

"Still. He was there. Others may come, also."

"Then I will go," Thorgils said suddenly. "I will live there, too."

It was silent in the Hall.

Auln looked again at Thorgils, one eyebrow raised. They had discussed what they would say before. Thorgils made no sign and sat impassively, as if the decision did not matter to him.

The gothi leaned back in his High Seat, rubbing his beard with one hand. He took some rabbit and ate it off the bone, chewing thoughtfully.

"Ulfar's land needs a man there," Thorgils said, pressing gently. His heart beat very fast.

The gothi swallowed his meat, and then stood. "There is merit in these thoughts." He pointed a finger at Helga. "You will return to Hvammr, woman. That is your place." Helga's face fell, and she blinked terrified tears from her eyes. "Auln shall go to live with you. Her sense will temper your folly, and so my daughter Halla will have a good example of the woman she should be, and the woman she should not. Hvammr is not close to the sons of Thorbrand, and she will be safe there, as she would not be at Ulfarsfell."

Halla's face whitened. She had heard the endless stories whispered about Thorolf's walking. Hildi put her arm around the girl and they held each other tightly, both weeping slightly.

"Thorgils, you are wise, as always," Arnkel continued. "You will go to live at Ulfarsfell and tend the land there."

Gizur put his head close to Thorgils as the gothi turned away to go to the door. "Hvammr is not far from Ulfar's farm," he whispered sympathetically. He had seen the anger in Thorgils' face.

Hafildi leaned over his dish of meat to look at him. "Better you than me, Thorgils. Bolt that door solid when night comes, and keep an eye over your shoulder."

Thorgils ignored them both. He stood and went with Auln to help her pack her things, kneeling beside her as she emptied the box under her sleeping bench. As she finished, she turned and whispered in his ear.

"Come tonight."

He nodded, his tongue locked by the rage building in him.

Auln and Helga rode double, with a pony behind to carry Auln's chest and bag. Halla wailed and spoke defiantly to her father, refusing to go, and he roared back, with Gudrid behind him adding her high pitched shriek to the scrap, accusing Halla of disobedience, and then cowardice.

"I am no coward!" she said suddenly, the tears drying instantly. Then she whirled, and went inside the Hall. She emerged moments later with a leather sack bulging with clothes. As she passed her father on the way to the barn, she struck his arm savagely with her fist, and then went on, pretending not to feel the pain in her hand. Her horse pounded out of the door of the barn and followed Auln's up the long slope to the ridge.

And so a kind of peace came again to Arnkel gothi's house.

Thorgils rode to Ulfarsfell.

In his hands he had his weapons; spear, axe, and bow with shafts, and he wore his good jerkin of leather. Two shields rode behind him, one on each side of the saddle, tied tightly. A small sack of tools and a bundle of sleeping blankets were tied to the pack horse behind him. With the horses, it was all he owned in the world. He spoke not another word to Arnkel, afraid that the rage in his heart would spill out onto his face. It was too short a ride to rid him of it, and so he goaded the horse ahead once he arrived in Ulfar's home field, driving with his heels and thighs until the mount galloped across Ulfar's pastures, onto Orlyg's farm, and then up into the hills, and still the anger would not go from his core. Ulfar's cold dark house had frightened him, too. Would the man's shade be waiting in there for him?

His mind showed him images of his knife going into Cunning-Gill's throat. But the face was Arnkel's.

With the rage there was a dark metal cloud of despair. His life had been in the shadow of a great man, and he had accepted that. Now he saw that all his loyalty was nothing. He was a game piece, placed now in the way of harm, to be expended. He had betrayed Ulfar, his friend. Betrayed him for Arnkel. He had taken that darkness onto himself for the man, and for that sin he received nothing.

He knew Auln was doomed. Sooner or later, she would meet the end the gothi planned for her.

He knows of the child, Thorgils thought. He must.

He went to the top of a long drumlin of rock and gravel, and at the top he let the horse rest. His spear rested on his thigh. He turned to face the setting sun, and watched the glowing orb with wide eyes until the brightness dimmed and he could readily see the movement in it, across its face. The moment it sank behind the horizon and left him blind, he said a prayer to Thor, and asked him for guidance.

His answer was a flicker near the darkening ground, to the north, towards Hvammr.

Elves.

They could only be seen from the corner of the eye, but he saw their movement, like a herd of motes within his eye, flowing toward something that drew them.

His heels drove into the horse and raced down the hill. Hvammr was a mile off.

Thorgils rode down into the dell of Hvammr in near total dark, trusting the horse to sense the way. The moon had not yet risen and only stars threw down a pale light. He reined in near the house, and heard screams from inside.

There was the sound of chopping, around the back of the turf Hall, where the body had been dragged out, and he rode there, his blood cold in his veins.

Thorolf stood by the wall.

He faced the newly laid turf, axe in hand, face no more than a foot from the wall, now hacked and broken. He wore mail and a helmet.

Thorgils backed away slowly, and then dismounted, drawing down the bow and his axe without once taking his eyes from the apparition. The elves danced about in the corner of his vision, insane in the presence of the unhappy dead.

An arrow found its way into his hands and he notched it, hands shaking with pure dread.

Auln was inside, and Thorolf wanted in.

"Thorolf!" he cried out, and raised the bow. "You have no place here! Go back to your howe. Go back!"

Lamefoot's spirit stood there, immobile, staring at the turf. Thorgils loosed the arrow. It flew out and struck the shade in the hip, rattling the metal rings with a thin clatter, and fell to the ground spent. The spirit turned immediately and walked slowly off, axe hanging from one hand. It vanished into the dark.

Thorgils held another arrow drawn to his cheek, arm trembling with the strain, until he heard nothing but the wind. He side stepped away from the back of the turf house, and lowered the bow, then ran to the door and pounded on it with his fist.

"Auln!" he shouted. "Auln! It is Thorgils."

The door wrenched open. Auln stood there, eyes wide with fear. She reached for his hand and drew him into the turf house.

A lamp burned on the High Seat, and one on the step of the dais. Thorgils heard whimpering and turned to see Helga and Halla with arms around each other. The older woman was witless, mad and staring, and Halla held her head, as if to comfort her.

"Was it my grandfather?" she whispered.

Thorgils nodded. The tears flooded her eyes, and Thorgils knew she would not spend a second night in the house.

A mass of broken benches filled the space behind the High Seat, wedged and jammed into place, chest high and impassable. Auln brought out a short stretch of timber from a side alcove, and threw it onto the pile.

"That's the last of what's inside. Tomorrow, we'll need to put stone and rock behind that wall." She stood, the fear very close, and looked at him. "Will you help me do it?"

IX
WINTER

OF THE WHITE BEAR AND HRAFN'S DISCOVERY

SEVEN MEN RODE HARD down the shore, the wet black sand shooting up behind the hooves of their mounts. Behind came the dogs, long tongues hanging from the corners of their mouths like pink banners as they tried to keep up with their master. There were four of them, as large and black as wolves. Back from the sand was much deep snow, and ice piled up thickly against the shore, jagged and impassable, but the beach was clear where wind had cleared it down to the ground. The frozen surface was perfect for riding. The men had cantered hard for most of the morning along it, and the horses were near their end. It had been glorious, an escape from the close fire and smoke of Helgafell.

Snorri gothi led them, his son Oreakja behind him, with Hawk, Sam the Fisherman, and another man called Styrmir, a farmer who had happened to be at Helgafell when news had come of the beast. There was also Kjartan, a friend of Oreakja, and the son of one of Snorri gothi's Thingmen. Last of all was Hrafn, his horse struggling under the bulk of the man.

They laughed at him, as they had laughed all winter, for Hrafn had been caught once again by the ice, that year come almost six weeks early. He found no comfort in the stories of toothless old men who said that it had been during their childhood that they had last seen the drift ice so early in the year.

All except Hrafn carried a pair of hunting spears, a short cross guard strapped tight across the shaft an arm's length below the head, with strips of precious iron bolted far down the shaft. The gothi had an axe tucked into his saddle. Word had come of a bear, spotted on drift ice that had come down out of the north. It roamed the shore, starved and dangerous. A terrified farmer, one of Snorri gothi's distant Thingmen, had staggered into Helgafell the day before. The creature had killed one sheep already that was known, and for that crime alone it must die. Then came word that the bear had slain a man.

They came at last to a farm hard by the shore, far down the Snaefellsnes peninsula. The tiny house and barn were sheltered from the harsh wind behind a vast outcrop of black basalt. Snorri gothi threw himself from the saddle and went to the door. He pounded on it, and called out.

The door was pulled open and a short bearded man glared at him, spear in hand. But then his anger faded when he saw who he had as guest.

"Snorri gothi," the man said, and stepped forward, lowering his spear. He looked up with sleep-gummed eyes to see the other men on their horses, spears held high, and he breathed out loudly in relief.

"Your name is Teitr, isn't it?" Snorri said.

"Yes, gothi," the man said. "I expected to see my own chieftain, Gudmund. He is no more than a valley away."

"My own Thingmen have called me to this place," Snorri said, hurriedly. "Where is the bear? Quickly now, before it causes more harm."

The man stepped forward and pointed up into the high pasture behind his farm. "Last we saw, it headed up to the meadows. Probably smelled the old sheep dung on the wind. Hoskuld found it outside his house, trying to get through the wall, into the whey vats, and it killed him when he went to stop it."

Snorri nodded.

They rode up the trail, a narrow, winding trench of trampled snow, a trough as deep as the horses' bellies. On one stretch they saw spoor, and Hawk came down from his saddle to look at it. He put his own large hand within the immense paw print, and it was lost.

"Thor's Blood," he said, in awe. "It's a big one."

The pasture snow was blown into drifts, with some as deep as a house, and in other places troughs easy to walk through, and they held to these, following the spoor, the dogs racing ahead to sniff the trail. The trail soon wound between two immense drifts, each taller than a mounted man and curved like huge breakers on the sea. The snow was packed hard enough to walk on.

The dogs ahead howled in excitement.

Snorri looked at the drifts. He pointed them out to Hawk, who nodded. "A good spot," he said.

They dismounted and Snorri asked Hrafn to take all the horses and lead them back down the slope and tether them to a stake in the ground far off the trail, in deep snow. He did this and then staggered back, looking about nervously. He found Snorri standing within the trough formed by the two drifts, spear in hand, and another at his feet, along with the great two-sided axe. He looked up at Kjartan and Oreakja on top of one of drifts, and Sam and Styrmir on the other. The four men perched on their knees and peered into the distance.

"Any sight?" Snorri called to his son. Hrafn ran up to stand beside him puffing with the exertion, sweating. It was cold, but not too cold and he had worn too many clothes.

"I see Hawk and the dogs," Oreakja said, looking up the slope from the top of the drift. "They are circling still. I still don't . . . ah, there it is! I see it!"

"Is it running upland?"

Oreakja watched for several moments before he answered. "No. It knows Hawk and the dogs are there, though. Keeps facing them and sniffing the air. They'll be up slope from it in a bit."

"How far?"

"Quarter mile. It's clear as air once you spot it."

"What are you doing?" Hrafn asked, putting his head close to Snorri's.

"Hawk is using the dogs to drive the bear down to us. It is a white bear, and they will always go to the sea for escape if the dogs press them."

"How do you know it will come to you, and not some other way?"

Snorri shrugged. "They are like men, in many ways. It will take the easiest route down, as it did going up. See the trail?" He pointed to the prints in the snow. "Now, friend Hrafn, take one of these spears, and go to stand with my son up there. He will show you what to do."

"It comes!" Oreakja shouted.

The boy grabbed Hrafn's arm as he scrambled to the top and pulled him down into the snow. The three of them lay in the cold, eyes peeking over the top of the drift. Across from them, the other two men had done the same.

Only Snorri gothi remained in sight, deep in the white ravine of ice, twice a man's height below. He held the long hunting spear like a pike, butted in the ground under his heel.

Hrafn looked at him, and at the men beside him, and their intention came clear to him then.

"Snorri gothi cannot stop the bear alone!" he said, and began to scramble to his feet. "We must help him!" Kjartan's arm held him down on one side, and Oreakja on the other.

"Be still! You will ruin everything!" Oreakja said angrily. Kjartan put his shoulder against Hrafn's as they lay. He was a relaxed, big shouldered boy, with warm manners, and was well liked at Helgafell. Snorri gothi saw his cool head as a good balance for his son's impulsive nature.

"More than one man will frighten the bear, and it will turn away," he explained. "Yet we must have one man there or it will not slow in its run from the dogs."

Hrafn nodded uncertainly.

"What do I do?"

"Stand ready. Keep low. When we go, you come with us, understand? The gothi will call."

Hrafn nodded again, irked that he was baggage in such a dangerous activity, especially to boys far less than half his age, and he had the urge to bring up his own war-like past in protest. But then he saw the gothi below him tense, and Kjartan pulled him back from the brink, leaving only a sliver of Oreakja's eyes at the top of the drift.

"Get ready!" Kjartan hissed through his teeth.

The barking of the dogs became louder with each second. The wind died to nothing and they heard a great rhythmic trampling of the snow, and huffed breath, coming down the trail. The steps halted. Suddenly, there was a deep bass coughing, as if a giant cleared his chest. Oreakja and Kjartan dug their feet into the snow, knees bent, like the start of a race, hands tight on their spears.

Kjartan put his lips to Hrafn's ears. "The bear is challenging Snorri gothi. It will attack any moment."

The dogs were almost on them. They could hear their steps in the snow, and behind them Hawk, running as hard as he could to follow. But they saw nothing, and waited, shoulders into the wall of snow.

There was long pause, almost pure silence, and then Snorri gothi's voice roared out in defiance.

"Odin! Give me strength!"

Oreakja and Kjartan exploded out of the snow, driving their legs into the drift, and Hrafn followed, a half step behind. They came over the top and saw the bear charging at Snorri, head down, jaws agape, the great muscles of its haunches writhing under the skin. The gothi stood like a rock, his spear point at the level of the bear's throat, head down and mouth open in the extreme passion of the kill.

The bear saw them come from both sides, slide-stumbling down the slope in a mad charge for each quarter of its body. It halted its attack and spun, roaring in fear and rage. The dogs swept in low and threw themselves at the bear's legs and throat. Distracted by a more understandable threat, it turned on the dogs, swiping with one paw and then the other. A broken body sailed through the air, howling in pain and spraying blood and ripped out fur, and came to a heavy rest in the drift. It squirmed weakly, almost dead.

Hrafn stood back while the five men charged in as one and impaled the bear with their spears, leaning hard into the shafts with their weight, their heads coming perilously close to the beast as it spun. The animal screamed a high pitched deafening shriek, insane with the agony of the mortal wounds. The men released the spears. It would have been death to hold them as the mountain of flesh writhed in a twirling dance, biting at the shafts. The bright red life blood spurted from one flank where Sam had pierced near the heart, and the gothi's spear hung from its throat.

"In the flank, Hrafn," Snorri gothi shouted. The bear lashed out with a paw and shattered the wood of one of the spears hanging from its side. The spear head remained in the body, but the shaft beyond the iron bracing exploded into fragments. Oreakja was too close, and the largest shard whipped into the boy's ribs and he collapsed, the air driven from his lungs.

The bear wheeled savagely, sensing a weakness in the trap around it even through its agony. The three remaining dogs saw it go for Oreakja and went mad, throwing themselves at the bear's muzzle. They tore the loose flesh to shreds. Another of them was maimed, bitten through its thigh and hurled away by the force of that great neck. Hawk came in. He was to the rear, too far from Oreakja to help, but he rammed his spear into the bear's haunches, to distract it with pain, and was thrown down by the twisting dance of the bear before he could release the shaft. He crashed into a drift, hissing from the agony in his wrenched arms and hands.

Hrafn put his teeth together and ran forward, heaving his spear into the flank of the bear with all his strength, behind its shoulder, feeling the spear head drive in up to the cross bar. He sprang back. The beast shuddered and collapsed, and then pushed itself up weakly for a last lunge at Oreakja, who lay on the ground pushing the snow with his heels as he tried to crawl away. His eyes were wide with terror, seeing the mangled jaws come for him.

Hrafn ran forward, waving his hands and shouting, hoping to distract the bear's rage to him.

There was a flash in the corner of his eye, and Hrafn saw Snorri gothi run forward, the great axe held high over his head. He leapt, high above the bear, and came down on two feet, square on the rounded shoulders, the axe descending in a blur.

It cleaved the great skull, spilling the brains of the creature out onto the snow.

The animal fell onto its belly with a rush, an instant collapse, voiding a great black mass of filth from its rear as it died. The gothi rolled forward into the snow.

Oreakja and Hawk lay on their sides, and the other men knelt, chests heaving, nursing their pulled and battered muscles. The gothi went to Oreakja, mouth tight with concern, but the boy waved a hand to show he was alright. He would have bruised ribs, but nothing was broken. Hawk nodded shakily. He was only stunned.

Kjartan killed the wounded dogs, slipping the knife in quickly, and he stood over them as they died, out of respect for their courage.

The gothi still carried the axe in his hand. His hands and arms were covered in gore. Behind him the two surviving dogs gathered to lick the brains and blood from the huge wound between the eyes of the bear. The beast lay with spears still jutting from it, bleeding out into the snow.

Hrafn stared at Snorri. He sat in the curve of the drift with his men and listened as they laughed and talked excitedly about the kill. They always paused to give their chieftain their ear, with instant respect, when he spoke a word.

The gothi's leap had been the most foolish thing Hrafn had ever witnessed. He had seen bears killed before, on hunts in the homeland. Spears and arrows and dogs, working together. A hard task, always, and that was what made it exciting. Never had he seen a bear killed with an axe. It was for the butchering.

Hawk brought up the horses, and they tied a web of ropes to the bear and cinched them to the saddles. The horses wanted nothing to do with the thing, reeking of enemy and blood, and would not settle, so it was a wild, unstable ride back to the shoreline. They could barely drag it across the ice and snow for the sheer weight of it.

"That's the largest bear I've ever seen," Sam said once, glancing back. "And I've seen plenty in my time, especially out on the ice."

Gudmund gothi waited on the shore.

He was surrounded by his retainers, all of them armed with spears, and some of them in leather armor. Gudmund was not happy to see Snorri.

"You've taken away the hunt from me, Snorri gothi," he bellowed darkly as they drove the horses onto the home field, and released the bear from its draw ropes. "And also taken the right of vengeance. It was my Thingman who was slain."

Snorri walked up to the man, and stood with his axe casually on one shoulder, so that all could see the blood on it. "My Thingmen called for help, too, Gudmund. What was I to do?"

Hrafn, standing off to one side with the others, leaned into Hawk. "Will there be a fight?"

Hawk smiled wanly. "Do you know nothing of Snorri, even after all the months spent in his company?"

In the end, Snorri gave the entire bear to Gudmund, and asked only for two claws from the front paw, one each for his son and himself. Gudmund grumbled, but it was plain that even his own

Thingmen thought Snorri generous, and he could not say no, although he loudly protested, saying that the whole pelt would be ruined by the maimed paw.

Snorri came back to them, a little grin on his face. "Well, I just saved us a long hard haul back to Helgafell." His men laughed, and agreed. Hawk said loudly that bear meat was tough on the jaws anyway.

Oreakja rode close to his father on the way home, his eyes bright with pride, until finally Snorri had him scout ahead with Kjartan for debris on the beaches and behind them, things they may have missed on their hard ride out. Hrafn moved up beside him and Snorri sighed, shaking his head at the young backs streaking away.

Hrafn laughed. "It is good to see a young man who thinks so highly of his father."

"He thinks nothing of the riches I bargained for him as dowry," Snorri sighed. "Nor of the wisdom I try to stick in his thick head. But a butcher's trick with an axe and I am a God to him."

"That is youth," Hrafn said smiling.

"That is most men," Snorri said sourly. "Act the beast and slaughter men by the hundreds, and you win renown and respect, and damn all else besides."

The boys found a pile of drift wood, and so they made camp for a meal, although it was late, and they could have made it back to Helgafell. It was a grand extravagance to build the flames up until they were higher than their heads, and they held their arms up to it, backing away from the heat.

On great chunks of broken log they sat and ate cheese and smoked salmon, and drank buttermilk from skins. Hrafn produced a skin of wine from his saddle bag, drawn from the large cask on his ship, and passed the rare treat among them. It was potent, far more potent than the mush of ale they usually drank, and soon their faces were red with more than just heat.

"I'm glad I don't live in the land where this was made," Hawk said, taking a long swig. "I'd be drunk every day. What was that place called again, Hrafn?"

"Anjou. In the land of the Franks."

"What's wrong with being drunk every day?" Kjartan sang out, and the rest of them roared with laughter.

The sun began to go lower in the sky, and they thought of moving, but the wine and food, and the drain of the fight with the bear had made them torpid. Long shadows stoked their unease, though, and each man began to look away from the fire, over his shoulder.

"They found another bunch of dead sheep the other day, down in Swan's fjord," Hawk said, spurred by the mood. Freystein and Illugi had come to visit in the boat a few days past, driven by boredom to leave the security of their farm. They had brought the news. "A Thingman of Arnkel gothi's swore that he saw Kili Arnusson walking with Thorolf's ghost across the pasture."

"The murdered always walk with the shade that killed them," Kjartan said with bold authority. "So my grandfather said. Was not Kili cut down by Thorolf's axe at Yule tide?"

"Not only shades wield axes," Snorri gothi said dryly.

"What do you mean, father?" said Oreakja.

"Nothing this shade has supposedly done could not be done by a man."

"Who would want to do such things?" Kjartan scoffed. Hawk and Snorri looked at each other, but said nothing.

The wind seemed to flow around the little bay, and so it was warm and comfortable. Oreakja said he would have camped there, if they had brought blankets or skins, or a tent. Kjartan offered to ride back to fetch them, and they fell to discussing it excitedly, two young men daring the spirits.

Snorri gothi shook his head. "No, you will stay at Helgafell, behind locked doors, until my dispute with Arnkel is resolved. It is not shades I fear out here."

The words sobered the men, and they quieted.

"But that could be years!" Oreakja protested.

The gothi spread his hands.

"That is the way of it now, son. You are not safe out here alone."

Oreakja stood angrily. "Then why do we not just finish it? Enough of this scheming. Go south and clean out Swan's fjord."

Kjartan nodded uncertainly and agreed, but the rest said nothing. Hawk sat still, saying nothing, staring into the fire. Snorri took the wine skin and drank from it, and then spat the large mouthful into the flames.

"Would you fight Hawk, son?" Snorri gothi said softly. "If he turned against me?"

Oreakja looked at Hawk, the man he admired more in life than any other, except his father. Then he thrust out his jaw. "If he was my enemy, yes." Hawk looked at him with hard eyes, and Oreakja quivered a little, but still stayed defiant. "But it would be a hard fight," the boy acknowledged finally, and the others laughed.

"Hawk, would you fight Arnkel gothi?" Snorri asked.

The man poked the fire with a stick. "Not if I could help it." He looked at Oreakja. "He's a warrior, that one."

"And he has other men, too," Snorri said, pointing his finger at his son. "Not as many as follow me, but there are some among them who would not hesitate to kill a young man or two who slept the night alone, away from thick walls, and no witnesses. You have only to ask the sons of Thorbrand how they like the feud they fight with Arnkel." He looked at Oreakja. "Kings may roll the dice of battle if they like. I will not. It is too uncertain."

Hawk nodded. "Yes, they missed the Autumn Thing at Helgafell. They thought that Swan firth would be ashes when they returned, if they left it."

Kjartan, Sam and Styrmir nodded in sympathy, knowing what it meant to miss the grand feasting and revelry of the Autumn assembly. There was little enough in their hard lives to give some joy, and they looked forward to the gathering all year.

"All the more reason to end it," Oreakja said, sulkily, sitting down. "We can take him down, like we did the bear today." He flashed the claw at his father, like a taunt.

"We want more than an end. We want victory. Only in victory is there honor."

The others looked at him, shocked, all except Hawk, who knew his chieftain. The gothi smiled grimly and pointed a finger at the two boys. "You have heard around the fire the endless stories of heroes fighting vainly to their death, and so you think that is what is best in life, that which makes a man. It is the fight that matters, you think, the courage and the will, not the result, for that is in the hands of the Gods alone."

They stared at the gothi, frowning, confused.

He looked round at them. "Fools die when they fight knowing they will lose, or when they have measured the chances in error. There is no glory in being vanquished. Where is the honor there?"

There was no more talk. Soon, they mounted their horses and rode back to Helgafell.

Later that night, sitting around the great hearth fire within the Hall, Hrafn turned to Snorri gothi beside him. "At last, I think I begin to understand you, gothi."

"Oh?" said Snorri, smiling. He filled Hrafn's horn politely, his long white hair covering his eyes as he poured. Both had much wine and mead in them.

Hrafn leaned forward conspiratorially, his elbow sliding unsteadily off his knee. "Yes. It strikes me that the sons of Thorbrand would have been very surprised to see what I have seen this day, up between the snow drifts. They might have changed their opinion of you to one of more respect."

The gothi said nothing, and only sipped from his horn. Other men sat on benches around them, talking quietly with each other.

Across the room, Kjartan clowned before the women and children with a tale of the slaying of the bear, and they sat enraptured by the story, listening with open mouths. Oreakja waited to one side, crouched behind a bench, with a hairy goatskin on his head to terrify them at the right moment.

"But you care nothing for that, do you?" Hrafn said, and his eyes were wide.

Snorri looked up. "I am like other men, Hrafn. I desire respect and esteem. But a man's reputation is merely a tool for his use. An edged tool that can cut him if not used correctly. I see by your face that you do not agree."

Hrafn sputtered. "A man's reputation is everything. It is all he has in life."

"It betrays him when he makes it the point of his life," Snorri said. "A reputation binds a man to certain ways of acting. It weakens him, Hrafn." The gothi smiled grimly, and leaned toward Hrafn, making the sign of secrecy to him, the finger and thumb together, and Hrafn nodded, knowing he was bound. "The sons of Thorbrand think I do not aid them now because I am afraid. What do you say, friend?"

Hrafn stared at the man. "Knowing you as I do now, I say you choose not to aid them, because you think they will lose, even with your help."

Snorri shook his head gently. "I choose not to aid them because I have a better way to win. A certain way. They care nothing for that, of course, and so I must give them a better reason to explain my lack of help, or they will rightly leave my service. Their respect carries a high price, you see. I would have to act in a way that is not best, to maintain that respect. How is this wise?"

Oreakja emerged with a roar, and the children screamed in joyous terror and hid their faces in their mother's laps. Hawk raced in, and speared the boy with his thumb and he yelped loudly. Hrafn and Snorri laughed with the others, and watched as Kjartan called himself the mighty gothi and slew the beast with an axe made of the long leg bone of a cow, pretending to beat Oreakja on the ground. The children then leapt on him in a pile.

Snorri smiled, and looked at Hrafn. "I jumped on the bear because I had to, to save my son, and for no other reason. It was need that drove me, not vanity, just as it was need that put me in the trough to draw the bear in. I am the least handy with a spear, so I was the best to use as bait. Except for you, friend Hrafn, but you were my guest. How could I ask you to take that burden?"

The gothi laughed at Hrafn's expression.

"You are an odd, odd man, Snorri gothi," he said softly.

"You have no idea, friend."

They drank late into the night.

X
SPRING

OF THOROLF, BURIED AGAIN AND LAID TO REST

THE WINTER HAD BEEN the hardest any could remember in Swan's fjord, and not only because of the weather, which had been cold, and the great amounts of snow which had fallen and made movement difficult, but also from the tensions of the feud, and the terror of Thorolf's ghost.

The short days heightened the pain, since no man would dare go out in the dark, after Kili had been found hacked to pieces on the pasture. Thrain Egilson claimed to have been chased through the dark by Thorolf, and only escaped by falling into a hole between two boulders. He had listened in terror as Thorolf's footsteps had crunched by, and then shivered to hear the vengeful howl of the ghost as it faded away into the mist. Only Arnkel gothi would dare leave the Hall after sunset, roaring that his father would not have the revenge on him in death that he craved in life. He would drag out the slaves or Thingmen to go with him to do the work at Hvammr and Orlygstead. Many times he even went alone, when all the men lay exhausted from work, although his wife and mother begged him not to go, fearing the ghost, and the sons of Thorbrand lying in wait for him along some path. He was stubborn, and would shake off their arms as he left, but would always return safely, and so it was believed that only he was immune to Thorolf's malice.

Thorgils always slept at Hvammr.

Arnkel did not approve.

"I said I wanted you at Ulfarsfell," Arnkel said to him darkly. They circled their mounts in the dim light of grey dawn on the ridge between Hvammr and Bolstathr. Arnkel had been warned by Hafildi of Thorgils' wandering ways and surprised him as he returned to work.

"As long as Thorolf means to slay Auln, I will stay in Hvammr Hall at night," Thorgils said stubbornly.

"By Odin's Blood, you will not!" Arnkel glared at his chief Thingman with open hostility, teeth bared. Thorgils stilled the bubble of fear that rose in him.

"I will," he said.

Arnkel stared at him a moment longer and then ripped his horse's reins away and rode off.

They hardly spoke after that day.

It came to be thought among the people of Swan's fjord that Thorolf walked the Earth because he yearned for the return of the Crowness, and would not rest until his family controlled it again.

As with all rumors, no one could remember who had first spoken the thought, but it was grasped eagerly by all who needed some explanation for the ghost. No one openly dared to mention Arnkel's treatment of his father's body, but that story drifted about as well.

The Thorsnes Thing was to begin in two weeks, and Arnkel's Thingmen grumbled that the feud with the sons of Thorbrand would cause many of them to miss the grandest event of the year. Many men spoke to Hafildi and Gizur as they went about the land, suggesting to him that they urge the gothi to settle the matter with the brothers quickly, and so end an unprofitable, unwinnable dispute.

Thorgils rarely went to Bolstathr. He busied himself at Ulfarsfell, and said little when he did come, only reporting on the state of the farm, and then leaving. Eventually even that stopped.

One fine morning, when the sun shone down warmly and had begun to melt the vast piles of snow that lay about, a dozen riders came to Bolstathr.

Most were from the next valley, but four of them were the kin of Kili, the Spirit-Slain, as he was known now, including Thrain, a quick speaking, intelligent man, disliked by many for his sharp wit. It was an impromptu visit, the idea born at a feast of Kili's kin the previous night. Thrain had raised the issue, and argued for it the most, and as the host pouring the ale, they let him talk. Full of drink, the men decided in the early hours to confront the gothi and bring peace to their cursed cousin, and also to their own houses, happy to see Thrain taking a position of leadership. They had ridden out to gather other men and found some willing to drop their work and come.

Arnkel met them out in the home field of Bolstathr, frowning darkly, axe in hand and leather jerkin on his back, and the sight of him armed made them hesitate. They had imagined welcoming horns of ale in the Hall. Hafildi and Gizur stood nearby, spears in hand, as if the group had been expected.

Kili's kin, led by Thrain, were very drunk, and they stood in the front, hoping the drink would keep their courage steady in the face of the gothi. The others hung back, wondering then if it had been wise to draw the attention of the gothi to them. There had been whispers that Thorolf's ghost would prey on those that displeased Arnkel, as it had Kili for refusing to carry Thorolf's body.

Thrain was pushed forward by the others.

"Why have you left your work, Thingmen?" Arnkel called out. "The days are short enough without wasting the light."

"We come to ask you for two things, gothi," Thrain said. "The first concerns the sons of Thorbrand."

"That is not your concern, it is mine." Arnkel said starkly, and the men chilled at the danger they saw in the gothi's eyes.

"It is our concern, gothi," Thrain pressed. "We find ourselves trapped by the feud. The sons of Thorbrand killed two of your strongest, and so they are fearsome. We must live together on one farm, all of my kin, out of fear of them, and that is nothing but waste and discomfort, and our wives complain of the crowding and the inconvenience. It has been a whole winter, gothi! And now the Thorsnes Thing comes and you have told many of us we may not go, but must stay to guard Bolstathr."

There was genuine grumbling from the men at this, and Hafildi and Gizur looked at each other, worried.

Arnkel said nothing. He stared blackly at Thrain. "The other matter?"

Thrain bit his lip, and then blurted out, "Your father, gothi."

Arnkel stepped forward and the men backed away, all except Thrain. The gothi stopped and said, "What of him?"

"We must settle his spirit, gothi. You must make good your claim to Crowness. This is clear." The men nodded, agreeing. "Also, Thorolf must be moved. Thorswater dale is not safe for such a restless shade. He must be taken far away, so far that he will lose his way back to Swan's fjord."

The other men looked at Thrain, wondering at the courage in him which they had not suspected before. He spoke boldly to the most dangerous man they had ever known.

Arnkel stood silently for a while, and then he dropped the axe to the ground. "Is this the will of my Thingmen, then? That I seek peace with Thorbrand, and with my father, and so give quarrel to Snorri gothi for the wood?"

The men roared out their agreement, lifting their spears into the air. Arnkel smiled and stepped forward, his arms out, and walked into their midst. "I will always listen to the will of my Thingmen," he said loudly. Then he invited them into the Hall, and called for ale and for meat, and the men stayed most of the morning.

Thrain was last to leave. He spent time with the gothi, talking quietly. When the others had gone, he raised his hand, as did the gothi and they made the handsal. Then he left, riding up the ridge, an eager grin on his face.

"Can you trust him?" Hafildi said doubtfully, watching the man disappear over the ridge line.

Arnkel shrugged. "There is no trust to abuse, except out of greed. He will cut wood in the Crowness for me, and his fee will be half the wood cut, to no more than twenty trees."

"Generous of you," Hafildi said, grinning. "I meant trust him to keep his mouth shut?"

"It was his open mouth that I paid for, Thingman."

A week later, Thrain was killed by Thorolf's ghost.

His cousins found him in the Crowness, savagely hacked beside a freshly cut tree, and they knew it was Thorolf protecting his wood. Three of them came to Bolstathr again, and found the gothi sympathetic.

He called for them to go on a task for him, at that moment.

Thorleif had spent the morning shearing sheep with Illugi and Thorfinn in their home field, while Thorbrand sat on the wall, in the sun, pointing out the ones that would be next.

His back hurt from the bending, and his right hand ached from squeezing the shears, which seemed to carry their edge less and less. One variety of their sheep lost their fleece naturally, but another, fully half of the flock, needed the shear, and that was work.

He stood, running the whetstone along the edge of the shears, easing his back. "There must be better metal to make tools from," he grumbled. "I spend more time sharpening and honing than cutting."

"Blaming your tools again, son?" Thorbrand said. Illugi broke wind loudly, and the brothers laughed, even Thorfinn, although he turned his head away at the old man's glare.

"Riders," called Illugi loudly, and pointed.

Four men rode down abreast from Ulfarsfell, moving slowly, so that they would be easily seen. The brothers ran for their spears and shields, and Illugi fetched his bow and case from where they leaned against the wall. They had carried their weapons close ever since the troubles had started. Thorleif shouted toward the house, and Freystein poked out his head, and then swore. In moments the rest of the brothers and all the slaves had come, and there were ten men ready to fight. They stood in a loose line, with Illugi just behind, near Thorbrand, who hissed at the boy every time he put tension on the bow string.

It was Hafildi, leading three of Arnkel gothi's Thingmen.

They reined in at the stone wall, but stayed in their saddles.

Thorleif said nothing, waiting. The three Thingmen looked nervously at Illugi as he twitched his bow.

"We come with a message for the sons of Thorbrand, from Arnkel Thorolfson, gothi of Swan's fjord," Hafildi said. Thorodd had come out of the house carrying spear and shield, and Freystein had a great club of wood in his hands, and both frowned darkly. Arnkel's men became more nervous.

"Deliver your message," Thorleif said, and waved his brothers and Freystein back.

Hafildi raised his voice in a formal chant.

"Arnkel gothi does call on the sons of Thorbrand for the ancient and holy duty of burial of his father Thorolf. His spirit lies heavy on this valley. The gothi asks that you meet him tomorrow at Ulfarsfell, so that we may take his father together to his new howe, and settle his angry soul."

The brothers were silent, surprised, not understanding. Thorleif frowned, peering at Hafildi for a clue, but the man's face was blank and set.

Thorodd was first to speak. "The gothi does not need us," he called loudly. "If he wants to dig up Thorolf and bury him again, he can do it himself."

Thorbrand spoke sharply, calling his son's name. Then he turned to Hafildi. "A moment, bondi, while I speak with my sons." He drew them off, back to the house and they spoke in low voices outside the door.

"What is this?" Thorodd hissed. "What is that bastard up to now?"

"He calls on you to help with the burial of his father," Thorbrand said. "Why he asks cannot affect our decision. We must agree."

"Damn him. I will not," Thorodd said angrily, and Illugi growled his agreement. "It's just a trick to draw us out and slaughter us." Freystein looked back and forth between them, and then at Thorleif.

"It is an ancient duty, as Hafildi said," Thorfinn the Holy said, slightly pompous as always when speaking of the Otherworld. "We risk angering the spirits of the land, and Thorolf's shade, and even the elves by refusing. We must help."

The other brothers shook their heads and spoke loudly against this, hating the words. Since the slaying of the Fish Brothers, they had all found it easier to speak their minds openly in front of Thorbrand. Only Freystein glanced at his master, nervously, anticipating the man's anger at his sons' independence.

"I'll go," said Thorleif.

They stared at him, and Thorbrand nodded with satisfaction.

"Freystein will go with me, to watch my back. Father is right. We have to agree, or be seen to be disfavored by the Gods. That will not stand us well in the eyes of others, and men will not be sympathetic to our fight here."

He walked to Hafildi and gave him the message to return. They would meet the gothi the next day, at Ulfarsfell.

The next morning, Thorbrand and Thorfinn walked with Thorleif and Freystein to the barn, shuffling slowly along with his staff, his hand on Thorleif's shoulder for support. The touch surprised Thorleif and he smiled a little. It was rare for Thorbrand to show warmth.

"Do you see the undercurrents, Thorleif?" Thorbrand asked softly, as they saddled their horses. "Do you think this is a simple request for help in the burial?"

Thorleif shook his head. "No. I think the gothi may want to discuss peace. The feud has been harder on them than us, by what I have heard."

The old man smiled, and then patted Freystein's head affectionately, like a favored dog. "It is good you bring this one along," he said. Then he looked at Thorleif. "Yes, you have it. When the sap stops running in the trees, Snorri gothi will cut in the Crowness again. He must. There is too much wealth there to ignore. A month, no more, and he will be there."

Thorleif saw it then, clearly. "One enemy at a time for Arnkel, eh?" he said blackly. Thorbrand nodded.

"Listen to his words," the old man said. "This can only help us. Snorri gothi will not be happy that we make peace with Arnkel. But what is best for Snorri gothi, may not be what is best for us, as I have told you all along. You begin to see this, I think. We have fought his battle without profit or aid for two seasons. Let him take the burden for a while." Thorbrand leaned forward. "He is still our best hope, and strongest ally. Bargain hard. Extract whatever you can from Arnkel. He will give much to have peace with us. But do not abandon Snorri gothi. Swear no oaths of alliance."

The morning was clear and fine, spring sunshine cutting through the night's cold, and warming them in their lambskin, so that by the time they reached Ulfarsfell, they had shed their coats and capes, and hung them on the back of their saddles. Thorfinn had decided to accompany them, and that was proper. Thorleif suspected Arnkel would approve that his brother and his ways of the Otherworld came with them, to add a kind of sanctity to the burial that had been lacking before.

Arnkel waited at the farm. He had ten men with him, and this made Thorleif hesitate. Two of the men were needed to drive the pair of oxen and sledge, because the oxen were fractious and full

of stubborn violence that morning, but it still seemed to Thorleif
to be too many men.

They rode slowly abreast to the wall of the home field and
stopped.

"We have come as bidden, Arnkel, for the burial of your father,"
Thorleif said formally.

Arnkel gothi nodded. Then he waved an arm at his men and
spun his horse about and they set out. Thorleif noticed how Thorgils traveled near the back of the party, where always he had ridden beside the gothi, in the place of honor, and he spoke with no
one. It was rumored that he and Auln had come together. Thorleif
thought the match a good one. He had considered Auln himself,
but she was too fierce a woman for his taste. But one day soon, he
knew, he would have to look for a wife, as Thorodd and Thorfinn
had done. He felt the urge for it in his deepest blood.

He rode up beside Thorgils, and the man nodded a greeting.

"Auln will be happy that Thorolf is moved," Thorleif said quietly. "I heard about his visit."

Thorgils shrugged. "I don't think he liked my arrow. He never
came back after that."

Thorleif rode along a while, considering that news.

Were the dead so much like the living, he wondered? Did they
still feel pain and fear? It was a terrifying thought.

Nothing was said on the ride up the ridge to Hvammr farm, but
it was plain from the first moments that it would be a troubled journey. The oxen fought the lead constantly. The sledge jerked about
from their resistance, once running up on a boulder, and it took all
the men to push it off and get it moving again. Two men on horses
backed the sled on the way down to Hvammr, the ropes taut with
tension. Thorleif rode at the rear of the group, with Freystein and
Thorfinn beside him, and none of the Bolstathr men spoke to them,
but Thorleif became less worried about treachery as the day wore
on. They had brought spears and shields and Freystein had put his
stout chunk of oak through his belt. Four of the gothi's men had

spears but they seemed more of an honor guard, walking at the front of the procession, while the rest trudged along glumly with empty hands or sacks of food and coils of rope. The gothi carried only his sword and rode behind the sledge, head bowed in thought.

They rested the oxen at Hvammr. One had begun to roll its eyes and the men rumbled their discontent at the omen, remembering what had happened to the last pair of oxen to pull Thorolf.

The ride to Thorswater dale tired the beasts quickly. They were both sick. Greenish dung shot out of them liquidly, and their breath came in gasps. The gothi called for several rest stops, but they were short. The animals no longer fought the lead. They were too exhausted for that and lowed with misery each time the drivers goaded them into motion again.

Finally they came to Thorswater dale. The group had fallen into a narrow column, forced there by the boulders and the shards of razor rock underneath, everywhere but the path. Freystein pointed at Cunning-Gill's house.

"Looks deserted," he said. The doors of the small barn were open, and there were no animals about. The melting snow lying about was untracked, even up to the door of the house.

A last drive took them to the howe. The gothi's men gripped their spears tightly and squinted fearfully into the crack within the earth. The dark holes of the caves lined the walls like patches of diseased flesh. A mist descended from the grey sky, the wind swirling it about in angry tendrils within the confined space of the crevice.

Arnkel had the sledge moved bodily by the men, and then turned the oxen team around, with their rumps toward the opening. Thorleif, Thorfinn and Freystein helped, as the sledge was very heavy. Then they worked the team backwards, the men heaving the sledge between the narrow walls of rock, until the oxen would not step down onto the sharp rocks.

Arnkel led them into the crevice and around the bend to the largest of the caves. They walked slowly. Snow had been pushed and gathered by the wind and was knee deep along the floor of the rocky chasm, melted to hard grains of ice.

One of Arnkel's Thingmen pointed down fearfully.

There were footprints, several trails leading in and out of crevice, all the same large size, the edges worn and ragged with the melt.

"Gothi . . ." Hafildi began, voice tight.

"Get your spears," Arnkel said harshly. He drew his sword.

The Thingmen scrambled back to the crevice opening to fetch their weapons. Thorleif and his men had carried their shields and spears in one hand as they heaved the sledge, unwilling to trust the Bolstathr men. Freystein breathed quickly, the club in his hand, terrified.

They came to the cave.

The crude rock wall had been broken down from the inside, piled rocks pushed out and tumbled, the bushes lying in dried heaps. Dead leaves littered the ground and snow.

Terror filled the men. Those with spears gripped them in two hands, crouched low as if expecting attack from the dark of the cave at any moment. Freystein pressed himself against Thorleif as a frightened dog would until Thorleif patted his shoulder and rubbed the slave's great head reassuringly, forcing a smile. The gothi had Hafildi bring up three torches from the sledge, and these were lit with flint and steel. He handed one of them to Thorleif, and the other to Hafildi, who took it reluctantly. The last he kept, waving a hand at the rest of them to follow as he stepped over the remnants of the stone wall and entered the cave mouth. Thorleif, Thorfinn and Freystein went after him, and then Hafildi. Three of the Thingmen would not come, shaking their heads with angry fear, but the others did, jeering at the three cowards, although they did it in whispers. Once in the cave they hurried after the light of the torches, not wanting to be in the dark.

The place stank of rotted meat.

Arnkel walked to the body, sword in hand and torch high. Thorleif stood beside him and the men crowded around, staring.

The face was desiccated, the open eyes milky with rot and sunken in. Around the neck were the shreds of the sack Arnkel had tied there, held in place by a cord.

"Odin's Blood, it's like he was put here a month ago," Hafildi whispered fearfully, eyes wide. "I thought he'd be bones!"

"He's only lain here half a year, idiot," Gizur said in his ear. "And much of that winter." Thorleif moved his torch a little and the feet became clear.

Snow crusted the corpse's boots.

The light of the torch glinted from something on the side of the body by the wall, under the arm and thigh. Arnkel sheathed his sword, and then reached out to roll Thorolf's hip back a bit to see the thing.

It was an axe, the head covered in a dark crust of blood.

The men backed away, hissing in fear, all except Arnkel and Thorleif. The gothi looked at Thorleif. "You are not afraid?" he asked.

"The footprints in the snow are old," Thorleif said. "So is the blood on that axe." He touched the leather jerkin. "I was told that Thorolf walked in armor."

"This is how I lay him here," Arnkel said.

Thorfinn spoke then, a quick request, and Arnkel nodded. From his pocket, Thorfinn brought out a curved needle and thread. He sewed Thorolf's eyes shut, shutting the milky orbs inside, then closed the mouth with thread and the nostrils, and then pulled over the ears and stitched them down flat. He grimaced in disgust at the putrid smell the work stirred up. Then he had Thorleif bind the feet together tightly and had Arnkel tie the hands on top of the body.

The gothi ordered his men to lay spears on the ground, close together, four of them spaced along the length of a man. They dragged Thorolf's body down onto the shafts, the body rolling obscenely as it fell, the guts audibly sloshing within the jerkin. Moving the body pitched the smell higher, and this made one of the men retch, gagging. Thorfinn pushed the body back into place with a great heave, and then four men took each side, and lifted. The spear under the hips cracked and sagged, but held and they shuffled out toward the cave mouth, breathing through their teeth with the effort.

"Thor's Blood, he's gotten heavier," Gizur grunted.

The ridge of tumbled stone at the cave mouth almost broke them, but they got over it, staggering, and made it to the sledge and lowered the body onto it heavily. Arnkel waved the men off when they went to pull out their weapons from under the body. "Leave them. We will have to lift him off it later."

Then began the long trip back.

Thorleif cantered up to ride beside the gothi as he followed the slowly moving sledge. "Where will you bury him?"

"Vadils Head," said Arnkel, and the men around looked up in dismay, knowing the long brutal climb ahead of them. Oxen would not be able to make most of the mountain journey. He glared around at them. "Would you rather I put him in Bolstathr, out in the home field? We need a place from which he will not find his way back."

They turned away.

By the time they reached Hvammr, the oxen were dying. It was clear. Only their driver, an experienced man, kept them moving, coaxing and whipping them in turn. He decided not to rest at the farm, to get the last out of the animals before they collapsed, but the gothi waved at him to stop.

He sent two of the slaves into the barn and they came out carrying squares of turf, thick and fresh. It was not building turf, from the marsh, but ordinary sod.

"I took those from the pasture, there," Arnkel announced. "A man must be buried in his own soil to truly rest."

The others nodded, and saw the sense in that, although it made the sledge heavier. There was a large pile of it, stacked beside the body, enough to cover Thorolf's corpse.

They made it to the top of the ridge at the gate that led through the stone wall between Ulfar's side of the meadow and Thorolf's. Then the oxen began to buck and circle, ignoring the whip, froth and green scum coating mouth and rear. Arnkel drew his sword and cut through the leads and harness moments before the beasts went mad and charged down the slope.

The men stood there, watching the oxen run past Bolstathr and then disappear down the shore to the cliffs where Cunning-Gill had died.

"They seemed healthy enough this morning," Hafildi said grimly.

"Shall I get the other two from the barn, gothi?" Gizur asked. "I'll only be a little while. Bolstathr is right there."

Arnkel shook his head as he sheathed the sword. "I will lose no more wealth to Thorolf's anger. We will haul him on the sledge ourselves."

The men looked at each other.

"Pile your weapons and coats here, and spit on your hands," the gothi said. He unbuckled his belt, and lay the sword down. "Now, pick up the leads, six of you, and we will haul, and take shifts doing it."

So they pulled the sledge down the slope of the meadow hill, and out to the shore.

It became a story told many times in later years, and any of the men who pulled that sledge would claim that Thorolf's spirit worked against them that day. His weight seemed to grow as they pulled, and stones would appear under their feet. Flat stretches of grass would suddenly be filled with rock. A wind came up. It blew hard in their faces, and the men grumbled that the Gods themselves woke that day to fight on Thorolf's behalf.

They fought with the sledge far past noon and finally came to Ulfarsfell, exhausted, just outside the home field, a long bow shot from the water of the fjord. The men stumbled away, some to sit on the wall, others down on one knee, gasping for air.

Arnkel looked up to the northeast, where Vadils Head dominated the sky.

Gizur and Hafildi both jumped to their feet when they saw his eyes. "Up that slope, gothi? Carrying Thorolf?" Hafildi's voice was filled with outrage and dismay.

"If we put him in a boat, and took him across the fjord to below the cliff, it would save us distance," Arnkel said, ignoring them. "But that path is steep. Otherwise, we go back behind Swan firth to the ford, and then up the mountain trail to the cliff." The gothi turned to Thorleif. "We could boat him to the ford from the headland there, if we have permission to cross your land."

Thorleif nodded. "Of course."

Arnkel nodded. He seemed to consider his words, rubbing his beard with a hand.

"I thank you for your help today, Thorleif," he said quietly. "It is what neighbors should do for each other." He paused, and his voice became hard, even wild, as if he could not stop his next words. "Rather than waylay them as they go about their day."

"Or steal their inheritance with guile," Thorleif said evenly. "And murder."

Arnkel gothi's eyes took on a manic gleam, but Thorleif would not step back. Instead of denial, or loud words, the gothi stepped forward a little more.

"It is said that your brother Illugi has an interest in my daughter, Halla," he said slowly.

Thorleif stared at the man, willing the surprise not to show on his face, trying for nonchalance. "He has seventeen years, and she is the closest girl in the fjord. What would you expect?"

"I think there is more than spring fever there," said the gothi. "Let it sit with you for a while. But now with spring arrived, and the Thorsnes Thing approaching, maybe it is time we put aside our quarrel and let our people live their lives."

He extended his hand to Thorleif, and the men watching held their breath, praying to the Gods.

Thorleif looked into the gothi's face, hating that he looked up into it, wondering at how a human being could come to be so large. He felt the immense weight of the gothi's will, the cold blue eyes measuring him.

The refusal welled up in him like a surge of rage, burning and potent. He wanted to prove to these men and to himself that he was no coward, but a man, a warrior, caring nothing for consequences. He wanted to deny the man's will, and so prove himself as good as the gothi.

The sudden insight staggered him.

He feared Arnkel.

All his defiance was a denial of that.

Odin's Blood, it's just as I was with him as a boy, he thought, aghast. Puffed out and pretending no fear, even to himself, when his very soul trembled at Arnkel's approach. He remembered those hard fists on his head, as boyhood tussle turned into a test of strength.

He saw himself suddenly through the gothi's eyes, contemptible, easily manipulated, hoping for a final insult to honor that could be avenged, then and there, with slaughter—the gothi content to break Thorleif completely with fear by the ultimatum of his outstretched hand hanging in the air, and so achieve a meek surrender.

It was very silent.

"Neighbors may share their wealth," Thorleif said, his throat dry. "Ulfar's hay is thick and tall, and you have need of only some of it."

The gothi stood with his arm still out, looking at him, still measuring. Then he said, "Then my neighbor Thorleif shall have half the hay from Ulfar's meadow."

"Three of four parts would be more fitting," Thorleif countered. The men looked from him to the gothi and back again. Three of four parts was more than just generosity. It was a payment, and they all knew it. Thorfinn put his hand on his brother's shoulder, cautioning, but Thorleif ignored it, meeting Arnkel's gaze, the vast hand hanging between them.

Arnkel frowned, staring at him.

He nodded slowly. "Alright, three of four parts."

Thorleif smiled broadly and stepped forward. He clasped the gothi's forearm warmly.

"Peace I also desire," he said loudly, so that all could hear. "Let there be no more violence between us." He shook the arm with great strength, showing his grin to the others, and the gothi.

The men around them exploded into a great cheer, and threw their woolen hats into the air. The two men were surrounded then, and their backs pounded again and again, while they looked at each other, each knowing that peace was only a word.

Nothing was settled. Thorleif knew that, as did the gothi. A little hay would not make up for land.

When the tumult had died down, Arnkel pointed to Thorolf lying under the afternoon sun. "We must attend to my father, before nightfall wakens him." The men became afraid at these words, and quieted. "Can we use your fine new boat to carry Thorolf to the ford?"

Thorleif nodded, but then held up his hand. "Our goal is to keep Thorolf from wandering. We do not need to go to Vadils Head to do that."

He pointed to the long point of land that ran out from the shore of Ulfar's farm.

"We can bury him there, on the farthest tip, layer stones upon him, and then close the gap of the spit with a wall. The dead do not walk on water, isn't that true, Thorfinn?"

His brother nodded somberly. "Ghosts fear water and will not pass it, especially sea."

"He broke down a wall once already, to get out of his howe," Hafildi said, full of gloom.

Thorleif spat in contempt. "That was no wall. That was a pile of stones that any sheep could knock over. Now, there. That is a wall."

He pointed again, but now to Ulfar's home field wall, each stone large, fitted and shaped. "I helped build that, and know it is solid. We will take the stones from it, and build it there, across the gap, and twice as tall as it is now, and twice as thick. No ghost will pass that."

Arnkel agreed, saying that it was a good plan.

He called for another sledge and for more oxen, and these were used to haul the stones and turf from Ulfar's wall, load after load that the men heaved to with a will, seeing how the sun was getting lower in the sky. Arnkel called for more men from Bolstathr and the surrounding farms, and soon there were twenty men, under the guidance of Thorleif, who was best with stone, guiding each piece into place. Thorolf's body was carried to the highest point of the peninsula, a mound of earth far above the tide mark, and was covered with the turf, and then the largest blocks, including a huge chunk of basalt from Bolstathr called for especially by the gothi and dragged down by the sledge.

"This one I called 'Einar's Stone' long ago, when I dug it up near the very spot he died," the gothi said to them, before he lowered the rock in place over Thorolf with his own arms, his face red and swollen with the vast effort of it. The men shouted excitedly at his strength. It had taken three of them to just slide it from the sledge, the rock as long as a man's leg and almost that wide.

"Now my grandfather's shade will hold him down, and that seems proper," he said breathlessly afterwards, resting on one knee.

The wall went up quickly.

The black, bubble-filled stones for it had already been shaped long ago with much effort, and no time was needed for that except for a chip here and there with the hammer. Most of Ulfar's wall was used, a quarter mile of fitted stone, knee high, with the same of turf on top of that. It was a short stretch across the neck of land. At the end, the wall was eight feet high, three feet thick at the top, flared at the base to four, and steady as bedrock. They finished the last bit, extending into the water of low tide, as the final gleams of light left the sky and the stars began to become clear. Four of the men volunteered, shivering to their knees in the cold water of the fjord as they bent to the work, but Arnkel called for skins of ale to be given them and soon other men were calling out to do the work, too. Thorleif walked along the top, testing it, but found no loose stones or instabilities.

"Like a Norman's castle," he said, jumping down.

Thorgils stood near the remnants of Ulfar's wall. It would be his work to build another, and an immense task it would be. The goats and sheep, and the milk animals would all need to be tethered or watched until it was made. He cast one glance at them over his shoulder and then headed back to the dark house.

As he left, Arnkel gothi rode up beside him, and looked down with his cold eyes.

"Now there will be no need for your axe at Hvammr, Thingman. I expect you will stay at Ulfarsfell, as I have bid you." The words were flat, spoken without any hint of negotiation.

Thorgils stared at the ground. "Most nights, I will." He looked up at Arnkel and his eyes were slightly mad, as if he had abandoned caution or reason, or both. Arnkel frowned, his immense confidence shaken a little. "But whenever the urge comes upon me, I will spend my night there at Hvammr, my axe and bow beside me for comfort. Who knows what nights those might be? Perhaps tonight." Some of the Thingmen were near and they listened open mouthed, wondering at the tension between the two men.

Thorgils went into Ulfar's house, and shut the door.

Arnkel turned away, composed his face and rode over to Thorleif, a labored smile on his face.

The gothi waved his hand up to Bolstathr, through the bustle of the men gathering their horses to leave. "It would honor me to have you come to my Hall and share ale and meat, Thorleif, both you and your brother and your thrall."

Thorleif put a foot in his stirrup and mounted. He looked down at the man on the ground. "Our duty is done here, Arnkel gothi. We ride back to Swan firth. I bid you good night."

He put his heels into the horse and it trotted away, whinnying in protest at the force of the kicks. Freystein and Thorfinn mounted hastily, seeing the frown on the gothi's face. They followed Thorleif, cantering to close the distance.

They found him grinning, his teeth white in the dark, the night wind blowing his long hair back.

XI
SUMMER

THE SLAYING OF HAWK

THORLEIF, FREYSTEIN AND ILLUGI rode the ocean rollers, steering for the mouth of Swan's fjord. In the trough of the wave they could see only the very tip of Vadils Head, and this Thorleif steered by, keeping it on his port quarter.

Sam had warned them of the weather, but the blue sky of the fjord had seemed friendly enough when they had rowed out in the early morning, and the wind had only come up in force a short time ago.

They were learning the ways of the sea.

Hrafn had been right about the boat. It locked onto the surface of the water, almost impossible to tip. Despite the anger in the sea and the wind, Thorleif laughed for the joy of riding the waves.

Still, there was need to be careful. Water pooped over the stern and threatened to swamp them. Their boots and pants were soaked, and the other two men bailed constantly. Errant gusts tugged the goose wings, small triangles of sail pulled down from the corners of the bundled sail. The wings were enough to give them steerage way, and luckily the wind blew straight toward the land. Thorleif was still a novice steersman. With the wind blowing off the beam or from the bow quarters he struggled to keep any heading. Tacking was something beyond him. Sam had shaken his head as they set off from Helgafell, and wiped his hands in the air, as if to say that he had warned them enough. They had laughed at him.

Eight large cod lay on the bottom, the slime already drying on their cold bodies. He would give some of those to Snorri gothi, and keep the rest for Swan firth, split open and dried. It brought him great satisfaction to use the cod lines and hooks of the dead Fish Brothers. Their boat had held a huge assortment of lines and nets.

The waves became worse as they neared the shore. Thorleif steered into the mouth of the fjord, well away from black rocks, riding the massive current of wind and water, and when deep inside brought the boat around the headland and ran for the sheltered beach near Helgafell. He missed it by a quarter mile, pushed south by the wind, and so that meant heavy rowing for Freystein and Illugi to come back north, with even the fragments of wind that escaped the headland enough to hold them back.

They hauled the boat up onto the sand through a mass of swans sheltered near the shore, and then stood, easing their aching backs.

"That's a long time to sit," Illugi said. "My arse is like rock."

"It will match your head, then," Thorleif said, and they threw stones at each other all the way up to the farmstead. As they rounded over the heights behind the shore, Illugi stopped, hand cocked to throw. He looked over Thorleif's shoulder.

"Snorri gothi has guests," he said.

Many horses filled the home field. One of them was tacked with silver, glinting in the sun.

They walked up to the great Hall. The gothi's men waved at them, and a man called Ketil came forward to greet them. He was a distant cousin of Hawk's, angular of face, tall and rangy, come the last season from the other side of the island after marrying Hawk's niece. It was odd that a man would move to the site of his new wife's home, instead of her moving to where he lived. He drew some ribbing for it, but it was not unknown, and his solid character seemed to deflect banter. For a young man of barely twenty years, he was very serious. A good worker, also, Hawk said, reliable and independent, and a welcome addition to the gothi's household. Hawk's niece was already pregnant.

"Welcome Thorleif, Illugi, Freystein," Ketil said. He leaned on his manure shovel, chewing the ends of his wispy mustache thoughtfully.

"Who visits the gothi?" Thorleif asked.

"Gudmund gothi. It seems he feels that Snorri gothi is in his debt, for his support at the Thorsnes Thing." He said this sourly. There was a roar from inside the Hall, and they turned to look.

Thorleif frowned. "Support for what? Snorri gothi had no dispute at the Thing, at least none that involved Gudmund."

"That is the answer Gudmund hears now, I think. Shall we go in? I think the gothi may need a few more men in there to keep matters calm."

The noise and warmth in the Hall washed over them, and for a few moments the bright sunlight outside blinded them to the drama inside. As their eyes adjusted, they saw Gudmund gothi standing in front of Snorri's High Seat, pointing an accusing finger.

"There will be reckoning for this, Snorri!" Gudmund said.

"Reckoning for what?" Snorri said softly, bending forward slightly from his seat. "What will the judges say? That I have reneged on my payment to you for doing nothing?"

"I stood ready. You knew that. Two hundred fair birch, each tree thicker than a hand length at least. That was the price for standing at your back."

Snorri stood. "And I will pay it gladly when you support me again, Gudmund. But I was not challenged by Arnkel at this year's Thing, much as that surprised me, and so I did not need your support, or your strength. You committed nothing."

Thorleif had been at the Thing, too, waiting with his brothers for the challenge to be offered by Arnkel for the Crowness wood. But the gothi had only sat on his bench, calmly advocating in several minor claims of his Thingmen, and showing no ill will to

Snorri at all. There had been upwards of five hundred men at the assembly and each had been waiting with much expectation for the feud between the two chieftains to explode.

Nothing.

When the last day had passed, and the men began to trickle home, there was much talk about it, and some men suggested that Arnkel had realized that he could never win against Snorri gothi's guile and had given up the wood, content with what he had taken from the sons of Thorbrand.

Now Gudmund had come, demanding his price. His eight Thingmen stood behind him, a couple of them nervous but most grim faced and holding their spears tightly. Hawk stood below Snorri gothi. He wore his new sword, and held an axe and shield, and other of Snorri gothi's Thingmen and slaves lined the walls of the Hall, a dozen or more, all armed, all standing tensely. Oreakja hovered near Hawk, legs planted wide and aggressively, staring at Gudmund from behind his shield. Kjartan carried a spear, also. He shuffled from one foot to another behind Oreakja, eyes wide.

Gudmund gothi glanced over as they walked into the main Hall. "Ah. Here we have other men you have betrayed. Maybe they will speak on my behalf." His tone was scathing, full of bitterness. "Sons of Thorbrand, what have you to say? Has your gothi shown his support for you? Has he paid his price in honor? What of your lands in Swan's fjord? Have you claimed them?"

"We will claim them yet," Thorleif said.

"Not with his help," Gudmund said, jerking his thumb contemptuously at Snorri gothi. He looked at the man for a minute and then spat in disgust and marched toward the door, hacking his arm at his men to follow.

"Gudmund gothi, wait," Snorri called out.

The man stopped at the door.

"It is not right that we dispute this in such a harsh manner and leave bad blood between us," Snorri said. "Let us settle this as men, with compromise and honor."

Gudmund turned. He spread his hands. "I would have put my honor and life at risk for you. That is worth a great deal."

"Intention can be noble, friend Gudmund, but if I were to pay every man for his good intentions, I would have no wealth left at all." That brought out genuine laughter, even from some of Gudmund's men, and the tension eased a fraction.

"One hundred and fifty trees," Gudmund said shortly.

Snorri shook his head. "Ten." He ignored Gudmund's look of outrage.

"One hundred at least."

They haggled for a long while, but Snorri gothi was stubborn and would not go above forty trees. Finally Gudmund threw up his hands in exasperated anger. He pointed his finger at Snorri gothi. "Those trees had better be at my farm in a week," he growled.

Then he stormed through the door, without even the handsal, and was gone.

Thorleif had watched silently, his eyes going between the two men.

Snorri gothi leaned back in his High Seat, and crossed his arms across his chest, while his men lay their spears against the wall and collapsed onto the benches, blowing out air from their pent up lungs. Hawk grinned at the gothi.

"I do love seeing that pissy old goat get shafted," Hawk said, banging his axe against his shield. "Pity he didn't want to fight."

"Save that savage spirit," Snorri gothi said soberly. "You will need it to go to the Crowness and cut the forty trees, starting tomorrow. It will take you more than a day to ready them all. Maybe two. Decide who you will take."

His eyes went to Thorleif and Illugi, and Freystein. Illugi was already with Oreakja and Kjartan, the three of them sparring and jostling like puppies.

"It would be a boon to me if the sons of Thorbrand would accompany Hawk to the Crowness tomorrow. There is much work to be done." Snorri waved his hand, welcoming them. "Stay the night, and we will cook those splendid cod that Freystein carries, and feast, and drink."

Thorleif did not answer, but he told Freystein to hand over the fish and he sat on a bench, accepting a horn of ale from one of the slaves.

They passed the afternoon talking with Snorri's Thingmen, and Thorleif shared a laugh with Sam about their adventure on the water.

"You were lucky," Sam said. "If the wind had come out of the east, you would be on your way to the homeland now. Did you have water on board?"

"No. A skin of ale, that's all."

Sam shook his head. "Well, a sailor needs luck, and you have it. But from now on always have a small cask with you, and some dried fish or some other food that keeps, well wrapped. Warm clothes, too, no matter how soft the weather seems. I've spent three days in an open boat, trapped by the wind. You could die of thirst, or cold, in sight of shore."

Sam peered at him. "It's got you, hasn't it?" he said. "The sea. It's in your eyes."

Thorleif nodded, appalled that he should be so easily read by a fisherman.

The idea had been growing in him that the Island need not be his whole life. He had traveled to Norway with Snorri gothi, long ago, but had always thought travel was a thing for youth. But even here in the Hall, he smelled the sea, and it worked on him.

Sam winked. "Wait till you spot the Sea People for the first time, playing in the shallows. You might change your mind."

"Sea People?"

"Elves," Sam whispered hoarsely, looking over his shoulder. "In the water. Strange things. Never stare at them, or act as if you've seen them, and never try to hook or spear one. They're not like the ones on land. The Sea People will follow you to your death. Your only defense is to sail out into the great ocean on a strong wind and outrace them, and hope they lose their courage in the deeps. There are some who think that is how the Island was found. Some poor fool running for his life into the big blue. They prefer to be near land, but they'll follow a ship anywhere, unless you can get away from them."

Freystein stood near, and his eyes were wide, as he heard Sam describe hull planks torn out of their rivets to let in the sea, and full grown men throttled in their sleep as they slept on the deck of a ship. He had enjoyed the boat until that moment.

The evening meal began, and Thorleif and the others helped to set up the trestles on their stands. It was short work, as more than twenty men had stayed for the meal, some Thingmen, and the farm hands and slaves coming in for their food after a long day's work. Large bowls of curd were carried out, and pitchers of whey. Then the fish were brought from the fire pit in the vast iron pot they had cooked in on the open hearth, carried by two struggling slaves. The steam rose like perfume when the lid was lifted.

"The last of Hrafn's onions, minced among the cod," Snorri gothi called out grandly. "To honor my guests."

The men lifted their eating knives in salute to the compliment. Oreakja walked down the trestles with a little wooden box of precious salt, sprinkling a pinch on each Thingman's food, while the slaves looked on longingly.

"Where is Hrafn, gothi?" Freystein asked.

"Down the coast, buying up as much seal oil and walrus hide as he can get, and selling his trinkets," said Snorri. "He should be back by summer's end."

The talk turned then to the killing of the bear, and Oreakja and Kjartan acted it out again for the men and the women and children. The story had evolved and now had lines for all the participants. Freystein was made to play Hrafn's part. Even the gothi spoke a line or two, smiling, while the onlookers clapped in appreciation.

"Thorleif, I have not heard your answer yet," the gothi said a little while later, when it grew quiet again and more food was brought out. Thorleif sat near the High Seat and the gothi had not spoken loudly, but in the silence of hunger his words carried. "Will you go to Crowness with Hawk tomorrow?"

All eyes turned to Thorleif, even as they chewed the smoked fish. An errant blast of wind pushed down the smoke hole, wrapping them in heat and sparks and smoke, but no one moved.

"I will ride to the forest with Hawk tomorrow," Thorleif said carefully. "Illugi and Freystein will take the boat back to our farmstead."

The gothi chewed contemplatively, staring at the roof beams, and then nodded. "That is well," he said, smiling. "Have some more of that cheese. It is old and strong."

Later that night as Thorleif crawled under borrowed blankets to sleep in the corner of the Hall, Illugi crept up to him and put his lips to his ear. "Thorleif, what about our truce with Arnkel? He will not like that we helped Snorri cut the wood." He held Thorleif's arm. "If there is to be a fight, I want to be there, too."

"I will do no fighting. Now sleep. I want you gone early in the morning, before Snorri begins his wheedling. Already he has asked for Freystein to join me." Thorleif put his forehead to Illugi's. "Do this for me, brother. Just leave in the morning with Freystein. Leave early."

Illugi nodded reluctantly and crawled back to his bench.

Thorleif lay a long time on his back, thinking, staring at the dim red glow of the hearth coals on the roof timbers. He fell asleep to the gentle snores that filled the Hall.

Illugi and Freystein were gone when he woke, although it was just grey dawn. He went out of the Hall, shivering, a blanket around his shoulders, and walked toward the edge of the rise that looked over the head of the fjord. The water was still as glass, not a breath of wind disturbing the light mist.

The boat was a point to the south, just fading away into the murk, with only the flicker of the oars to reveal it. Thorleif nodded, satisfied. He stood by a rock off the path and urinated a long time, and felt very good at the end of it, not cold at all. Elves jumped about in the corner of his eye, but he ignored them, knowing it was only the smell of his piss that roused them. Foul things, he thought. He would rather have rats than elves. At least you could catch rats and rid yourself of them for a while. It was said that they killed the elves in the Christian lands, hunting them down, and that did not seem such a bad idea. It was the women who would object here, fearing for their children in the cribs, throttled and dead.

He walked back to Helgafell and found Hawk with some slaves preparing the pack horses in the home field, a dozen of them, the strongest of the gothi's animals and the only ones that could take the weight of the sectioned logs.

"Three loads," said Hawk, darkly. "That's what it will take. I don't want to go there three times, but we'll have to do it. They have a man watching the woods, always. I've seen him myself once, pretending to be a shepherd, but it was that damned Hafildi. I might be able to get away with one trip without being caught. We might have to make a night visit, elves or not."

"Take some more men with you," Thorleif said. He felt uncomfortable, knowing what he must do to Hawk later.

"Hah. That's a good one," Hawk spat. "They all had other business. They were happy enough to gorge on the gothi's food last night. They have gone. No man wants to go to the Crowness, not after Thrain was found there looking like a bear-killed seal. So I must take slaves, because they have no choice."

"Thorolf is properly buried now," Thorleif said. "I know that for a fact."

Hawk glared at him.

"It's not some fat shade that worries me, man."

"I know."

"Well, at least I have your arm with me," Hawk said, and slapped his shoulder.

Thorleif said nothing. He went in to the Hall and packed his gear and threw on his leathers. Then he took his shield and spear and walked to the barn. Hawk lent him a riding horse and saddle. There were four slaves to do the cutting, three of them terrified, and Hawk threatened one of them with his fist when he dallied tacking up. The last slave was called Cwern, a big, black-haired Celt with a scarred face who cursed the others for their cowardice. They were Britons like him, and he felt they should show themselves better, and said so in broken Norse. It was a show to impress Hawk, but the man still thumped the slave's shoulder and praised him.

"Get your rears mounted, and start acting like this one here," Hawk shouted to the others, pointing at Cwern. "The sooner this job is started, the sooner it is done. It is loyal thralls like him that soon earn their freedom!"

Hawk led, his spear butted on one thigh, and a shield hanging from his saddle, with Thorleif beside him. The slaves each led a string of three horses in file behind them. The gothi came out of the Hall to wave at them as they left, and Hawk nodded.

"Three trips," he muttered to Thorleif as they turned away. "Snorri owes me for this. I expect a whole skin of ale on the table before me at every meal for the next month."

"He has a different view about debts than most men," Thorleif said, and Hawk looked at him, but said nothing. He knew it was true.

They rode down the slope, staying to the broad trail until it split, one path heading west to the high country that circled south to surround the fjord, and a narrower one leading to the Crowness.

Hooves sounded behind them, and Hawk and Thorleif wheeled about sharply, lifting their spears. One of the slaves bolted, dropping the lead of the string of horses, and raced down the western path despite Hawk's shouted orders. But it was not an attack.

Oreakja and Kjartan came out from a draw behind some boulders, grinning.

Each carried a spear and a shield, and Oreakja wore a helmet of iron.

Hawk swore darkly, and then laughed, an aggravated bark.

"You pups go back to Helgafell," he shouted. "Do you hear me?"

The boys rode up to him, still grinning, and jostled Hawk on both sides.

"We ride with you, Hawk," said Oreakja. "We'll watch your back, and no one will bother us."

"Your father will bother you, lad. He'll tan your hide when he sees you've taken his helmet. He told you. No. Both of you!"

The boys would not move. Oreakja set his jaw stubbornly.

Hawk glared at him. Then he spoke, and his voice was not angry, only somber. "Lad, you and your friend both have guts, I'll grant you that, and I'm proud of you." Oreakja grinned, and nodded, happy to hear the words.

Hawk shook his head. "This is no game. Killing a bear seven men on one is one thing, and great sport. Fighting men is another." He looked both in the eyes. "You could both die today."

Kjartan swallowed, seeing for the first time the grey sky and the blackness in Hawk's face. He had been pulled along by Oreakja's bravado, but now even Snorri's son cooled, hearing those words. The slaves trembled and looked over their shoulders.

"Oreakja . . . " Kjartan began.

"Shut up." He looked at Hawk. "We're going," he said. The grin was gone.

Hawk nodded and grimaced. "Your father will have words for me tonight."

"Go back, Oreakja," Thorleif said, his heart aching. "Hawk is right. This is no place for you."

The boy ignored him.

The slave who had run came back, peeking over the rise, and Hawk angrily waved him over. He cuffed the man hard over his head, and sent him to hold the string of horses.

They came to the forest.

A clearing had been hollowed out, and wood lay stacked with spacers within the cleared space, a dozen sections of log twice the length of a man. Scraps of bark and shavings lay everywhere, unharvested.

"This is where Thrain was found," Hawk said to Thorleif. "We'll take those dozen there. That will save us a day."

The slaves led the horses in and tethered them on a picket line from stakes pounded in the soil. Then they took axes from the packs and went to the nearest trees. Two men worked each tree, chopping at opposite sides, one cut slightly higher than the other to guide the fall. Hawk stood with Oreakja and Kjartan, spear in hand. They peered through the dense tangle of branches and shrubs. The hilltops that surrounded the forest could just be seen. It was very quiet, the wind absent, and so the axe blows rang out loudly, echoing through the wood.

"We had no trouble last time we came here," Oreakja said to Hawk, seeing how that tough man watched the forest so warily.

"Different times, boy," Hawk said, without looking at him. He kept his eyes on the surrounding forest and especially toward the hill. A long section led straight southwest, paralleling a stream, as if it were a road through the forest, and they could see clearly to the top of the highest rise of land. "Thorolf was alive then. Shut up now, and just keep your eyes open."

He peered up at Thorleif, still mounted.

"Going to stay up there all day, man? If you are, ride up that stream a bit and keep watch."

"I'm leaving," Thorleif said.

The men looked at him, and the sound of the axes stopped as the slaves straightened to listen, alarmed.

"What?" said Hawk, frowning. "What's that?"

"I'm leaving. I told the gothi I would ride to the Crowness with you. So I have." Thorleif hated the look in Hawk's face and the vast disappointment in Oreakja and Kjartan, who stared at him with open mouths.

Hawk still stared at him. "Get off that horse," he said, grimly. "That's the gothi's property." Thorleif dismounted and slapped the horse away.

Hawk put his spear point to Thorleif's chest. The sharp point hurt, cutting through the cloth.

Thorleif stayed in place, although the blood soaked into his shirt from the cut. His shield hung down loosely on his arm. "I will not fight again for the gothi's rights until he fights for mine. Tell him that. You know he has abandoned my family, Hawk."

The spear point held for a long moment, and then dropped. "Get out of here," Hawk spat, and turned his back.

Thorleif walked away from the clearing along the open section that led to the hill, trying to still the black despair in him. The axes began their rhythm behind him again, slowly fading as he walked farther away. The water spoke to him as it ran by, mocking him, calling him coward under the gurgle of the current around the slick stones. He felt the elves lurking under the nearby bushes, pressing in, feeding on the stink of treachery in his soul, and he slashed absently at them as he walked, without raising his head.

"You know nothing," he hissed at them. "Leave me be!"

He came to the edge of the forest and began to mount the hill, picking his way up the loose scree of sand and stone, glad to be free of the oppressive air of the wood. It was a hard climb along the broken ground, but finally he reached the summit, just as the sun broke free of the clouds and mist and shone down on the land. A light wind touched him, cool and fresh. The way to the mountain paths that led eventually to Swan firth and safety were further to the west, hidden in shadow and distance. It would be a long walk home, and farther still because he would need to go high up into the hills to avoid the forest and Bolstathr, and pass through Thor-swater dale to home. He still did not trust Arnkel.

He was alone. That would be a mighty temptation to his enemy.

Turning, he could see down the stream gully to the tiny figures working the wood, and caught sight of a tree falling. Others lay on the ground, the men trimming branches and hacking the logs into sections.

He crinkled his nose, smelling something, and looked down at his feet.

It was the skin of a smoked fish, peeled away and left, still fresh and aromatic. Thorleif crouched and tipped it curiously with his finger, and found bits of curd underneath.

A man had been here, recently, and left the remnants of his lunch. Nearby, just over the rise and down the reverse slope, he spotted horse pellets.

A man watching. A man who had ridden off.

He looked to the south and his heart froze.

A rider came.

One man, small in the distance, riding the top of the cliffs near where Cunning-Gill had been slain.

The rider was far off, but he could see the upraised spear, and the round shape of the shield on the man's arm. Sunlight glinted off the metal armor and the helmet.

It was Arnkel gothi.

———

Gizur came hurtling in to the home field at Bolstathr, and jumped down from the horse. He ran into the Hall and found the gothi sitting with his mother and wife, and playing with his daughter.

"Gothi!" he cried out. "They are in the wood." He panted, tired from the hard ride. "I will gather the men."

"No." Arnkel stood, and picked up his daughter under her arms. He nuzzled her until she laughed. She gripped his beard tightly in her little fists.

"Are you going to wrestle the bad men again?" she said, eyes wide.

He nodded, and lowered her to the ground.

"Will you win?" she asked, peering up at him and he ruffled her hair until she batted his hand away, her lower lip thrust out defiantly.

"I always win, child," Arnkel said, looking down at her. "Go to your mother now."

He walked over to a chest by the wall and flipped it open.

"How many, Gizur?" he said over his shoulder.

"Four with weapons that I saw, gothi. Others cutting trees, maybe three or four slaves." Gizur paused, confused. "You don't want me to gather the men, gothi?"

"I'll go alone."

Gudrid immediately protested. Her sharp words set off a round of coughing, and she bent over double, and Gizur's protests came through the hacking. Hildi put her hand over her mouth.

Arnkel ignored them. From the chest he lifted a heavy oiled skin package and unwrapped it. With a shrug of his shoulders he put on the mail armor he had taken from Thorolf's house. Next came gloves, thick leather gauntlets flared past the wrists to the forearms. Then greaves of bronze, strapped behind the calf. He turned to face them, the helmet hanging from his hand, and they were silent, staring at him.

Gudrid became silent. Then she turned and pulled the sword from the wall, and the belt that hung below it. She brought them over to Arnkel and cinched the belt around his waist, and handed him the blade.

He sheathed it.

The sunlight grew suddenly bright through the smoke hole. The gothi sensed it, and smiled at his mother. "You see? Odin himself urges me on." He touched her cheek with a finger of the gauntlet. "Rest now. You need to rest. Your face is white."

"I will rest when you are home." She smiled. "Einar smiles on you now, my son."

Hildi's hand touched his arm as he passed her on the way to the door, and he smiled down for a moment at her. She nodded, determined that her eyes would stay dry.

The men in the home field stared with open mouths and backed away in fear as Arnkel walked out the door of the Hall, the helmet on his head, and mounted Gizur's bay. The animal had recovered its wind and cooled, and now wanted the excitement of the run again. Gizur ran out with the gothi's shield and spear and handed them up.

He meant to say some word, a wish of luck, but Arnkel's power made such a thing seem worthless. He watched the gothi ride off.

———

The view was glorious from the top of the cliffs. Arnkel took all of it into himself, his vision unnaturally keen. He saw every bird wheeling above, every fragment of dust blown by as he raced to the forest, as if the visor of the helmet was made of the clearest glass. The horse's rhythm rocked his soul, bringing back the past. His heart was settling into its rage, and he remembered Thorolf's words to him long ago as they rested against the walls of Hvammr Hall, their blades drooping from their hands, the sweat covering them.

"After battle, nothing is the same," Lamefoot had said, staring into space, and his words rang in Arnkel's ears as if the man spoke them from the very air that rushed by his face. "The ale is not as sweet, the sky not as bright, and your blood never as warm as the first time you fight to the death. After that, you crave it, always wanting it, knowing it will destroy you one day, and not caring."

You're right, bastard, about one thing in your wretched life, he thought.

He wanted that taste again.

Far across the fjord he saw the mass of Vadils Head where Onund was cairned, his cleft skull now bare under its covering of stones, rotted to nothing, and he lifted his spear in salute to the man's spirit, and thanked him for his death.

I will kill them all, he thought wildly. Every one of them.

"Odin!" He screamed it to the sky, wanting the God to see his face and know it was him.

He saw a man waving his arms frantically on the hill top to the left, signaling to someone down in the forest. It was nothing to him. The helmet funneled his vision forward, and he searched only for the narrow trail that would take him to where Gizur had said they worked. He began to hear the axes.

The brush of the forest closed around him, whipping by in a green and yellow blur.

His horse exploded through the undergrowth into the clearing. He threw his leg over the saddle, pulled his shield off the hook, and turned to face the men.

They stared at him, shocked. Three of them clustered near the center of the clearing, the ones with spears and shields, and he strode toward them. On the edge of his vision men dropped their axes and ran into the woods, while the armed men shouted at them to return

He saw Hawk.

Snorri's headman stepped forward, still barking at the others over his shoulder, his eyes full of wide rage and fear, spear lifted high, shield tight to his body. Arnkel put his own shield up, and reared back his spear. Just before they struck, he heard Hawk's shout to the other two armed men.

"Run!"

They came together with a crash, each man thrusting down hard at the other, the heads of the spears smashing off the boss of the shields. Hawk swung his shield around in a wide cut with the edge, but missed, and Arnkel thrust again, catching the point in the wood. They backed away for an instant, circling slightly, and then rushed forward again like two raging bears. Arnkel's spear shattered, the tip catching the metal of Hawk's shield edge at the join with the wood, and shivering the shaft into two long jagged pieces. Hawk drove in just over Arnkel's shield and caught his shoulder, hard.

The mail stopped the point. Arnkel grunted with pain from the impact. He reached across and gripped the shaft of Hawk's spear. With one inhuman thrust of power, he wrenched it away, snapping it off behind the head.

He pitched the broken thing away behind him. They drew their swords, panting with effort, circling, crouched and wary. Neither man noticed the struggle near them, as Cwern and Kjartan held back Oreakja, gripping his arms and dragging him back toward the horses.

Arnkel saw Hawk's inexperience with the blade. He held the point too low, like a knife, with his arm too far extended. Arnkel moved in, and feinted with a horizontal cut to the man's shield side. Hawk raised the shield to take the blow, and Arnkel twitched the blade off a fraction as it flew through the air, under the shield and around. The extreme tip of his blade cut into Hawks sword hand. There was a ring of metal and a glare of sparks. The blade fell to the ground, and Hawk's thumb with it, the blood jetting out from the hideous wound. Hawk's hiss was almost a scream, and he staggered back, holding the shield up blindly.

Arnkel stepped forward and slashed under the lower lip of the Hawk's shield and into the man's thigh, cutting through the meat to the bone. Hawk fell back, tripping on a tangled mass of birch branches, madly scrambling backwards with the one good leg, clutching the other, blood trailing in the leaves and wood chips, and spurting up, brightly red. The gothi stepped forward slowly, as if savoring the moment. He kicked away Hawk's shield and stood over him. The man lay white-faced, shocked by the loss of blood and the pain. His mangled hand trembled, held close to his chest.

Hawk spat at Arnkel as the gothi hacked down. The spittle covered the gothi's face, to mingle with blood that sprayed out from Hawk's broken skull. He cut again, and again, and then stood to watch the shuddering of Hawk's body fade away.

He heard the shouting then, as if through a long tunnel in the Earth, curses, and angry weeping.

Oreakja had almost broken away from the two men at the sight of Hawk's death. Cwern barely held one arm, and Kjartan held desperately to his spear.

Arnkel strode toward them, covered in blood, the sword hanging from his hand. Cwern ran then, stumbling, and only Kjartan was left, teeth gritted in fear and effort, his heels dug into the soft loam of the forest floor as Oreakja twisted in his grip.

"Oreakja! He will kill you! Stop!" He was desperate, seeing the gothi come to slay them, but there was no sense left in his friend. At any moment he would break free. Every part of Kjartan said to do as Cwern had done and leave the boy to his fate.

"Gothi," he cried desperately. A fevered thought gripped him. "You have won! It will be blood feud forever if you slay him!" He warmed to it, imagining that he saw Arnkel slow slightly. "Snorri will never give up if you do this. There will be no settlement. He will fight you forever!" He screamed it with all his strength. "You have won!"

Oreakja broke free then, and ran at the gothi, spear high, teeth bared and his face filled with madness. But his shield was held wide, his chest open, throwing all caution away as he leapt forward. Kjartan grimaced, waiting for the sword to kill his friend. He stepped toward Arnkel, bringing up his spear, knowing he was also dead.

The gothi easily blocked the spear thrust, and then cut upwards, a quick backhanded slash. Oreakja fell back hard to the ground, stunned, his face cut open to the bone from the corner of his mouth to the temple, just missing the eye. For a long moment there was no blood, the force of the blow pinching the veins, and then it poured out redly, coating the boy's face and neck in a flood.

The gothi stood over him. "You have more courage than your father," he said. He toed the boy's boot. "I have given you a token to remind you of your hero, Hawk. The same gift I gave him once, long ago."

He looked up at Kjartan, and the boy forced himself to meet the man's gaze and not tremble. He saw death in the cold blue of those eyes glinting behind the metal of the visor.

"Tell Snorri I spared the boy's life, and your own. Tell him this wood is mine. Understand?"

"Yes, gothi."

"Take him home. Then, tomorrow, come to Bolstathr. There you will find your master's horses. I am not a thief, as he is, and will only use them to take the wood to my farm."

"Yes, gothi."

When Kjartan had pushed Oreakja up onto a horse and led him away, Arnkel mounted Gizur's horse, and rode out, brushing by a startled Kjartan. He cleared the edge of the forest and came to a rise of land and looked around, pulling hard on the reins to spin the horse about. Towards the Knolls he saw the three slaves who had run. They walked across the ragged green of the pasture land, and he spurred toward them, riding hard. The black haired one had vanished into the forest. Arnkel's horse was nearly blown. He could sense its weariness and cursed himself for not taking Hawk's horse back in the grove, but he had wanted nothing untainted from this day, no implications of wrong. He would catch these men on his own mount.

They caught sight of him near the Knolls. One was limping along, and the others left him behind, scrambling up to the heights where the footing would be treacherous.

Finally the mount turned on him, and would go no further, except at a walk, the froth pouring from its mouth. It was too clever to kill itself for him, even though he whipped it, and screamed in its ear.

He turned and headed back to the grove, swearing blackly. But soon he brightened, seeing the blood on his armor, and he partly drew his sword to look at the gore that coated the blade.

It had been a good day.

He smiled, remembering Kjartan's desperate words to him.

Of course Snorri would have settled, he thought. The man was a coward to the bone, and even his son's life would be counted in cows or sheep. Oreakja and Kjartan lived because Odin had cried out to him then, telling him to spare the life of two brave warriors not yet grown, and because fear would live longer among others from the sight of Oreakja's scarred face, than it would from one killing. Hawk's bloody death would start the fire. The boy's face would feed it for a very long time.

He put the pack horses in long string, the half dozen that had been already loaded with wood. The other six he whacked on the rump and sent back to wander their way to Helgafell.

They waited for him in the home field of his farm, a crowd of his Thingmen and his family. It was very silent as they watched him come, except for the whispers that grew when the blood that coated him became clear, and the long string of laden ponies, and the sight of Hawk's shield and sword hanging from his saddle, the rightful spoils of combat.

He dismounted and they watched him, their faces full of awe.

"Gothi," Hafildi and Gizur said together, and they bowed their heads with the others.

XII

WINTER

OF THORGILS' CONFESSION, AND THE
SCHEMING OF THORLEIF

HILDI BEGAN THE WORK at dawn, boiling the baby's diapers clean and pouring the reeking water over the mud of the cabbage patch, where it would grow the leaves thick and rich when summer came. Hvammr had better soil than Bolstathr, and she knew the garden would yield well. She tied the squares of cloth to the line, working quickly. It was not that it was cold, but there was much to do with Auln still abed with fever and the pains of childbirth. The bitter chill had left the wind, and although it was not spring, it smelled as if the long dark days were coming to their end. She worked happily, singing under her breath.

The joy of being out from under Gudrid's heel was exhilarating. She had borne the burden of it so long that she had forgotten how to be content. Vigdis worked the loom inside, also glad to be away from her grandmother, and Halla she had sent out to the pastures to herd sheep. It was man's work, but that mattered little. There, Hildi knew, she met with Illugi. She had seen them once, nose to nose, thinking they were hidden, happy together. It soothed Halla to see the boy, and that was good. She had been irritable lately, pestering Vigdis unmercifully, and so much like her grandmother that Hildi and Vigdis had giggled into their hands together when she turned her back. Little Unn and Rose played nearby, hiding behind the rock wall.

She drew water from the well for another pot of boiling, and staggered inside with it.

Auln's eyes were on her, startling her.

"You're awake," Hildi said. "How do you feel?"

Auln watched her silently from the bed, until Hildi became nervous and went to adjust the blankets.

"I dreamed, Hildi," she said quietly. Auln's eyes were bright, too bright, and they seemed to pierce Hildi to the core.

"You have winter sickness, Auln. Wait a day or two and it will pass." She pulled the blanket over Auln and felt her forehead with a hand. "You're a little cooler, I think, but the fever is there still."

"The baby?" Auln said.

"Sleeping with mine," Hildi said, smiling. "See?" She pointed to the crib across the room where Auln's son and her own little daughter lay hidden under warm blankets.

Another daughter. It had felt almost like revenge to see the look on Gudrid's face. If only Arnkel had not been so sad. But he had held the baby tenderly, and said her name would be Gudrid, and this had stilled the old woman's bitterness for a little while.

"Thank you, Hildi," Auln said softly, and held her hand. "You have been a good friend."

Hildi smiled again, uncertainly, and turned away as Auln fell again into sleep.

Outside, she went about the work of the day, milking the goats, and coaxing the children to help her feed them. Thorgils had brought two immense swans he had killed with a bow and they hung in the barn, waiting to be plucked and cleaned. One would go to Bolstathr, but the other she would roast at Hvammr. She had decided this boldly, enjoying the independence and the responsibility.

She had been a slave too long.

Gudrid had shrieked at her when she left Bolstathr, calling her many foul names, saying she abandoned her husband.

"Auln is about to bear child," Hildi had said patiently, her satchel in her hand, speaking to Arnkel, and not the bitter old hag. He sat on his High Seat glumly, forehead furrowed. "She needs my help. Halla does not know what to do." She had taken the hands of the little ones who watched the scene with wide, unhappy eyes and left. Behind her she had heard Arnkel trying to calm his mother.

Auln had birthed well, and the baby was healthy, a boy full of good flesh.

He had Auln's look, but his hair was black, and nothing like Thorgils' red shock and beard, although both said it was his child.

It was Ulfar's hair. And his face, too. The mouth had the same full softness, recognizable even through the tender baby fat.

She worked, trying to put her tasks in front of her thoughts. But no matter how fast she ripped the feathers and down from the swan, she could still hear the whispered words between Arnkel and his mother, plotting. She still could hear the words between Thorolf and Arnkel, long ago, when Arnkel still pretended he was son to Thorolf's father, scheming to take Ulfar's land.

That was life, she told herself, painful and without mercy, and Arnkel fought for his family.

But it was still hard to meet Auln's eyes when she called her friend.

Thorgils came at noon, as he always did, after the chores at Ulfarsfell had been done.

She wondered how long Arnkel would let that name stand for the farm.

Thorgils went about his work with a nod to Hildi.

She said nothing to Arnkel of his visits, knowing her husband did not want Thorgils at Hvammr. Hildi had asked him once why he did not approve of the two together, even though their attach-

ment was obvious to all. He had frowned and told her not to concern
herself with such matters, but she had asked before love, while he
still desired her and had his hands on her skin under the blankets,
and so she had coaxed the whisper from him that Auln was Ulfar's
kin, and that her claim was as wife, and that Thorgils would become
ambitious if married to her, and take up her case for the land.

It had surprised her, at first, that Arnkel should have any dis-
trust for Thorgils, who had been beside her husband for as long as
she had known him, and seemed like one with him. But then she
remembered that only he had spoken against taking Ulfar's land
by trickery, and Arnkel had scorned him, and called him weak in
front of Hafildi. She knew that Hafildi mocked Thorgils when he
was alone with Arnkel, calling him Christian, and monk.

That had not seemed right to Hildi.

Thorgils helped her clean the other swan after he had tended
to the barn, and they sat silently at either end of the bird, the barn
door wide open to let in the white light. Winter was an easier
time for work. When the cow's milk began to flow again with the
growing grass in spring, then there would come the long days of
milking and making skyr, and carrying it down from the pastures,
and there would be no time for leisurely chores.

"Gizur says he found seals on the far side of the fjord, sunning
themselves on the ice, where the floes break on the shore," Thorgils said. Outside they could hear the shrieks of laughter from the
children as they ran through the snow of the yard.

"It is rare to see them here," she said.

"Yes. We'll try to get one or two tomorrow. The ice is still thick
to walk on."

They worked in silence for a while, and then she said, "Thorgils,
the baby is Ulfar's." She could not meet his eyes. It was not news a
man would want to hear, and he knew what it would mean.

"I know."

He plucked another handful and stuffed the feathers into the
sack at their feet.

"There will be other children, Hildi," Thorgils said. "And they will all be kin under our roof, bearing my name."

Hildi looked at him a long time.

"That is good," she said finally. "But it is not your love for Auln or the child that I worry about, Thorgils. There are other things." She stared at him sadly. "Arnkel will not be pleased that Ulfar's son lives."

"I know that, too."

There was a whisper of leather on snow from the door of the barn. Hildi looked up in surprise and saw Auln, leaning against the barn gate, a blanket around her shoulders. Thorgils turned and saw her, and he stood to help her, and tried to get her to sit down on the stool he had been using.

She shrugged off his tender hands and remained standing.

It was very silent in the barn.

Hildi smiled awkwardly. "Rose is up to trouble. Hear that screaming? Enough to frighten the spirits." She went to the door to peer out into the yard, clutching her shawl around her shoulders.

Auln watched her with red-rimmed, angry eyes.

"I had a dream last night," she said. "A vision. You had blood on your hands, Thorgils."

He could not meet her eyes.

"That was Cunning-Gill's blood, Auln," he said.

He pulled his eyes up slowly and found her staring at him

"It did not feel that way," she said, her voice hollow and haunting. "Ulfar walked with me, and he seemed so sad. I asked him if he hated me, for what you and I had done in coming together, and he told me that he only wanted happiness for me. And even for you, Thorgils, though you betrayed him. He still sees you as his friend." Tears ran down her cheeks. She put her hands to her ears, her eyes closed in pain "The elves! They speak so loudly! They speak of treachery!"

They watched her, shivers of terror running through both of them.

Thorgils felt ill suddenly, as if a gnawing beast within him had decided to find its way out at last.

"Do not say such words, Auln," Hildi whispered fearfully. "The things will hear you and come."

"Why will Arnkel be displeased, Hildi?" Auln said suddenly, her fevered eyes opening. Hildi pretended not to hear, and called to the children. But Auln still stared at her and said again, "Why, Hildi? Why would he be concerned? Why should the gothi care whether my child is Ulfar's or Thorgils'?"

Thorgils turned her, so that she would face him, and held her face in his hands. She shook herself free and batted away his hands. "The child cannot be hidden forever a quarter mile from Bolstathr," he said. "One day the gothi will see the child, and that hair, and he will know that Ulfar has left a child. A male child."

His voice was grim, his mouth twisted. He took her arms tightly, though she fought him. Hildi looked on sadly.

"I don't care if the gothi knows he is Ulfar's," Auln said. She broke Thorgils' grip again and backed away. "Why should that matter? He owns the land, doesn't he? What threat is a little child?" The words were like a chanted litany, a profession of failing faith. She shook free of him again.

Auln turned to the sunlight, her hands on her face. Her mouth worked strangely, as if she tried to form words that would not come.

"Arnkel is not the man you might think him, Auln," Thorgils said hesitantly. "He is a chieftain. Such men yearn for power above all things. And power is land."

She stepped quickly toward him and slapped his face.

He stood silently while she glared at him, panting, and then at Hildi.

"No!" she shouted. "This is a stupid discussion! The gothi is honorable. He has always treated me with respect, and Ulfar, too." She looked at Hildi. "You would speak of Arnkel gothi like this, in front of his wife! He is no child killer like Thorbrand."

"Thorbrand?" said Thorgils, frowning.

"What do you say to that, Hildi Arnkel-wife?" she grated wildly, ignoring his question.

Hildi said nothing, the tears running down her cheeks.

"She would say that Lamefoot hated Ulfar, and Arnkel used that hatred for his own ends." Thorgils said the words without emotion, flatly. "She would say that Arnkel sent Cunning-Gill to kill Ulfar, and so I was sent to kill him and keep the secret forever."

She slapped him again, harder, and cut her hand on his teeth. She gripped the cut tightly and bled onto the ground, the drops coming quickly.

"I'm sorry, Auln," Thorgils said, his voice grey as ashes. Blood welled from his sliced lip. "It has been in my heart, and I have hated it. There is the truth." The nausea inside threatened to take him. He could barely stand.

She stood a long time, her face broken with shock, mouth trembling. Then she spun and ran out of the barn. The sickness slowed her, but her rage drove her ahead. She collapsed to the ground, face wrenched as if in agony, and then scrambled up to run again.

Thorgils and Hildi stood in the barn, watching her stagger toward the house and disappear inside. Thorgils touched a finger to the blood on his face. He looked at Hildi, and it was in his mind to tell her that it did not matter who had fathered the child. Any child of Auln's was doomed, as long as Arnkel gothi lived.

Auln came out of the Hall carrying the baby. Wrapped in wool and fur, it made a tight bundle, and she cradled it gently as she mounted Thorgils' still saddled horse. He went out of the barn, frowning.

"Auln, where . . ."

She said nothing. The horse bolted off at her insistent heels. He started after her, running along the path of trampled snow, easily keeping up to the mount. Auln was not a good rider, and nearly came off on the long slope up to the ridge line, but then slowed the horse, and disappeared over the ridge. Thorgils settled in behind her, thinking she went to Ulfarsfell, but instead she turned down the path to Bolstathr, to Arnkel gothi's Hall.

He frowned, alarmed.

"Auln," he called. "Do not do this."

She did not even turn her head.

The path became wider and smoother as they approached Bolstathr, and the horse pulled away a touch. She went into the home field, through the gate, and two slaves working the sheep in the pens looked up curiously. Thorgils struggled through along the icy path, but he knew he would not be in time to stop her going in the Hall.

She disappeared inside.

He forgot caution and footing, and hurtled ahead, falling heavily once, but came to the door finally and burst in.

It was the first time he had been to Bolstathr in nearly half a year.

Gizur stood there, and gawked at him as he passed by. If it had been Hafildi, the man may have tried to stop him and then Thorgils would have killed him. But Gizur had followed him too long. There was still respect. He backed away a little and nodded him in.

Auln stood in front of Arnkel gothi's High Seat.

She held a knife.

Gudrid stood near, staring with open mouth, and several Thingmen also, and Hafildi had put himself between Arnkel and Auln when the knife had come out. The gothi waved the man back. He leaned forward.

"Auln, what madness is this?" he said. "Why do you stand with a blade drawn in my Hall?"

"I have come to claim the debt you owe me, gothi," she cried out, pointing the knife at him. "The debt you acknowledged with your own words, when I helped you to claim Orlyg's land for Ulfar, and yourself."

"My son owes you no debt, woman . . . " Gudrid began, but Auln hacked the air with the knife in her direction to silence the woman, without taking her eyes off the gothi.

Arnkel waved his hand at the Thingmen, ordering them away, and they filed out reluctantly, not wanting to miss the drama, peering curiously at Thorgils as they passed him. Thorgils could hear them gathered at the door outside, ears up against the wood. From the roof came the rat-like rustle of men climbing the turf to listen at the smoke holes. Only Hafildi, Gudrid and Gizur remained.

Arnkel's eyes turned to Thorgils.

"How fairs my property at Ulfarsfell, Thorgils?" he called out. "All is well?"

"All is well, gothi," Thorgils answered uncertainly.

"Good. And my property at Hvammr, Auln? How fairs that?"

Auln stared at him, confused, her eyes mad with fever.

"All is well?" Arnkel insisted softly.

"I have not come to talk about your property," she spat out.

He stood suddenly, cutting her words off with a chop of his hand.

"Yes, my property, Auln. My land, known as such by all! What do I care for the meager claims of others to it?" He stepped down from the dais toward her and came close, ignoring the knife. He rubbed a lock of the baby's black hair between his calloused finger and thumb before Auln pulled the child back. "It is said that Irish monks lived here, on this spot, when my grandfather claimed this land, and he killed most of them and drove the rest into the hills to die of hunger. Should I sail to Ireland to slaughter all monks there, to quiet their claim?"

Auln said nothing. She wept silently, looking into the gothi's eyes for truth.

"I have no need to slay this child, Auln."

She thrust out the handle of the knife to him.

"Do it now," she said, weeping. "If ever you intend to take my son's life, do it now, and spare me the torment of waiting."

She shook the knife, holding it out.

"Do it now!" she screamed

The gothi turned, and walked back up to his seat. He sat and faced her, saying nothing, his great hands resting on the arms of his seat.

Thorgils came up behind her and took her shoulders. She turned and slashed at him. The tip cut his hand. No man said a word as they left the Hall. Auln led, and her mad eyes parted the men outside like a herd of sheep. Thorgils waited while she mounted her horse and then led it back over the ridge to Hvammr.

Rounding the ridge line, Auln nursed her baby in the saddle, speaking in a soft voice to the little thing.

To one side she saw a movement, and looked up.

It was Freystein, crouched behind a boulder, peering down at Bolstathr.

Thorgils saw him then, too. The man stood, grinning like a child caught while playing tag. He waved. A moment later he turned and ran away south along the ridge, towards Swan firth. They stared after him.

Thorgils looked up at her.

"They are watching," he said to her.

She said nothing to him.

In her heart she swore she never would again.

Arnkel gothi walked outside with his mother that evening, in the gloaming, while the others sat down to second meat. The men watched them go with wide eyes, knowing what they meant to do. He put her on his horse and they rode together along the narrow paths until they came to the Crowness, the edge of the forest, where the trees were still thin. On the pack pony, a little goat bleated mournfully at the indignity of its fate, its legs tied over the saddle.

"I see them," she whispered. "Always in the corner of my eye."

"It must be done," said Arnkel gently. He took the little fold of cloth from his pocket and gave it to her, and led her by an elbow. In it was the hair he had plucked from the child, the hair he had shown each of his Thingmen later, so that they could see it was black as coal, hair like Ulfar's.

They walked a short way into the wood, to the stone altar Einar had built for her many years before. Such a place could never be close to the home, as the altars to Odin and Thor that marked the hill near Bolstathr could be.

This was a place of the elves.

Gudrid shivered as they walked into the gloom. "You have men," she whispered. "Send one of them to do this thing that needs doing." The cold was in her lungs, and she coughed, bent with the force of it.

Arnkel frowned, and put his lips to her ear as they walked. "What will the tales people tell each other around the fire name me then, mother? When I am dust, and only my reputation lives on in song, what will they name me? Not the slayer of Hawk, the humbler of Snorri, the Great Chieftain Arnkel gothi. No, I would be Arnkel, the child killer. I may then have a reputation for ruthlessness, but it is not the way I wish to be remembered.

"But if the elves do it, then I am free of such accusations."

She nodded miserably.

They came to the stone cairn. Trees surrounded them, the bare branches splattering the little light left into darker patches of shadow. It was cold, the wind cutting them, flicking dead leaves past their feet.

She looked up at Arnkel. Her strong son stood impassively, unaware of the shadows moving about them. "They may not accept your sacrifice, Arnkel. They know you have no love for them, that your heart is given to Odin."

"That is not true."

"Yes, son. You are blind to the ways of the Otherworld. There is too much life in you, like all people of strength. The elves are ancient, part of the Earth, from before the time of the Gods. They are far more real than the Gods, who are just men and women, their lusts and desires magnified beyond reason."

Arnkel gothi frowned, and looked up at the sky cautiously. "Hush, woman!"

She looked at him, knowing her words were true. Yet they were here, in the wood. Arnkel gothi had made certain that all his household had seen them go to do this sacrifice.

He met her eyes. "What?"

"You must swear to me that you will give the elves their time to do this thing, if I ask them."

"Swear? Why?"

"Swear it!"

So he did, to Odin.

She frowned at him, knowing he still did not believe.

"Now, you must swear not to question the cost of it," she said.

"More oaths?" he sighed. "Take a cow, take two. Whatever it needs."

She stared at him.

"I swear it," he growled, and she nodded, satisfied.

It was quick, a few words to the things darting about just out of her sight, and the cloth left with the hair, and jetting blood from the neck of the goat, its little body left draped over the stone as they left.

They turned to leave, and Arnkel's head twisted slightly to look at something in the near dark. "I thought I saw . . . "

"Come!" Gudrid said, and pulled his arm. It was not healthy to see the elves clearly.

They rode back to Bolstathr.

Gudrid went to her bed, shivering, coughing painfully, and there was blood, as there had been for some months, little granules of black. She had hidden it from Arnkel and the others, but she knew that she could not live another winter.

Arnkel sat in his High Seat, and that night he drank many horns of ale, and slept heavily, trying to forget the shimmer of unnatural eyes peering from a crack in the ground.

Gudrid lay awake a long time, waiting for the rest of the household to fall asleep.

Goat's blood would not be enough.

She had not told her son that. It had been an easy thing to hide the slash to her hand in the deepening gloom of the forest. Mingled with the goat's blood was her own.

The elves would not take human life as a boon without human life given, she knew. Not many could pay that price. It was a foul and ancient bargain.

Her own blood had only been a promise, to hold them to the purpose a little while.

So when the snores filled the Hall, she crept out the door, stifling her cough in a great wad of wool. She took no shawl, or coat, and went barefoot in the snow. It would only prolong her agony to dress more. There would be too much a chance of waking someone by bringing a horse from the barn, so she walked to the forest.

The pain in her feet was overwhelming for a while. She wept from it, and it was soon gone into the cold. She stumbled along, clumsy, her limbs stiffening, until she lurched along as if someone had pulled her from the grave and set her to walking on some unholy purpose.

"Oh, Freya," she moaned to the Goddess, "Grant me your strength."

It was so cold. Spring had not yet reached the night time.

More than once she almost gave up, to return to the warmth of the Hall and her bed, to die there. The ice cut her feet, but she felt nothing through the numbness. By the time she reached the altar in the forest, life was already leaving her.

Gudrid lay herself across the cold stones, weeping in agony, onto the frozen red ice of the goat's blood.

"I do this for you, my son," she whispered.

At the end she felt Freya's strength come into her, a soothing warmth that filled her with light, and banished the chittering of the voices around her. Fear and loathing left her, and she rested.

———

Thorleif, Illugi and Thorodd fished the waters of the fjord, near the mouth of the river. From ice fishing, they knew where the bottom dropped away and it was there that the best salmon hung, just off the bottom, waiting for what the river spewed out to them. The wind was fresh and their stone anchor dragged slightly, but held enough that they could fish a long while before moving.

Ice piled on the windward shore, huge floes ground up against each other and mounded like fallen shingles. The wind had come up in the last week, and cleared the ice in one grand blow, breaking the lock of winter on the fjord, and exposing the inky black water. It had been a sight to see.

Soon they would need to put aside their pleasure and start to attend to the sheep and the cattle. It was spring, and the wool needed to be collected, and the cows taken to the upland meadows. The large vats and barrels in the milking sheds on the meadows would need to be checked for leaks, and repaired. Then would begin the endless cycle of milking and carrying the milk down from the highlands to make skyr, and butter and cheese. All the work would need to be started before they left for the Thorsnes Thing, and that was in less than a week.

Thorbrand scowled at them each time they pushed out the boat, and called them scoundrels for shirking work.

"Find a wife for yourself, too, at the Thing," he had said to Thorleif. "A good strong one who knows how to hold an udder. One with a good dowry, and a low bride price. She can make up for your laziness." He threw one last bitter insult. "Soon I will call you the new Fish Brothers."

Yes, spring was the time to find a wife. His father was right about that, at least. The warming weather set the blood to boiling. The cracking the of the ice always set him off and that year he was determined to find a woman.

Illugi was often near Hvammr, looking for Halla.

Freystein had spent much of the winter watching Bolstathr. He had seen interesting things.

The gothi had become bold after the slaying in the Crowness wood. He often rode out in just the company of a pair of slaves to attend to work at Orlygstead, or at Hvammr, although he rarely stayed more than an hour or two in one place. He was always armed, with sword and with spear and shield, as were the slaves. The man was tireless, working into the evenings, and he drove his men to do the same. And sometimes he was alone.

One day he caught Illugi at Hvammr, sitting with Halla. Freystein had run down the hill, his club in hand, thinking fearfully that he would have to save Illugi from a beating or worse, but the gothi had only sat with them and spoken, and so Freystein had ducked out of sight.

That night, around the hearth fire at Swan firth, they had demanded that Illugi tell them what had been said.

The boy grinned. "He asked my intentions."

"What did you say?"

Illugi laughed. "I said I wanted to wed her."

They had stared at him, open mouthed.

"Well, I couldn't say we'd been kissing in the barn and I had my hand in her dress, could I? He would have killed me!" He grinned again. "What a waste that would have been. It took me all winter just to get that much, with Hildi chasing me off all the time."

The men had roared and even Thorbrand had smiled, his wife's arm around his shoulder. The old man stayed up far into the night, thinking.

"It is time for a betrothal," he announced the next morning, to all their surprise, and Illugi had leapt on the man in joy, and almost wrenched his back.

They beached the boat when they saw Thorbrand come out of the Hall, wearing his best shirt and boots, and his fine cloak of harbor vathmal, woven with many colors. Freystein followed, dressed well also, with his hair braided. Thorbrand waved irritably at Thorleif and Illugi. "Get yourself dressed, and washed. You stink of fish."

They dove into the icy water and jumped out again. It took only a few moments to change into their best cloth and leathers. Thorleif put on his one good robe, red vathmal hemmed with gold thread, fastened at the shoulder by a silver clasp.

He rode beside Thorbrand. Illugi followed far behind with Freystein. The two laughed and sparred with their spears from the saddle, circling their horses about each other. A bright spring sun shone down out of the blue sky.

Thorbrand's face became hard as stone as they rode slowly across Ulfarsfell, close by Thorolf's wall. He looked over his shoulder at Illugi, frowning at the boy's antics.

"He's just happy, father," Thorleif said. "He truly loves the girl, I think."

"Love will not make us more wealthy," the old man said blackly. "A generous dowry might. He should be more serious. It will be hard to bargain a good settlement if he acts as if the marriage already is set."

Thorleif nodded, but said nothing. He knew Thorbrand would see little value simply in his son's contentment.

"Arnkel will not give away anything of true worth to marry his daughter," Thorleif said.

"Perhaps. I think he will."

Thorleif looked at his father. "What's in your mind, father?"

Thorbrand smiled without humor. "Still you flail about in your fog. Will you never know wisdom, son?" When Thorleif said nothing to this, he continued. "The Crowness, man. The forest."

Thorleif frowned, surprised. "The land he has killed for? You think he will simply give that up to us?" He looked at his father uncertainly.

His father snorted in open contempt. "A dowry is not land given up. It is wealth invested, and it is still within the family. The greater family. Do you think the matter of the Crowness is settled, son? Snorri gothi claims that land, still. So Arnkel has won a little victory, and shed blood? What of it? Arnkel is no fool, and he knows that the forest is the most exposed of his possessions, and would be the first to be lost to his heirs, if he were not about. Who would fight for it for his daughters? Hafildi? Hah!"

The scathing sound of his laugh rang in the air. Freystein and Illugi looked toward them, and their laughter died for a moment. Thorleif looked away, to the clear blue sky, trying not to hate his father.

"Thorgils might," Thorleif said.

"Not anymore. The word is that he and Arnkel have fallen out over Auln. Good news, that."

"So he would want us bound to the Crowness, to help guard it for his heirs?" Thorleif said, forcing reason and calm into his voice. Thorbrand nodded, and looked sideways toward his son. "Now you see it," he said grudgingly. "He would also assume it would drive a wedge between Snorri gothi and our family, as well. It is the wisest choice for him."

Thorleif saw Arnkel in his mind, the man he had known as a boy, dominating all around him with his will, calling Odin to his aid. But not really needing him. He could not believe that the gothi would ever be able to give up something he had fought with sword and spear to take, not even for the most cunning of reasons. It was not in his soul. How could he make Thorbrand understand that? It shone out of the gothi's eyes, like one of Ulfar's songs, clear as day. His father had never stood in front of the man with weapons in hand.

"So are you ready to abandon Snorri, father?" he asked.

His father shook his head, sighing. "No, son, although your actions in the Crowness may have given him that impression. We will see what happens from that. Perhaps it will be to our advantage. I had not expected that from you. You surprised me." Thorleif swallowed and tried not to show his pleasure at his father's words. You have thirty years, man, he thought. Stop acting like a boy looking for approval.

"But our interest in the Crowness would become something to bargain with him," Thorbrand continued. "We could sell it to him for other favors, and must. It would be foolish to deny Snorri." Thorbrand looked at him, a gleam of avarice in his eye. "With Illugi married to Arnkel's heir, Bolstathr and Hvammr would be in our grip, with Snorri's backing to beat down the mewling of his daughters. We will own Swan's fjord from the river to the forest."

Thorleif rode on. He could hear the elves in the grass mocking his lack of guile, and he cursed them. Would he never match his father?

Would he want to?

He could smell the bitterness of the poison Thorbrand had sprinkled into the honey, as if it came off his father's robe.

Do I want to become a man like him?

He glanced over. Thorbrand rode hunched, his seamed face twisted and taut, and he turned, feeling his son's eyes on him, as if he could see the thoughts behind the skin and bone.

"You have much of your mother in you, Thorleif," Thorbrand said. "She is a strong and full of goodness."

"But that is not enough," Thorleif said bitterly.

"No. It is not enough. To be a gothi, you must . . ."

"I don't want to be a gothi," Thorleif said harshly.

His father rode silently for a moment, and then reached across to touch his arm.

"You must begin to act like one, if your family is to survive." He pointed to Bolstathr ahead. "That man must die."

"I know that."

"What have you done to make that possible?" Thorbrand said. "Nothing."

"I have set Freystein to watch the gothi," Thorleif said calmly. He would not let his father goad him into anger. "I have lulled him into thinking we have given up our claim."

"And all other men, as well," Thorbrand snapped. "Soon, no man will remember that it is our land."

Thorleif looked at him, frowning. "He drove eight men out of Crowness, and killed the best of them. Alone. He is not like other men. We cannot kill him ourselves."

Thorbrand grunted scornfully. "Perhaps you should just bow your head to him, and become his Thingman."

"Better than Snorri, at least," Thorleif said. To his surprise, his father did not become angry, but merely rode on, silent, head hanging low. They caught sight of Thorgils, as he worked in the home field of Ulfarsfell, shaping a black rock with a hammer, his bare, sweating back to them. He placed the rock into the slowly growing wall and jostled it steady.

Thorbrand turned to him. "Son, my days are numbered and I will soon be gone, and you will head our family." He touched Thorleif's shoulder again. "Know this then. Snorri gothi is like a vast hearth fire, the kind that burns on its own without fuel or care, for many days. Pour water on it, and it will steam, but soon the fire burns itself hot again. His power ranges across this land, subtle and immense, his influence everywhere. Men listen to him at the Thing, son. Not every gothi has that respect. Certainly not Arnkel, who would be looked upon as a danger and a menace. He is merely a white hot glowing ember, outshining the rest of the fire for a little while, soon to consume itself. Snorri gothi will be here long after Arnkel."

"Poetry," Thorleif said.

"Yes, poetry." Thorbrand pointed a finger at him. "It is not enough that you have abandoned Snorri. That has hurt him, but will not influence his decision. He will never fight Arnkel with the sword unless he thinks there is no longer any other way to defeat him."

He looked at Thorleif. "You must remove the choice from him."

"How?"

"Where is Snorri strongest?"

Thorleif bent his head in thought. Into his mind came the picture of Snorri gothi handing silver to Thorolf, long ago.

"At the Thing," he said. "Within the Law."

Thorbrand nodded. "Then you must take that from him." He pointed at Thorgils. "There is the result of a lifetime of loyalty to Arnkel gothi. Cast aside, and made into little more than a servant. The same fate awaits you, if you take up with that man. Or worse. Remember Ulfar."

Thorgils turned at the sound of their horses. They rode aside a little to speak with him. He nodded politely but kept working, chipping at the next stone. Fifty paces of knee high wall lay already done, but there was twice that to finish yet.

"The wall looks strong, Thorgils," said Thorbrand.

The man nodded again.

"I'll fetch turf for it when it warms a little more." Thorgils spoke without interest, his voice dead, as if the conversation held nothing of value to him. Illugi and Freystein came up then, waving at Thorgils.

Thorleif saw the man's grief. "We heard about Auln's baby, Thorgils. It was an awful thing. Is Auln alright?"

Thorgils chopped savagely with his hammer, eyes down. "It has been three weeks since the child died, and still she weeps at night."

Thorbrand held his hand up. "It is best when a weak child dies early, rather than later, when food and care have been wasted on it." He seemed not to notice the glare of rage Thorgils sent his way. "The child should have been left out in the cold when born." Thorleif hastily pulled Thorbrand's shirt and tugged him into motion, nodding good bye to Thorgils.

They rode to Bolstathr.

"The baby was fat and strong, father," Illugi said. "I held him myself, you know. But Auln found him smothered that morning, the same day they found Arnkel gothi's mother in the wood."

Even under the bright sun, it made them shiver with apprehension. The Otherworld's hunger was a curse that all men had to bear. Trying to harness it always brought disaster. They all knew what had happened. Arnkel had given his own mother to kill the child.

There were men working in the home field and they ran up to the wall, two of them holding spears in both hands, as if to attack. Gizur was one of these and he stared up at Thorbrand, and eyed the spears of Illugi and Freystein warily.

"What business do you have here?" he said suspiciously.

"What a welcome!" Thorbrand sneered. "We come in our finest to speak civilly with the gothi, and we find only his slaves threatening us. Is our feud not ended?"

Gizur spat on the ground, and waved his hand at the rest of the men. "No slaves here, Thorbrand. These are all bondi."

"Bondi, eh?" Thorbrand said contemptuously. "Well, free man, go and tell the gothi that Thorbrand and his sons, the masters of Swan firth, come to speak with him."

The shouts had drawn people out of the Hall, and the gothi was one of these, standing with fists on his hips by the door, watching the discussion. Gizur trotted up the slope to him and they spoke quickly. He came back down, walking slowly, while the gothi went back inside.

"The gothi welcomes you, and asks that you join him for the morning meal." Gizur growled reluctantly. "You are to leave your spears outside. And that club." He pointed at Freystein's belt.

Thorleif glanced at his father, but Thorbrand nodded slightly.

They tethered their horses by the door and leaned their weapons against the turf wall. "No one touches these," Freystein said to the surrounding men, and he pointed his thick finger at all of them. Thorbrand frowned. "Then you had better stay out here and see that no man does," he said.

Freystein kicked the dirt in frustration, knowing he should have kept his mouth closed around Thorbrand. He had a big man's appetite and had been looking forward to the food. Illugi laughed at him, and then promised under his breath that he would bring a bite out.

"If I remember," he teased.

The bright sun shone through the smoke holes, illuminating long trestles loaded with pitchers of skyr, and bowls of cheese and butter. Whey-soaked beef had been cut into chunks and lay on a platter, ready to be eaten with fingers.

The gothi met them as they came in the door. He took Thorbrand's outstretched arm, and the two men stood a moment, looking at each other.

"I bring my family's condolences regarding the death of your mother, Arnkel gothi." Thorbrand said. "Gudrid was a noble woman."

Arnkel nodded. "Thank you for your words, Thorbrand. Come to my right hand here, and tell me more about Gudrid. You knew her in her youth. Tell me something of her. A child remembers things differently than a man, and I was only a boy when she was young."

So they sat around the long trestles and ate, while Thorbrand told them about Gudrid, and her passion for life and fiery temper, and Einar's love for her. He also told of Einar's exasperation with her iron will, how she would insist on her way in all things, directing Einar's men about their chores when her father was not there to check their work.

"She was not yet twelve years, and yet the servants and slaves dreaded her coming, even more than they did Einar who was a jovial man and easily forgave laziness." Arnkel's men laughed at that because the gothi was much the same as his mother, although none would point it out. Thorbrand verged on insult to Einar's memory with his comments. He seemed not to know what his words did to the gothi, clutching his staff along his cheek, his long white hair hiding his lined face as he spoke. Arnkel knew his men's thoughts. It pleased him that they thought he was a hard task master, but at that moment he wept, his head bent, and all of them were silent to let the gothi have his grief for his mother.

"Finally, Einar gave her to your father, Thorolf, thinking that only her beauty and strength could tame him and that his violence could be restrained. But we all know that tale." The men sighed in relief when Thorbrand avoided the story, knowing the madness in the gothi. They had all seen Thorolf stagger out of Bolstathr, his face cut like a piece of meat.

"It has been a fine thing, hearing of my mother, but it seems we have other matters to discuss," said Arnkel, wiping the water from his eyes, and he waved a hand at Illugi and Halla, who sat at either end of the table, their eyes on each other at every moment.

Thorbrand nodded. "My son seeks a wife and Halla seems a good match. Further, they both seem to approve of it, and though that is hardly necessary, it does make it more certain that they will be happy together, and there will be no need for divorce at a later time, with all the difficulties that go with that."

The gothi nodded, and soon they were deep into a discussion of the bride price. Halla was to be sold, as cattle might be, and the gothi wanted a steep price for that.

"Fifty cows!" Thorbrand gasped.

"My daughter is a prize worth having, Thorbrand," Arnkel said dryly. His hand touched her cheek affectionately, and she smiled at him.

"Of that I have no doubt, gothi, but the price is barely one we can pay," Thorbrand answered. "We would be paupers and my family would go hungry." He leaned forward, lips pursed. "The dowry of the bride would need to be ample to offset that."

Arnkel gothi sat chewing his meat slowly, as if ruminating on what wealth he would send with his daughter to another man's hearth, to keep her in comfort.

Thorbrand leaned and put his mouth near Thorleif's ear, his eyes on the gothi expectantly. "Fifty cows. The Crowness is precious to him, but it is ours now." The last words whispered into his ear as Arnkel stood from his seat and wiped his mouth on a sleeve. He looked down at Thorbrand, and at his son.

"Orlygstead," he said.

And he smiled.

It became very quiet in the Hall. The sons of Thorbrand gaped at the gothi, while their father stared at him, his mouth open in shock. A moment later he gritted his teeth, keeping the rage from his face with every shred of his will.

Thorleif sat still. He should have felt dismay, but all he could feel was the cold laughter inside at the look on his father's face.

"My daughter and the boy could live there and work the land," the gothi continued, hand on his beard. "It is fair land and green, and the sheep do well there. Of all my lands, it is the best to give to the bridal pair."

Thorleif glanced at Illugi and felt pity for the boy, who still did not understand. He saw only the frowns of his older brother and his father. Halla looked frantically from one to the other, seeing that the air in the Hall had soured. She stared at Illugi in despair.

"Such a dowry would not be appropriate," Thorbrand said harshly. He pushed himself from the table and stood. Thorleif stood with him. "It is not yours to give."

Illugi still sat, his usual temper quelled by his dismay. But then he came to his feet and went to back his brother and father, his face twisted with remorse. He looked once at Halla, and then away.

The gothi's men were standing now, and Gizur and Hafildi and others were reaching for the spears that lined the wall. Arnkel frowned.

"It saddens me that we must come to this again," he said loudly. "Must all my legal and rightful claims to land end in blood?"

He stepped down from the dais. Thorleif watched him, knowing it was all drama, all an act.

The gothi's eyes went to Thorleif.

"You have seen where that will always end, son of Thorbrand," the gothi rang out, and his eyes were like blue coals of rage. He pointed his finger. "Kjartan says that you left the Crowness before I arrived and I saw you on the hill and so I thought you had wisdom. I thought you would heed the judgement of the Gods themselves on my side."

"The judgement of men will be a different matter," Thorbrand said blackly. "We all know that Snorri gothi has made formal appeal over the death of Hawk. You will have to face him at the Thorsnes Thing, and you will lose much." He paused, his mouth twisted bitterly. "We could have made something here. Something of worth."

"I care nothing for the judgement of men," Arnkel said. "Who will enforce the Thing's decision? Snorri?" The gothi snorted with contempt. "A man must have strength to hold what the Law says is his. He does not have that strength. Nor do you. The Crowness is mine. Orlygstead is mine. Ulfarsfell is mine."

He looked once more at Thorleif, and stepped forward, challenging.

"Was it wisdom, Thorleif? Or was it cowardice?"

Thorleif said nothing. He thought he should have felt fear, seeing that God-like man readying himself to kill. Or perhaps he should have felt rage. A warrior would feel rage, he told himself.

But all he felt was icy calm. The dark laughter of the gothi's men was nothing to him.

Thorbrand glanced at him, and then spat at the feet of the gothi. "You speak of cowardice. You take our spears away and then challenge us over meat, in the peace of your Hall. Fine courage that is!"

Arnkel gothi waved his hand grandly. "Then go. Go in peace today, for tomorrow there will be none between us."

They rode back to Swan firth.

Thorleif led them at a hard canter, and Thorbrand did not argue that he took the place of leader. One look at Thorleif's face outside the Hall had quieted him.

"He cannot win, son," Thorbrand said on the ride back. "Snorri will rally his supporters against the man, and he will lose the judgment."

Thorleif said nothing.

When they arrived at their farm and dismounted he turned to his father. "What does it profit us if Snorri wins? If he gains the Crowness in Law, and extracts a fine for killing Hawk, how does that aid us? Where will Arnkel turn then to make up his losses?"

Thorbrand looked at him evenly, listening.

"You spoke wiser words, father, when you chided me for loyalty to Snorri, long ago. And when you told me to strike Snorri where he is weakest."

Thorleif turned and faced Freystein and Illugi. "Get Ragnall and Egil. Pack the boat with enough food and water to take you out to sea and down the coast."

He told them what he planned, and what he wanted them to do, his words calm and clear. They stared at him in surprise as he spoke. Even Thorbrand blinked at his words.

He went to the barn, saddled a horse, and prepared a pack pony. In the Hall, he put on a leather jerkin, and a thick leather hat on his head. He took a shield and a spear. Thorbrand met him outside, as he mounted the horse to leave. Freystein had prepared the four other riding horses for him, all saddled, and these he attached to Thorleif's horse with a line.

"This is a bold thing you do," Thorbrand said, peering up at him. He smiled grimly. "It is something I would have expected of Snorri gothi."

The rare words of praise broke the ice in his heart a little and so he looked down, and took his father's outstretched hand. He saw the age in his father's face, and the relief in his eyes, that his son had finally seen the grim facts of life. "Let us hope I have not become too clever," Thorleif said.

"Can't I go with you?" Illugi asked, handing him the reins.

Thorleif shook his head. "No. I want the time alone. I'll see you later." He grinned at the boy to reassure him. "Halla is not lost, brother. We'll find a way to have her back for you."

He went to the upland pastures first, taking most of the day to reach them, and spent a few hours going through the flock. He sent the dogs to pick out all of his and led them to another pasture, far from the others. He needed time to think, and the job needed doing, anyway, with the feud about to renew. One of Arnkel gothi's Thingmen was there, checking his own sheep, but they only looked at each other over the long stretch of rocky grass. The man even waved as Thorleif rode off, and this made him smile grimly. He knew nothing of what had happened in the lowlands.

Thorleif waved back.

The trail to the next valley split many times, heading to different farms and meadows, but he took the highest one, that led through the cold rock up to the mountain and then to the frigid desert of the interior. Men went there sometimes to commune with the Gods. He avoided anyone he saw and rode till nightfall. He spent a long night, dozing fitfully inside his lambskin with the dogs huddled around him, sometimes waking to stare at the stars, the thoughts flashing through his head. Elves came about once and set the keenest of the dogs snarling, but he had nothing for them in his heart and they heard that and went away. By dawn he had settled all he would do and say. The paths were covered in pebbles and scree, and he could not ride quickly for fear of turning one of the horses' hooves, but he wanted to be on time. He came down into a valley far from Swan's fjord, and rode for the largest farmstead he could see from the heights.

The workers and slaves came to greet him as he arrived, and one ran to find their master. He came out of his Hall, still munch-

ing cheese, and wiping his hands on fine cloth. His fingers were
covered in gold rings, and he wore a fine robe of ermine.

Thorleif raised his hand. "Greetings, Gudmund gothi," he said.
He dismounted and unstrapped the large keg of clean honey he
had taken from his father's store. He offered the gift to the gothi,
who took the keg and handed it off to one of his men with barely
a glance.

"Yes, I remember you from the Thorsnes Thing, bondi, and
from Snorri gothi's Hall," Gudmund gothi said in his loud voice.
"You are far from your home. I would have thought a man in your
predicament would stay close to it, for protection."

"That is what I have come to speak to you about, gothi," Thorleif
said. "By the way, I see you are hard by the river here. You would
have need of a boat!"

He pointed down the river to the speck growing there, coming from the sea, sunlight flashing from the water falling off the
swinging oars and then turned back to see the greed in Gudmund's eyes.

XIII

Of Snorri Humbled at the
Thorsnes Thing, and Auln

THE RAIN LASHED DOWN upon them without mercy as they rode to the Thing, and both man and horse dripped, the water pouring over their waxed wool cloaks, soaking everything from boots to tunics. It was a cold, savage rain and Snorri gothi was glad of his broad brimmed hat that kept neck and back at least partly dry, but he still felt the chill in his bones. Oreakja, Sam and Klaenger rode along beside him, hunched and miserable. Behind him followed fifty or more of his Thingmen, picked up in ones and twos as they had ridden. More would come. The ride had begun before dawn.

Kjartan and Ketil had been sent ahead to the Thing with Cwern and two other slaves in the early hours, during the dark, their long string of pack ponies loaded with tents and wood, and food. At least they would have comfort waiting for them when they arrived. Oreakja had wanted to go with them, but Snorri had held him back. The cut on his face had healed well, a long red welt just beginning to lose its crust to the new flesh underneath. It puckered slightly, and gave the boy a ferocious look.

"It's not your health, son," Snorri said. "It's your hot head I worry about. All of the house of Bolstathr will be there, and I think you may do something rash if I am not at your side, especially with those new tricks you've learned from Hrafn."

Oreakja's smile was hard. He knew his father only feared Arnkel would finish his work on him. He said nothing to the polite excuse his father made. For days after Hawk's death, he had lain in his cot, the pain of the wound burning him. He had not struck even one blow, he thought. It had shamed him, and aged him.

He had sought out Hrafn.

The merchant had returned weeks before, after the drift ice had retreated, in ample time for the Thing, claiming that his best luxury trade was then. Oreakja had come to him at a quiet moment, knowing of his warrior past and his loyalty to his father, and had spoken to him.

"So you want to learn weapons better, eh?" the man had said over the rim of his horn. "I don't blame you, with your face like that."

Oreakja had blushed furiously, frowning, but Hrafn had held up his hand. "I mean no insult, lad. I have met Arnkel gothi. You've been very, very lucky, walking away alive, and without a wound that cripples you for life."

He stood, and pulled a spear from its rack. He held it in two hands, and then reached up to touch the tip of it.

"First lesson then," he said. "A spear is more than just the sharp point at the end of a stick. It's a slashing weapon, not only a stabbing one, when you fight men. Did you know that?"

"No."

"Then we'll begin with that."

So for that first day he learned to cut with the edge of the leaf shaped blade, arcing it about in cunning weaves, blocking with the shaft, slashing at imaginary leg and face, and throat.

"Experienced fighters will wear their helmet, if given a choice of one piece of armor to wear, beyond a shield," the merchant said. "Rip open a man's scalp, or his face, and he's done. Only then can you seize the moment to stab him."

Snorri had watched, as had the other men, and soon the others were copying the drills Oreakja went through, although with not as much diligence. Even the gothi had picked up a spear and practiced. Hrafn had Kjartan spar with Oreakja using sticks and wooden blades, like children, but they ignored the laughter of the other men and worked at it grimly. Both of the boys had sobered after that horrible day in the Crowness, humbled by their weakness, when they had thought themselves so strong.

Snorri gothi had nodded, satisfied by the new maturity in his son. Alone, he sacrificed a calf to Odin on top of the mountain, and thanked the God for saving his son's life.

The riders came over a rise and saw the flat-topped green hill of the Thing, hidden in rain and mist.

Many tents dotted the lower areas, in clumps. Smoke leaked from most of them as the men huddled out of the weather.

They rode down to the lower areas looking for the Ketil and Kjartan, and the red striping of the gothi's main tent. Snorri sent out ten men, searching about, but one of the riders returned quickly with bad news, his horse sending up waves of water from the hooves.

"Olaf gothi's men are over there," said one of them, a farmer named Hordur. His round, beefy face was pinched with worry as he pointed. "They say that some men drove off our pack horses. Ketil and Kjartan are out collecting them, down the shore. Some have said it was Arnkel's men."

There were angry shouts at this, and a few of the men urged the gothi to attack Arnkel then and there. Most looked at each other nervously. Snorri waved the angry ones into silence, water dripping in rivulets off his hat and the cuffs of his coat. "We know nothing of this except the words of others. Before I have us draw swords, we need to find Kjartan and Ketil."

So they rode down the shore, and found the two of them, and the three slaves, just returning with the last of the ponies that they had found. The three men were very relieved to see the gothi, and his many Thingmen. They were exhausted by the long search through the night, soaked and chilled.

Ketil explained, his voice taut with anger. The five men had rigged a picket line for the horses, and unloaded the gothi's tent. While they pounded in the stakes for it and prepared the guide ropes, someone had slipped in and cut the picket line and driven the pack ponies off with yells, and cracks of whips. The animals had scattered, terrified, including their saddle horses, and so they had begun the search on foot.

"Could you see who it was?"

"No, gothi. It was still dark."

They had left the tent lying where it lay, half the stakes pounded in. But when they came to it, they found that all the guide ropes had been cut off the waxed canvas, close to the grommets. Each would have to be re-tied.

Snorri gothi calmed them again, palms down. "A prank, a stupid prank. We will not roar about and give them the satisfaction of knowing we are bothered by it. Not until we know who it is."

They put up the tent, and the others as well, and Snorri ordered the loaded firewood to be lit in each one. Soon the smoke and heat was filling each one and the men began to warm themselves. Tempers cooled a little.

The choosing of the judges was delayed until the next day.

Hromund gothi had sent a man bearing the carved whalebone of official messenger around with the message, and Snorri had sighed with relief. He had spent other years choosing men and settling cases in rain and wet, but the water thundered down without rest, pressing in the canvas, and snakes of water crossed and re-crossed the tent bottom. Nothing could be done in weather like that. The message said that the judges would be selected, the sacrifice made, and the cases of the Court of Prosecution begun that same day. It would be a long day, but time would have to be made up.

He rode out at one point with Ketil to speak with his usual supporters, preparing for the next day's work. Olaf gothi welcomed him loudly and warmly, horn in hand, and Snorri sat with him for a while. The seal hunter had been drinking all day in his tent, and could hardly say a word without slurring it. Snorri looked at him tensely, wondering if he should warn the man to slow his drinking, as the next day would be a hard one, but thought that the cautioning words would be insulting.

There was something new in the man's horn, not smelling of the pulp of ale.

"Wine!" Olaf roared out. "By all the Gods, it has a kick to it! I'd never drink anything else if I could get it." He drained the horn in his hand, the red running down his neck as if he had been slashed by a knife, and then called loudly to one of the slaves to fill him up. "Your Thingmen brought it for me this morning, the sons of Thorbrand. What's the oldest one's name? Thorleif? Says he got it from your merchant friend." He peered at Snorri, one eye closed suspiciously. "What do you think he wants from me?" He instantly forgot the question when the slave arrived with a skin of the wine.

Snorri left finally, irritated. The tail of his words reminding Olaf about his case against Arnkel the next day was drowned under the gothi's roared greeting of one of his favorite Thingmen.

Ketil looked at him worriedly as they walked out into the rain.

Gudmund gothi's vast tent was crowded with many visitors and Thingmen. Its fine weave and thick oiling kept the place under it dryer than any other on the plain. The place steamed with the heat and smell of many bodies. Snorri waited impatiently for a while, pretending to drink ale with Ketil, until it became apparent that the gothi would never notice him in the press, or chose not to do so. Gudmund sat in a vast wooden chair, laughing with men at his elbow. The chair had been made on the spot from disassembled pieces hauled with great effort to the Thing. It irked Snorri to approach the man as if he were a supplicant to some king on his throne, and even more that he would have to play on the man's vanity. He was damp and tired, and his patience was fading quickly.

"Gudmund gothi, greetings," he said, putting one foot up on the dais. "Might I have a word with you?"

"Of course, Snorri!" Gudmund said loudly. "How may I be of help?" The crowd of men around him looked at Snorri curiously.

Snorri glared at them.

"A private word," he said shortly.

Gudmund waved his hand at the surrounding men. "How can I so treat my Thingmen and guests, Snorri, to send them out into the rain? Please speak your mind openly. They will not mind."

Snorri stared at him, frowning. Gudmund had twice forgotten to speak his title. "Did you receive my gift last month, the twenty seal skins, and the oil made from them? And the message with them?"

"Yes, they came. Thank you for the gift. I still await the forty trees promised me from before. Also, it seems unlikely now that you will be able to provide me with the further one hundred trees your messenger mentioned, given the danger in the Crowness."

There were the pursed lips of suppressed smiles all around Gudmund, who winked broadly at one of his Thingmen.

Snorri frowned again, and spoke quietly. "Tomorrow, or the day after will be a day of reckoning. Wouldn't you agree?"

"Oh, very much so," came the reply.

"Perhaps we should discuss in detail what will happen. . . . "

Gudmund interrupted, raising his hand. "I have no doubts as to my duties tomorrow, Snorri. Rest easy." He gestured to one of the slaves near him, a man carrying a skin. "You there, earn your keep. Fill the man's horn." Then he bent his head to one of his Thingmen and began talking.

Snorri turned away, and left the tent. He rode quickly, silently, Ketil looking at him again and again. On the way back he stopped off at the tent of another gothi, a lesser chieftain from the west called Ingulf, and spoke with the man for a while. Ketil waited outside, miserable, hunched in his seal skin cape, trying to hear through the patter of rain on canvas.

Snorri emerged a short while later, his face grim.

"What news, gothi?" Ketil asked nervously.

Snorri laughed bitterly. "It seems the only news that has traveled about this winter is the legend of Hawk's death. Did you know Arnkel killed Hawk even though the man had a dozen shield men at his back?" He spat on the ground.

The lightning and thunder came that night, ripping the sky apart. Oreakja and Kjartan squatted at the door of the tent, peering out, trying to spot Thor amid the clouds as he threw his bolts, each man putting on a brave face.

"Hrafn is sailing in that," Oreakja said to Snorri. The merchant had planned to make his way around from Helgafell with the ship, and anchor offshore of the Thing, so as to be closer to all his goods.

He was there the next morning, ship held tight by double fore anchors under the clear blue sky and steady but mild wind. Steam rose from the soaked ground, and had added to the morning sea mist, but it all soon burned and blew away. Men emerged with relief from their tents, stretching and groaning, shedding the wet clothes they had slept in.

Breakfast fires soon burnt outside. Most men simply ate cheese or curds. The messenger came around again, the chunk of whalebone held on his shoulder like a man porting a spear. All gothar were requested to gather on the hill top within the hour, he said, and trotted off importantly.

A steady stream of men began to walk up the hill, gothar and their key Thingmen, and interested onlookers. More than one feud raged on the Snaefellsnes peninsula, and some of the gothar had many men with them, carrying spears and shields. A brief argument broke out over the seating along one of the rocks, but Hromund gothi's sharp words soon settled that. The old man watched with hard eyes as the chieftains arranged themselves about him. He was trusted as an honorable man, fierce to all, strict and thorough about protocol. His five sons stood near, armed with axes, and armored in boiled leather cuirasses and iron helmets, ready to back up their father's authority. A dozen of his Thingmen were there, armed as well.

Snorri settled onto the bench that his Thingmen had carried up the hill. Ketil sat near him, and Sam, and Klaenger, with Oreakja and Kjartan standing behind with the others, spears butted on the ground.

Olaf gothi was nowhere to be seen. A few of his Thingmen stood near, but most were absent. None of them could tell Snorri anything. He stood on the bench and looked toward the seal hunter's tents on the plain. There were men stirring about down there, making fires, but no Olaf.

He bent his head and whispered to Ketil. "Run to Olaf gothi's tent. Wake him if he sleeps, and tell him that the Thing begins."

The man ran off down the hill.

Arnkel arrived, striding along at the head of a wedge of his forty Thingmen, and more coming up behind. He wore fine clothes, red shirt and green trousers, his hair tied tightly into braids, and his sword hung from his waist. The man behind him carried his shield, and all the rest came armed with spear and shield. There were much murmuring and whispered words from the crowd of men, and they looked back and forth between Snorri's party and Arnkel's. They were not quite across from each other in the circle. Benches were put down by Arnkel's men and he sat, a slight smile on his face, Hafildi and Gizur beside him. Thorgils stood with the pack of men in the back.

The circle filled slowly as each gothi arrived. Gudmund made his way up the hill, and there were many whispers at the grand clothing he wore, a robe of purple Byzantine silk, with gold wire worked into the hem, and shirt of fine white linen. He walked over to the space beside Arnkel gothi and imperiously pointed to where he wanted his benches to be placed.

Snorri watched, appalled, when the gothi nodded to Arnkel.

Ketil returned, gasping for air and put his lips to Snorri's ear. "They cannot wake him, gothi."

"What's that you say?"

"They cannot wake Olaf. He lies there as if dead, hardly breathing, and his Thingmen cannot rouse him. One of them even twisted his toe and poured water on him. Nothing!"

Snorri's heart fell out of his chest. In a panicked moment he leapt to his feet, thinking to race down the hill to wake Olaf himself. He forced calm on himself, looking about for some idea that could save him.

The sons of Thorbrand came up the hill, Thorleif leading them. They carried their spears and shields, as Snorri had ordered, and made for the gothi's group. Hromund began the first rituals of the Thing behind him, calling on the Gods to witness the choosing of the twelve men, his arms upraised, turning slowly about in a circle. Thorleif came up beside Snorri, his face set in stone, and he nodded to Snorri.

"We have come to stand beside you at the Thing, Snorri," Thorleif said formally.

Snorri stared bitterly at him. "Do not think that this makes up for your lack of loyalty in the Crowness, Thorleif."

"My loyalty has never been the issue, gothi," Thorleif said quietly. "Do you wish to argue this now, in front of the Thing?"

Snorri gritted his teeth in disgust. He turned and sat down, his mind churning, trying to think.

Thorleif looked down on him, trying not to let his nervousness show. He squeezed the shaft of his spear tightly for control, and looked across the circle to where Arnkel gothi sat, laughing quietly with his men, and then to Gudmund gothi, who sat as if bored by life itself, scanning the horizon for distraction.

The selection of the twelve judges began immediately

Snorri's four candidates were chosen without argument, Arnkel gothi merely nodding at each man's name, and Gudmund gothi raising a hand languidly to approve. The other chieftains cared not at all, since few opposed Snorri at that Thing, and they all nodded their agreement.

Snorri argued against each of the other men.

He stood as each man was announced, and for each one had questions concerning his reputation and suitability. At first men simply listened in surprise that Snorri was so much against the men chosen. The first man was one of Arnkel gothi's and that was understandable. But the second was Olaf's candidate, and men frowned, confused that the gothi would dispute the choice of a man who followed his best ally.

By the seventh man, the circle of men were tired of Snorri's talk, and men yelled out in dismay when he stood again. The shouts of derision drowned his words, although he tried to speak through them.

Hromund frowned and came up to Snorri, speaking quietly, disturbed at the loss of respect for a prominent gothi.

"Why do you delay, Snorri gothi?" he said quietly. "The men want the cases to begin. We have lost a day to rain, and men need to return to their work."

Snorri waved his hand grandly, as if agreeing to grant a favor. "I will certainly allow the selection to move along, if you would delay my suit against Arnkel gothi for the slaying of Hawk to the last."

Hromund frowned again. "Do you merely delay, Snorri? Is that what this is all about?" The old man peered around him at the crowd. "I see that your good friend Olaf is missing." He looked at Snorri again. "Your suit arrived at my Hall before any other this winter, and so it must take precedence, but if Arnkel gothi agrees to postpone his defense until later, then I shall allow it. It is his choice also, as it is his honor being challenged, but if both parties agree, it may be changed."

The old man sent one of his fearsome sons over to Arnkel with his father's message. They spoke for a short time, while Snorri waited hopelessly, knowing it was pointless.

The son trotted back over, the bangles of metal on his leather jerkin ringing out in the silence. Men spoke in whispers, eyes going back and forth between the two men.

"Arnkel gothi agrees, father," the son said. "He will wait for the case against him, if Snorri gothi agrees to all of the next judges without delay."

Snorri listened, astonished.

By Thor's balls, he thought with immense relief, he would sit by Olaf that night, and bind his hands if needed to keep them away from drink, to make the drunkard ready for the next day.

"I agree," he said, elated at Arnkel's stupidity. He saw no more of the man's Thingmen in the pool of judge candidates waiting nervously to one side, so there was no danger in allowing a quick selection. Gudmund gothi had two men in that group, and other gothis one or two.

The men were chosen quickly after that, although one of Gudmund's men was refused by Hromund gothi. He had slain a man in feud the other year, and one of the victim's family had a case at the court that year. It was a clear conflict of interest, and he was told that carefully, and thanked many times for his application.

The bull was led to the altar on the other hill and sacrificed properly. The blood filled the enormous copper bowl. Snorri helped with the blessing, sprinkling handfuls of the blood on all the men, as did the other gothar, until the warmth had left it and it lay inert, mere flesh. He saw Thorleif near him, and purposely avoided throwing the blood toward him even as the man watched him. But another chieftain's handful caught his face, and Thorleif wiped it away thoughtfully, eyes on Snorri. The bull was butchered quickly with a dozen knives and hand axes, and the fat burned on driftwood.

Oily smoke still poured off of the altar when Hromund called them all back to their seats on the other hill to begin the Court of Prosecution. The sun was well into late afternoon by that time, and Snorri watched it imploringly, urging it forward in his mind.

Hromund took his place in the center of the circle as the men settled themselves again. When the conversation had died, and their eyes were on him again, he pointed to Arnkel gothi, who stood immediately. He walked forward a few steps in front of his men and stood, looking at Snorri. There was a buzz of talk.

"The first case to be presented is thus," Hromund intoned solemnly, turning slowly. "Arnkel of Bolstathr does make counter suit against Snorri of Helgafell for the onslaught of Hawk, Snorri gothi's retainer, on Arnkel gothi's person."

Snorri stood, eyes wide with rage and alarm. He pointed his finger accusingly, and shouted, "This case was to be delayed until later, as agreed. Are you not a man of your word, Arnkel?" His men surged forward behind him, spears held in their hands now, and they yelled out supporting Snorri's words. Hromund held his hands out, palms down, signaling calm, and when the noise had died a little he spoke.

"It was your claim against Arnkel for the killing of Hawk which was delayed, Snorri gothi," Hromund called. "However, Arnkel gothi has applied to this court for a counter claim to your own charge, as he is entitled, in which he claims that he was assaulted with the intent to cause his death by your Thingman, Hawk, and by your son, while they and others in your service did take wood from his lands of Crowness." Hromund's rheumy eyes were hard and pitiless. "That suit has not been delayed."

The world spun about Snorri in a slow dance. He heard the old man's words ringing hollowly in his ears.

The case began.

Arnkel stated his position plainly, telling how word had come to him of thieves in his forest, the land that belonged to him by inheritance from his father, and that he had ridden forth armed to repel and possibly kill the thieves in the very act of the theft, as was his right.

"Still, I had no desire to attack the men, who far outnumbered me, and wished only to warn them off. It was then that Hawk assaulted me with spear, and wounded me slightly."

Arnkel pulled off his shirt and stood bare chested, pointing to the small raised puncture scar on his shoulder, turning slowly so that all the men could see the ugly mark. It was not large, but enough to see.

He had shown restraint and mercy in sparing Snorri's own son, Arnkel continued, and his thick finger pointed at Oreakja's scarred face as proof of his mercy. The boy's face went red, and he looked around fiercely, but it only made him look like a scoundrel, and so Ketil told him under his breath to cool his temper.

Arnkel sat down, and put his shirt back on, while Gizur and Hafildi pounded his back.

The case against Arnkel for ownership of the wood had been something Snorri had planned for, and Sam and Klaenger stepped forward as witnesses that Thorolf had handselled the land to Snorri, and then reminded them all, his voice full of reason and calm, that they had all heard what Thorolf had said at the Thing two years past.

Arnkel countered, leaping to his feet and shouting that the handselling had been arfskot, the theft of his inheritance, and he brought up several witnesses to support his claim that he had always spoken against it, the men all saying that Arnkel had shown anger when first told of the deal.

"But you do not need these men to tell you that!" He roared the words out after the last witness had spoken, turning to speak to all of them, and then faced the judges. "You all heard my rage when Snorri gothi handed Thorolf my silver and I heard the cost Snorri gothi had wrongly put on Thorolf, and my anger has never passed away. The Crowness is mine, by Law!" He put a hand earnestly to his chest. "I went to my land to order thieves away, and one came at me with spear and shield, and then another. Was I to stand there and be slaughtered, with my feet planted in my own soil? No, I fought, and defended myself. Is it a crime that I was successful?"

Gudmund gothi stood.

The buzz of talk fell to nothing.

"It seems to my ears that Arnkel gothi has spoken wisely in this matter," he said slowly. "His claim as Thorolf's heir to the Crowness was never surrendered, and it is widely known that he sent ample warning to Snorri gothi to avoid the forest, at his peril. Also known is that Arnkel gothi went to the men cutting the wood in the Crowness alone, the simple act of a land owner asserting his rights, and was attacked. If he had meant harm, or expected it, would he not have brought his Thingmen with him?"

"The Law seems clear on this matter."

He sat, carefully folding the fine robe under him, and sat with his fist on his thigh, staring at the sea.

The many eyes turned to Snorri gothi.

"Will any other men speak on this matter?" Hromund said into the silence.

Still there was silence.

The sun was now very low in the sky, and the men facing the northwest sat with their hands over their eyes from the glare. Most of them had had enough of the stiff formality of the day and they all yearned for the night's fire and drink and laughter. The other aspect of the Thing beckoned to them, and so no one else would say anything that would prolong the case. It seemed clear who was in the right, in any case.

"Then let the judges decide," Hromund said.

The crowd of men turned to each other discussing what they had heard, and the judges sat with their heads bent, listening to one another speak their opinions.

It was over quickly.

The head juror stood and said that Arnkel gothi was due compensation for the assault. However, since no harm had come to him, and one of the attackers had been slain and the other seriously hurt, honor had been served.

There was an immediate roar of disapproval from all sides. Arnkel's men stood and shouted that some other payment was due, while Snorri's railed back that the land question was not settled. Both sides began to shake their spears at one another. Snorri's men had grown to more than a hundred, but Gudmund's and Arnkel's together outnumbered them greatly, and the masses of men began to sway closer together, like puddles of blood oozing along the ground to merge. The more wild at heart or simply drunken men surged forward, while the rest crowded behind them, content to posture and make noise. The shouts among those in the front became more personal, insults and challenges, and at this Hromund stood on a rock and sent his sons and Thingmen between the two groups.

The noise died a little at the sight of Hromund's grim faced men in front of them. Arnkel gothi's men stood down first, at their chieftain's waving hands. He turned to the congregation, arms up to show that he wished to speak.

"The Court has made its decision. I am not happy that a man who defends his honor receives no apology, no recompense and nothing but the satisfaction of having kept his head and taken another's, but I will abide." His face became grim. "I had thought that Snorri gothi should be required to state that the Crowness is my land, by right of inheritance. But that is not necessary." He turned away to his own men. "Not necessary at all," he said over his shoulder.

It was gloomy and quiet around Snorri gothi's fire that night. Few men drank, expecting some kind of trouble. Hrafn sat near the gothi, but the chieftain sat with his head down, chin on his hand, staring into the red embers of the peat fire saying nothing, so Hrafn took himself around to other fires, his large pack filled with goods on one shoulder, two of his men following with a similar burden. The best time to sell trinkets of tin and glass was

in the dim light of nighttime, when men were drunk and the fire
gave a glitter off anything metal. He had said that before. The wild
laughter and shouting from Arnkel gothi's encampment a short
distance away filled the night until very late, and finally other men
shouted to them to be quiet.

Snorri slept not at all.

At dawn he rode over to Olaf's encampment. He had not trusted
himself to go before, thinking that his rage would spill over and
that he would do or say something he would regret. It was time
to be especially clever, especially cunning, and not give in to rash
impulses, he thought.

Olaf lay in his bed, sick. His face was whiter than Snorri had
ever seen it, a death pallor under the wind burnt brown. The
healer who sat near him said the worst was over, however. The
tent reeked of vomit.

"It was the wine, gothi," the toothless man squeaked at him. He
lifted the empty cask in his two wrinkled hands. "It is a very great
amount to drink. Too strong. Too strong. I have never drunk wine,
but the few drops I tasted from the bottom seemed bitter. Is it sup-
posed to taste this way? Perhaps it is the nature of the drink."

"Bitter?" Snorri said frowning. The man held out the cask and
he touched a finger to the moist inside and put it in his mouth.
Yes, there was something there, but it was hard to tell what it was,
really, from just wet wood.

"A very great amount for a man to drink," the healer repeated,
shaking his head.

Snorri spoke to Olaf's chief Thingman and told him he would
arrange passage back to Olaf's Hall by Hrafn's ship, to spare him
the brutal ride towed by oxen. The man was immensely relieved,
and took his hand gratefully. It was odd to see such a tough man
unnerved, but the loss of a gothi was always to be dreaded.

The next day was a blur of minor cases, some of which Snorri
was required to speak on. Men would not care about his own
troubles. He had many duties to his Thingmen and others, and

he took them seriously. There was the future to think about, and men would not come to him as friend and advocate if they thought him undependable. Arnkel gothi and he did not acknowledge each other that day, or the next.

Snorri quietly withdrew his case against Arnkel. It was pointless to continue.

On the final day of the Court of Prosecution, Hrafn sailed away with Olaf.

Snorri went down to the water to see the merchant off. Thorleif went with him. His brothers had camped among Snorri's men, but he had been far away by himself, without a fire, watching the sky and counting on his dogs to listen for footsteps. There were many among Snorri's men who put Hawk's death at his feet as much as at Arnkel's, and a few hotheads, especially Sam the Fisherman, who seemed especially incensed. Sam had drawn his knife when Thorleif had first appeared at the Thing, and only his brother's shouts and Snorri's stern command had made him sheath it again.

The two men picked their way among the rough boulders down to the beach sand. Sam had made a point of handing the gothi's axe to Snorri when he saw Thorleif arrive at Snorri's tent that morning. Snorri used it as a walking stick now, his hand gripped on the head. Olaf had been floated out on a raft already and lay on the deck, still sleeping, a half dozen of his men with him. Hrafn came to the rail when he saw them, and called out through hands cupped to his mouth, saying he would return in a week's time. He had been more than happy to take Olaf back to his home, knowing that his generosity would be repaid with a good price for the man's seal oil.

"I've had enough of the drunks here, too," he had said, grinning, showing them his skinned knuckles. "There are men here who think that a merchant is a weak, helpless creature, because he smiles at them, and so his goods are for the taking."

They watched as the ship's boat warped the vessel out to deeper water where the wind bit. The sail went up, and in a short time it was scudding down the coast, riding the waves, the bow breaking the sea into white foam .

"Freedom," Thorleif said, eyes fixed on the ship.

Snorri gothi nodded. "Yet we must stay here to face our fortunes."

They looked at each other.

"You have changed much, Thorleif Thorbrandson," Snorri said quietly. "I see a different look in your eye than the one I once saw." Snorri smiled grimly at Thorleif's blank expression. "I had not thought that Arnkel was capable of such subtlety, to turn a powerful gothi from his greatest ally so easily, or even to think to do it."

It was a struggle to say nothing, but Thorleif stayed silent. His father's voice was in his head. "Revenge does not need the spice of gloating, unless one is a child. It is sweet enough alone."

Still, the temptation to tell the gothi of his long night with Gudmund almost overpowered him. He had ridden with Gudmund's messenger as far as the home field of Bolstathr, and watched him make his way down the hill to Arnkel's farm.

"Perhaps the hundred trees denied him before tempted him," was all Thorleif allowed himself. "Arnkel can provide those now, easily, and Gudmund does love his wealth."

There were shouts behind them, and they saw Thorleif's brothers jumping down the rocks to the beach.

"Damn, he has gone!" Illugi said breathlessly, staring down the coast at the speck of the ship. "I wanted to say good bye!" Thorodd and Thorfinn ran up and looked curiously at the gothi and at Thorleif, and at the axe in the gothi's hand. Freystein had his club as always, and his hand went to it, thinking there was trouble.

"Is everything alright?" Thorodd said cautiously, peering at them.

"We were discussing freedom," Snorri gothi said. "Like all good things in life, it has its own unique price."

He threw up the axe in his hand, and held it out to Thorleif. "Courage is the price, Thorleif. Take this axe."

Thorleif put the long shaft into his hand, and hefted it. It was beautiful ash, with a large double bladed head, the edge sharp, but not so sharp as to cling to what it cut, gleaming with oil.

He whistled it about his head, cutting diagonally to and fro.

"It is the finest weapon I own," said Snorri, and he looked at all of them. "It has the longest reach, but no matter how long the handle, it will never reach Arnkel's head when he stacks hay in Bolstathr, when you swing it all the way from Swan firth."

The brothers stared at Snorri.

Thorleif smiled grimly, his eyes bright with triumph. "Do not think I will hesitate to heave this at Arnkel when you decide to come to seek revenge for Hawk," he said, "Nor that my brothers will hold back."

Snorri nodded, and turned to leave, walking slowly up the hill. "I will be waiting your word."

Thorodd and Thorfinn looked at each other uncertainly. Illugi grinned at Thorleif and took his arm. "That's it, then?" he said.

Thorleif nodded, grinning, too. He hefted the axe up to his face to look at the blade.

"What do we do?" Thorodd asked.

"We continue to watch," Thorleif said. He patted Freystein's shoulder. The reflected sunlight off the steel of the axe was bright in his eyes. "And we wait." He smiled at his reflection. "A chance will come."

Thorgils rode at the rear of Arnkel's troop as they headed back to Bolstathr from the Thing. He was there by choice, really, but the other Thingmen knew that he had somehow fallen out of favor with the gothi, and they avoided him, beyond a polite word or two.

Hafildi had taken to calling him 'Ulfar' the last few months, whenever he came from Ulfarsfell to report on the farm. Then the bastard would pretend horror at his slip. He tried it once on the ride, and had a few men laugh, but a slight shake of Arnkel's head stopped him.

The gothi said little to Thorgils anymore.

Thorgils wondered when the knife would come. He hoped Arnkel sent Hafildi. It would be a joy to kill him.

He knew it would come, some day, when least expected. It had bothered him at first, when hope had filled him along with Auln's love and he had suddenly so much to lose. But now, it mattered little. Life was simply meaningless work, and fruitless care for a woman who no longer saw him.

Auln had become mad.

She crept about the hills, on her hands and knees, calling in whispers to the elves, returning at night to Hvammr with her hands and legs bloodied to sit staring into nothing, or at the sky. No one could hear what she said to the creatures of the Otherworld, but her tokens of cheese and smoked meat were found perched on boulders and field walls all about the fjord. Men and women avoided them, as they did her, except when they crept to Hvammr to beg a blessing, or a curse against another. The mad were considered holy and close to the Gods.

Thorgils knew now that the mad were simply that. Mad.

He found small statues of clay, cunningly made, arranged into little vignettes of violence on the ground. All showed an unmistakable Arnkel, helmeted and holding a sword, and a trail of small figures coming out of his shadow. He knew instantly that it meant to show the gothi's line, his heirs. One of the smaller figures, the first male, was always decapitated. Evil reeked from the things. He would always smash them, the fear and loathing choking him. Some people said Auln begged the elves to return her dead child. Others said she hunted the elves, like a Christian, seeking vengeance. Thorgils would bathe her cuts and rub salve onto them and wrap them in bandages, and this she would allow, like a tame dog, although she would not meet his eyes and would pull away screaming if he tried to put an arm around her for comfort.

Hildi became too afraid to approach her any longer. Auln would kneel outside the door of the Hall where her baby had smothered, touching the planks of wood for hours, as if communing with the spirit of the child inside. Hildi awoke once to find Auln near her, knife in hand, staring at her. Arnkel heard of it. Hildi returned to Bolstathr with Halla. The girl hated the return. Although Gudrid was no longer there to torment her, it became nearly impossible for her to see Illugi. Arnkel sent out a reluctant Gizur to run the farm, with two slaves who feigned every possible sickness to avoid working in the cursed place. Olaf the slave even claimed to have seen Thorolf's ghost again, but the gothi nearly killed him with his fist for saying it, and the man crawled away to the barn, battered and bloody.

"My father rests in peace!" he had roared at the slave writhing at his feet. "He is satisfied!"

Hildi begged him to not to evict Auln from Hvammr.

"Where will she go?" she said to him, and she knew from the hard look in his face that he cared little. He granted Hildi's wish, though, and Auln stayed to haunt Hvammr as thoroughly as Thorolf had once done.

Well, Arnkel's mood would improve now, Thorgils thought. The gothi had all he wanted.

They came into the Crowness and the gothi dismounted. He walked among the trees, marking with chalk the ones he wanted cut down. Gudmund had demanded a high price for his support, but Arnkel would cheerfully pay it. He would pay, and pay again, now that he saw what the wealth of the forest could do for him. Gudmund's messenger had arrived unannounced, and had been brought to Arnkel. The gothi had listened to him, his eyes widening when he heard the offer of alliance from the most forceful chieftain in the peninsula, and the most influential, after Snorri. Thorgils had been there in the Hall, reporting on the hay yield of Ulfar's meadow, and he stood close to Arnkel. In his excitement, the gothi had forgotten for a moment how he had made Thorgils

virtually an outcast, and had spoken to him as he had in the old
days, as his closest confidant. Hafildi had looked on, eyes blazing
with jealousy.

"What a chance!" Arnkel had crowed to him in a hoarse whisper, when the messenger was seated on the other side of the Hall,
drinking ale. "Snorri will have no inkling of how I have flanked
him. I'll take his last coin if he challenges me!" Arnkel had leaned
forward. "Do you see it?"

"Do not ask for too much from Snorri," Thorgils had said, falling into the old habit of retainer. He had not known why he spoke
out. Perhaps it was just distraction from the emptiness in him.
"You are the wronged one, seeking only justice. Do not appear
grasping or vengeful. Such men are not respected, and it will hurt
you in the long run."

Arnkel had nodded, sitting back with his hand on his beard,
his eyes thoughtful as they looked down on him.

But nothing had changed, really. He lived at Ulfarsfell, alone.

The last tree marked, Arnkel mounted. Hafildi was given the
task of taking the trees, and several Thingmen were asked to join
him, for a share of the wood.

When they arrived at Bolstathr, Thorgils went to leave without
a word, and turned to the path up towards Hvammr. His duty had
been to get the gothi home safely, and that was all. There was little
danger, anyway, with the sons of Thorbrand isolated and Snorri
gothi frightened of his shadow. All of Arnkel's enemies seemed
vanquished.

The gothi saw him ride by, and held up his hand casually, as
if to give an instruction. Arnkel stood by himself, the other men
busy stripping the saddles and tack from the horses.

"Why did I lose your loyalty, Thorgils?" the gothi said, looking
up at him. "Did you love Ulfar so much? Or was it your yearning
for Auln's love that fouled your friendship with me?"

Thorgils reined in the horse, stunned by the plain words.

He looked down at Arnkel, and caution left him.

What point was there in caution?

"My father Gunnar was a freedman, gothi. Your own grandfather freed him, and he served Einar loyally. He was a carpenter, a good and useful man, like Ulfar." Thorgils let a little of his anger show, for the first time. "I am bondi, a free man, because of your grandfather. But Ulfar will never have sons to be free, and that is not right."

Arnkel's eyes were cold and pitiless. "High principles for a simple bondi. But I must deal with life and death." Arnkel pointed his finger accusingly. "Do not think yourself so noble, Thorgils. You had as much to play in this as I did, and you have your prize up there at Hvammr now, crawling about in the mud to call forth the Darkness. She is the treasure you wanted so badly."

Thorgils stared at Arnkel, hating him, hating himself.

"You knew Ulfar's fate from the moment I first sent you down to his farm to be his friend," Arnkel said harshly. "You are sentimental, and that is your weakness. It is something I realized too late about you. Sentiment drives a man to invent reasons for his actions. You betrayed Ulfar for what was his, but could not live with yourself, and so you would blame me for your guilt." Arnkel spat on the ground. "Sentiment makes a man a liar, even to himself!"

"Bastard!" Thorgils shouted insanely. The rage exploded in him. He threw himself off the horse and at the gothi, his fists windmilling, head down, weapons forgotten, hardly feeling Arnkel's hammered blows to his head and side. But his own fists bit, and he felt the flesh and teeth of Arnkel's mouth mush under his knuckles. They fell back from each other a fraction, to hear the yells of the men rushing at them, and then were at each other again. Thorgils' head seemed to explode with light and pain even as he struck his knuckles again into Arnkel's face. He stumbled back and found his arms held by Gizur and other men, and the gothi was held also. Both writhed in the frenzy of rage, and the men let go Arnkel's arms as he shouted at them. Blood dripped freely from the man's swollen lip and eyebrow. He spat out a tooth with a spray of bloody mucus. Thorgils felt the swelling of his brows already, and the blood poured from the cuts in his cheek and from his broken nose. His head spun painfully, and the air would not come into his lungs.

"Go! Go back to your lies!" the gothi raged at him.

Thorgils threw off the men's arms and pulled himself up into his saddle. He rode off without looking back.

He went directly to Hvammr.

There was no one there.

It was already near to sundown.

Thorgils came down from the horse and walked about, his head spinning with pain and nausea, calling Auln's name. The fire in the great hearth was cold, and it was dark as pitch inside. A long match had been made to store the embers. He broke open the long tube of tightly wound grass and lit the fire using it and put on peat, setting some whey and meat to slowly cook over the fire in an iron pot. Then he mounted the horse again and began to ride around the farm in ever expanding circles, searching between the boulders and into each little vale.

There was nothing for a half mile out. He was tired, wanting sleep and food and rest, his head pounding under the drying blood, and so he went to the top of the highest rise and let his voice roar out her name again one last time.

A sudden certainty struck him then, through the extremity of his pain. He knew where she was.

It was not that far a ride, but in the gloaming his fear rose and began to choke him. The Crowness was a tangle of white birch, trees like glowing bars on the black cage of darkness behind it, the wind rustling in the leaves above. He brought the horse close by the outermost trunks, calling Auln's name loudly, knowing that he would attract the elves before long with the smell of blood on him. If he kept moving then he would not have to see them, so he rode along, calling into the wood.

He caught a flash of white in the failing light, deep within the trees, different from the flicker of elves. One deep breath braced him, and he goaded the mount ahead. Like any horse, it feared for its eyes among the brush and branches and kept its head down, fighting him.

"Auln," he shouted. "This is no place to be at night. Come to me!"

He found her on the ground, near the old stone altar. She lay as if asleep, her head on one outstretched arm, the other arm curled tightly to her chest. Blood covered the front of her dress, a black wetness. His hands went over her frantically, looking for a wound that could bring out so much of the blood, but found only cuts on her wrist, still seeping. He tore a strip from her hem and bound the wounds tightly, then heaved her up onto the horse, and sat himself behind her. He held her upright with arms about her as he rode out. Only then did he hear the angry sibilance seeping through the grass behind him.

"You will not have her tonight!" he raged over his shoulder, and dug his heels into the horse's flanks.

Once out of the forest, he slowed. He felt answering warmth from Auln's back, and knew she was still alive, but she was limp and would have fallen except for his arms. Finally they came to Hvammr. He carried her inside the Hall and lay her on a bench with blankets over and under her. There was a little precious drift-wood on the peat pile, and he threw it on the embers of the cook fire to make a decent light.

The bleeding had nearly stopped, but the wounds were deep, two ragged punctures a thumb's width apart, just back of the hand, on the wrist. He washed them, and bound them again, and then slipped the blood-soaked dress off her unresisting form, trying not to let his heart flame at the sight of her breasts.

Her eyes opened as he covered her with blankets.

"Lie down with me," she whispered.

He swallowed. "You are near death."

"Lie down with me."

Her hand pulled at his shirt weakly. In moments he was naked with her under the blankets, his heart pounding with lust. They moved against each other frantically, and he slid on top of her and entered, his mouth moving on hers.

"I am cursed," she cried softly, at the height of their passion, as he thrust into her again and again.

"No," he said, appalled, but he could not stop taking her, too far into the heat of it.

"All those who love me, or whom I love, die," she whispered. The wounds on his cheek opened and dripped blood onto the hollow of her eye and ran off down the curve of her face.

He spent himself bitterly, crying out as if in pain.

They lay a long time in each other's arms and then slept.

Thorgils awoke at the dawn.

His stirring roused Auln. She pinched the blankets around her chin, and curled for warmth while he dressed.

Her dark eyes were on him.

"I dreamt of my mother," she said.

He moved about the room, lighting the fire from a few remaining embers, to heat the food in the pot. His stomach growled its emptiness and added to the vast pain in his head. Both his eyes were black and swollen, so much that he could hardly see. "Was it a good dream?" he asked softly, almost in a whisper. He did not want to disturb the mood that had brought out the first words from her he had heard in months.

"There are no good dreams," she said. She seemed lucid, although her voice was very weak. He saw her eyes on him, sane and human again, if only for a moment.

"Thorgils, if you stay here with me, you will never know happiness. And you will die."

"No."

"I have what I needed of you, nestled in my belly, growing even now." Her wounded arm came out of the blankets, the bandages gone, the wounds open and savage. "I have made dread bargains." Her eyes went cold, and the haunted gleam crept back into them. "And I have seen what you did with Arnkel."

He stared at her, his mouth twisted as if in pain, the wounds in his head throbbing.

"Do not speak of it," he said desperately. "Daylight is here."

He rushed suddenly to her side and knelt.

"There is still a life for us," he pleaded into her ear. "There is more than just this one little valley in the world. We can go together. Forget the past, and go together."

Auln felt her arms on him, but her mind was filled with the scent of her child, the new flesh so clean, so perfect, and then so cold under her hand. She heard Ulfar's voice calling to her, and then saw her mother's face, her eyes silently pleading as she floated away on a ship to her death.

"I cannot leave my family," she whispered, hanging limp in his arms.

"What?" he said, puzzled, drawing back a little. "What did you say?"

She drove the knife toward his throat. He caught the flash of it from the corner of his eye, and his arm went up instinctively, meeting her wrist, the tip of the knife sliding in a fingernail's length into the large muscle of his neck. He gasped with the pain, and forced her hand back. She was weak, and so it was easy to take the knife from her. He stood back, panting with the shock of it, his hand to the wound, feeling the warm red pulse against his fingers.

Auln blinked dully, as if drugged, and lay her head to the pillow.

He staggered out the door, retching onto the ground, and fell to his knees in the yard. The wind blew strongly, racing the thick clouds across the world, and on it he heard a voice speaking his name, faint echoes in his mind. He knew that voice, and put his head back to look into the sky.

"Ulfar!" he screamed. "Ulfar!"

Auln closed her eyes and slept.

XIV
Winter

The Battle at Orlygstead

Winter had come hard and early. Snow lay piled around Bolstathr, blown to deep drifts. The fjord had frozen well before Yuletide over a space of two days, the ice and the water below perfectly clear, so that when the sun was high it seemed as if a man walked on air as he moved over the ice. Fish could been seen moving in the shallows, and the men used the rare vision to hunt them through holes they chopped with axes. The children shrieked as they walked over the slick surface, thinking they would fall through, but it was thicker than the length of a man's forearm within a week. Arnkel had made ice skates for his children from leg bones of a goat, and the men saw this and made their own, pushing themselves along with their spears, shouting insults to each other at each tumble. The mood was good at his farm, and Arnkel gothi looked on his lands and his people and thought that perhaps he could begin to think that life had become as he had once wished it could be.

Despite all his success, though, he was restless.

His men spent most of their time hunting and fishing, not wanting Arnkel's frown on them for sitting about the Hall. Bringing back even a lone duck or salmon was enough to justify a man's day. Hafildi and Gizur went on sealing trips, spending three or four nights away, when the gothi's worst temper was on him. The

slaves were worked in the barn, mucking out the stalls and feeding the crowded animals, and the gothi was usually there, when
he was not setting out to Orlygstead, or to Hvammr to check the
state of the farms there. He scouted the Crowness often. More
than once he had taken the bowl of curds from under the nose
of one of his slaves as he tucked into it, declaring that only men
who worked ate. That was Olaf, who growled under his breath,
and would go to the barn to pout and clutch his empty belly, the
other men laughing at his bad luck.

Thorgils began to spend more time at Bolstathr, at Arnkel's
request.

He went, caring for nothing. All his rage was gone. There was
only himself to hate.

They had stared at each other the first time they met, and then
Arnkel had stepped forward, his hand to the scar tangling his
eyebrow.

"You hit like an ox kicks, damn you," he had said, smiling
slightly.

After that, it was like sky clearing after the storm.

Later, Hildi embraced Thorgils and told him that she was glad
to see him again, her voice full of genuine welcome. Arnkel's wife
had changed very much since Gudrid had died, he could see. She
walked and spoke with far more assurance, and her way with the
men was stronger. She put her lips to his ear as she had hugged
him. "I've had enough of that Hafildi. He's an uncouth bastard,"
and she had laughed.

Hafildi sulked at his return and mocked him. Most men said
nothing to that, afraid of Hafildi's bulk and temper, but Gizur
was happy enough to see him return, and the other men quickly
fell back into the habit of deferring to him when the gothi was
not close by.

Still, much had changed.

It was obvious that Arnkel had missed Thorgils' ear and opinion. Their way with each other was more formal than before, as if

the gothi realized that Thorgils was not a fixture of his life, to be treated with gratuitous contempt. Usually they spoke of mundane things, related to the farms and the livestock.

Never again did they speak of Ulfar.

But, once, the talk became far more serious.

"So you don't think Gudmund gothi would back me if I actually attacked Helgafell?" Arnkel said at the conclusion of a long session one night.

"No gothi would do so. Such a thing would only bind them all against you, even if Snorri raised not a hand. He could be dead and you would be hounded out of the land." Thorgils had hidden his astonishment that the gothi even considered such a thing. Attack Snorri? For what?

It came to Thorgils then the Arnkel saw the world as something to be conquered. His victories had made him hungry for more victories. "He will never come here, then. He will stay safe in his hole." Arnkel rubbed his beard thoughtfully. "Gudmund gothi has over five hundred men he can call on!" Arnkel said to him. "That is power! I need more men!"

"Gudmund's men are farmers, as are your men, with land of their own to make food. He has only a few more men on his home field than you do. There is no food to feed more. This is not the homeland," Thorgils reminded him patiently. So the gothi drove his slaves and servants harder, and worked long hours himself, even in the winter, hoping to make some surplus, and take on men. Arnkel missed the strength of the Fish Brothers.

Every night Thorgils would ride out to Thorswater dale to see Auln. Arnkel had allowed her to live there alone, after he had moved Hafildi and his wife and all their stock to Hvammr to make it productive again, and she spent most of her hours at the loom within Cunning-Gills' abandoned house. She paid rent to Arnkel for the house with the vathmal she made. Now and then she would disappear for a day or two, and then be back without a word.

She never said another word to Thorgils after that terrible day.

He worked hard making the place a good home for her, building a wall for her few goats and the cow he had bought for her child's milk. He repaired the turf of the walls and roof. He brought in sheepskins and furs for the floor and walls and benches, and had hauled the heavy loom along the broken track, borrowing Arnkel's oxen and sledge for the task. He had brought peat he had dug with his own hands from the fens, and packed on ponies. To all that she said nothing, and gave him not a glance. It was is if he did not exist in her eyes.

He had dozed once, sitting in the corner on a bench, repairing a broom for her. He woke to find her inching closer, the knife in her hand, steps away.

It was a mad existence. He knew that, but his heart would not let him leave it. One day Auln would forgive him. He would wait for that day.

No one can hate forever, he thought

He told himself that, but then he would look at Arnkel, and his certainty would fail.

Auln's belly grew larger each week.

Arnkel knew of the child coming. He had found Hildi making a cover for the child. She had not hidden it quickly enough. Thorgils had spoken plainly to him, when they were alone.

"If the child dies, I'll kill you, Arnkel," he said, and the gothi saw the truth in his eyes. The rage had filled Arnkel then, and he had stepped forward, his hand on his sword. "So I am hostage to any fever or chill that can take a baby's life, then? You can try to kill me, if you can, Thorgils, but you will die!" They stared at each other for a long moment. "How will you know it is not just fever, or the croup?"

"Auln will know."

To that Arnkel had no answer.

It was a flash of dispute between them, but the next day was calm, as if the gothi had forgotten Thorgils' challenge.

They would plan the work together and assign the men to their tasks. Ulfarsfell was rented to Gizur, along with his wife and his children, and they ran the farm as their own, paying the gothi in produce and in coin for it, but it was still Arnkel's land, and he went there often to see how the work went. Orlygstead the gothi kept to himself. Being so close to Swan firth and the sons of Thorbrand, he wanted to spend as much time as he could there, to make his presence felt. More than once he had chased off Freystein and Egil, and he knew the brothers and their father Thorbrand still plotted against him.

Sometimes he would send Thorgils there with slaves and servants, to tend to the animals. In winter, the cows and sheep were close to home and needed to be watched constantly. One of the rams had become aggressive and was tormenting and injuring some of the gelded males. The fear and stress was not good for fattening them, so he needed to be watched. Once, chasing the ram, Thorgils found Egil, the slave of Thorbrand, asleep in a nestle of boulders near the farm, a cloak of white feathers wrapped tightly around him.

Was he only shirking work, or was he watching, as Freystein had been?

All these things he said to Auln as he sat with her. It became habit for him to go on and on about the news and his day, and never would she answer him, or even look his way. The silence unnerved him though, so he would talk.

It also kept him awake.

The baby came just before Yule tide. He found Auln lying on her bed, writhing with pain, the birth fluid soaked into the wool blankets, and had raced down the paths to Bolstathr to fetch Hildi. She and Arnkel had both ridden with him to the little house.

Auln had screamed at the sight of Arnkel in her doorway, and had pointed a shaking finger at him. "Out! Out, you murdering bastard! Out, or all your children will die!" Hildi had drawn back

from her, but then gritted her teeth and ordered the gothi back
into the night, and then went to help her. Thorgils went with Arnkel, and they stood in the crisp hard snow of the yard, their feet
slowly numbing in the cold.

"She knows everything," Arnkel said finally. Only starlight lit
the snow and so Thorgils could not see his face, but the voice was
soft with wonder.

"She has the Sight," Thorgils said. "Everyone knows that."
He would never tell Arnkel of his confession to Auln, and Hildi
wanted only to forget that day, he thought, looking at the man
without expression. Let the gothi think Auln could see his soul.

The birth was quick, without complications, and they heard
the cry of the baby come clearly within the hour. Thorgils went
in then, Arnkel following him, and they closed the door quickly
behind to hold in the warmth of the dark house. Auln was asleep,
her face shining with sweat, blankets to her chin.

Hildi knelt beside her. A single oil lamp burned, and only the
two women could be seen, the rest of the house hidden in shadow.
Hildi held the child in her arms, wrapped in wool. Her face was
drawn with strain.

"It is a son," she said, looking at them.

The shadows whispered from the dark corners, and Hildi looked
around fearfully. "They are within the very house," she whispered,
her teeth gritted in terror. "But Auln would not say the words to
make them leave. Arnkel, you are gothi and priest. Can you not
forbid them from this place?"

The gothi hardly heard her. He stepped forward and used a
finger to pull the cloth from the infant's tiny head.

"I see your likeness in him, Thorgils," he said.

Arnkel's eyes were wide and open as he looked down into Hildi's
arms. His hand crept lower until it covered the whole lower face of
the baby, the mouth and nose and eyes. "It has always struck me
how frail a shell holds the life there," he said quietly, as if to himself. "This body, so easily erased from the world at this moment,

could grow into a thing of iron, filled with hate, and vengeance, and ambition."

"Gothi," Thorgils said. He stepped forward, a single step, his hand on his knife suddenly, without thought.

Arnkel looked at him, his eyes misted and dull. His hand dropped away. He went out the door into the night.

Thorgils stayed that night, to feed Auln and to watch over her. He meant not to sleep but it came over him near the dawn. He woke lying curled around himself on the earth floor, stiff with cold, to find Auln sitting beside a little fire, the child in her lap. It cooed contentedly.

"Awake at last," she said, and for a moment he was happy, blinking the sleep from his eyes. They were the first words she had spoken to him for two seasons. Then he froze, staring.

She held the knife in her hand, close by the child's throat.

"Do you see how it would have gone?" she whispered. "My child and Ulfar slain, and so your child would die for that." She wept, the tears rolling down her cheeks and onto the face of the infant. "But I cannot do it. When I saw Arnkel's hand on him, fear and horror filled me. My heart is not as hard as his." She looked at him, and even her hate was something he cherished. She saw him. "Not yet."

"This is my child, my blood."

The knife dropped to the ground and she held the swaddled infant close to her face. Thorgils stepped closer to her, to put his arms around her. Her nails slashed at his eyes as he came close, and he jerked away. The baby startled at the sudden motion and began to wail. Her eyes were cold and dead as they looked at him, and then they turned away from him forever, and left him standing there while she cradled the baby and whispered to it.

That was his life.

Weeks of winter passed.

After Yule tide, it warmed slightly, and clear skies reigned for nearly a week. It was glorious to have sun shining, even for the few short hours of day, and the children spent most of their time on the ice, sliding about, shedding their lambskins and furs even when their mothers scolded them for it. Halla had been given charge of Arnkel's two smaller children, and the younger sons and daughters of Hafildi and Gizur. She was a good ward for them, firm and loving, although she could be short of temper like her grandmother. Arnkel found her once shouting at Hafildi for tacking up her favorite horse with the wrong bridle, and he grinned at her in pride, loving her spirit. Hafildi spat on the ground and cursed, and said he served Arnkel, not a woman, and this set her off on a new spasm of rage. Finally Arnkel was able to draw her off to let her cool.

"You cannot deal with men that way," he told her patiently.

"Why not?" she said, slapping away his hand on her cheek. "You do." She stormed off, but returned later to put her arms around him as he worked in the barn.

"I'm sorry, father," she said stiffly. He touched her shoulder, understanding her unhappiness.

Swan firth lay close, but so far away.

"The marriage cannot happen as things stand," he said sadly. "You must see that."

"Must it always be like this?" she said. "Always fighting. What is the point of it?"

"The point is power, and land and wealth, and that is our future," he said. "One day you will understand."

The next day an awful thing happened.

Halla played with the children on the ice, pulling them along on a little sled, and spinning them in circles, while they egged her on. The ice was still clear as glass, and thick. She went hurtling along one smooth patch, and then slid to a stop, peering down into the ice. But only for a moment.

Then she was striding to the shore, the children complaining that the game was over so soon. She shushed them and sent them inside, and then went to find Arnkel. She found her father in the barn with Thorgils, tending a sick cow.

"Father, you must come. There is something under the ice." Her eyes were wide with fear. The two men looked at each other and followed her out.

The bright sun shone down, piercing to the sand on the bottom. Halla led them farther out, into the depths, where the water became dark as night, searching about, and then pointed ahead.

"There it is. See there? That white shape." She stood, her hand trembling as it pointed.

Arnkel and Thorgils walked out slowly, looking down into the ice. Both carried a spear for balance, but now they clutched the shaft in two hands, as if to fight. A billowing white moved slowly below the surface, wafted about by the currents pushing up from the bottom. Arnkel knelt, and the shape came up from the depths until it butted against the under side of the ice.

"Sea People?" Thorgils hissed.

Arnkel said nothing.

It was Cunning-Gill.

The body floated on its back, humped up obscenely in the middle where the gases in the torso buoyed it. The faint currents moved the arms, bending them and straightening them, flaring the loose cuffs of the shirt. It seemed as if the body beckoned them to join it in its cold wet grave. The face was barely recognizable, blown and fish eaten, the eyes gone, the flesh jelly.

They stared in horror. Arnkel felt Halla come up behind him, and his arm went up to block her.

"Go back, child," he whispered. She ducked under the arm and looked down.

A swirl of current seemed to animate the corpse, and it spun to move itself below Halla and Arnkel, the hands brushing against the ice, grasping, hungry.

They ran.

Arnkel dragged Halla by an arm, and they stumbled and slithered to the shore.

"No one goes out on the ice anymore!" Arnkel gasped.

They sat inside the Hall later, in the afternoon. Halla had told the story to everyone and no one wanted to go outside when the light began to fail. Arnkel began to drink, his eyes open and staring, and the men muttered, knowing how strange it was for the gothi to be so disturbed. But they were happy be inside, when the gothi usually drove at least some of them to work at one of the farms even in faint day light, and sometimes even in the dark. They began to eat and drink, and the slaves snuck a horn of ale, too, seeing the gothi distracted. Olaf guzzled one horn after another, his grin large and glassy.

Thorgils finally began to speak about the next day's work, if only to distract the gothi from his mood. Arnkel answered in short words at first, but soon put down his ale, and leaned forward.

"The hay is low in our ricks here at Bolstathr," he said to Thorgils, making an effort to speak through the ale clouding him. "I had planned to go to Orlygstead today with the oxen and sledge and haul back a good supply." A roar of laughter came from the other end of the room, and the gothi noticed the red faces of the men.

"Never too late for work, eh?" he roared out to Thorgils with a wink, and he stood. "Hildi, bring me a good supper, and one for Thorgils, too! I will be out tonight under the full moon at Orlygstead, doing a man's work!"

The laughter ceased abruptly when the gothi pointed down the Hall. "Olaf! You and Dim will come with me. The rest of my men have worked hard this day, but you must earn all that ale you've put in your belly. The moon will not rise until late, so you will have that long to sleep and rest yourselves. Then we will go."

The slave's faces dropped at the words, and they hung their heads, terrified that they would have to go out at night with ghosts about. Hildi came out from the private space of the house carrying a platter with curds and smoked fish. "Husband, what kind of madness is this, to work in the middle of the night?"

Arnkel touched her cheek. "It is a sure thing that the sons of Thorbrand will be sleeping when I am at work near their lands, wife," he said softly.

She smiled. "Oh yes, that's true." She was pleased to see caution in her brave husband. When she walked away, Arnkel leaned toward Thorgils. "Dead or alive, Cunning-Gill is nothing to spend worry on. I'll spit in that bastard's eye if I see him."

"I said much the same thing, once," Thorgils said in agreement.

For a long while he sat, watching the gothi eat.

He stood.

"I will use the rest of the light to reach Thorswater dale, if that is alright with you, gothi," he said.

Arnkel chewed quickly and swallowed, surprised. "You will have no food?"

"I want to make sure Auln is alright," he said.

Cunning-Gill might come out of the water for Auln, knowing his care for her, Thorgils explained, and so he wanted to be there with her.

Arnkel grimaced sourly. "That witch has nothing to fear from ghosts, bondi. But do as you like."

The gothi's hand came down on his arm as he turned to leave.

"It is good that we work together again, old friend," Arnkel said, looking up into his face. "We should never have been torn apart."

Thorgils looked at him a moment, and then nodded. He left.

He took his spear and shield and saddled a horse in the barn, thinking on the gothi's words to him, wondering if it meant anything to him anymore.

The path was a worn snake of ice and rock, and he had to goad the horse up it, but it was the only way. He would be able to ride most of the way there with light at least. On either side was deep crusted snow that would cut the legs of the horse terribly. Near the summit the light was much better as the setting sun struck the ground from the south west. He caught a flurry of movement right at the wall that had once separated Thorolf and Ulfar's halves of the meadow. The movement was too noisy to be elves. He heard the scrape of metal on rock, a man trying to hide, surprised by a rider coming by. Thorgils was glad of his weapon, but he made no sign of having seen the man and rode on.

Auln's door was locked, but he knocked on it three times, as he always did, and it was unbolted from the inside. She always unlocked it, but never opened it for him.

He leaned his spear and shield against the wall and crouched by the peat fire, holding out his hands to warm them.

"Cold out there," he said.

No answer. He expected none.

He began to talk then, as always, and the first thing he thought to speak about was of Cunning-Gill in the water. He stopped quickly, realizing that it would remind her of Ulfar. She worked her loom as he spoke, the baby sleeping in the little crib beside her, and the clacking rhythm never changed, as if the thought of slaughtered men returning to the world were an everyday thing. He told her then about the gothi's plans to work Orlygstead with his two slaves later that night under the full moon, and about the man he had heard on the trail by the meadow wall.

"Probably Freystein, or that Egil one," he said.

The loom clacked away for a while after his words faltered. He could think of nothing more to fill the quiet. He sat in silence, turning his hands in the heat and putting on a brick of the loamy peat. Then the loom stopped and Auln stood. She went to Thorgils' spear and shield and took them from the wall. She opened the door to a blast of cold and pitched the weapons out into the snow, like garbage, and then walked back to her loom leaving the door slightly ajar.

It was a simple thing to understand.

He left.

When the sound of his horse had faded to nothing, she dressed herself warmly and then wrapped the child in the snug bundle of fur and wool that Thorgils had made for her. The straps went over her shoulders and under her coat.

She began to walk down the slope. The child slept, rocked by her motion, and soothed by the warmth of her body. The path was as quick to walk as to ride with the uncertain ice and snow, and in some places the crust beside the path was strong enough to carry her quickly. In an hour she was past Hvammr, listening to the murmured voices of Hafildi and his family inside, and then up the slope to the ridge line.

She came to the meadow wall.

It was still very dark, the moon rise still hours away. She could see nothing.

"Who is there?" she called. "Enemies of Arnkel, come out."

Freystein stepped out of the shadows, a cloak of white swan feathers drawn over one shoulder, large enough to cover his whole body in the snow. He looked cautiously down the path and then stepped closer to her.

"Auln," he said gently. "How do you fare? We have missed you."

She held up her hand. "I have a message for your master. Go to Thorleif and tell him this news."

Snorri gothi was sleeping.

Bears reared up all around in his dream and he cut at them with his axe. But one had him by the leg and it shook him about. He could not make it release him no matter how hard he struck at it.

He woke to find Freystein at the foot of his bench, shaking his leg, standing well back from the gothi's arms. The slave crouched cautiously, not wanting to be stabbed by mistake. He knew the gothi always slept with a knife at his side.

"What in Thor's name are you doing, man?" Snorri growled. He sat up on his elbows.

Freystein still wore his cloak and furs and reeked of the cold outside.

"My master Thorleif sends me, gothi. He says to tell you that he will meet you at Orlygstead tonight," Freystein said. "Arnkel gothi goes there with oxen and sledge with two of his slaves to gather hay from the barn, when the moon rises."

Snorri stared at him, still fogged with sleep and dreams. Then the words struck him and he sat up quickly.

Oreakja and Kjartan lay near and had woken at the words. They held spears in their hands, and they leapt to their feet. Snorri brought himself to his feet with a grunt of effort. He rubbed his hair sleepily, and then called for Ketil.

"You two," he said, eyeing the boys grumpily. "Put on your leathers, and those helmets I bought for you."

Ketil came running, and Snorri sent him out to the two houses near Helgafell on the shore where Sam and Klaenger lived with their families. Then he dressed himself, and pulled on the cuirass of boiled leather he had bought from Hrafn, wearing it over his inner clothes. On top of it all he wrapped a thick warm cloak of wool lined with leather, thick enough to turn an uncertain knife. He took a pair of spears, a shield and an axe from the wall. By the time that Ketil had returned with the fisherman and their two eldest sons, he was ready. Lamps had been lit, and cheese and ale were brought out by some of the servants. Already there were cries of alarm from the sleepy children waking to find light and noise in the middle of the night.

"We must go before the whole house wakes," Snorri said. "Is your horse outside, Freystein?"

"I walked, gothi," Freystein said, grinning. "Or ran, rather. Along the ice."

"Eh? What's that?"

"The ice is flat and safe, gothi. I would not ride a horse on it, though. We will make good time walking along it, and we will not lose our way. I could see clearly the whole way from Ulfarsfell."

There were nine of them.

The moon had just come up over the mountains, and its light covered the world in highlights of ethereal white. Their shadows on the snow were crisp and clear. They trudged in single file along the path, retracing Freystein's footsteps, following the familiar paths south until the footsteps verged off to the east and headed south to the frozen water, just north of the Crowness.

They walked along the fjord far out from the broken ice along the shore, where the way was flat and even, the ice beneath covered with packed and powdered snow. It was quiet, their footsteps muted by the snow, almost without sound, and as they passed the forest they could hear the slight wind above their heads whistling through the bare branches far over to their right. Under that was another sound, the awful sibilant hiss of the elves' voices. They filled the wood, and each man turned his eyes away, knowing he was watched.

Freystein came up beside the gothi, the swan feather cape draped over his head to hide his face.

"They know where we go," he said, fearfully.

Snorri shrugged without comment. He glanced once at the forest, and seemed undisturbed.

"Hawk tells them," Snorri said. The men raised their spears high to honor the man's ghost.

"Snorri gothi, forgive me but may I ask a question of you?" Freystein said.

The gothi nodded. The men walked a few steps apart, to spread their weight in case the ice might thin in one spot, but the words carried easily in the crisp stillness of the air. They had all been silent, knowing what a thing it was they marched toward, and the forest had reminded them of Arnkel and his strength.

"What are the elves? Why do they haunt men?" Freystein said, almost whispering, and the men looked fearfully at the wood, as if the disrespectful words might be heard. But they listened. The old people rarely talked of them, out of fear, and so they had the same question in their minds. Where stories of Thor or Odin or Freya would be spun again and again, only fierce, hushed warnings would come from children's questions of the things that lived in the corner of their eyes, never quite visible, always present.

Snorri said nothing for a time, and Freystein almost thought he was ignored. Then the old man cleared his throat. "They say that the Otherworld fades in Christian lands, that the elves have fled in the face of the Tortured God. The Christians have their saints, and their demons, and perhaps these have driven them away."

"But what are they?" Freystein insisted. "Why can we never truly see them?"

"They are the children of our terror, Freystein, as is all the Otherworld, born from us, living in us. And the Gods are the children of our wonder. Together they are the fruit of everything we cannot explain with our eyes and ears and mind."

Freystein walked alongside him a while. "You make it sound as if they are not real," he said finally.

"Oh, they are real, fighting man," Snorri gothi said, laughing darkly. "As real as the thoughts in your heart."

They made very good time down the flat of the fjord ice, far faster than the treacherous paths would have let them go, even on horseback. Toward the south end of the fjord the snow had blown away off the ice, and for a short while, in the strange light, it seemed as if open water waited for them. Freystein waved them ahead.

"The ice is thick and good. I walked it myself this night, as I told you." He pointed ahead, to the headland where Thorolf lay buried. "There, by the base of the wall, in the shadow. That is where Thorleif said to meet him."

Freystein took off the white cape, and stuck it inside his pack. They all wore dark clothing and leather, and against the clear ice and black water they were almost invisible. No one would see them from the shore until they came very close. Snorri sent Freystein slightly ahead to lead, and they followed him in file, moving quickly and quietly. In a short while, they had made it to the little beach by the headland wall, and were scrambling over the broken ice, and into the shadow of the wall.

Thorleif and his brothers squatted there.

All six of them had come, and then knelt grimly, spears and shields grounded, their eyes bright in the shadows. They formed a circle with Snorri's nine men, facing each other, shoulders against one another. The gothi looked around at the dim faces, trying to gauge their readiness.

"Egil returns," Thorleif said to him shortly. The slave ran across the snow, keeping out of sight behind boulders. He came to the deep shadow of the wall, gasping for breath.

"They have started to take the hay out of the ricks," he said, speaking in short bursts between breaths. "It is as Auln said. Two slaves and the gothi only. No horses, just a sledge and oxen."

"How are they armed?" Thorleif asked.

"Spears I saw, and the gothi had a shield. He has his sword, but is not wearing it. I heard no ring of that steel armor, though, and he has no helmet." Egil grinned. "They came to work, not fight."

"Then it is time," Snorri gothi said.

He and Thorleif looked at each other.

"Tonight we settle many scores," Snorri said. "For Hawk, and for my son, and for the shame that you have suffered at this bastard's hands." He looked round at all of them. "Know that you will all have my protection for this, and my influence."

Thorleif and Snorri gothi clasped hands.

They stood.

"Freystein, Egil, you will not come with us," Thorleif said and held his hand up when they protested. "Slaves and servants will have little protection for what will happen after this night. Even the gothi will not be able to save you, though he says so now. You do not have rights, and we go to slay a chieftain. The consequences will be harsh even for bondi."

He told them to follow behind most of the way and hide out of sight nearby, so that they could carry any wounded men back to Swan firth. His words sobered the men. Thorleif crouched and drew a half circle in the snow with his finger, and a dot at its focus. "We go in a line, like this, between them and Bolstathr, Snorri gothi's men on the right side of the arc, and us on this side. This dot is Arnkel. Keep in line and advance together."

"Why not surround them?" Snorri said frowning. "That way there is no escape and it is sure."

"I want the slaves to have a place to run. They will run, seeing all of us with our shields up. If they are trapped they would fight. Better fifteen to one than fifteen to three. And in a line we can see each other at all times, and no one will become lost in the dark."

"What if the gothi runs?" Illugi asked.

"I don't think he will run," Oreakja said quietly. They all looked at him and the awful scar on his face.

"No, I don't think he will, either," said Thorleif. "Arnkel believes Odin himself favors him. He will fight."

The other men's eyes widened at that. "Is it true?" said Kjartan.

"Of course it is true," said Thorleif, smiling broadly. "Also true is that Odin often calls His favored sons to the great Hall early in life, to share His company. Why else would he have sent us this opportunity, the gothi alone, and without his armor, and time for us to gather?" Thorleif raised his axe high. "We go to do Odin's bidding for him."

Egil lead them all towards Orlygstead, pointing out to Snorri's men the best places to move, and they ran slowly, keeping their arms and shields from rattling. They threw themselves to the ground on the reverse side of the long ram's perch and peered over, only their heads exposed.

The gothi and the slaves heaved bundles of hay from the ricks to the ground. A pile lay on the snow, almost a whole sledge load.

"Wait until they come down and start to load the sledge," Thorleif whispered.

There were only a few moments of delay. As the three men stepped down from the ricks and moved to the pile of hay, Thorleif waved his hand and the men stood in line and advanced, the outermost men stepping out faster to arc the line around the home field at Orlygstead. They crunched across the snow openly, forgetting stealth, although no man called out. Each of them knew what a struggle they would soon have and faced it in his mind. They had crossed half the home field before one of the slaves straightened from the labor of loading hay and squinted across the field into the dark.

He stumbled backward, shouting, his arm upraised to point at the men.

So it began.

Arnkel felt the warm sweat of work on him, and told himself that he would make a point of nighttime work from then on, when the full moon was high. The light was good enough for most kinds of outdoor tasks, and when the sun shown so little, the most had to be made of the day.

The slave's shouting irritated him, and he turned to curse the man, not wanting to give warning to those at Swan firth. There was still an hour's worth of chores to finish.

His blood turned cold when he saw the line of round shields coming toward him. He turned to left and right and saw shields everywhere converging, no more than thirty paces away. Both his spear and shield lay off to the right against the barn, and his sword with them. Dim and Olaf backed away, mouths open in terror.

"Damn you two, hold your ground! Pick up your spears!"

He saw in their faces that they would be no use. Their eyes had lost reason. Dim turned to run.

"Olaf!" Arnkel shouted. "Run to Bolstathr! Rouse the men!"

The man was gone then, into the dark around the corner of the house.

Sudden rage consumed him, rage at himself for his thoughtlessness, and rage at the murderers out of the dark. For one brief moment he looked into the darkness behind him, to where the slaves had run. Then, he bent down and with a great heave flipped the heavy sledge up on its back, spilling the hay in a great flood. The oxen shied away, lowing in terror at the odd stretch on the harness. One stomp of his foot and then another broke the runner off the sledge, a large square timber of good morticed oak, nearly twice his height, curved at the end and filling his hands. He tucked one end under his arm and turned to face the men.

They came at him without words, spears high and he swung the timber about with both arms like a huge mace, crashing it into the shields of the three nearest men. One man screamed, his arm shattered by the wrench on it, and another fell back to the snow stunned. The third jabbed over his broken shield and narrowly missed Arnkel's throat, cutting his neck. Arnkel brought the timber back and sent the man flying into a snow bank. He fell heavily and only slowly came to his feet, shaking his battered head.

Arnkel turned and saw Thorleif coming at him with an axe, Illugi and Thorodd beside him with spears. He swung again, and Thorodd staggered back, his shield crushed around his arm. Arnkel turned quickly and leapt up onto the thick wall, whipping the great beam back and forth like some horned animal at bay. Thorleif leapt up to the wall with him, waiting for the beam to swing away so he could duck in and slash. The rest of the men were close now, surrounding the wall, and they began to jab at Arnkel's legs. He broke one spear with a swing and then another, the beam flicking about as if it were made of air instead of solid oak. Thorleif darted in low under a swing and tried to hack at Arnkel's leg. He was clubbed aside for his trouble, the shield boss crushed in and his hand and arm numbed with the blow. He fell off the wall, dropping the axe and shield, and then scrambled after the axe desperately on hands and knees as the men closed in on the gothi. It was a silent battle except for the grunts of effort and the hisses of pain. Arnkel's teeth were bared like a lion, his eyes red and raw, blood pouring from his neck and from a deep gash in his thigh. He swung at Snorri gothi, a vicious killing sweep. Snorri twisted out of its way by a hair, and the beam crashed into the wall. It broke at the mortice, hanging in two clumsy pieces.

Thorleif found his axe just as Arnkel pitched the remnants of the beam at two men and jumped over their stumbling forms to the barn wall where his sword and shield leaned. He was chased by stabbing spears. Illugi's spear tip caught his calf before he turned with the shield, cutting deep to the bone, and Arnkel cried out in pain and staggered another step, then wheeled around. He warded off Illugi's next jab with his shield, and leveled the boy with a foot to his stomach. Illugi fell to his knees, gasping, exposed, but Arnkel only backed away, sword up, panting, limping badly.

Sam and Klaenger came at him suddenly from his right, and he raised his shield to them and slashed at Klaenger, catching him across the arm so that the fisherman cried out and dropped back, clutching his torn flesh. Sam's spear broke against the shield, but in that moment Oreakja stepped forward and slashed with his spear diagonally at Arnkel's open side. The gothi's face and neck opened up, and blood sprayed out from the terrible wound, bright in the moonlight.

It was the end. His shield stayed up, but he cut weakly, backing away, and hard up against the barn wall they finished him, Snorri cutting the shield from his broken arm, and Thorleif swinging his axe to Arnkel's head. The massive blow felled Arnkel like a slaughtered bull and he toppled against the wall, and slid heavily to the ground.

The spear men stepped forward, stabbing again and again in the blood frenzy, the gothi's body jerking with reflex spasms of agony as the metal pierced his body.

Finally they backed away, panting, and the wounded men fell to one knee, heads bent, leaning on their weapons.

Arnkel lay with legs splayed, head and upper back against the barn wall, arms limp at his side, though his sword was still in his hand. One eye lolled at them, the blood coming from mouth and ears and the ripped mess of the other eye, his clothing soaked with the blood of the spear wounds. Thorleif's axe had cut a hideous slash across the cheek and ear, and caved in the bone of the skull.

Somehow, life was still in the man.

The eye moved about, looking at all of them, and then the hand came up and pointed weakly to Illugi, and collapsed again to the ground. Arnkel's mangled mouth tried to form words. Illugi looked at the others, and at Thorleif, and then stepped forward, his spear ready.

"Careful, boy," snarled Thorodd. "The beast still lives. Let's finish him." He stepped forward. Thorleif held him back with his arm.

Illugi crept near and then knelt by the dying man.

Arnkel's empty hand came up, and even wounded as the man was, Illugi pulled back in alarm. But the hand settled on his arm.

"Will you care for my daughter Halla all her days?" Arnkel said hoarsely, the blood in his mouth and torn lips slurring the words.

Illugi's eyes went wide.

"Yes. Yes, Arnkel gothi," Illugi said, his head near Arnkel's. "I swear it!"

"Then I give you my blessing," Arnkel whispered, and his vast hand rose and lay on Illugi's face and forehead, smearing it with blood.

The arm fell away, and he died.

They stood a long time in the night, looking down at the gothi, humbled by what they had seen, the taste of victory ashes in their mouths.

Silently, they lay down their weapons and carried the body to the wall. Snorri gothi and Thorleif carried the shoulders, and Illugi cradled the head. Sam and Klaenger struggled with his massive legs, and their sons held his middle. Thorodd and Thorfinn lay a bed of hay on the stone, thick and comforting, and onto this they placed Arnkel's body, hands across his chest, feet together, and put his sword in his hand. Over his legs and waist they spread the hay, like a cloak, so that he would be warm on his journey.

When it was done, they stood a few moments, their hands on his body, remembering who he had been.

Dim ran off into night, filled with terror, and fell over a rock as his head was turned to look back. He was found days later, frozen and dead, the blood from his scalp having frozen his head to the ground.

Olaf circled back to Bolstathr, listening to the sounds of the battle, the rasp of steel and wood, and cries of pain, and as the fear left him he began to walk.

What hurry was there, he thought? To save the man who had shamed him and made his life misery?

An hour later, after a long stroll about the land, he braced himself before the door of Bolstathr, and then burst in. He pitched his voice high and fast so that they would think him terrified.

"The gothi is attacked!" he cried out, waking the house.

Thorgils led the men, but found nothing at Orlygstead except the gothi's body, covered in hay and a fine robe of swan feathers.

XV

Endings

Many things changed on that winter night at Orlygstead.

Halla ignored her mother's fear and went to the Thorsnes Thing that spring. Thorgils went with her, Hildi begging him to go. He stood by her as she brought suit against Snorri gothi for the death of her father, killed foully in the night. Many men were appalled to see a woman arguing Law, although they acknowledged that it was her right to have compensation for her father's killing. Still, Halla could find no support, as Thorgils had told her she would not.

A woman needed strength to take what the Law said was her own.

Gudmund gothi happily sought his trees from the man who now could provide them and so had no interest in her offers.

She returned to Bolstathr with only one result.

Thorleif stood forward and claimed the killing had been by his hand alone, as he and Snorri had arranged. So it was not foul murder, without honor, but simply manslaughter, a dispute between men settled honorably in blood. The gathered chieftains were not happy to see one of their kind destroyed by a simple bondi, however, and Snorri knew that far better than Thorleif.

Thorleif was banished from the Island. The term was three years, never to set foot in the Free State or he would forfeit his life to any man who would want it, without penalty. Thorleif stood shocked as the sentence was delivered. Snorri gothi had assured him that all the trouble could be settled by simple payment of goods.

Snorri spoke to him after the Thing, on the beach near Helgafell, while Hrafn waited to take his friend with him to sea. The chieftain's Thingmen surrounded them, Sam and Klaenger staring at Thorleif without sympathy while the good sailing breeze tossed their greasy locks about into their faces. Arnkel's death and three years of exile hardly paid for Hawk's soul in their minds. The sky was roiling grey, but patches of blue vaguely promised the hope of clear skies.

"Well, at last you have your freedom," Snorri said to him, smiling benignly.

"And you have your vengeance on me," Thorleif said.

Snorri gothi shrugged. "Vengeance? An expensive indulgence," he said, and walked back up to the Holy Mountain, and there he sacrificed to Odin, and to Thor.

Thorleif went on ship with Hrafn and had many adventures. In time, he returned to the Island, to help his brothers wrest life from the harsh land of his birth.

It took a year, but Halla softened her desperate, angry denial of Illugi's courting, lulled by the little lies told by the sons of Thorbrand and by Hildi's quiet words. In the end, Illugi had hardly taken part in the slaying of Arnkel at all, at least in her mind. They married, but she would not live at Swan firth with her father's killers. Illugi accepted her terms and went to live at Bolstathr. Never once did he sit in Arnkel's High Seat. Halla insisted on that. Gizur and his family came back to work at Bolstathr, as the sons of Thorbrand came forward to reclaim the lands that had once belonged to their former slaves, Ulfar and Orlyg, and no one opposed them. Hafildi stayed at Hvammr, and Thorgils would collect the rents from him. It gave him a certain satisfaction to take the man's money.

Even more satisfying was the growth in his son. His son. He said the words under his breath, as if he could not believe them.

Thorgils would hunt swans by the shore, and the boy would carry his bow for him proudly, stumbling with its length. Auln had given him no name, and called him only "boy," though it was obvious that she loved him, in an absent, incidental way. So Thorgils called him Gunnar, after his father, and the boy answered to it. Thorgils hoped his father could see his grandchild. The boy never asked why his mother never spoke to his father, or looked at him, or touched him. As with all children, life was simply life, and that was explanation enough.

Halla and Illugi had many children, all of whom grew into strong men and women in the fullness of time, and together they mingled the two families and bound all the lands of Swan's fjord together.

All but the first child.

He was an adventurous boy from the beginning, always exploring, always in trouble of one kind or another and was greatly loved for that by his grandfather, Thorbrand, for whom he was named. The old man would take him on his horse into the hills and to the mountains, and fishing out on the fjord. The little boy had Arnkel's strength in him and the wit of Thorbrand, even from a very young age. Many in the valley who saw him predicted a great future, perhaps even one too large for the Island to contain. He was the one Halla would lift onto Arnkel's High Seat. She would whisper in his ear, "You are the heir of Arnkel. You will fill this chair properly, in time, and take back all that was ours."

One day he wandered off, and was never found, although the men searched the whole valley.

All that was found was his torn and bloody shirt. It rested on Thorolf's wall, not seen for many weeks, wet and faded from the weather.

Inside it was wrapped a little jar of Thorbrand's honey.

It was said later that Thorbrand went mad when the shirt and the jar were brought to Swan firth. He rode up into the hills, although no one knew why then, and Illugi followed him, thinking that his father had some knowledge of his child's murderers.

He went to Auln's home at Thorswater dale, naked sword in hand. Thorgils worked in the field of Bolstathr, and as the path went by there, he looked up to see the two men ride by, and the gleam of metal in Thorbrand's fist. A sudden certainty filled him and he raced for his own horse to follow them.

Auln waited in her yard, as if expecting them, her hands on Gunnar's shoulders.

Thorbrand walked to her, sword high. Illugi held his arm when he saw what he meant to do, shocked. When Thorbrand shook him off in a spasm of rage, Auln pushed the boy toward Illugi.

"I give him to you in payment for your son," she said, her voice broken and raw. "I ask no forgiveness. It had to be. With one stroke I cut Arnkel and Thorbrand to their souls for what they did to me." A shadow of her old self passed across the mad assurance of her face. "I am sorry, Illugi."

She faced Thorbrand squarely, her face calm as death, even as he raised the sword over her. He killed her with one stroke.

She fell without a sound.

Thorgils rode up at that moment.

Illugi stood appalled, clutching the boy to him, and in his horror at death and his sorrow for the child he had loved, he stopped Thorbrand from killing Auln's son, his strong hand clutching Thorbrand's upraised sword arm. He forced the man away.

Thorgils threw himself from his saddle and came for Thorbrand bare handed. He would have killed him there under the blue sky.

Illugi shouted to him then, his voice torn with grief.

"She killed my son, Thorgils. She killed my only son." He held tight to Gunnar as if it were his own lost child, who only stood, staring at the hacked body of his mother.

Thorgils stopped. He fell to his knees beside Auln's body and held the blood-soaked thing to him.

Illugi stepped forward as Thorbrand staggered away into the field, his sword dangling from one hand, forgotten. The old man vanished into the rocks.

Illugi took the silver band from his arm and dropped it on the ground, and beside it he lay his sword, bought just that season, a fine blade of good Frankish metal.

Vengeance needed to be stayed.

Blood did not need blood to wash it away. Wealth would always serve among men of restraint and honor on the Island of free men.

Illugi took the boy's arm gently and led him to Thorgils. "I will give no more for Auln's death, except the child himself. He is your son," Illugi said. The lines of pain etched his face, and even through his own agony Thorgils saw the wisdom in the man's face, the holding back of his rage. "Here I give you your future. That is payment enough. It is more than I have."

Thorgils rode the long trail up to Vadils Head the next day. He wound up through the many grave cairns until he came to the cliff, leading the pack pony and its grisly load.

He buried Auln beside Ulfar, piling the stones deeply onto her cloth wrapped body.

When he was done, he walked leadenly to the cliff edge.

The summer sun burned brightly on the sea, lighting the foam of each breaker in a line of pure white until it smashed onto the black beaches. Swans circled below, eternally dancing with each other, and with the gulls and terns. The whole of the world stirred in the rare warmth, burning its life while it could before the long winter would return.

Thorgils balanced on the cliff's edge, gusted about by the wind. He stared out into the world and then down to the rocks below. It would be a short fall, a brief spell of terror and then oblivion. The elves whispered behind him from among the graves, urging him on, exalted by the scent of despair.

Something turned his head, a blur of purpose near him. He turned.

Ulfar stood by his grave, and Auln beside him.

Thorgils looked a long time at his friend and at the woman he had loved, feeling no fear or dread. He did not see hate, or betrayal in Ulfar's eyes, only a kind of weariness, that the man's spirit was forced one last time to come back to such a dreary thing as his old life, and that he did it only for his friend, one last favor, to show him that he wanted nothing more, and that all debts were paid.

He saw nothing but sadness in Auln.

The voices of the elves faded into disappointment and then silence.

Auln's arm went up slowly, and she pointed, down, down to the valley below, down to Bolstathr, where life went on, where their son lived.

Then they were gone, and only the wind remained.

Thorgils mounted his horse and rode back down the mountain, the sun warm on his back.

Acknowledgments

I am indebted to Professor Jesse Byock (and to his publisher, Penguin Books) for permission to adapt his detailed map of Swan's Fjord and the local region for my use. His book *Viking Age Iceland* (Penguin Books UK, 2001) is a profoundly thorough resource for anyone interested in further reading on the topic of medieval Iceland, and an interpretation of the events of the sagas.

I would also like to thank my wife, Jane, for her love and support, and honest critique of the novel, and my children, Maddy and Duncan, for their inspiration.

Finally, my thanks go out to Jordan and Anita Miller of Academy Chicago Publishers, and the rest of the staff there, for their trust and hard work on my behalf.

GLOSSARY OF PLACES AND TERMS

Arfskot: a legal term in Norse culture, referring to the unlawful transfer
of land title to another without consultation and permission of the
original owner's heirs, or rightful inheritors. Land was always considered property of the larger family, rather than specifically that of an
individual. Ulfar was bound to Thorbrand as his former slave, and so
committed arfskot when he gave his land, which should have gone to
Thorbrand on his death, to Arnkel instead. Arnkel himself was guilty
of arfskot by accepting.

Bolstathr: the small farmstead of Arnkel *gothi*

bondi/bondar: a bondi was a free man, unbound by inherited or devolved
duties and obligations, and held full rights as such in Norse law

The Crowness: one of the last stands of birch forest in Iceland, of immense
value, belonging to Thorolf

The Free State: medieval Iceland, c.970 A.D.

gothi/gothar: The gothar were chieftains in Iceland, men of importance and
sometimes wealth who used their influence to resolve disputes, among
other duties. A man would "sell" his dispute to a gothi, who would
then take on the conflict as his own. The office was transferable, and
could be sold. Less than fifty positions existed in the tenth century.
The extremely egalitarian nature of Iceland's society meant that these
men required craftiness, charisma, and an understanding of people as
primary traits. They competed with other gothar to attract followers,
and yet could not command these followers, as the agreement between
Thingman and Gothi was voluntary, and as easily broken as made.
These chieftains did not rule. They facilitated, to their own profit and
that of their followers. Until the twelfth century, those who tried for a
more traditional Scandinavian chieftaincy involving greater personal
authority generally had as their reward a violent end to their lives.

handsal/handselled: the handsal is the traditional Norse conclusion to a
deal or bargain, a strong and obvious striking of the palms of the two
parties, once with hand high, once with hand low. It is still practiced
in various forms in the many parts of Europe settled by the Norse
(British Isles, Brittany, parts of Spain, Normandy and of course, Scandinavia). It was legally binding, in essence the signing of a contract in
a pre-literate age with a strong code of honor.

Helgafell: the large and wealthy farmstead of Snorri *gothi*, near the Holy
mountain

Holmganga: the Norse were a feuding, warrior culture, and personal dis-
agreements were often settled violently, within a code duello. The

Holmganga was a duel, generally fought on a small island if one was available (the term stems from the words "island bound"), with weapons defined and agreed upon by both parties.

Hvammr: the decaying farmstead of Thorolf Lamefoot

Jarl: a lord or noble in Scandinavia, of elevated status

Knarr: a generic term for the many styles and types of sailing vessels used for trade, rather than war, by the Norse. They were stable, wide craft, clinker built, with a large carrying capacity. Sails were the main form of propulsion, though all carried at least a few pairs of long oars. They were used in the colonization of all the Atlantic islands, Greenland, Iceland and North America.

The Knolls: last of the highlands before the coastal lands begin near Helgafell

Landnam: the "land-taking." This is the period of fifty years beginning about 870–880 A.D. when the migration from Norway to Iceland took place, hundreds of families uprooting and settling in an untouched land.

lyke-help: the closing of the eyes and mouth of the dead

The meadow: a hay meadow on the ridge line between Ulfarsfell and Hvammr

nefatfl: a traditional Norse board game, often compared to chess. The two sides represent the king and his guards versus the assassins. The king piece must escape off the board for the king side to win. The assassins win by preventing this.

Orlygstead: the farm of Orlyg, brother of Ulfar

Skald: a poet, and a singer of odes

Skyr: a nutritious food made from coagulated milk, much like yoghurt, and used as a drink when thinned with whey

Swan firth: the fertile farmstead of Thorbrand and his sons, near the mouth of the river that empties into the southermost tip of Swan's fjord

Swan's fjord: a deep, glacier made rift along the north coast of the Snaefellsnes peninsula of Iceland, known for the large population of swans that gather there

The Thing: early Norse society relied on popular assemblies for much of its decision making, called 'Things." Consensus was important in order to mediate violence.

Thorsnes: the great spread of coastal lands along the north edge of the Snaefellsness peninsula

Thorswater dale: a spring source in the rocky hills above Hvammr farm, with little pasture, and the rough home of Cunning-Gill

Ulfarsfell: the well kept farm of the freedman Ulfar, next to Bolstathr